ASCENDERS

HIGH SCHOOL FOR THE RECENTLY DECEASED

Life + Love,

C. L.

♡

ASCENDERS

High School for the Recently Deceased

C.L. GABER

Cover by Adrijus G - RockingBookCovers.com

ISBN: 978-0-9962420-2-8

Formatted by: Tianne Samson with E.M. Tippetts Book Designs
emtippettsbookdesigns.com

To Ron for yesterday, today and all the tomorrows

Clowns to the left of me, jokers to the right,
Here I am, stuck in the middle with you,
Yes, I'm stuck in the middle with you.
—Stealers Wheel

Listen, there's a hell of a good universe next door, let's go.

—E. E. Cummings

INTRODUCTION

1.

I was there. And then I was gone.

My mother gave me no notice that we were relocating. Suddenly, we had just moved without all that annoying planning and packing. Somehow my clothes were thrown into boxes with shoes that were missing mates. Someone had packed my books and CDs, and had even reached under my bed into that secret hiding place I counted on to protect my treasures; like the iPod loaded with the best and worst of everything from Nirvana to the Stones, plus my lucky green rabbit's foot—because you just never knew when you would need a little extra luck.

My mother must have remembered the family photo album because there it was on our brand-new living room coffee table that I passed on the way to my very own bedroom and a bed I had never slept in a day in my life.

It was strange because we could barely afford to pay the rent each month, let alone buy something as nice as a hand-carved oak table imported from someplace far, far away. When I had looked, the tag didn't say from where. It was just imported.

It was one of those times when you go from A to Z so fast that you hardly remember any of the in-between. Or as I—Walker Callaghan—senior at Kennedy High School in suburban Chicago and news editor of the school paper the *Charger* liked to say, "Maybe it's not about the happy ending. Maybe it's about the story."

Flopping onto my new, handsome, four-poster bed with lovely little tulips carved into the wood, I thought it was so unlike my mother, the master planner, to do something this off-the-cuff. My mother was a woman who made a battle plan to go to the local 7-Eleven for almost-expiration-date milk. Even weirder was the fact that we had moved farther away than anyone imagined. *A lot farther.*

"So run this by me one more time, Mom," I shouted. "I must have been heavily medicated or feeling really sorry for myself. We moved? You pulled the trigger. Bang-bang—relocation?"

I didn't give her time to answer.

"A new school in my senior year of high school?" I called out to her on a murky, cold winter morning on Burning Tree Court.

Even though I was letting the heat escape and Mom had always said we didn't live to "support Commonwealth Edison," our old electric company, I still opened my bedroom window wide and found that the air drifting in was stun-your-senses Arctic cold. It smelled green and fresh outside and those dense marshmallow patches of white fluff in the sky could only mean serious snow because they were roasted dark on the bottom.

I tried to shiver, but couldn't. I was perfectly warm despite the window and the fact that I was wearing faded jeans and a well-washed blue cotton tank that read: Normal People Scare Me.

In true dramatic fashion, I couldn't resist needling the one

12

person responsible for our fate, our new house, and everything in it that was unknown and strange. "Mom, new school. Senior year. I'll have no friends here. Are you trying to kill me?"

Without knowing how or why, I was now enrolled in this elite-sounding new school called the Academy, which sounded quite upscale and serious to a girl whose educational pursuits consisted of a generic public-school education outside of a big melting-pot city, where you were either rich (if you were lucky) or you were normal (if you were like everybody else). Our family worked hard at being desperately normal.

"Great, it will be a bunch of rich, stuck-up snobs who will hate me—and cheerleaders. There are always cheerleaders. They're like cockroaches. You can't get rid of them," I concluded, yelling from my new room to hers, which was somewhere down a hallway that I had never really navigated before.

"I hear it's quite fancy," Mom called from her room. "A Callaghan going to a private school. Imagine."

I didn't have to imagine it as I was living it. Of course, I didn't know it at the time, but when I had asked that question, Madeleine Callaghan, my mom, the mover and shaker in my life, had cringed and then cried hard into a brand-new washcloth she didn't recognize—the thick kind we could never afford. The weeper was the one who had given me the odd-for-a-girl first name, which was her maiden name before she married my father, steel worker Sam Callaghan. We weren't just blue-collar, but faded blue-collar from clothes that had far too many seasons of washings. In our family, the rule was "Don't throw it out unless it's dead-dead."

Running my finger along the smooth wood of my expensive new dresser with the intoxicating just-cut-tree smell, I ducked down on the ground to read the label on the bottom. Imported from R-19877. Really? Did we win the lottery? And what was with the secret spy code?

"Honey, please, I'm begging you," Mom answered after appearing in my doorway. "For once, let's not do the Diane Sawyer investigation act. I can't do twenty rounds of questions. Not today." Her voice sounded thick like she had a cold, so I closed the window.

"There is no need to insult Diane who probably doesn't even have a dresser this nice," I replied.

"Walker, let me make you some breakfast," Mom said. "Everything is always better after a little oatmeal and orange juice. You'll see."

2.

Back home in suburban Chicago, Principal Amanda Stevens was toying with the loudspeaker at Kennedy High School. It was time to make an announcement that drifted across her desk once or twice a year (every year)—and it always pulled her heart right out of her chest. She couldn't dwell on herself, but had to think of her students. Many of them knew this girl from her work on the school newspaper. What would she say about her? Principal Stevens went through the usual lines in her head: It was a terrible shame. A waste. A tragedy. It was all those sentiments that meant nothing really because they were just words.

This was a heart ripper—dead at seventeen. Good night, Irene.

Ms. S knew that she better just do it. So she clicked the on button on the PA system, took a deep breath, and said what needed to be said. Nothing more. Nothing less.

"I regret to tell the student body that we lost one of our own last night. Walker Callaghan, a well-respected senior and news editor of the *Charger*, has died."

She released the on button and grabbed for a bottle of extra-strength aspirin, wishing there was something stronger. Then she clicked the PA back on again. "Of course, counselors are available," she added.

CHAPTER 1

1.

I was told to unpack us, which was bad enough because everything was a jumble of disconnected things. I just couldn't believe that Mom had blown out of Chicago in such a disorganized way. I found the big black frying pan in the dining room hutch and my bright-pink mini blow dryer in the kitchen pantry. Maybe this is how it starts with parents. One day they're messing up the packing, the next they don't know your name.

With all the hills surrounding us and the nearby sound of rushing water I heard in the distance, we had obviously moved to the upper part of Michigan or the UP as the Yuppers called it. Gazing out my bedroom window far down the quiet tree-lined street shadowed by what seemed like hundreds of tall pines, I wondered what suburb of Michigan I now called home. *What was my zip code? What was my address? Was I a cheesehead now? Nope. That was saved for those who called Wisconsin home.*

A quick trip outside didn't help. I could see that a few of the neighbors' lawns were covered in crunchy piles of orange-and-red autumn leaves, while others appeared to be strangely green under what looked like a few inches of snow from the previous night. As far as ecosystems went, this one was a doozy and that probably explained why no one was outside today.

Wandering back inside, only one question remained and it swirled around so many times in my head that it should have made me a little dizzy.

How could she do this to us?

Maybe I was being a little too hard on my mom, a second-grade teacher for twenty years, who had a lot on her plate since my dad died of cancer when I was just five years old. Then again, I couldn't help but feel a new wave of resentful washing up because it seemed like everything I counted on was suddenly gone.

How in the world was I supposed to graduate high school without my best friends Madison and Ashley? We'd been stuck together like industrial-strength Krazy Glue since kindergarten; and they had been essential when Ashton Hamilton broke my sophomore-year heart by announcing that he wasn't just seeing someone else, but someone else named Fred. *Way to call that one, Walker.*

Now that I was out of sight, Madison and Ashley would forget that I had bad taste in guys and could lift my right brow, Mr. Spock-style. They were my closest friends at Kennedy High. It was only natural they would move on and find new friends and create fresh stories where I would never become even a supporting player. My role was simply cut. Erased.

For a sad, feeling-sorry-for-myself moment, I thought about how I never really had the chance to say good-bye. Now we would never graduate together. And forget about taking all of those dorky prom pictures next year where you smile until it feels like your teeth will fall out. I was sure my friends would be over me sooner rather than later because our lives moved that fast. Friends were like text messages—one day you were on the screen and the next you were simply deleted, letter by letter until you never really existed at all.

Gone meant gone.

Wasn't that always the case when people moved?

I wasn't about to just accept my new situation without a hell of an argument. "I'll hate the new school. I won't know anyone. Hey, Mom, I know the last thing on your mind is the fact that your daughter is about to go straight to complete social exile at age seventeen," I huffed, carrying a box of clothes to one of the two back bedrooms. *Since when did we have extra bedrooms? Back home I had to sleep on the living room couch and now we had a guest room for actual guests.*

"I want to go home and live with Aunt Ginny," I announced.

Aunt Ginny was my mom's much older sister who smelled like she did a cannonball into a bottle of Listerine. She spent part of her life flossing and the other part watching *Law & Order* reruns over and over again. The theme song was basically burned into all of our brains by now—which wasn't a good thing.

Mom moving away from her only sister was odd because she was a creature of routine. We ate tuna sandwiches with Ginny every Monday for dinner and spaghetti and salad on Sunday. We brushed upon waking and read before retiring. Mom ran our lives in writing. Everything was jotted down in her worn, plastic-covered Day-Timer with the cheerful red-and-white polka dots on the cover because schedules were kept and change was to be avoided at all costs. She believed in bedtimes, manners, and a code of living. "Your word is your promise," Mom was fond of saying. "You can never break your word."

Her frugality was another sacred trait, which was why these

moving boxes were strange to say the least. There wasn't some handwritten scribble across them, but actual typed announcements of exactly what was inside. Since when did my mother take the grocery shopping money and buy some expensive labeling device when a black marker would do?

In my new room in exile, I pulled back the tape on one of the boxes and the jumbled mix inside was even more curious. Who packed a math textbook with a hairbrush, hair ribbons I hadn't worn since I was six, and the ashes of my precious black Labrador, Jake? Clutching his box of ashes to my chest, I noted that it felt lighter than usual. This bothered me, so I shook the box, but it still felt like nothing was in there but air. It was as if the J-man had evaporated or something.

When in the world did Mom have time to do such schizophrenic packing? How long has she exactly known about this move? Passing my mother in the hallway, I called out for good measure, "Did I mention that I hate it here already—and I wanna go home?"

"Only a thousand times. In the last hour," Mom responded, removing the forks and knives from the box located in the bathroom. "I'm sure the new kids will be very welcoming and lovely. Hopefully, it won't be much different from your old school."

"Yeah, right," I said. "Keep dreaming."

"There's no point in being so dramatic, honey. It won't do you any good. You think it's easy for me to pick up and leave this way? There was just . . . no choice." Mom turned away quickly to dab at her eyes, which made me instantly feel like pond scum.

Bill collectors, I thought, suddenly feeling sad for my mother who really did carry a heavy load. My father actually died of some rare cancer that no one studied, meaning there was no chance in hell of any hope or any cure. I knew that my mom had been struggling for what seemed like forever and occasionally we got some annoying call during dinner announcing that the Visa bill was late and now the card was cut off or that someone "forgot" to pay the electric that month. It was an "accident" when our water was actually turned off and no one could shower for three days, but that nice man from the city did show us how to turn it back on in a pinch. "Neighborhood people stick together," he said, winking at my mother who wasn't in the mood for any extra services. My Dad was her one true love, and even a man who provided "city services" didn't rate.

As for our financial status, Mom never wanted to alarm me and always assured me that it was just some big clerical mistake on the other end, and the lady on the line was actually looking for some *other* family who was eating mac-and-cheese from a five-boxes-for-a-dollar sale on a Tuesday, like every other Tuesday, and calling it a feast. And she made it feast-like by growing oregano on the windowsill, and putting a fresh leaf on top of our carnival-orange noodles like we were dining in a five-star restaurant.

The Recession, the Depression, the Big Lie, or whatever they were calling it, officially made for tough times when you were a single mom on an elementary schoolteacher's salary trying to raise a teenage daughter. Eventually, our two-bedroom house was sold and we moved into an apartment in the suburbs of Chicago, although no one in the burbs lived in apartments. In the land of expansive front lawns and block parties, people lived in massively big houses with purple and white petunias poking out in the spring, and neighbors were far enough away that you didn't smell what they were cooking for dinner.

Our apartment wasn't even strictly Callaghan-women territory, but belonged to my strange-smelling, lonely Aunt Ginny and her antisocial cat, Prissy. That's when I was sent to sleep on the couch in the living room with a comforter that smelled of old-lady Pond's cold cream and catnip. Of course, I never told my friends about our living situation and took the bus into the city everyday to go to school. It was just too embarrassing to admit that we were now boarders in someone else's world.

Extras became nonexistent and staples became struggles. The ancient, sun-faded, garage-less blue Honda did not become a trendy new electric car that didn't guzzle gas, but got two new tires and a pat on the dashboard as a prayer to please run another ten thousand miles in harsh wintery conditions.

We lived in a suburb called Arlington Heights, which was biblically cold and miserable in January with winds whipping hard and ice covering streets and sidewalks. The grayness of it all crept into your soul until you felt like there would never be another sunny day.

It was no wonder that Mom must have saved up her extra tutoring money and moved us here, which was on the outskirts of my new school. This choice was smack-dab in a place that was green and lush, with rolling lawns and white fences, but also strangely cold to support that kind of vegetation. *Michigan. Why the hell did Mom move us here?*

I had only been to Michigan once when I was a little girl. In a rare vacation, we spent a week in the summer at this cute little rustic rental cabin in the middle of the woods. The trees seemed to converge in a way that made me feel protected; and the lake was so beautifully calm that I spent half the time just drifting around in a little canoe. It was one of the rare times in my life I remember Mom truly relaxing as she sat in a rocker on the porch, did her crossword puzzles, and told me to be extra careful. "Don't go too far out in the water, Walker," she yelled. "I don't ever want to lose sight of you."

"I know. I'll avoid the swamp creature," I promised, and then took my little boat so far out that Mom looked like a dot with the green pine trees swallowing her whole.

And now we were back in Michigan once again, but I couldn't

remember any details of our move here. Maybe it was the pressure of school and passing trig class in Chicago that had finally warped my mind. Or maybe it was the fever from the respiratory infection I had that turned into actual pneumonia. It was so severe that my wheezing self spent a week in the hospital where I was actually put on oxygen and spent most of my time in some sort of drugged-up, steroid-induced fog. I couldn't remember much from my time at General Hospital (yes, its real name). I had murky memories of Mom driving me home, giving me some killer knock-you-out pills, and tucking me into bed. Last night when I retired after taking my pills, I thought it was my old bed, but maybe now I was the one who was losing it.

I took a deep breath.

In Michigan, I could breathe easily and that fact made me giddy with happiness.

Staring out of the new living room window into the small garden in my foreign front yard, I wondered how in the world Mom could afford my medical bills and an upscale home complete with four bedrooms, a cozy living room, fireplace, and an actual old-fashioned front porch like the one we had at the cabin. This one swept around most of the house and it was lined with a few pink petunias that were proud and perky, poking up from terra-cotta pots, obviously a gift from the last occupants. The sassy rosebush didn't even seem to mind a moderate dusting of snow.

Someone had also tended nicely to the small, perfectly manicured, vibrantly green lawn outside our new white Craftsman home. Truly, it was a dream house on a quaint, tree-lined street, except that it was far away from what we knew as home and whom we knew as home, which made it feel like we were secret invaders.

Trudging from the front of the house to the back for the trillionth time on perfectly distressed, dark hardwood floors, I looked at the six boxes full of my stuff and dug in. Soon, all my favorite zombie books were neatly on the little white shelf over a lovely antique desk. My best outfits, including my jeans jacket, a black wool skirt, and a Cubs T-shirt, were already in the closet. There was even a brand-new navy-blue peacoat with a wide collar and big black buttons. I guess it was for me, although I never saw it before tonight. Shimmying into it, I noted that it fit like a glove, as Aunt Ginny would say.

Finally, my eyes hit something I was dying to find. In the pocket of my old denim purse, I hit pay dirt just like I was hoping. Pressing the on button of my cell phone, I watched the lights blaze on, the Sprint logo flash, and then waited as the phone tried to find service. "No service available" it flashed. *Maybe Mom didn't pay the bill—again*, I figured, tears springing to my eyes. If there were ever a time to cry, it certainly was now.

Crushed, I ripped open another box that contained my slightly beaten-up red plaid robe and those stupid Christmas slippers with reindeer heads that my grandmother Renee sent from New York via UPS last year. It was strangely comforting to slip them on. Last, but not least, there was a box with my old high-school yearbooks. Flopping down on my bed, I opened one to exactly the right page where Madison and Ashley grinned back at me. Tears rolling down my cheeks, I slowly closed the book.

There was nothing else to do but open the window for a brisk breeze, climb into this bed with the white comforter that felt like sinking into a cloud, and call it a night. In the dark room with the frigid air, my bones didn't ache from all the hard labor and I wasn't really that tired or cold. In fact, I was wide-awake and raring to go despite the fact that I had just helped unpack an entire house.

All in all, it was a pretty busy day for a girl who should feel half-dead.

2.

Badgering doesn't begin to describe it. "Mom, I need to know what happened. Why are we here? And where are we?" I demanded for the millionth time the next morning. Her only response was to stand there and look at me stone-faced. My inner reporter kicked in, as this was the ultimate challenge: a subject who refused to talk.

"Mom, I love it here," I said in a soft, sweet voice. "Where are we?"

Nothing.

When I added a few decibels, she gave me that stern motherly gaze like I was crossing some kind of invisible line from loving daughter to spoiled brat. *I would break her. I had to break her.* All day long, I cajoled, begged, implored, and flat-out asked my mother question after question about our relocation. Her silence was unusual and it felt strange and uncomfortable. If nothing else, she was the ultimate open book.

So I decided to check out my new private bathroom, the first I didn't have to share with my mom. Almost immediately, Mom was invading my space; so I made my best twisted-up, Grim Reaper face. Recoiling a bit when she put both of her chilly hands on my face, as if she was checking for damage, I laughed nervously. "Mom, I swear, I'm using the acne stuff," I said. "Do you see any zits? And since I've been so great about teenage skin care . . . care to answer a few questions?"

Nothing.

Even as her eyes did a second check on me, I knew all Mom could find wrong was my attitude. "Want to tell me why we moved now?" I asked in my sweetest voice. "And if we can afford this house, can I have a raise in my allowance?" It was an inside joke. I didn't really get an allowance at all, thanks to the economy. Bus money was my allowance.

Mom walked away sighing in relief, only to double back two second later. She was there again, just staring intently at me. When she began to run her hands down my arms, I mentioned that perhaps she was really losing it. "Mom, did I grow a second head?" I demanded. "Do you think I'm my own evil twin? Have I turned into a pod person?"

"I just love you, Walker, and want you to be safe," Mom whispered.

"I'd be safer if you let me take a bath in peace," I said, pouring some body wash into a new claw-foot tub. My occasionally too large hazel eyes fluttered shut and with a sigh on my lips, I whispered, "We can bond later. Oprah will love it."

Mom had to smile because I was the same old Walker who, in the most charming way, found my mother utterly annoying. Then on her way out I thought I saw her wince, which caused me to yell out, "You okay?"

"Fine. Fine. Never worry about me."

She was okay, but soon she wasn't alone. After a long soak, I put on my worn Chicago Bears sweatshirt and black leggings, tucking my long, straight, red-brown hair into a pony. And that's when I heard the voices coming from outside the front door. At that moment, I knew exactly what to do, which was to open the little slider window near the door and listen to every word.

I counted two other voices speaking to Mom in quick, hushed tones. One introduced herself as Abby and apologized profusely that they hadn't arrived earlier, but "storms always made for a crazy, busy night and we're the welcome wagon."

Then a gravelly voiced woman, who sounded like a smoker, announced that her name was Maggie and she was a counselor.

When I peeked through the curtain, I could see that she looked like your average suburban mom in yoga pants; her large "bee-hind" jutting out from of a bright-fuchsia jacket. She had a beige reusable grocery bag slung over one shoulder.

"It's not about being stuck. You're just transitioning," Maggie said to Mom.

Great. Another busybody life-coach type. Or financial counselor, I thought, *trying to tell Mom—the widow with the teenage kid—how to get her life back on track by just spending her last dollar on counseling.*

"It wasn't your fault," Maggie said. "But we can talk about that later. We only have a few specialists who help the parents because this place is really for the teenagers, or the Unformed as we call them. What's important now is that you go about things in a normal way. Walker can't know. Not just yet. You know how teens are . . . Ultraemotional!"

"School is mandatory for all teens. Act like nothing has happened. Don't get into the details of your relocation—she can't handle it yet. Remember, Walker gets upset when her Gmail won't work. She's seventeen. And her mind isn't fully formed yet. The human mind doesn't fully form until you're twenty-four. It's a proven scientific fact—and it's why she's here," added Abby. She wore jeans, a red jacket, and had earbuds dangling around her neck with some strains of Pink's "So What" drifting into the night air. *So, so what. I'm still a rock star. I got my rock moves. And I don't need you. Na-na-na-na-na.*

"What if I feel just as lost? I can't handle this—not now, not ever," Mom said with tears rolling down her soft cheek.

"You're the adult. You're forty-three. You will handle it," said Maggie. "Walker needs to keep learning. She's what they call on Earth . . ."

Her voice trailed off.

"A work in progress," said Abby, as she reached for Mom's hand. "Think of it this way. You're already on your journey. For Walker, it's still just beginning. Her story remains unwritten."

Mom nodded. I heard one of them say it was all about coming to terms.

What the hell was this? Obviously, these women were talking Mom into sending me to this new school. An Academy. So that's what this was about. Mom was finally shipping me off to boarding school, which she always threatened to do when I had a really big mouth. I knew we couldn't afford it, but maybe this was just a trial period where we would see if I could win a scholarship or something. If we had to pay, forget it. No dinero. This whole sales pitch was going to fall upon deaf ears.

A few weeks in this school and then the bill would arrive in the mail. If I knew my mother, and I did, I'd be back on Aunt Ginny's couch before summer.

CHAPTER 2

1.

At precisely 6:35 a.m. on Tuesday morning, Mom drove the blue Honda through the center of what looked like a sleepy, Michigan vacation town. Tall pines obscured our view of what was described on our INTRO channel as "a land of wonderful wilderness complete with waterfalls and icy trout streams."

Just like Hemingway wrote, I imagined that the trickling stream we passed to the right was "a rising cold shock." Not that I was planning to do any swimming in icy-cold waters today. As we got closer to the actual town, I saw how civilization sliced through the heavily forested lands, but a touch of the wild remained. A large deer stood by the side of the road and just glancing at him sparked a shiver that snaked from my lower spine to my neck, but he didn't dare us with the idea of his darting out. He was content to just stare like we were the animals in the zoo.

I could smell the freshness of the air mixed with the pleasant aroma of natural wood-burning fireplaces that seemed to leave a scent trail drawing us closer to the action. For a long moment, I imagined curling up in front of one of them with a warm blanket, a good book, and a large cup of hot chocolate.

But I didn't dare. I had school today. And just like in the past, Mom was driving me there on my first day.

I noted that the car was in perfect working order and suddenly without a dent or scratch on it. Maybe she took it to a body shop before skipping town. Hanging my head a bit out of the window which was no longer broken, I saw that the two-story buildings were charmingly inviting. Some were made from old red bricks and others were carved from clean white stone. Sky-high alpine and elm trees were regal and mature and the pine smell was so fragrant and fresh that it was as if Christmas was happening this very minute.

The two-lane road simply dubbed "Main Street" was actually lined with mature pines and tall budding cherry trees—quite unnatural for this region—along with white hydrangeas in white planters, despite the weather report of below-zero temperatures last night and tonight.

That's right, Mom had made sure to watch the weather, although here a teenage weatherperson (certainly an intern) said that today would be, "Sunny, cold, and a bit warm with a chance of precipitation, despite being dry." What a smart ass.

There wasn't real news on any of our three new televisions, only weather reports and informative feature stories about cooking, nature, and how to explore your inner passions for yoga, guitar playing, or river rafting. Or you could just explore your passion for chowing down, which was reportedly big and highly caloric here since the local stands on this Main Street carried hot dogs, curly fries, root-beer floats, and frozen custard to name a few of my favorite food groups.

This place was also apparently known for having twenty-six of the most beautiful waterfalls—or the Falls, as the locals called them—ever seen. As for the rest of the channels, we seemed to be able to find any TV show or movie we searched for at any hour of the day. It was obviously one of those "move-in specials" where they try to get you hooked on the premium channels so you splurge for the bigger package when the trial period is over. Last night, Mom and I watched a marathon of *Everybody Loves Raymond*. It felt safe because Ray lived in a zone where no one ever had a problem more pressing than who ate the leftover lasagna.

That morning, Mom had dressed quickly and cooked me some delicious oatmeal with fresh nuts, cinnamon, and raisins that had been waiting in the cabinet—along with farm-fresh whole milk that tasted like delicious thick cream, and pulp-free orange juice from the fridge. Then like any other school day, we got in the car and pulled out of the driveway. Today I had a small map in my hands, although there were only a few roads to navigate. We were instructed to "take Main Street until it ends and you'll see the Academy from the road because you can't possibly miss it."

2.

Main Street was like a throwback to those quaint little all-American cities before the recession when small downtowns still existed and were actually flourishing. Only a few younger people lined the two-lane street, and I saw them stopping every now and again to say hello or duck into one of the quaint stores like Flipside Records where they sold real vinyl or Mel's Milkshakes where a sign touted, "One thousand flavor combinations." Obviously, this Mel liked to brag. Someone named Trotter had his own café here alongside a few welcoming coffee shops that were just opening for business, with store owners in front sweeping the light snowfall away from their front doors with large brooms.

A young man in a striped shirt and rainbow suspenders was doing his mime act in a gazebo that sat in a small park just off Main. As we passed, he jumped onto one of the stone ledges that lined the park and lifted one white glove as a greeting. When I looked back, I could see him smiling. He looked so happy.

One of the coffee shops called Perks promised a free blueberry muffin or toast with "exotic jams" along with a large cup of hot cocoa made from real melted chocolate. If you were extra hungry, they offered ground meat-and-potato pies made with Cornish pastry. Finish it off with what they promised were "heavenly cookies."

Strangely, every single place offered free drink refills, plus seconds and thirds on the food. How did these people earn a living? Then again, there weren't many people in sight, but it was early.

Still, this felt like a ghost town.

When we stopped on the weathered street for one of the few traffic lights, Mom and I could smell the fresh brew wafting into the car and it seemed like salvation. My eyes darted to the local movie house, which just had one title. No multiplexes here. And there was a small sign in the window that there would be a Q & A with an actor from one of the Batman movies. "They should take that old sign down," Mom said. "Such bad taste." The name of the actor who was lecturing on Saturday (no date given) was Heath Ledger.

"Mom, can we drive like we actually want to get there?" I asked with a little smile. *What was up with Mom's driving?* It was even worse than before because now she had gone from snail slow to

31

old-lady crawl. Mom was creeping along as if she had finally found the small-town life of her dreams complete with yarn stores, a corner market, soda shop, and that white gazebo.

Why is she driving like a snail? I wondered, glancing at the speedometer to see that she was only going ten in a thirty-five zone. She continued the inch-along crawl on the rain-wet pavement until she reached the bottom of a hill where Main Street ended and transformed into an unnamed road that slowly climbed upward. Now the car was moving so slowly that for a moment I wondered if we would just slide backward again to the bottom. At least that way, we could stare into that quilt store that caught Mom's eye.

At that frustrating moment, I zoned out entirely and began to think about what my old friends and I would have been up to on a Tuesday morning with a fresh school week looming. Just about now, Ashley would be standing at the locker next to mine trying to figure out if she could write her own note saying she had some fatal disease in order to skip out of gym class. I'd have to remind her that her period wasn't a fatal disease and impending brain surgery didn't seem entirely plausible.

My happy memories were interrupted by the fact that we had indeed reached the end of the road.

Two large, black steel gates, that were obviously the entrance of my new doom, were imposing to the point that it was obvious we'd soon be entering a fortress or a billionaire's private mansion.

What the hell is this place? I wondered, gazing up at the stately white-bricked mansion that was far off in the distance. At first glance, the school looked like an estate house or a castle. It was timeless in its architecture and a bit on the arrogant side. The main building broke through the clouds, so I craned my neck in an attempt to determine how many stories high it went, but that exercise was futile. Instead, I gazed in awe at the gray, weathered stones and peaks jutting up higher than the eye could see to announce a rather imposing presence.

The sign in front of my face looked like it just received a new coat of white paint and it was far too plain for a place this grand.

In simple, black painted letters it read: **The Academy**.

I shuddered for a second as the main gate creaked opened because it wasn't just intimidating, it was awesome. Through thick pine trees I saw manicured grounds that were the same luscious summer green as my front yard. Tulips and crocuses were in full bloom, although the temperature outside was only twenty degrees according the DJ on the radio who played oldies that sounded a lot like "newies."

We careened the car up, up, up what seemed like the longest driveway in history. The place looked so old and stately that I half expected to see horses and carriages or moats and dragons. When we approached a small green booth, a second checkpoint, the long, cold steel mechanical arm that kept what belonged outside away was down.

Inside the booth sat a kindly looking older man in a black suit, starched white shirt, and crisp muted-silver bowtie with a nameplate on his chest that proudly read: Harold.

"Walker Callaghan?" he demanded with a twinkle in his eye, startling me because his familiar tone felt like I had known him forever. As the confused newcomer, I simply nodded. *How did he know my name? Was I the only new student in ages?* I couldn't know at the time that twenty newcomers had arrived in the last hour.

"We just arrived over the weekend," Mom said, filling in the blanks. "We're from Chicago . . . and I don't know exactly what to do now."

"Well, it's quite easy," gate-guard Harold advised with a slow smile that seemed to match his kindly old man's face. His eyes were brown and sparkled when he looked at you. "I think the next step is to hit the gas, go up the driveway, and check out the school. It's just that simple. Enjoy your time."

"Sounds like a plan," said Mom whose voice began to get all quivery again, so I gave her my best and biggest "Yes, I really am a trooper" smile. I knew this must be a proud moment for her because no one in the Walker family had ever gone to private school. She couldn't even afford music lessons for me, let alone a place that looked like a boarding school out of some turn-of-the-century novel. I wondered, *Did Mom knock off a bank and forget to tell me? Did she donate a kidney to medical science? Did she marry a billionaire? Was my new name Walker Buffett? Please don't let it be Walker Trump.*

"Proceed to the double doors at the end of the driveway and you'll be met by our head counselor, Miss Maude Travis. She'll take it from there," Harold said. "And if you don't want your blackberry pie for lunch, which is what they serve on Tuesdays, you can always bring it to a hardworking gate guard. We always have pecan on Wednesday. I love me some pecan, too!"

Before I could question that one, we were off—slowly driving past manicured evergreen bushes until we reached the top of the driveway where students were lingering with books in their hands and wary looks on their faces as they stared at our car. My heart began to pound like was five years old again on the first day of kindergarten. In an instant, I knew that there was nothing private about private school. Two blonde cheerleader types were blocking the front entrance and seemed to be comparing their new leather boots and short skirts while gazing into the car window to size me, and my current fashion statement, up.

In an annoying singsong voice, one called for the other whose name was apparently Amanda, but by the looks of her and her constant whining about everything, I already dubbed her *Demanda.*

When I half fell out of the car in my old, black winter wool skirt that fell below my knees and a crisp, nondescript white collared shirt, Demanda and her BFF looked at me and then gazed at each other with sympathy. The looks of pity on their faces were undeniable. "I didn't know we were admitting the Amish," Demanda whispered in a way that was loud.

"So, cliques are cliques anywhere . . . make that everywhere," I whispered to Mom who was right beside me like the other specimen in their science project. I knew that Mom had already flunked the chic parent contest. She always wore navy skirts, white turtlenecks, and a little white cardigan sweater that was as soft as a newborn's cheek.

"And how old do you have to be to go to this school?" I asked her. "There's a little kid over there that looks like he's only nine or ten. What's he doing here? Is this some baby-brat boarding academy?"

"Just give it a chance," Mom said, ignoring my last question.

"Keep an open mind. Don't judge. Always flush and floss. I know, Mom, I know," I said, reciting some of her greatest hits.

3.

Kindly Miss Travis interrupted future words of wisdom from the slowest driver in town. She appeared out of nowhere, a near eighty-year-old gray-haired grandmother type holding an efficient brown clipboard and wearing a miles-thick red cardigan that had a few pulls on the side from wear and tear. Her skin was crinkled everywhere and there wasn't a stitch of makeup on her face. Silver hair was tucked neatly into a small bun.

Eyeing me, your standard five-foot-four girl with long, glossy reddish-brown hair that fell stick-straight halfway down my back, blunt cut bangs, and big hazel eyes, Miss Travis took immediate charge of the situation. What I would learn later was that this was exactly what she did precisely 365 days a year with all the girls and boys in her care; although she tried not to get too emotionally involved because it could be a heartbreaker. Still, she loved the job.

"Walker, may I be the first person to welcome you here to the Academy. We have your transcripts," she began in her brisk, no-nonsense manner. Miss Travis masked emotion with her great efficiency.

"So fast?" Mom questioned.

"Oh, immediately," said Miss Travis.

"And from these transcripts, we've enrolled Walker in a few classes that should expand her grasp," Miss Travis went on. I waited to hear the horrifying list of what I would be stuck with for the rest of the school year. As a senior, certainly, I would have to take trig, chemistry, computer science, and maybe even one of those impossible macroeconomic classes that I would surely flunk. The doom cloud returned and my eyes hit the pavement.

"You'll start by taking music theory, art appreciation, chemistry, and pop literature. Ever read *Divergent*? Or that book where those lovely young ladies swap the magical pants? So entertaining, although in the case of the latter not absolutely hygienic, if you ask me," Miss Travis rattled off, adjusting her cat-eye glasses that hung from a string around her neck. "In the afternoon, we thought you might enjoy physical education, taught by a former athlete, a lovely man named Walter, plus you'll have an independent study period and something we call fruit appreciation."

"We learn to appreciate fruit?" I asked, my eyes a little wide because I never expected my conservative mom to enroll me in some hippie place where you actually talked to your banana and communed with your cantaloupe.

36

"Oh dear, don't make me laugh," Miss Travis said. "It's just our way of saying it. It's your standard computer class taught by a new teacher who has an odd sense of humor, but he possesses one of the most brilliant minds in history."

My brain began to race. "What will I be studying independently?" I asked in a meek voice, trying to sound curious.

"Why, you'll study whatever interests you, dear," Miss Travis said. "If you're interested in the relationship between Charlie Brown and Snoopy or how Earth was created, feel free. Explore to your heart's content. Expand your horizons. Isn't that what all the hipsters say?"

"So, I'll have to write term papers for final grades," I pondered aloud.

"Oh no! How silly!" Miss Travis smiled. "The knowledge you gain will be judged by only one. Just you."

My eyes went wide because I just couldn't believe it. My bookworm mother had actually found the one progressive school in the nation and she wasn't rallying against it? "When are midterms? I guess I'm already a bit behind since I'm starting a few weeks late," I said, sadly. For some reason, I was suddenly determined to put my best foot forward here, as my mother would say.

Miss Travis was now ushering us up the stairs toward the front doors and began to talk again in that whimsical voice of hers that made her sound like Mary Poppins's much older sister.

"We don't do midterms or finals here, dear," she finally said. "We don't believe in tests. Not even the SATs."

"No tests," I mouthed. "How will I ever get into college?" There was no time to contemplate that one because suddenly we were walking through enormous, heavy doors that were at least twenty feet high and sporting brass handles so tall that they could be gripped by five people at the same time. From my first glance, I knew this wasn't like any school I had ever attended.

This place was fantastic with a big dose of fabulous rolled right in.

We stepped through two carved oak doors into a fancy parlor that looked like the drawing room in a stately old mansion. The creamy white walls supported a seemingly endless collection of famous oil paintings including what looked like the Mona Lisa and some Van Gogh landscape I studied in Chicago in art class. Thick, gorgeously patterned Asian rugs in deep reds and vibrant blues were strewn on the chestnut floors that were so highly polished you could see your own reflection looking up at you.

A large mural of peaceful, winged angels hovered on its own over a white stone fireplace so enormous you could actually step into it. As I frowned at my feet, my reflection glanced back up, smiling like the floor had suddenly transformed into a mirror that could alter your mood.

A winding hand-carved ebony staircase shot straight up through the center of the school and the walls leading upstairs offered even more elaborate oil paintings and sculptures of men, women, and even animals like regal Dobermans and milky-white greyhounds.

Miss Travis was the perfect hostess, insisting that we take a seat in the lavish sitting room where steaming hot tea was waiting in two sky-blue porcelain cups on a long wooden table. Real gaslight fixtures cast a warm glow over her face.

Mom and I sunk into an overstuffed, red velvet couch while a butler named Edward, an old man in a black tux, quickly entered to ask if we needed anything at all. He looked exactly like Alfred from the Batman movies; a right-hand-man type, who was always at your side whether you needed him to bring tea or push a secret button that led to the Batcave.

Miss Travis encouraged us to settle in and relax while she went over a few reminders about the rules of this place. "You'll be

38

in school from eight a.m. until three p.m. every single day. That's nonnegotiable," she began.

"What if I get sick and need to take a day off?" I asked.

"That's not an issue here, dear," Miss Travis said. "You won't get sick."

"If you say so," I said, resisting an eyebrow arch. *How could she possibly know that I wouldn't get sick? I was just* really *sick.*

"The rules are simple. You're here to learn and to be curious," Miss Travis added. "If a subject interests you, then please explore it. Enjoy learning. It's one of our greatest joys."

"That's it?" I said.

"Please be courteous to your fellow students," Miss Travis added. "And don't litter. We are a green school. Recycling trucks come on Thursdays."

I nodded and Miss Travis stared at my mother. "You can pick her up later or she can simply walk home. There's no crime here, if you don't count the . . . well, we'll get to that later, but she should be fine as she acclimates," Miss Travis said, sounding a bit nervous for the first time.

It was much too soon to bring up anything undesirable or—as I would find out later—what Miss Travis dubbed, the Element. I would find out soon enough.

"Mom, I'll walk. I want to explore the town a little bit," I said. "Remember, free real hot chocolate with a blueberry muffin. Seconds and thirds."

"Well, just be home before dark," said Mom who stopped herself suddenly. My mother stood, hugged me, and then nervously walked out of the sitting room. For a minute, I was tempted to follow her because although it sounded good, a new school was still like walking into the vast unknown.

"I'll show you to your first class. This one offers a variety of teachers throughout the year and this morning a fresh instructor has arrived. So today's class will be new to all, not just you, my dear," Miss Travis rambled as she led me through a maze of smaller parlors until we arrived at the bottom of that beckoning, winding staircase. She pushed a button and one of those little chairs that carry the elderly suddenly appeared along the stairs. "I like to conserve energy—my own," she told me. "You need your exercise. See you on floor seven."

4.

A few minutes and a lot of huffing proved her right although I wasn't really breathless. Maybe I was huffing from habit. I quickly made it upstairs where she directed me to room 710, an intimate classroom where ten students sat in twos at highly polished, long mahogany tables. The cheerleaders were there, including Demanda and her posse, whispering to each other while looking everywhere but at each other. Glancing at their bright green-and-blue manicures was also a major obsession and made them look like mermaid rejects.

I walked past some nerd-type who had a full head of Brillo-pad red curls, plus arms and legs that went on for miles and about zero-percent body fat or muscle. He had his head in a book, but I could feel him glance up as I passed him and he flashed me a genuine smile, which I returned with a quick sincere one of my own.

"Hi, I'm Arnie. Enter at your own risk," he said, extending one of those mile-long arms.

"Hi Arnie, Walker," I replied.

"Walker . . . odd, but appealing. Your name, not you, " he

40

replied, returning his nose to the book. I guess that's what passed for flirting at this school.

The other kids looked pretty normal and around my age including one fine-boned ballerina type with supermodel glossy blonde hair and lipstick that was red-black. She wore what looked like a pale-pink leotard with matching leggings and covered herself with an additional layer of a thin sweater and one of those dusky-pink skater skirts. I heard someone call her Tosh, and she even smiled up at me sort of warmly before saying, "There's only one table left in the back. You'll have to share it with Mr. Personality. God speed, newbie. Don't hold him against the rest of us."

I had no idea what she meant, but wandered to the back of the classroom and plopped down at the table in the corner, which was empty. Eventually, I reached into my brand-new leather backpack that had appeared during the move and was filled with every school supply anyone would ever want, from paper to a slim laptop and an iPad. Again, I wondered when my mom had time to get all these school supplies, including a backpack that looked like it cost some serious change because it smelled like real cow flesh. There was about two thousand dollars of electronics in my possession. I was trying to figure out how much Mom spent in total in my head when I was jolted out of my self-imposed mental shopping trip by the class bell.

The same moment the sound echoed, a broad-shouldered student in a black leather jacket blasted into the class, which caused the cool girls to start whispering. Looking around the room, he obviously noticed that his formerly empty table in the back now had another occupant. "Damn," I heard him whisper under his breath as he walked closer. "Just what I needed—a squatter."

Tossing his book onto the wood, he didn't miss the new dark-haired girl jumping half out of her skin, but trying to look bored at the same time. Although I tried to calm myself down, he had to

41

know that I was petrified—by the fact that my hazel eyes were as wide as saucers. I didn't know then that he had been in my shoes several years earlier when he had arrived with his brother and sisters.

"Walker," I said, cutting to the chase and trying to look into his eyes, which were cast downward so my gaze met the middle of his chest. Extending my hand felt foolish now and I allowed it to plop to my side in defeat.

For a few long seconds, he said absolutely nothing and stayed in the same position of epic rudeness. Then he slowly forced himself to look at me. The impact of it had me backing up a few centimeters. He was much more rugged than I would expect from any private school student, with a thin scar that ran across his chin to his lower lip and several light-green tattoos sneaking out of sleeves that were haphazardly pushed aside. This wasn't your average high-school senior. He looked too weary and too wise. If you told me that he was a senior in college, I might have believed it.

"Daniel Reid," he finally said with freezing calm, running a hand through jet-black hair that was shorter on the sides than on the top. That hair looked recklessly hand-combed off a masculine, square face that was marked by about a day's growth of facial stubble; you could barely see it, but the shadow was there and made him look older and dangerous. I figured he was about six three or four with serious arms but a lean frame that fit nicely into snug, faded Levis.

Obviously, he worked out. I could imagine the six-pack and the sinewy muscles than ran from his thighs down the sides of his muscular legs. Almost blushing because I was a little too deep into the detail of a total stranger, I decided to focus on the fact that he dumped his leather jacket in a heap on the floor, slammed down his stool, and once seated, stared straight ahead.

"So how long have you been going to this school?" I whispered loudly, shifting nervously on my stool as if I wanted to dig a hole out of there. Obviously, I wasn't such an expert when it came to small talk and I could tell that he preferred we didn't talk at all.

"Forever," he said in a harsh tone as I stared at the side of his sculpted face.

"I'm already liking this idea of just learning what you want," I blurted.

"Yeah," he muttered and nodded numbly.

"What about SAT prep?" I asked. "It's hard to believe that we really don't need to take the college prep tests. Whose leg are they pulling here? Not your leg. You're too tall." My thin attempt at a joke seemed to annoy him.

"We don't do that here," Daniel snapped, pretending to be suddenly engrossed in the pen he was tapping loudly on the table.

"What don't we do here? Joke around—or take tests?" I demanded and heard him swear under his breath.

I wasn't done.

"College applications?" I blurted again. When he looked up again and stared hard into my eyes, I was rendered speechless. It was almost as if he put one of those large hands gently across my mouth, but that wasn't the case because the wide palms and long fingers were planted firmly on his knees. I couldn't contain the rush I felt. It continued to sizzle under my skin for several impossibly long minutes. His eyes weren't just blue; they were gray-blue, a surprisingly soft, inviting, gauzy color that you only find on the most perfect cloudy day on the beach before a good rain.

But there was nothing else inviting about Daniel Reid.

"Do I look like the welcome wagon?" he practically hissed. I saw his eyes go from soft to almost metallic. When I looked honestly hurt, he shook his head, swore again, and continued to speak under his breath.

43

"Screw college," Daniel said with a sigh. With those words, he had exceeded his friendliness quotient for the day. Maybe the year. "If you need to know any more go talk to a counselor. You know. For guidance. Or whatever girls like you need."

Girls like me? Asswipe.

"So, wait a second. No homework. No SATs. No college applications?" I said, ignoring his obvious lack of social graces and that grim, hard mouth. In that moment, I knew his game. He wanted me to brand him as one big douche and get on with it so I'd leave him alone. So, I decided to have a little bit of fun with him.

"I can't get over no homework," I repeated with a slight upturn of my bottom lip, trying to kill him with unwanted kindness. "Is this heaven?" I asked, tossing him my most dazzling grin. I sealed it with a wink. What was with the flirt? I had little success with the opposite sex in Chicago, so I was sure it wasn't that dazzling or dazzling at all. But I had to do it.

Those broad, muscular shoulders pivoted in my direction and those steel-gray eyes seemed to drill through me. I'm not sure why, but in that moment I glanced over at the cheerleaders who were giving me stabbing looks for talking to the hands down most gorgeous man any of them had probably ever seen in their entire lives. He made David Beckham look like the ugly older brother.

Obviously, the cheerleaders had their own dibs . . . and they weren't about to share, although he totally ignored the fact that they even existed.

"Is this hell, Danny?" I said, looking ahead at the rah-rah brigade, rolling my eyes and catching their disgusted looks. No way did they miss my eye roll. Pleased with myself, I turned my full attention to his annoyed gaze and those full lips.

"No, this isn't heaven. It isn't hell. It's high school," Daniel said. He was frowning again in a way that made it seem like he wanted to toss me out the nearby window. But I wasn't giving up, which was a trick I learned in my short career as a newspaper reporter. If at first you don't succeed, just stay relentless.

"By the way, it's not Danny. It's Daniel. And do you have a last name?" he asked, but without any passion.

"Walker Callaghan," I said with a genuine smile, offering my hand to him again. He ignored it for the second time.

"Pay attention, Callaghan. Learn something," Daniel said, pointing to the front blackboard. I tried to tear my eyes away from him, but somehow I was frozen in place. He took it upon himself to rectify the situation, gently grabbing my chin with those big hands and slowly moving it in the direction of the front of the room like he was guiding the big hand of a watch into place.

"Don't move. It will be worth it," he said.

At that moment, the teacher finally arrived, but he wasn't any educator that would have worked at Kennedy High. For starters, he had longish, dirty-brown unwashed hair that matched his ripped jeans and faded brown flannel shirt.

"Music theory one-oh-one," the teacher scoffed. "What bullshit."

"You really want to know about music?" he continued. Even I perked up and stared at him because he looked so familiar, especially when he turned his back to us and started writing notes on the blackboard. When my hand flew to my mouth, Daniel turned his head ever so slightly and I felt his stare down to my bone marrow. *It was . . . no, it couldn't be. How could it be?*

"So, I'm Kurt," he said. "I used to have this band."

CHAPTER 3

1.

Once again, in fruit appreciation class, I was forced to sit next to the only person with no tablemate; so I took my position next to Mr. Charm much to his exasperation. I even raised my Spock brow to Daniel Reid who gave me a quick glance and then began to pay rapt attention to the fruit teacher guy like they were kindred spirits. The truth was that the class wasn't about fruit at all. It was about computers and all things high tech.

The teacher was some lanky, overly excited guy who told me, "Just call me Steve. I used to work at a company named after fruit. Go sit in the back. Learn something real."

What he passed out that day wasn't exactly homework but, instead, interesting reading of some very heavy books about prospective technology that sounded futuristic in a completely fascinating way.

"The human race will soon be able to give up cars and the

never-ending oil crisis and just teleport everywhere just like 'Beam me up, Scotty,'" Steve said. "People will just use a device called an iPorter." A little buzz went through the classroom because this did sound pretty cool and cutting edge, but it also sounded a bit crazy.

"You think beaming oneself places was just for a TV show or the movies?" Steve asked, adjusting his wire-rimmed glasses for emphasis. "Think again, but do think about it. That's your assignment for the evening."

All we have to do is think? I thought. *No one puts your thoughts on your permanent record. Thinking is not homework.*

What I loved about the class was that it wasn't just about technology, but also about philosophy. This Steve guy loved to veer wildly off the topic at hand and just talk about life—something we never got to do at Kennedy High School, which was all about teaching for standardized tests.

"When I was seventeen, I read a quote that went something like: If you live each day as if it was your last, someday you'll most certainly be right," Steve said, nudging us in that annoying thinking direction again. "It made an impression on me, and for thirty-nine years since then, I have looked in the mirror every morning and asked myself: If today were the last day of my life would I want to do what I am about to do today?"

Then he careened closer to me during a waltz around the room in his bright-blue Nikes and said, "Whenever the answer has been 'No' for too many days in a row, I know I need to change something. Food for thought," he said with a challenging lift to the last three words.

When the bell rang, he tossed out what I would later learn was his trademark line, "Get out of here. Stay hungry. Stay foolish."

I just knew I had heard those words somewhere before, but I couldn't remember where or why or how.

2.

By three p.m. that day the final bell didn't ring, but chimed like an orchestra was now announcing the end of another day. A deep-sounding voice came on the PA system, but without the usual barrage of high-school announcements. "Enjoy your time," a man said in a rich baritone.

It's weird that none of the other kids are walking home, I thought when my feet finally hit the endless grassy front lawn. In fact, most of them were still somewhere inside the school, which was even more enormous and endless than I realized. There were countless floors filled with winding mazes of classrooms, libraries, study nooks, a gymnasium, a theater, a swimming pool, and even dorm rooms because most of the students didn't have families in town.

Earlier in the day, one of the nice girls from music class named Gracie, a willowy fifteen-year-old redhead, engaged me in a little lunch-line chitchat. "Most of us actually live here at the school in various quarters like dorm rooms at a college," she told me. "There are very few families accompanying the students. Hardly any of us live off campus. Your new friend Daniel lives off campus . . . with his family."

"He's definitely not my friend," I interjected. And she smiled.

"I wish he was *my* friend," she purred.

"So, it's a boarding school? You only go home for the holidays?" I asked, promptly changing the subject. I didn't know much about this guy, and I wasn't sure I wanted to know anything at all.

"Most of us live here year round until we graduate, I mean, move on. The dorms are pretty sweet," Gracie said. "Maybe someday you'll need a roommate."

"Well, my mom moved here with me," I said. "We live in one of the houses by Main Street. It's not half bad."

"Your mom?" Gracie said in a longing tone. "That's really nice. I wish I could see my mom, but not really. She's off doing her . . . thing."

"There's always Thanksgiving," I offered, but Gracie just looked away sadly and said that she might even pop in on her mom that night. *iChat*, I thought. *Her mother must have paid the Internet bill.*

Then I asked Gracie a simple question, "So how long have you been here?"

"About a thousand years—or it feels like it," Gracie said in a wistful tone. Her voice perked up when she announced, "You should really try the brownies. The ones with the nuts are the best. Do you like nuts?"

I better, I thought, noting that there was a mixed variety of human ones at this new school.

With still a ways to go before exiting the campus, I passed that nice gate guard, Harold, who was still in his booth. He gave me a big friendly smile and a thumbs-up; he even lifted his fork to show that he got some of that pie he was coveting. I had been planning it all day, and couldn't wait to retrieve something out of my backpack. Harold was delighted when I tossed a little plastic baggie on his ledge. "Chocolate cream," I said with a wave.

"This is the beginning of a beautiful friendship, Walker Callaghan," he replied, tipping his head.

After I passed him, the real boredom set in as I trudged along toward home. By the time I walked off the lavish grounds of the Academy and onto the cobblestones of Main Street, I felt like a total idiot for hoofing it because the walk was certainly longer than it seemed from the short drive that morning.

The wintery sun was dipping low now and the sky had taken on a pleasant pink-purple canvas. Before I knew it, I was in the heart of Main Street and popped into Perks coffee shop where the smell of fresh brew enveloped me like a warm, delicious blanket that just came out of the dryer. The counter girl, who introduced herself as Angelina, was only a few years older than me and she was rocking out to Coldplay on her MP3 player. She could have cared less that I took forever gazing at a menu that seemed endless, but I finally narrowed down the seemingly infinite choices and ordered a vanilla soy latte with extra whip.

Suddenly, it dawned on me that I didn't have any money. I didn't even have my purse, which was odd because I never forgot it back in Chicago. *Oh my God . . . was it lost? My purse had the fifty dollars I was saving for Christmas, plus a ten dollar gift card from Starbucks. Where was it?* I got that sinking feeling in the pit of my stomach. How could I be so stupid and order with no cash on hand?

"I'm really sorry, but can I still cancel . . ." I began, and Angelina, who had long wavy auburn hair down to her butt and looked like a granola eater in her acid-washed jeans and peace-sign T-shirt, just waved her hand in the air and said, "On the house, sweetie."

Friendly town, I thought.

In the corner there was a computer and an offer of free Internet. Finally! A Christmas-morning feeling swept over my entire body. Now I could e-mail Madison and Ashley and tell them what was up and ask if anyone missed me. "I'll bring your drink over to you," the waitress promised as I made a beeline for the keyboard and began to type away. First, I tried to sign into my Gmail account, but it wouldn't come up at all. So I went over to Yahoo and created a new account for myself, which took about one minute. I typed in Madison's email address: mad4life@gmail.com.

Mad, you won't believe where I am. My new school is pretty cool, but I don't know about this town. We do have a new house and this totally hot guy sat by me in music class. Tall, dark, brooding.

You know the type. Gorgeous! Pretty rude. Of course, I want to see him tomorrow. I'll try to get pix. By accident, I hit the send button before I was done.

Whoops, I thought, pausing to start a new e-mail to Mad when a message bounced back. It was a mailer-daemon that read "Message undeliverable."

I shrugged and decided to write to Ashley first.

Hey Ash, is Mad still flirting with stupid Cade Boyer? Miss you guys. Is it still freezing outside? It's cold here, but strange. You can go out without a coat and you're fine. And there's green grass at school, but no snow, which is also weird because there are piles of the stuff everywhere else. Can I call you over the weekend? Maybe you can even take the bus and visit. Hitting send again, I waited. A minute passed and I received another mailer-daemon.

I continued to type.

Greetings, Aunt Ginny. Hope you're doing well. I have a quick favor. Can you make sure to get my mail and put it in a pile in Mom's room? I'm waiting for a reply from a magazine I sent a story to for publication. It's kind of a big deal.

I typed in her email address only to have it bounce back again as undeliverable. At that moment, the latte arrived. "Is there something wrong with this computer," I asked the waitress. "Everything is bouncing back. I'm in tech hell."

"You're not in hell. Not even close," Angelina said, chuckling, as she passed me a few real-sugar packets. "Sorry. Bad joke." She paused when she noticed my surprised stare at the little white packets. "We don't do sugar substitutes here. Why bother?" she said. "It's only the good stuff. And speaking of good stuff, do you want free biscotti with that? They're peanut butter. Really good. No trans fats and the peanuts are sourced from sustainable farms."

I shook my head and said, "Thanks, but not today." It was a reflex action since I felt guilty enough about the one freebie.

I didn't really have time to think about food because of the commotion that blew into the front door like some sort of mini-tornado. Two young girls with jet-black, stick-straight hair flying behind them were racing each other and burst through the glass door, which slammed into the wall with a loud thud. Granola girl looked up for a moment, but then went back to separating sugar packets.

The oldest girl shoved the younger one, who pretended to trip, but instead gave her rival a big bear hug across the knees, which caused her to fall forward. "You lose, Jenna," said the younger girl. "I got here first, which means I get the first hot chocolate. Get out of my way. *Loos-uh.*"

"Why are you guys such raging idiots?" said a teenage boy, who was next to burst through the doors. He was the male equivalent of both girls and obviously their brother because he had the same onyx hair, although his was much shorter, cut in a longish buzz. He grabbed each of his sisters by a shoulder and tried to make some order of their chaos. All three had pale features and icy blue-gray eyes, making them each striking and beautiful in their own way.

"Can you clowns please knock it off," said a deep voice attached to a tall form that stood in the open doorway allowing the cold air to blow inside. This time the leather jacket was back on, and the hair was slicked back off his face like he had just gotten out of the shower. Did he really need the black Ray-Bans?

As Daniel Reid stepped into the coffee shop, the look of disdain on his face was clear. He didn't even see me because he was too preoccupied with restoring the peace. "You!" he said, pointing at Jenna and removing the shades. "Sit there. Act normal. If that's possible."

"You," he repeated, pointing at the younger girl. "Go order. Try to stay out of trouble for five seconds. I know that's impossible, Andy, but pretend you're actually well mannered, which we all know is a lie."

"Peter, you carry the stuff," he commanded.

"Why am I always the slave?" the younger boy asked.

"Fine. Don't go get the stuff. Let it rot up there. Just stare at the drinks," Daniel said, grabbing a local newspaper.

"So, whadda you want?" Peter asked his brother.

"A vacation from all of you," Daniel responded.

"You know you don't really mean that—although if you say it enough maybe you'll get your wish," said Peter in a strangely serious voice. For a minute, it sounded like his voice actually cracked. Then again, he was at that age, maybe fourteen or fifteen, when boys temporarily sounded a little like girls.

"No, I don't mean it," Daniel said, walking over to give him a brotherly shove sideways. "But go sit down before I strangle you. That, I do mean."

Peter picked a table near me, but I noticed that his older brother didn't follow. Instead, he decided to lean against the counter and flirt with Angelina who was tossing her head back and laughing like they had some kind of souped-up inside joke. For some reason, I couldn't tear my eyes away. Disgust was the next emotion to register because it truly wasn't any of my business why she was touching his arm. A minute passed. Still touching. Why did it bother me? Quickly, I looked away because I didn't want to be that girl from music class who was seemingly stalking him since this was our third encounter of the day.

Soon, I was slumped forward and frowning at the screen while holding back my tears when I saw that my second-attempt e-mail to Aunt Ginny had also returned.

"Damn it!" I said, a bit too harshly under my breath.

Of course, he stared at me, and I took that as a signal to either spontaneously evaporate or say something utterly fascinating. I chose to slump down even further behind the screen because evaporation seemed like the better choice.

53

But I didn't have a real chance to drop out of sight completely because this girl called Jenna was suddenly at my side. "So, you're new," she said, plopping down in the chair next to me and gazing in that adoring way younger girls do when they meet an older soul sister. "We're your neighbors. We know everyone on our block and I saw you moving in with your mom. She seems nice. We haven't had a mom on the block in a long time," the kid rambled. "Does she bake? Cook ziti? Are you Italian? We just love when we get the moms. And we're not Italian. We're Irish. Do you have any questions?" Jenna said with a grin.

CHAPTER 4

1.

Of course, I just listened as the girl rattled off her questions, although my mind was stuck on the fact that this kid actually thought there were no mothers on their street. *How could there be no mothers on the street?* Come to think of it, I hadn't really seen many adults on my street or even in town, which looked like it was pretty much run by high-school seniors. Of course there were older people at school, but nowhere else, but that was common in boarding school situations. Mostly, it was just kids in small groups either walking or driving to the Academy. In a way, it was as if this was some sort of hip orphanage where you got your own house if you weren't sent to live at school.

How in the world . . .

"I'm Jenna Reid. I'm thirteen. That's my idiot little sister, Andy, over there. Peter is barely housebroken. We think of him as our overgrown human puppy. We just feed him constantly and give him a chew toy," she continued, laughing at her own joke. "And then there's big-bro Daniel, who pretends to be mean and in charge. Don't call him Dan or Danny. He'll freak out on you," she blurted out. "It's so cool all of us live off campus. Who needs the dorms? Do you like vampire books?"

I had to do what came next.

"And Angelina behind the counter. Is she your brother's girlfriend?" I asked, because I could never not ask.

"Girlfriend!" Jenna whispered like this was the funniest thing she had ever heard in her life. "She probably wishes, but he doesn't have a girlfriend. He has us."

"Jenna," Daniel admonished her while walking toward us from across the room. "Can you keep the questions down to just five or six hundred? She just moved here and you're like the FBI and CIA rolled into one."

"Oh, I forgot to mention. Daniel's also the comedian in the family," Jenna said with a smirk. "And he's just so NOT funny. Ask anyone."

"Where are you from?" Jenna continued her interrogation, beaming at me like I was a movie star who suddenly landed at her local coffee shop for a quick meet-and-greet with fans.

"Well, I'm from Chicago, really the suburbs. This place called Arlington Heights," I said and Jenna vaulted out of the chair she had scrambled into and now began to literally jump up and down like a pogo stick.

"Kill me now!" she shouted, twirling as she jumped. "Us, too! Chicago by way of Lake Forest. Ever hear of it? Ever go there? Do we know you? Who is your dad? Who is your mom? Am I asking you too many questions? Am I blowing your mind?"

"Easy clown," Daniel said, now standing above us, shaking his head.

I had to laugh. "Uh, let's see. Ok, Lake Forest as a town—heard of it. Never been there. Too fancy for me. I don't think we know each other, but nice to meet someone from the Land of Lincoln. My dad was Sam. Died when I was little. My mom is Madeleine. She's here with me. You can never ask too many questions. That's my motto."

I looked up into Daniel's steel eyes, which were locked on me, before answering her last question. I wanted to look away – really – but he had me on some sort of lock.

"No one blows my mind," I said slowly.

Daniel didn't move.

"What does President Lincoln have to do with any of this?" Jenna interrupted.

"She flunked history, but got an A in being annoying," Pete shouted, carrying the drinks to their table.

Obviously Daniel knew the only way to restrain her was to physically lead her to their table, so he placed one of those large hands on her tiny shoulders and steered her away like a car being turned in the opposite direction. My pulse quickened and I tried to keep my mind off his blue-back hair that he was shoving out of that chiseled face and the fact that he smelled like pine trees and hot coffee. His light-gray eyes burned as he put his sister into a mock headlock for her final steps to their table and sipped his coffee.

"Hey, don't call child welfare. I beat on them all the time," Daniel called out to me.

"I figured," I shot back. As a response, the younger boy, Peter, stood up and did a karate kick that missed his older brother by mere inches.

"I'm the real tough one. Did you know I learned everything from Bruce who came last month to teach," Peter chimed in, now standing by his brother's side. "He really did. Bruce. You know, *Bruce L...*," He didn't finish the last word. With that dangling,

Peter moved back to show me a few more karate moves. Without thinking, I gave him a quick round of applause because the kid did a mean roundhouse kick that looked like it could really hurt someone.

"Pete. Shut up and stop before you break something," Daniel said.

"You mean hurt yourself," I added. "At least that's what my mom would say.'"

"We can't really hurt ourselves. Didn't they tell you?" Pete interrupted. "No rules. No conseque—"

Daniel took a hand and put it over Peter's mouth before he could finish what he was saying. His voice was muffled when Daniel lifted his hand a little bit, but I could have sworn the kid added, "No limits! Ya-hooo!"

"Callaghan just arrived yesterday," Daniel told him. "Cool it—and you know what I mean. Go get your drink. Do something useful." It wasn't so much a suggestion, but an order.

So, he did remember my name.

"You know . . . if Bruce Lee is the gym teacher . . ." I began.

"That's next week," said a sarcastic Daniel. "And our gym teacher is a guy named Walter. Used to play football until… well, until he didn't." Then he looked down at the linoleum as if he felt he was saying too much.

When Jenna asked me to come sit with them, there was no choice but to relocate my seat. Sitting next to him seemed to be my karma for the day. Why did it have to feel so good? So right?

2.

Half an hour later, I learned everything about Jenna's obsession with British boy bands, her hatred of Miley Cyrus, and that there was some boy in her yoga class at school that she thought was hot-hottie-hot. *Wait. They taught yoga at this school?* Andy was mostly quiet and extremely shy, but somehow found the nerve to ask me how I got my hair so long and straight, which was sweet. "If you actually washed yours then you would have pretty hair, too," Daniel said.

I made immediate eye contact with the wood on the table. *Was that an actual compliment?*

Pete went on and on about his love of karate and Jenna continued to inform me of every like and dislike she had ever experienced. Daniel spent the time just keeping them in line, which wasn't hard because they were rambunctious but not unruly kids. In a way, he was like a dad and big brother wrapped up in one handsome leather jacket and surly attitude.

When my latte ran out, I half expected him to do something nice like get me another one. Of course, he just sat there proving that my day of contact with this handsome stranger had been ninety-five percent chance and five percent a made-up story in my head.

"We'll walk you home, Walker. You live real close," Jenna insisted. "Plus, it's dark and the woods can be creepy."

Daniel stood abruptly like this was settled without his consent and certainly without his approval. "Let's go," he barked, nodding to Angelina who blew him a quick kiss as all of us walked out the door. I was the last one—the odd man out.

3.

It was dark now and Daniel's three younger siblings raced ahead to continue the battle they had been having before they walked into that warm and cozy coffee shop.

"So, what do you do for fun around here?" I asked Daniel, walking next to him as we crunched over fresh snow. Now that the sky was a dense black with absolutely no stars, I was a little afraid I'd never find my way back to my house; so I didn't want to lose the guy with the long strides who walked so quickly I was almost jogging to keep up. We were off the main road because he insisted on a shortcut across an expansive field that butted up against the back of our houses.

"You're looking at it," he said. "We go to school. Hang out. Walk around. Go to town. It's a pretty basic existence, but nice and uncomplicated," he said. "That's the way I like to keep things. Uncomplicated."

Was this a warning? If so, he could take his concerns and . . .

"And your parents? What do they do?" I asked before allowing my temper to bubble over.

"I don't know what they do anymore. They used to only do things that made them money, so they could become even richer. But that doesn't really matter now," Daniel said. "They're not here."

"You mean they're on a trip?" I asked, crunching down a snowy embankment so steep that I happily accepted Daniel's hand when he held it out. His hand was strong, firm and made my pulse bounce when I grasped his fingers. It wasn't a romantic move, just a way for me to navigate the small hill we had to climb down until it bottomed out into what looked horrifying to me. At the base of the hill was a giant lake that was heavily iced over; it was the size of a football field. There was no way to walk around it and, frankly, I didn't have the energy to climb back up the hill or the skill to find my own route.

"Is it safe?" I asked Daniel before taking one tentative step onto the frozen ice covered with a fine coating of filigreed snow. It looked like someone had sprinkled powdered sugar on what looked like a river.

He didn't speak, but took three giant steps in front of me onto the ice and continued walking, all two-hundred-plus pounds of him, crunching over the surface in his black military boots. I had no choice but to double-time it to keep up as I slid and clomped over the slippery surface. It wasn't easy to get the hang of it, which defeated my inner Olympian skater girl who lurked deep in the recesses of my dream life wish list.

Now that it was absolutely dark, I felt like the world had faded to inky black. I didn't have any idea where we were walking, but knew I had to get home before my mother became frantic and called the cops, which would be mortifying in a new town.

"So, how long have your parents been gone?" I asked, sliding along and breathing not-so-heavily, while thinking that maybe his mother and father had a time-share in Miami or Palm Springs during this time of the year and had just snuck away for the weekend or even dumped the kids on him for a week.

"How long have they been gone?" Daniel pondered out loud. His laugh was beyond sarcastic; it was vicious. "They've been gone years, months, and days. Who cares about them? I certainly don't."

Of course, he was kidding. Parents didn't take vacations from their four children for years. It was called child abandonment and there were laws. *Wait, maybe his parents were in jail for breaking the law. Embezzlers? Ponzi scheme?* My journalistic mind was in overdrive. "So, it's just the four of you kids in the house? For years.

61

Home alone." I said with a little laugh. "Obviously, that was a bad joke."

"No joke. It's just us four—we're a family. Intact. For the most part," he said, quickly walking ahead again. He really didn't want to get into it now.

Intact? I thought. *Now this was really getting interesting. I knew he was the exacting type, and his choice of words was deliberate.*

My next question would have to wait.

In what seemed like an instant, my back foot caught on a large fallen tree branch and I fell forward with all my body weight. Crashing hard onto my hands and knees, I cried out, but I wasn't in any real pain. Before I could stand up, I slipped again until my stomach slammed against the surface of the thickly iced-over pond. The cracking sound was like thunder. Then, in what felt like a sickening surge of broken glass and rushing water, the ground suddenly ceased to exist. I didn't have time to scream as I dropped into the dark, lifeless, icy chill of wintery water.

I braced for the first slap of bitter freeze, instantly calling up some stupid fact from science class at Kennedy High where we learned that Titanic survivors described hitting the freezing ocean water as thousands of tiny knives stabbing every inch of their bodies.

I expected excruciating pain, but there was none. There was just numbness as I entered the earliest stages of being converted to ice.

Resistance was only natural and I fought hard as my hands flailed through the water trying to keep my head above the murky freeze, but it was pointless. The water was hungry that night and my thrashing almost made a game out of its impending conquest. It only took a second or two of my desperate survival dance for the lake to swallow me whole.

CHAPTER 5

1.

Daniel must have heard the crack and he stopped in place. Slowly, he turned around as I struggled to pop up again, but by putting up a fight I only succeeded in making it worse. As my body was being carried under the heavy sheet of ice in an involuntary dance, I could see Daniel above, the soles of his black boots carefully following my route as he calmly watched me drown.

In a way, it was fascinating to watch him ever so gradually shuffle along as my hands desperately reached from under my new icy roof for the bottom of his boots. The only thing that separated us was about five solid inches of deadly winter soup. By the time he found me in an even darker spot where the lake mingled with several dead, embalmed trees, all he could see from under the thick coating was my face looking up at him, frozen in horror. He saw my pouty mouth almost kissing the ice and frantically trying to say one word to him.

"Help!" I mouthed.

I gulped down murky green water, ingesting long tentacles of lifeless leaves and thick clumps of sludge-dirt, and it all slid easily into my lungs while *he just stood there. He. Stood. There.*

Frantically, I maneuvered away from the spot by the trees, which made it worse because now I was pinned under even thicker ice, my milky-white face pressed up against eight to ten inches of immovable crystals.

Casually, Daniel walked to where I was wildly waving my arms underneath the water. When I looked up now, he was a hazy dark blur that made me suddenly dizzy. That's when I shut my eyes to wait for the inevitable.

But I didn't black out. Long minutes passed, my eyes sprung open, and I continued to push upward again as the water became midnight black. For some reason I was still alive, but I still couldn't free myself from this wintry prison.

My mind raced. *How much time had passed? How much time could pass before I would be brain-dead? How much time before I died?*

Daniel still stood above the ground and calmly watched me struggle. "To hell with this," he finally said, loud enough for me to hear him under the ice. Was he telling me to stop struggling and just accept that I lost?

After another endless minute passed, he shook his head and, though apparently talking to himself, said even louder, "Okay, enough . . . but you need to know."

Kicking through a thinner spot of ice, he made a small hole and then pummeled it into a bigger passage with those clomping boots. Reaching down into the crack, he offered me a strong hand and a tat-covered, muscular arm. Somehow through the dark water, I saw human fingers moving and grabbed them like they were my only lifelines, which is exactly what they were to me.

All it took was one big hoist and I was in his arms, pressed body-to-body up against him, soaking wet, freezing cold, and mad as hell.

With my right hand, that had absolutely no feeling in it, I slapped him squarely across the jaw as hard as possible. When he didn't budge much, I slapped him again, which made my hand tired, but it didn't hurt. When I attempted to punch his face, he grabbed my hand in a firm way that signaled we weren't going another nine rounds.

"Easy there, tiger," he said with a smirk that made those soft eyes twinkle. "I guess you're a fan of the Rocky movies."

"Why . . . you bastard . . . why . . . you didn't even try to save me," I sputtered, but I wasn't really coughing and certainly my brain was perfectly fine. For a split second, I counted to five backward. Again, it was amazing that my mind was still functioning. Maybe the water was cold enough to save me. Is that how it worked?

"I saw you. You were just standing there! Watching! Watching me die!" I screamed, shoving him again. This time, I took him by surprise and he landed butt-first in a pile of snow.

Calmly, he stood up, lurched forward, and grabbed both of my arms, holding me against his rock-hard chest until I stopped struggling and gave up the idea of trying to knock his block off. He held me tightly like he was protecting me from some danger worse than what just happened. Tears formed in my eyes and I began to touch my arms and then tested my breathing, which was perfectly normal. He still refused to let go. Big white puffs of my breath filled the dark sky and I watched them evaporate slowly like little clouds. Then I looked up.

"Why aren't I dead?" I said in an anguished voice.

Daniel took a deep breath, carefully released me, and then answered slowly.

"Because, baby, you can't die twice," he said.

2.

I'd be lying if I didn't say that I wanted to slap him again, but I was too busy running my hands all over myself. I had no idea why I was still breathing or talking or looking at this asshole as if he were some sort of lunatic, which is exactly what he was . . . a lunatic *who just stood there looking gravely concerned and even a little bit sad.*

Nothing seemed weird or broken on me, except I was soaking wet standing in the snow and not shivering one bit. I knew my mom was going to kill me for coming home drenched. But first I had to send my new music-class buddy off to the men in white coats. "Yeah, we're all dead inside. Teenage agony. All the pain. Being this age sucks," I ranted, taking one step closer to him to look into his eyes for some clue that he was just kidding—a mean, kidding, maniac who almost let a girl drown right in front of him. *No Boy Scout points for that one, jerk ass.*

"No, you're dead—inside, outside, upside-down dead," he said, looking hard into my face where I'm sure the only thing he saw was my utter disbelief.

I made a mental note to tell my mother that we were packing up and moving back to Chicago first thing in the morning. Whatever these people up here had could be contagious.

"You need a shrink."

He only smiled sadly.

Then he did the one thing I couldn't possibly see coming. He pulled off his jacket, yanked off his shirt, scooped me up in his arms, and walk-raced toward the spot where I had fallen into the freezing pond. I could almost swear that his boots had turned into blades and he was setting some speed-skating record on that lake of doom. The oppressive black night sky minus a moon or any stars made his face look dark and formidable.

"So, you're the kind who needs proof—just like me. I'd say kindred spirits, but that would be a really bad joke," he said. Looking down, I could see that I was hovering above the hole where I had landed in the lake just moments ago.

"You wouldn't!" I shouted as we teetered above the rushing water only inches below us. "If you do this and we live . . . then I will kill you!" I announced in a calm voice.

"Famous last words," he said with a half smile. "I prefer, Remember the Alamo!"

As his words rang through the night, he bent his knees and jumped hard into the air, landing both of us in deep freeze. The splash was epic, and so were my last words. "You are so dead," I mouthed.

CHAPTER 6

1.

The great splash began with a loud roar and then it settled into an even louder nothingness. My heart began to pound because this time I didn't even have a moment to catch my breath, but I knew enough now to conserve what little oxygen I had inside my lungs. It was more of a reflex when I reached wide for both of his shoulders, which were rock-hard; I held on with the tightest grip possible. For what seemed like five minutes, we just floated underneath this chilled-out amusement park.

When my eyes cleared a bit under the murky darkness, I could see that Daniel was smiling in a way that made his eyes crinkle at the corners, which made him devastatingly handsome. On the inside of his arms, near his biceps, I could see tattoos that read, Jenna, Andy, Peter . . . and Bobby. *Who was Bobby?* And then there was a strange tree tat that started on his right wrist, the thick trunk looking half-dead and black as it raced up his arm and past his thick bicep. Curiously, the closer the tree climbed to his shoulder, it came alive with supple summer leaves that were wide-open and vibrant green. They cascaded on thin braches lushly onto his shoulder and then seemed to multiply past that area as they rained halfway down his chiseled back like falling stars.

Under this water—that should have turned me into a human ice cube, but actually felt warmer now—I didn't have time to memorize it all because Daniel shocked me again when he reclined all the way back like he was a human raft. It was a reflex when I settled onto his chest as if I was riding on him. Our bodies fit into the right grooves like puzzle pieces. His hands settled on my hips and our faces were only inches apart as we sunk much deeper into the dark abyss.

A moment later, his body disappeared and I began to plummet down into what seemed like a bottomless pit. That's when I felt his right hand grab my wrist and hoist me hard into protective arms. When we were face to face in the drink, I watched his look of concern fade into what was mischievous wonder. At that moment, he took his hand, placed it on top of my head, and dunked me as if we were two kids playing some sort of game in the deep end of our community pool.

Only one thought went through my mind: *Revenge.* He moved like a human eel, too fast to catch, easily slipping out of my grasp.

Time passed slowly as I tried to calculate the minutes we were under the water. *One. Two. Three. Ten.* Finally, I saw a finger that motioned me to swim after it. Given no other choice, I obeyed, blinking my eyes twice when I saw what seemed like just a vision, but it was real. A brand-new murky figure had swum up next to us and I stifled a scream; but it wasn't a prehistoric swamp creature. It was Daniel's kid brother, Peter, who was now underwater and having a grand time of it. He bypassed us to grab his younger sisters who were also swimming near us and were engaged in a watery wrestling match.

With a thick roof-like plank of ice overhead, but posing no real concern, Peter did a breaststroke near me and then mouthed words I could easily read, but couldn't believe at the same time.

"Marco Polo," he taunted, opening his mouth and drinking a big gulp of water. Then he rubbed his belly as in, "Man, that was tasty."

At that point, I just closed my eyes and waited for the world to go black. When I realized I hadn't moved an inch underwater in what seemed like ages, I wondered if I would just freeze in place like some sort of teenage mermaid on her last swim. My mind was racing, but my body was in absolutely no distress. Placing my hand over my heart, I felt it beating *ba-dum-ba-dum-ba-dum* in a resoundingly normal way. *How? Why?* Without any answers, Daniel grabbed for my free hand and yanked me to his side where we swam under the ice until we could see the night sky drifting through the open hole.

The suction of the water was great as we shot like human darts to the surface. I found myself in his arms once again, and then gingerly deposited back on land in a nice, fluffy snow bank. Around us, the wind whipped in our faces, but I wasn't freezing cold; despite the fact that I was soaking wet and probably in some sort of shock or in the middle of a really bad dream. "I'm out, angel. The rest is up to you to find out," Daniel said, wrenching his shirt back on before shrugging into his jacket and shaking water droplets off his face in one animalistic movement.

"You're out—of what? The rest—of what?" I said in an exhausted voice as he picked up his backpack and shoved mine into my arms.

"The rest of everything," he said, walking away from me.

There was no choice but to stand up and follow him.

2.

We walked home in total silence. *One foot and then another.* It was dream walking. Until I thought I heard Daniel grumble something about reaching my front step, which didn't look the least bit familiar.

"Jenna, stop needling your sister," he yelled to the girls tromping behind us and then stopped for a moment to reign in Peter who was now throwing hard-packed snowballs at both of them. Then he turned to me and pointed to a red front door. Obviously, it was mine. "Home sweet home, princess of the sea," he said.

I stepped onto the porch, but before I opened my front door I gathered the courage to ask him one more time, in a voice that wasn't much above a whisper.

"Dead in what way?" I demanded. "Dead, as in socially dead? Dead as in DOA, when it comes to having friends in this town? Dead as in dead to you? Which is what I should be because I plan on never speaking to you ever again—after you let me drown twice."

"No, just plain dead-dead, Callaghan," Daniel said with a little smile as if he got my sense of humor and appreciated it for some strange reason. "You're standing here bitching me out, which means, for purposes of historical accuracy, that you haven't drowned – and you're still speaking to me."

"I hate it when I'm right," he said.

"You're an idiot," I told him, continuing my rant. "And who told you that I was dead? Did you read about in the newspaper or was it on the local news? Did it make the CNN crawl?"

"The fruit appreciation teacher told me," Daniel said in a

cautious voice. "He's the only one who has . . . universal Internet access for all time. Don't ask me how he arranged it, but he covered that one before he even arrived," Daniel said.

"He told you *what?*" I demanded, still occasionally checking for signs of brain damage from being under for so long. While half listening to Daniel, I began to recite the French national anthem that I had learned French 101 class. The words came easily in both English and French. *Let's go children of the fatherland, the day of glory has arrived.*

"Are you even listening to me?" Daniel demanded and I snapped out of it for a moment, quite certain that all my brain cells were indeed intact. "If you're listening, it's something Steve showed me; something he reads about every new student before they arrive. He printed it out for me since we're neighbors. But I don't think this is a good idea because you already know too much for your second day."

"Second day where?" I demanded. "There are actual rules for your second day in Michigan? Did someone forget to give me the guidebook?"

"Michigan!" he said in an astonished voice. "I've never heard this place called Michigan!"

"It's not Michigan?" I demanded.

"This isn't Michigan," Daniel said.

"Just read this damn thing," he insisted, pulling a piece of paper from his backpack and shoving it into my hand. For a moment, my heart actually did stop in a way that made the icy lake seem like a swim in soothing tropical waters.

It's not every day that you stand on your front porch, ready to go eat dinner and do some homework, but first you must do one more annoying thing: read your own obituary.

CHAPTER 7

1.

Bursting through the door, I didn't even say hello. I had no intention of beating around the bush until I saw my mother at the stove cooking dinner like this was just another normal night in our otherwise ordinary lives. She was stirring what smelled like chicken noodle soup and I was surprisingly starving. On second thought, maybe I'd wait for tomorrow or the next day to confront her with this one. Tonight, it might not be a bad idea to just get the lake smell off me, eat a tuna-salad sandwich with a side of soup, watch a movie, and go to bed.

Very shortly, she was going to notice that I was soaking wet. Cue my mom. Actually, it only took about five seconds until she started in like the worst fate in the world was wet clothes and a wool coat that was soon going to stink up a storm from mud and algae. I made it to the fridge to grab a 7UP and then waited for the interrogation that went something like this: "Honey, you are soaking wet! Did you fall in a lake? Are you hurt? Do you have frostbite? Should we go to the hospital?"

My mother was nothing if not perceptive, and also dramatic because her words were laced with utter horror. Casually, I clomped in my wet socks over to the cabinet to get out two bowls for the soup she was stirring and then I started to set the table like it was my number-one priority to fold cheap paper napkins in perfect rectangles. In one corner of the room, a radio was set on low and I could barely make out the strains of the Rolling Stones' "Jumpin' Jack Flash" and how it was all a "gas, gas, gas." Without knowing it, I did a little hip sway in my soggy argyle socks that squished loudly on the tile floor and left puddles in my wake.

Mom dropped her line of questioning and our conversation for the next few moments was punctuated with trivialities. *How was my day? Did I meet anyone nice? Did I meet anyone not nice? Did I make any new friends? Were my teachers friendly? And knowledgeable? And nice? Did I join the swim team?*

I gave her the CliffsNotes: *Interesting. Yes. Not really. Not really. Sort of. Surprisingly so. Uh huh. I don't do sports.*

And then I blurted out four words: "Mom, am I dead?"

2.

I held my breath as the round, brass clock on the wall ticked in a way that each second sounded like a bomb going off. Centuries passed as I waited for her to break out into hysterical, snorkeling laughter to confirm this was the single, dumbest thing I had ever asked her in my entire life. It would go down as my second stupidest question *ever* next to the all-time classic, "Can I have a brand-new red Camaro for my sixteenth birthday?" That didn't happen either.

Her response wasn't in words. Her answer was clear, and punctuated by the shaking of her shoulders, which was the only thing I could see because she instantaneously spun around and turned her back to me. Like tiny earthquakes, her bones shook uncontrollably, which forced a cold chill to sprint up my spine.

The answer was yes. I was dead.

I.

Was.

Dead.

Swaying forward, I caught myself before I fell down; and then I poured my entire body into one of the hard, oak kitchen chairs. Desperately needing to do something with my hands, I grabbed one of those napkins and began to shred it into paper snowflakes until I balled up the leftover wad of paper and destroyed the thing. For some reason, I couldn't accept what happened in the lake as proof of my demise. *Wasn't there something about cold water freezing your organs and you could stay alive for a long time?* I didn't put a hundred percent merit into that obituary Daniel had handed me. *Maybe it was his idea of a sick joke to freak out the new girl.* But my mother's response, her tears, made it real.

I tried it on for size.

I.

Am.

Dead.

As a dead woman, I could only do one thing, which wasn't to haunt a house or fly through the clouds. I walked up to the back wall in the kitchen that led into the living room and tried to walk through it. I couldn't. All I did was bash into it hard, which sent me backward a few inches. It didn't hurt, but I was wounded inside from humiliation. So, I returned to the table and just sat there and watched my mother stir some pepper into the soup, then cut little tabs of butter to put on our bread. Deep down, I wanted to race out the door, run as hard as possible, and keep running until my lungs burst out of my chest. Then I could evaporate into the universe. But I didn't. I didn't do any of it.

I finally asked one question. "Are we having salad with dinner tonight, too?"

My entire life was over and the first thing I did was go into the pantry where I knew someone or something had stocked us up with the wide-cut croutons and real Thousand Island dressing. Mom just sniffed, and shook her head up and down as I searched the shelves.

My mind racing, I thought, *Dead. Gone. DOA.*

It didn't even seem possible.

It didn't seem possible at seventeen years old, going on eighteen, when the map of my life seemed to stretch out so endlessly in front of me. I couldn't see a finish line because I was barely out of the gate.

"So, what happened?" I asked her in a soft voice as I walked out of the closet with the Thousand Island, even though I was dead and maybe didn't even need to eat healthy things like lettuce anymore.

"We were driving home from your doctor's appointment, where we got the all clear when it came to your lungs. I suggested that we stop at the old-age home to drop off materials they needed for a pillow-making project," Mom said in a robotic voice, as she continued to stir mindlessly. "It was snowing. I took Milwaukee Road because I was afraid to drive on the expressway. It was icy and I didn't see the truck. I've always been a terrible driver, and the truck startled me, so I hit the brakes. And then I swerved. Sideways. I froze. I lost control." She almost whispered all of it as she took silverware out of drawers and lettuce out of the refrigerator like some kind of whirling creature who had to keep moving in order not to think or burst into spontaneous flames.

"We slid into the oncoming lane. Right into headlights," she whispered, spreading the butter on our bread. "All my fault. All . . . my . . . fault."

I wanted to rage at my mother, but somehow I couldn't find it inside me.

"Do you think I'd ever want this for you . . . ? Do you think I'd ever wish this for us?" Mom suddenly shouted, which was so uncharacteristic for her. She never lost it, but this was way beyond the norm. "I'm responsible for you. And now I don't know what we're supposed to do and why we're here . . . or where this 'here' even is," she continued her rant until her voice broke.

I wanted to scream at my mother for killing me, but I also felt badly for her, the woman with the dead kid. So, I did what I always did rather naturally, which was to make a joke out of the entire thing.

It was just my way.

"Well, I guess," I began, "this is as good an excuse as any for missing midterms at home."

And we did the impossible in that next moment. We actually stood there and laughed.

My mind flashed on my old friends. *Did they know I was dead and gone?* They certainly knew I wasn't on a winter trip to Hawaii or the Virgin Islands. They must have thought I got sicker with my lung condition—until it was curtains. Wait, they didn't think that because maybe our accident made the evening news. My end was probably reduced to a one-minute story of a woman and her kid who got killed followed by the forecast and then sports. *How long had we been gone?* I couldn't remember a moment of the accident or how we got here.

Was there an announcement at school? THE announcement?

At that moment, I had to get out of there. Racing out onto our back porch, I stood outside where I wasn't cold despite the fact that I could see my breath, I still hadn't changed out of my wet clothes, and it was chilly enough to freeze ice cubes in my hands.

The sky was cloudless and completely starless, but I could see red roses poking up through the snow. "Where the hell am I?" I screamed at the top of my lungs.

I didn't hear my mother walk out behind me, but suddenly she was there next to me, shivering like she was freezing, and with her always-loving arms wrapped around her soggy daughter. It dawned on me in that staggering instant: She was dead, too. When I put my arm around her back, she actually winced like it hurt her, but how was that possible? I knew now why I couldn't really feel cold or pain. I was dead. At the very least, I could feel one thing: sorry for myself. But then there was her life, too.

"Mom, are you alright?" I asked, wondering if that question even applied now. *Why was she still in pain? We were dead, damn it!*

She didn't answer. At least not for a long time.

"Look, Walker," Mom said. "Tomorrow we'll find out more. We've been summoned."

The note was simple: *We would like to invite you and Walker to meet Principal M. King in his office at 9:00 a.m. Refreshments will be served. Answers will be given.*

"Tonight, I think we should just take a deep breath and leave it at that. I know that I'm tired and my back is killing me."

Numbly, I nodded.

Suddenly, I didn't feel anything.

Inside or out.

3.

I spent most of that night in my room mourning myself and everything I would miss about my old life back on Earth—or whatever they were going to call my so-called prior existence. I would miss my friends, my Aunt Ginny, my annoying grandmother in New York, Tater Tots, juicy hamburgers, and deep-dish pizza from Lou's.

I'd miss chocolate-chip cookie batter that was going to kill me or make me as fat as a cow. I'd miss my prom, my graduation, and college, moving out, falling in love, getting married, having children, getting old, and then ending up somewhere else like here. I ran my list of nevers in my mind: never smoked, never really drank, never had sex, never worked for the *New York Times*, never won a Pulitzer—never ever, ever, ever. And never would.

I'd miss it all. Why in the world did I ever find it all so boring when I had it all in the palm of my hand?

Later, I checked on my mom who was tossing and turning. In her sleep she started talking to someone, so I stood over her listening and worrying. One thing about death I was quickly learning: It didn't absolve you from your fears. It didn't make you feel much different either. I was still eating, drinking, peeing, sleeping, worrying, and feeling chills—although I banished all thoughts of Daniel Reid for the moment. Why the hell was I even thinking about that jerk?

"Yes, I can hear you," Mom muttered in her sleep. "I can't . . . I won't . . . No, you can't make me. Walker, she needs . . ."

Make her do what? What do I need? I thought.

When she rolled over, the conversation continued.

"Go home," Mom muttered to no one in particular. "You look so tired. You need to go to sleep. Leave me be. You look so tired. Go home . . . I can't. I won't . . ."

Again, I didn't think she was talking to me.

I left her muttering and slid back into my own bed to have one last good cry for all those nevers before dawn.

CHAPTER 8

1.

His office was located in the tallest tower at the Academy, it's regal, blue-coned roof shooting so high into the sky that it looked as if it was piercing other solar systems. The elevator was out of order after the twentieth floor, so Mom and I had quite a hike up five more staircases. She did it with her hand on her lower back, but never complaining. I decided to take the stairs in twos, strangely not that breathless today. I felt stronger as each day passed. It was like I could move mountains and crush steel.

Finally, we reached the twenty-fifth floor where we had been told to enjoy some tasty little vanilla cakes and wait. Just like any other principal's office there was a little bench outside where you could stew about your fate, fret over it, or lament it. The heavy wooden door outside the office was closed shut. It was fitting for the man who was in charge. That large, heavy wooden barrier looked like you would need ten people to budge it open. A small brass nameplate was in the middle of the door announcing this institution's fearless leader was none other than: Dr. M. King.

Of course, Miss Travis was there before we arrived, bustling around in her red cardigan with the runaway threads and snags everywhere, and promising us that this was the day we would be given the answers we craved. When my mother saw the name on the door, she gasped and whispered, "Is that who I think it is? Is it really *that* Doctor M. King?"

"Oh dear, everyone thinks that at first. But in this case, it's simply not true," said Miss Travis, chuckling and giving my mom that adult "knowing" look. "He's not *that* M. King. He's just a former principal from Detroit. I'll let him tell you the story—it's a doozy."

Minutes later that heavy door started to open slowly, and a man stood behind a large oak desk to greet us, his face flushed with excitement. I had no doubt that this was the M. King in question. He was a tall, bony, extremely spry black man in his sixties with merry eyes and a wise smile. He didn't look too ethereal in black pants, a starchy white shirt, and a beautifully tailored black suit jacket with a white handkerchief peeking out of the pocket.

"Walker Callaghan, please come in before you break your bones sitting on that hard bench," he said with a laugh in his voice that took some of the edge off the fact that he was more than "large and in charge" at what I guesstimated to be almost six foot three inches tall.

"Now, what kind of name is Walker? Are you from the South?" he posed, motioning for my mother and me to sit in two of the cushy leather seats in front of his desk. Mom touched her back as she sat, which caused Dr. King to lift one eyebrow but he never inquired about her health. Miss Travis seemed to just disappear.

"It's a family name, sir," said my mother shaking Dr. King's hand and ignoring her pain. "And no, we're not from the South, but from Chicago. That's where we . . ."

For a moment, I saw something in his eyes—a glimmer of remorse—and then the twinkle entered again. "It's actually my maiden name," she explained, "and I wanted to name my only child after my father's family."

"Well, Marvin is a family name, too," he said, turning to me. "My father was Marvin Senior and my grandfather was even more senior than him. Me? I'm just plain old Doctor Marvin King, a pleasure to meet you both."

I smiled back at him because he was easy to like, although, at the same time, he had that principal aura around him that made you want to spit out your gum, sit up straight, and confess to something that would surely get you detention. *Do they even have detention in this place? Could I get expelled for attitude?*

"Let's get right to it like we would in Detroit, the Motor City. Great town. But that's beside the point. You want answers," he said.

There was no beating around the proverbial bush.

"Walker, you're dead. You were in a car accident in Chicago. Your life on Earth is no longer. Just like you, it has ceased to exist," he said in a blunt tone and then he paused as if he was giving me the minute I needed mentally to catch up.

I'm not sure why, but I couldn't even cry. I just sat there with my hands folded in my lap nodding like I was in the dentist's office hearing that I had two cavities and had better start flossing—or else.

"Dead is such a bad word," Dr. King continued. "I used it because you're used to it. But the truth is your life back home is what's dead—not you. You've just moved on."

"Sir, what I don't understand is where . . . where did I move to?" I blurted, then looked at my mother as she sat mesmerized while waiting for our next marching orders.

Dr. King just smiled warmly, walked out from behind the desk, and sat on the ledge by one of his windows that offered no views because of the thick clouds.

"This isn't heaven. This surely isn't hell. It's somewhere in the middle. You're in what I call the Midst," he said, answering the questions before I could even ask them. "This is not what you know as Limbo or Purgatory. That's something for grown adults. This Midst, as we call it, is for teenagers, because you're not fully formed yet. You're still growing in every which way. For you, one door is closed, but the possibilities are still infinite." He looked at me cautiously before he continued. "The prevailing wisdom from Up Above is that you need to keep growing and maturing in an environment that feels normal until it's time to move on."

And then, as if he knew he was about to be hit with the ten million questions swirling through my cerebral cortex, Dr. King put up one finger politely to stop me. He still needed to say his piece. "I can't tell you about what's next. That's not in my job description. We're not union here, but close," he said with a chuckle. "I can't tell you how long you will be here—or what you're here to learn. It might be another five minutes—or much longer. I can only tell you it will be an epic adventure. It will be the adventure of an after-lifetime, as I like to call it."

"Then again, that sounds like the brochure we can't really put out because naturally we're nonprofit," he said grinning.

My mouth dropped open.

This was just what I needed: A wise, but hip principal who looked like Morgan Freeman in *The Shawshank Redemption*. I could hear Morgan's voice. In fact, it sounded a lot like Dr. King's vocal intonation. For a second, I imagined Morgan saying his famous words from that film: "Get busy living or get busy dying."

Obviously, I was getting busy on the latter.

"Every year," Dr. King said, the smile fading fast, "good kids like you pass for one reason or another. An accident. A fire. Abuse.

Cancer. Disease. Bullying. Stupid stunts gone wrong. *Jackass* filled a whole wing here with new arrivals."

"Some young deaths are intentional. Some kids fight like hell to stay back on Earth, but they have to give up the good fight for one reason or another. Some kids spit in the face of life—only to find out that other forces spit back much harder. It doesn't matter, except I wish I could tell living kids to stop saying, 'I wish I could die' or 'Kill me now.' You never know when your fondest wish will be granted. All those kids end up here first in order to develop into the people they were meant to be."

Sensing that I was about to combust, he stopped for a minute to let me ask a few questions. "Then why is my mother here? She's not a teenager. She has surely developed into the person she is supposed to be," I asked.

Dr. King looked—in a word—impressed.

"Walker, I'm not going to underestimate you," Dr. King said with true admiration in his voice. "That's a great question. Then again, I wouldn't have expected any less from you because I know you're a news reporter."

"News editor of the *Charger* at Kennedy High School," I interjected.

He just laughed warmly. "Duly noted," he said. "And the answer is simple. She came with you—it's rare. It's special."

"That's why you were sent to that lovely little house, which I hope you're enjoying. She came to be with you, which again, isn't the norm, but sometimes that happens when family members pass together—but not always."

Dr. King could see the question marks in my eyes and said, "I'm so sorry, but the rules aren't hard and fast. They're playground rules. It feels sometimes like we're making them up as we go along. But there are rules here—and we'll get to that in a moment."

"The house is beautiful, sir," my mother piped in, coming out of her trance undoubtedly caused by all of this information being much too much for her to comprehend. Her natural politeness broke through the surface, however, and she had to comment on our lovely accommodations. When she moved her leg to shift positions, she grimaced. My attention ricocheted from her face to the narrowing of Dr. King's eyes. *Why did he seem so perplexed each time he looked at my mother?*

Without skipping a beat, he directed his laser-beam stare back in my direction as Mom settled back again.

"Walker, we can't possibly cover everything in one session, but I do want you to know that I'm here to help you anytime you need me," Dr. King said.

"If I'm dead," I blurted out to this man or whatever he was, "Then what *exactly* are you?"

"Oh, dead," he said in a matter-of-fact voice. "School shooting. Dead as a doornail."

2.

Death Story: Dr. Marvin King
Age of Demise: 52

Dr. King was a born storyteller and his rich, deep voice told his tale well.

They called me a thirty-year man at Lennox High School in Detroit, home of the Fighting Lemurs. Bet you didn't know that lemurs fight?

During my time there, I worked my way up from history teacher to assistant principal, which pleased me and all those other Marvins in my family to no end.

86

The town was always struggling economically, but never so much as when the bottom dropped out many years ago.

Saw the whole town go from bad to worse during the Great Recession or Secret Depression, as I like to call it. Good kids and their families were suddenly foreclosed on and kicked out of their homes. I was the assistant principal at Lennox High by then and I never would take a promotion. They asked so many times but I wanted to work with the kids, not scream at adults at policy meetings. The kids needed me more. When the depression hit, many of my students were living in motel rooms with their families—or worse.

Some lived on the streets or in their cars. School was the only constant in their lives, and they used the sinks in the boys and girls bathrooms as showers. Kids who weren't joiners signed up for after-school activities in droves as a way to keep warm for one more hour on a winter's afternoon. Never before had the chess club swelled to over a hundred members.

Hard times bring hard problems. One day a young man I liked very much named Jackie Silver was plunged into his own recession story. He was a sophomore living with his father. His mother had left years earlier to LA to chase after some boyfriend. You know how it goes.

Jackie and his dad were doing just fine until the local steel plant started laying off workers. They lost their house and went to live at the Motel 6 by the highway. When they couldn't afford to pay that tab anymore, they moved into an old Chevy Tahoe that was in danger of being repossessed. Jackie's room became the backseat of a truck.

Of course, I didn't know any of it. Jackie's dad said that they were trying to save their house and swore they were still living there. I didn't know that Jackie only ate one meal a day, which was his school lunch. Anyone could see how Jackie was getting to look like skin and bones and I personally told the nice cafeteria ladies to make sure that Jackie's belly was full each day. It wasn't the first time I saw a young *man get tears in his eyes when he was given a tasteless burger and some greasy french fries for free. We lied and said that someone had to eat the leftovers and he was actually helping us out.*

Most important of all, I didn't know that his daddy—the man who couldn't afford to feed his son—refused to sell one of his prized possessions: the semiautomatic gun he kept in the Tahoe, just in case.

One day, we were having a school pep rally and the entire student body was gathered in the gym to cheer on the fact that the Fighting Lemurs football team was on its way to play in the Michigan State Championships. The band was on stage breaking my eardrums. The cheerleaders raced up there, gold pom-poms flying, legs kicking. The student-body president, a wiry, red-headed kid named Arnie, was at the mike telling his fellow students, "We need to win because they've taken so much away from us this year in Detroit. We have to give something back to ourselves that money can't buy. Our pride."

At that point, a young man in the sixteenth row stood up, looked left, then right, and with his right hand pulled a semiautomatic gun out of the waistband of his Levis.

Jackie Silver, fueled by eating two burgers that day, aimed at the stage and struck Arnie first, killing him instantly, and then hit two cheerleaders who lived, although one would never walk again. Jackie did this before whirling around and shooting into the rest of the student body. Miraculously, there were several flesh wounds, but no deaths in the audience.

People were screaming, running, and pushing as shots flew into the crowd. All you could hear was the pounding of feet like a herd of wild animals. Kids were trampled as they ran for the gym doors and teachers hid behind the steel of the bleachers as if this provided some barrier between life and death. I saw the school principal slip out a side door and run toward his SUV in the parking lot.

I would have none of the ducking or running. I had a responsibility to these kids, and something had to be done. I walked to the edge of the stage and shouted, in the most commanding voice I could muster, "Young man, you listen to me. Jackie, you're going to give me that gun and then come to my office to talk about what's bothering you. We'll fix it together."

I took one step off the stage and then another while Jackie stopped shooting for a long minute to think about it. The students had fled by now—he and I were the only ones left standing in the gym.

I continued to walk toward Jackie, reaching out one arm for the gun as I approached him. I thought I saw a little remorse in Jackie's eyes, but at the same time, I was afraid of the trancelike stare that seemed to possess him.

"Do we have to tell my dad?" Jackie asked, tears starting to roll down his face. "I just want to go home. I don't want to tell my dad."

I didn't have a chance to answer. Jackie dropped the gun on the floor, and allowed his upper body to crumple as if he was trying to touch his toes. Breathing a sigh of relief, I took another step closer to kick the gun away from him because it was still too close for comfort. Jackie never touched that gun again. Instead, he pulled a small handgun out of his sock and shot me squarely in the chest. Twice. I died instantly.

After surveying the damage he had done—the three lifeless bodies on the stage, and mine on the floor in front of him—Jackie lifted that same small handgun his father also kept, just in case, and shot himself in the head.

3.

"So yes, dead as a doornail, I am," Dr. King told me as I tried to hold back the tears that had formed. "School shooting. A modern-day problem. You read about them in the news all the time, sad to say."

"Applied for this job the minute I heard about it," he continued. "I knew that the Academy was my calling. And I got a promotion to boot."

"So, are we in heaven?" I asked Dr. King, although I knew he already explained it once; but I didn't comprehend exactly what he had said to me. I learned in my Reporting 101 class that asking a question a second time often produces a completely different answer. Why not test the guy? He seemed used to it.

"Walker, we don't think in those terms here," he said. "Let me explain it this way. There is nothing above us or below us. We're right here where we belong—in the center of things."

"Kids go, they come, they stay awhile," he said.

"And the teachers?" I asked.

"For the most part, they're here because they want to be here," he said. "And there are some great surprises when it comes to who is making the lesson plans and conducting classes. We really do recruit the best of the best. Let me just tell you that at the Academy, Elvis never really leaves the building." He paused and added, "Sorry, that's a bad inside joke."

I wasn't done with my line of questioning. "Why haven't I ever heard of this place before?" I demanded.

"People have known about this place for years," Dr. King chuckled. "What do you think Rod Serling was talking about when he said, 'It's a place of imagination.' Do you really think he was just talking about some TV series called *The Twilight Zone*?"

"I thought it was just a show," I said.

"It was more than a show," he replied. "At least in concept."

Dr. King walked back to his desk and leaned against the side of it, so that we were only inches apart. "There are people who are well aware that this parallel universe exists," he said, scanning my face for any recognition.

"Certain things also travel through a parallel universe. Think about this for a minute: How do you think Twitter gets a tweet from Iowa to Alaska in less than a second? Do you really think that's just technology without any boost? There are things in this world that seemingly have no explanation at all, but there is an explanation," he said. "Most people just get tired and stop looking for the answers."

4.

Now that my mind was swimming, I waited as Dr. King offered us some pleasantries like warm tea and more vanilla cake before getting to the other reason why we were here today.

"During orientation days like this one, I like to personally sit down and talk to each student about the rules at the Academy," Dr. King began.

I swallowed hard.

"Technically, there are no rules," he said, looking at me for a reaction.

"It has come to my attention that someone else has already explained to you that you cannot die twice. That's actually true—although I will talk to Mr. Reid about his methods of introducing you to that concept." Dr. King added. "That brings us to a dangerous fact of your existence now. You're a teenager with absolutely no consequences for your actions . . . almost no consequences."

"I only ask you for three things," he continued. "The first is not to engage in obviously destructive behaviors because I don't admire recklessness. The second is not to litter because after living in Detroit, I need a clean environment. The third is the most serious request, but it's not really just a request. It's the only rule and one that must never be violated. Your spirit and its future journeys depend upon you paying heed here."

My face lifted and this time I stared hard into his compassionate eyes, which were hard and steely now.

"You cannot, under any circumstances, attempt to go back to the living realm," Dr. King stated. "You cannot try to return to life as you knew it for any reason. I'm sure you've thought about it—and you will think about it again. Push those thoughts out of your mind the minute they appear."

"There is no going back," he reiterated in a hard tone. "There are elements here who will talk to you about going back. They will tell you that it's possible, which isn't true. It's never possible. No good will come out of this exploration or contemplation. If you even try to think about going back, expect great anguish—mentally and physically. I want you to promise me now on your word of honor, Walker. I need you to confirm that you understand."

"Don't do anything nuts or destructive," I began. "Don't litter."

"I'm not as concerned about those dictates because everyone breaks them. It's only human. I want you to repeat the most important rule to me—and give me your sacred promise," he stated.

"There is no going back," I said. "I won't look into it. I won't explore it. I won't think about it."

Dr. King smiled warmly. "Now, get out of here, Walker It's-a-Family-Name Callaghan, and go test the limits. Everyone does until that gets boring, which is why limits were created in the first place. Meanwhile, I have to see about a young man who bungee jumped to his death off a crane in Ohio. A high-school senior with a scholarship to Ohio State in physics, of all the ironies."

He shook his head. "What kind of reckless risk seeker do you have to be to rig your body to a rope and plunge a hundred feet off a crane, just hoping that you'll survive it?" Dr. King muttered under his breath.

"Did the rope break?" I asked, suddenly curious, because each member of this student body was a miniseries of his or her own.

"The kid jumped before they tested if the lock was working. It wasn't. You'll see him tomorrow in fruit appreciation class," he said in a practical voice, adding, "I better get the paperwork started."

CHAPTER 9

1.

I spent the rest of the day going to my new classes as if nothing out of the ordinary had really happened. In other words, it wasn't like a dead assistant principal, who had his chest blown out by a former student, just told me what seemed unthinkable. I was officially dead; and it was time to take some risks in what remained of my life in another form in a different realm. I was dead and on a rather upscale winter vacation. At least, that was one plus about being here.

He wanted me to test the limits? Fine. When no one was looking, I snuck to the cafeteria between periods and ate half a red-velvet cake, three brownies, and a cup of creamy, handmade chocolate ice cream. I washed it down with two slices of pizza and a frothy vanilla milk shake garnished with a large handful of rainbow sprinkles. My stomach felt just fine and dandy, thank you very much. Tums were obviously not required in the afterlife.

Back in English class, I really looked around at my fellow students—who were also total goners as in dead-dead—and the jaw dropper was that they looked physically better than anyone I usually saw at Kennedy High. I was used to a student body that mostly looked tired and pale from too much time in front of a computer screen and no sun or fresh air. A big chunk, no pun intended, of Kennedy High was obese. No one looked tired or stressed or even pudgy here. No one even had a zit. They weren't overweight or too skinny. They were perfectly perfect as if a fairy godmother came around and bestowed upon them the world's most amazing makeover. At the Academy, their eyes were bright and their faces were glowing with possibilities. I had no doubt that they still had hopes and dreams for the future—in whatever form the future presented itself.

There was a muscular kid named Brian who had a heart attack on the football field in Dallas, Texas, at age sixteen after two-a-day practices. To me, he still looked like the MVP, most likely to succeed in any realm. He was sweet and kind, and even jumped up to help our English teacher, Miss Louisa, get some books off a high shelf. "It's nice to have a strapping young man come to the rescue. I love all my little men here," she said.

"What's your catastrophe?" I asked Tosh over lunch at the school cafeteria about an hour after my large snack. That didn't stop me from ordering a large chicken potpie—and I already had big chocolate-chip-cookie plans for dessert. I could see that Tosh was packing it away when it came to the meatloaf and potatoes, and a mound of apple brown betty on the side. "Eating disorder," she said between bites. "Pretty stupid, huh? I starved myself to death back at home because I thought I was fat. The truth is I was a size four, but my mother was always going on and on about how I looked a little too chunky to her. I pretty much survived on diet soda and air in those days."

The student body was one fine drama after another. It made me sad to meet Emily, a sophomore, who on the day she finally received her driver's license (after two tries at the San Jose, California, DMV), decided to text and drive. She didn't see the SUV in front of her until she plowed into it. When she woke up later that night, she was in a dorm room at the Academy.

2.

In chemistry class, it was time for class projects. I saw Arnie, my music theory classmate and school-shooting victim, in all of his glory. Before his future was blown away at that pep rally, Arnie always planned on becoming a nuclear physicist or curing cancer because he lost almost everyone in his family to the disease. He continued those quests at the Academy because saving humanity remained his number-one priority. Number two, Tosh told me, was finding a hot girlfriend.

Today his class assignment was to give an oral report on combustible fuels and their impact on the environment. Arnie couldn't think of a better way to spend an afternoon than dealing with things that went *boom*.

"You better back up for this," Tosh warned, moving both of our books to the back row in the classroom. She put on knockoffs of designer Gucci sunglasses as our science teacher placed a giant piece of what looked like plexiglass in front of Arnie. The kid who planned to cure cancer was busy setting up his magic potions.

"Now that gasoline costs five dollars a gallon back at home," Arnie began, pouring some regular-old gasoline into a large beaker. "It's time to get rid of our dependence on this unnecessary fuel forever."

To prove his point, Arnie actually took out a match. Gasping under my breath, I knew that this kid was much too smart to actually light a match around gasoline. Glancing sideways, I saw Daniel Reid wordlessly slink into the room late. It was the first time I saw him all day and he gave me a curt nod as he backed up to lean against a closet door. I returned the nod with a half smile for telling me the truth. He reached out a hand to grab the handle of that door. Why was he bracing himself?

Arnie struck his match.

What happened in the next minute horrified me. He touched the tip of the fire stick to his beaker and it exploded in a tiny fireball that not only shot into his face, but also engulfed his entire body. Stifling a scream, I could hear Tosh giggle and then saw Daniel shake his head like he had seen this before. A second later, our chemistry teacher, a handsome young man named Mr. N, with long blonde curls, soft brown eyes, a deeply sloping nose, and a dimple in his chin, was dousing Arnie with white foam from a well-placed fire extinguisher.

"How very illuminating, Arnold," he said. "Now, according to the laws of motion, every object in motion will stay in motion until acted upon by an outside force. Why don't you stay in motion for a few seconds longer until you're no longer on fire? I don't want you to overheat."

Tosh whispered to me, "Oh, Arnie is always blowing himself up in science class . . . because, well, he can now."

The outcome was like nothing I had ever experienced in my life. Despite being on fire seconds ago, Arnie was absolutely, positively fine. Nary an inch of him was burned or even blackened by the fact that only a blink ago his entire body was engulfed by fuel and flames. *It was like it never happened.* It was as if someone pushed a reset button the moment he was hurt. There wasn't even a plume of smoke in the room. And Arnie looked as normal as possible—for Arnie, chemist and future heartbreaker.

Time seemed to stop and rewind itself. It was all just one giant do-over because there were no consequences. You couldn't die twice. *Obviously that meant that you couldn't even get hurt. You probably couldn't even get a hangnail here.* Why not test all the limits indeed?

"Tomorrow, I will combine sodium, water, and chlorine gas," Arnie said with glee. "Sodium is a highly combustible element and the addition of water can make it explode. Pretty cool, huh?"

"Arnold, please give it a twenty-four-hour rest. My heart can't take any more booms today," said Mr. N, before starting the day's lesson. "Now, everyone, please write this down. To every action, there is an equal or opposite reaction."

3.

We called it gym class in Chicago, but at the Academy, the standard term was PE or physical education. Bronze-colored uniforms with a big A hand stitched on the front were required. In the locker room, it was like being back at Kennedy High School. There were the more developed of our female species including Demanda and her friends, Amber and Blythe, admiring themselves in the mirror while the "others" like myself slipped on the school-issued shorts and T-shirt with record speed. Public nudity was never my thing. In addition, PE was never a favorite subject of mine because I'm more bookish than athletic, but I figured there was no choice.

At the Academy, physical education was a core class.

The gymnasium was so large it could have fit two football fields inside. I looked around and saw a few familiar faces, but not Daniel Reid.

It didn't take long for my eyes to lock on an amazing-looking middle-aged man who was sinewy and strong, plus well dressed in a Chicago Bears T-shirt and matching navy blue sweats. His smile was wide as he ushered everyone onto some wooden bleachers in a corner of the gym and began roll call. He announced Daniel's name three times. "Another tardy for Mister Reid," he fumed, walking in my direction—fast.

This guy really knew how to move.

"Welcome to the best damn class at the Academy," he said, and my heart seemed to stop. As a Chicagoan, I knew him. Everyone loved this man whose nickname in life was "Sweetness."

"That's Coach Walter. He was a football legend," whispered Arnie who was sitting next to me on the bleachers gazing at me adoringly, although I had pasted on my best "let's just be friends" smile.

"Oh, I know. Number thirty-four," I whispered back. "In Chicago, he was everything—and then he was gone."

"Today, our quest will be dodgeball," Walter said, mocking the shocked look on our faces by bugging out his eyes and putting a hand in front of his face in fake protection. "I'm warning you kids that this is the last week of this silly game. Next week, it will be full-tackle football—girls included. No pads. Let's make it interesting."

My eyes went wide at the thought of it and then I remembered that it was impossible to actually get hurt. Arnie whispered, "I suck at dodgeball, but I'm hopeless at football. Not that it really matters. Even when I get beat up in the locker room, it doesn't really hurt anymore. Well, I guess it just hurts my ego, though we're not supposed to care about that anymore. But I still do."

Obviously, death didn't overcome teenage angst.

"The rules in dodgeball are you must sit down once you're hit," Walter continued. "Anyone who tries to hit the teacher will face serious repercussions, Chicago style." I wasn't sure if that meant he was going to force-feed them deep-dish pizza or call Al Capone to go medieval on their asses. I could see Walter hauling an assortment of balls out from the equipment closet.

Maybe I was seeing things, but it looked a lot like we were going to play dodgeball with regulation-sized small, hard baseballs. *Was he insane? Someone could lose a . . . well, lose nothing.*

"Oh, they don't do gym in a normal way here. In gymnastics, they flip themselves off the roof. With dodgeball, you better move fast because you'll really know when you're hit," said Arnie who quickly pointed to a senior named Matt who was climbing the rope up to the gym's ceiling.

"Big deal. Kids climb the rope all the time at my school," I said.

"It *is* a big deal," said Arnie. "Just watch what happens."

Matt, a former basketball player, shimmied up that rope like he was born in a jungle and climbed trees every day. But when he got to the top, he screamed, "Look out below" and just dropped to the gym floor. No pads. He just let go and crashed to the ground, landing flat on his back. A moment later, he dusted himself off, smiled, and said, "That was fun. Now, let's play some dodgeball."

Arnie was sent to the A team while I was on the B team. Before he left, we did a quick vow that we wouldn't target each other.

Meanwhile, Demanda just snickered from her vantage point on top of the bleachers where she was busy filing her nails. Obviously, bloody dodgeball was one of her favorite PE activities and she was even sharpening her talons for it. There was no choice but to make eye contact with her on her saunter down the stairs; she took them like she was auditioning for *America's Next Top Dead Model* while I clomped on down.

"So, you're the new girl. I'm just flushed with excitement. Where are you from?" she asked me, stopping for a minute to give me one of those totally demoralizing head-to-toe-inventory type of stares.

100

"Chicago," I said. "And you?"

"Phoenix, Arizona, but I spent a lot of time in Los Angeles," she said, her voice a mixture of arrogance and aloofness. "I was a cheerleader at my high school until I relocated, as I like to say. Of course, there are people at home who still aren't over it. You should see the display of flowers they left at the forty-yard line." My lack of emotion for that not-so-amazing game-day display of floral arrangements seemed to bug her.

"Obviously, you weren't a cheerleader."

I held my ground and forced my gaze to remain steady. Without seeming the least bit interested, she couldn't resist asking, "By the way, what did you in? Bad fashion? Social suicide?"

"Serial killer—one of my victims shot me back," I said in a light tone like it didn't matter anymore. Her impossibly big eyes popped wider. The last thing I needed was for her to know any of the details of my life or my death. It turned out that I didn't need to worry about garnering any of her sympathy because she obviously didn't have any remorse for anyone, except herself.

"I'm sure your death was still not as spectacular as mine," she said, one-upping again. "You might have heard that it was a car accident—and it was. But bigger."

Death Story: Amanda Peck
Age of Demise: 17

I didn't want to hear the story because I didn't really want to know her, but there was something so fascinating about hearing the details of someone's demise that I just couldn't turn away. Plus, Demanda liked having the spotlight, and later I'd learn that she told the story to all newcomers because few had as dramatic a death. She called it five-star spectacular. I preferred to call it a cautionary tale.

Let's start with the obvious. As I said, I was a cheerleader. To clarify, I was head cheerleader at Mountain Ridge High, voted the girl with the best bod and the best ass, but that last one was unofficial because it was only an Instagram vote. Still, that means it was an international vote. In terms any losers like most of you could understand, there was only thing more popular than my phone number at Mountain Ridge—summer vacation. Winning the lottery probably would have come in a close second.

You should know that being Queen Bee is a hundred percent commitment and endless maintenance. I could barely find time for actual schoolwork because . . . well, because.

That day, it was bitch hot, but what else was new in the hell on Earth known as Phoenix, Arizona? Adding to the pain was that it was homecoming weekend and 115 degrees in the shade which made it impossible for even the best of foundations not to just slide off your face.

Important note: Naturally they didn't need a competition to decide who would be crowned the homecoming queen. Someone should have just mailed me the idiotic crown.

Daddy, being Daddy, naturally knew that I needed wheels for my senior year of high school, and I had cheer camp that previous summer, so he surprised me in June with a bright, new, shining Mustang in cherry-bomb red.

Daddy didn't screw up often, but he must have had a massive brain fart when he bought me a hardtop. Chrome wheels. Tinted windows. But still a .... hardtop.

Yeah, I know. Bummer.

"Honey, I didn't think you'd want the wind in your hair," he apologized. And I chose to forgive him because he didn't screw up like this too often. So what if those weren't the all-time perfect wheels. The rest of it could have been optioned by Hollywood.

Perfect future. Perfect social life. Perfect boyfriend in massively built Jimmy Weaver, QB of the Mountain Ridge Cats. He was dark, brooding and got straight Cs, which was an accomplishment in the Weaver family. He was a less handsome Daniel Reid, but let's not go there.

It was near perfect everything in those days—except for one thing that I was cursed with since birth.

I should have been born blonde, but we all have our handicaps.

That day, I jumped in the 'stang with my disgusting black roots that were dying to ruin my yearbook photos. It was Saturday afternoon of the big dance and I boogied down to the local CVS to find my fairy blonde godmother named Clairol. But number 729, Blonde Bombshell, was out. WTF?

Really? Did I need this bullshit on the day of a maj social obligation? I didn't have time to run to every drugstore or beauty supply in town and good luck getting a hairdresser to give you a touch-up on such short notice.

It was that little old lady counter woman who told me what to do. "Dear, in my day, we covered our roots with a little bleach and peroxide. For under five dollars, you'll be the blondest of them all."

I liked the way she said it. The blondest of them all. It sounded like a Disney movie.

I spent $4.99 on my blondeness and an extra seven dollars on a package of Marlboros.

Then Jimmy started in on me. It was your basic panic call.

His tux didn't fit right. His stupid asthma was acting up. He didn't get a haircut. "Jimmy, what part of this do I really care about? Just fix it," I yelled into the phone. Daddy would have fixed it. Except for the car, he fixed everything.

Jimmy pissed me off so much that I wanted to hurl a cheer kick into his rib cage, but he wasn't there in his fine flesh. So when I got to my car, I slammed the bag from CVS so hard into the backseat that it bounced from the fine black leather seats onto the floor with a tiny thud. The cigs even popped out, so I tossed them in my purse and threw it down as well.

Jimmy was still on my celly bringing more dark clouds. "Baby, I forgot to get us a res at the Four Seasons," he said. "Coach has been real hard on me this week."

"Jimmy, one day when you're working at the local gas station filling tires or living in a box by the side of the road, you'll be melting in the hot sun thinking about how you could have slept with a homecoming queen, but she dumped you the night of the dance," I yelled.

I told him to call Kathy Blake and take her to the dance. Kathy, of course, was the fattest girl in school.

In the middle of this misery, I started driving. And I took the back roads on the way home, so I could let the car rip over a hundred as I screamed at him.

"Jimmy," I shouted, "you better get down on your hands and knees and pray that I still go to this damn dance with you. And you owe me big for all this BS."

"Sure, baby," he pleaded. "Whatever you want. And one quick question: Would you even consider staying at a Hilton?"

"Go sleep in Paris if you want to stay at a Hilton," I yelled. Click. I hung up on him and blasted the radio, not noticing what was ahead of me. All of a sudden, this motorcycle came out of nowhere.

Yeah. You're thinking this is how I bit it.

Not even close.

I swerved around the damn motorcycle, which was going too slow, and when the driver looked up, I flipped him a quick middle finger. What a wad!

By now, I was far from town, a rocket jet flying through ranch territory. Why the eff not? These roads were always empty, so I punched it even harder. The 'stang could rip at 140 miles per hour, and I needed fast because I was furious.

Asswipe Jimmy. He made me so mad.

"Shit!" I yelled, after reaching into the passenger's seat, where my purse was nowhere to be found. Then it dawned on me. It must have ended up in the backseat and this was bad because my purse meant my cigs.

I took my eyes off the road for a second to reach back for the purse. Finally, I found it on the floor, but I would have pulled over if necessary. I needed that kick. Badly. The matches were in the cup holder next to me.

"What the eff!" I yelled to no one in particular when I noticed that my Prada bag was soaking wet on the bottom. It was new and I hadn't junked it up yet with too much stuff and I'd never put liquids in it.

In that moment, I knew what had happened. That stupid old bitch in the pharmacy had probably knocked the bottles open when she put them in the bag. Or maybe, just maybe, when I pitched them into the backseat, they may have opened somehow, although I doubt it was my fault.

Placing a Marlboro in my mouth, I hit the gas again until my foot touched the floor of the car. The speedometer registered 145 miles per hour and I couldn't go any faster if I wanted. The windows were up. The air conditioning was pumping hard. My heart was pounding.

I struck the match.

Ka-boom!

After, you know . . . after . . . I stood at the side of the road watching myself and my 'stang turn into a giant fireball that probably reached thirty feet high while it was kissing the sky. A rancher on horseback came riding up hard, but it was too late. No one could tell where the fire ended and I remained. The second explosion seemed to put a period on it.

I stood there. On the side of the road. Feeling fine. Yelling at the rancher.

"Hey, asswipe. I'm right here," I bellowed.

He never turned my way.

Dr. King explained it to me later that day—but I still don't totally get it. I guess I was in a confined space, meaning a small car. Hydrogen and bleach release toxic gasses when they're open. Those bottles spilled. I struck a match, turning my car into an actual bomb.

It was the worst science experiment in history, but even worse was the fact that I died at seventeen with black roots. The paper called me the ultimate dumb blonde.

I hate science.

She waited for me to respond. And for some reason, I couldn't resist.

"I'd write a mean letter to Clairol," I muttered.

Those weren't the words she wanted to hear. "You should watch yourself, Walk-her," she said. "Is that your real name? What a weird thing to call a kid. Walker. Like you're old and need a walker. Or you're a dog who needs to be walked. And by the way, I don't believe that serial killer crap."

"Uh-manda, in Chicago we're very good at watching ourselves," I replied, grabbing two baseballs and wishing that I had a better arm. I could go one better that would seal the deal. "By the way," I asked. "Who became homecoming queen?"

Even in death, her look froze my blood.

"Chicago?" Walter said, breezing by to tell us to line up. "A hometown girl! Amanda, you better watch your butt because we make 'em tough where I come from. Now put down your nail polish and line up. Walker, is it? Walk with me."

I nodded. And walked.

He motioned me to help him push the bleachers back.

"One word of advice, Walker," he said in a low voice. "People don't change very much at this point. They are who they were. Trust your gut. I'm sure your gut is telling you right now that Amanda is *one of those girls.*"

"A total bitch?" I said.

"Language, young lady," Walter said without any real punishment in his voice. "I was going to say that she's a . . . well, I better not. The Academy frowns on us instructors using language that I used every single Sunday on the field."

For some reason, I couldn't resist saying what I was about to say.

"Why didn't you get a new liver?" I asked him, because I knew. I read about his story and how he died so young while waiting for a transplant. How could someone so famous and rich not move right to the top of the list? Everyone wondered when it came to Walter.

"Well, now," he said, "what makes one man worthy of a new liver and another not worthy of it. I don't think it comes down to the size of his wallet. Anyway, life gets real complicated, but in the end we're where we're supposed to be in this crazy, mixed-up universe. The truth is, I always planned on becoming the world's coolest gym teacher when I got older. I just got that job a little sooner than I expected."

"Physical education. You're a PE teacher," I said with a smile.

"Where we come from, Walker, it's always gonna be gym class and soda is always gonna be pop," he said, nodding for me to join my team.

An hour later, I wondered why bruises weren't forming. As predicted, Demanda nailed me in the first round when I took a hard ball directly to the center of my stomach. It didn't really hurt, but I doubled over from habit, which caused her girl posse to high-five each other with glee. After the impact, time seemed to reset itself and I was absolutely fine, but still tagged out.

Walter was right. Even in the afterlife, you still had to watch your butt.

4.

The library at the Academy was a dark, somber place with amber lights that cast shadows everywhere and bookshelves that reached ten-stories high with first-edition tomes that could only be reached by using small transport pods that shot students upward like mini-elevators until they found the reading material of their choice. I couldn't wait to go for a ride and made a mental checklist of dozens of books I needed to check out. "Dear, you need to take a driving lesson first," said the librarian, a round-faced, older-looking woman whose name tag read "Maya."

"Did you drive at home?" she asked. "I had a Prius. Terrible shame about my passing. I was smack in the middle of a new book. My sister, I didn't really like her, got the Prius. Still bugs me. I hope Gertrude is doing well."

"Your sister?" I asked, brushing away my hair that I was perpetually growing out, but mostly now it just fell into my eyes.

"No, Gertie was the name of my Prius," she said.

"A bike. I drove a Schwinn," I said and Maya smiled. As I glanced over her shoulder, the rest of my words got lost somewhere between my throat and my heart and those mile-high stacks of books.

Daniel had that rumpled look of someone who appeared to have spent a long day at the library. If I was being honest, I'd admit to myself that I was a little disappointed when I didn't see him in our fruit course this morning, or at gym—not that I'd admit that to anyone but myself. "Thanks, Maya. I'm sure Gertie misses you, too," I said, my eyes refusing to leave the little wooden table across the room where a very familiar leather jacket was splayed on a chair and what looked like a motorcycle helmet was tossed in the corner. "Um, I'll do pod ed . . . tomorrow," I said. "Got to work my way up to it. I'm a city girl. I take the bus—I don't drive it."

"Wonderful," she said. "Enjoy the library. Enjoy your time. You never know what you'll find. Or whom."

She wasn't kidding.

Be cool about this, Walker. You don't know him. You don't know many guys at all. At least not guys that look like this—or was it "that?" This was no time for worrying about proper English, although I was in the library. This could be . . . complicated. Not the driving. He could be complicated. Those little shivers he gave me plus my natural dorkiness around even vaguely cute members of the opposite sex were definitely a recipe for postmortem disaster.

Why was it that walking was also complicated now, as the library carpet seemed to slow me down like trying to swim backward through quicksand? One foot in front of the other. Why was I such a clod? Was I walking cool? Or like some geek ghost? Certainly many other girls in this school thought he was technically attractive. Yes, that's what I would brand him: Technically red hot. I was maybe cute at best in any realm, including this one. Why couldn't I just float like some sort of sexy airborne Cameron Diaz?

The good/great news was that he obviously didn't sense my presence, feel it, or welcome it as I plodded over—my new black boots feeling heavier with each nerdy step. As I got closer, I could see what looked like hundreds of pieces of paper scattered like big white tiles that had been tossed recklessly all over the table. Even pointing a fan at his work wouldn't make it any messier. I couldn't help but focus on what he was reading, which was certainly easier than focusing on that shock of black hair that was falling forward. For some reason I wanted to reach out and run a hand through it to smooth it back so he could continue on with his studies. *Uh huh.* I wanted to do this as slowly as possible while feeling the warmth of his skin and the silk of those glossy black locks. I remembered those moments in the water in his arms. *Walker, get a grip. You are not living a RIPD (rest in peace dork), romance novel. Plus, you've never—ever—gone past first base, as they say. Why are you even bringing baseball into this?*

I was very good at internally yelling at myself.

Gather the facts. You're a reporter. The facts were simple: teenage slob, Caucasian, definite attitude issues. The facts were that he wasn't studying English or chemistry. It wasn't even technology or music that excited him (Kurt would be so disappointed). It looked like he was studying physics. *Really? The guy was into physics?* The last thing that came to my mind when I thought of him was the word scholarly.

"So, hello, Daniel Reid," I said, trying to chase my vocal geek away, but the crack in my voice cemented the fact that I was not too cool for school.

He didn't look up.

"Callaghan," he said, his nose buried in his papers and those broad shoulders hunched over. "Come a little closer."

This was not the greeting I expected and my feet absolutely refused to move. Was there a pod for this moment?

"I won't bite," he said, making it worse.

My face flamed red. Always.

Somehow those boots moved a little bit as his head remained buried in a book that, when I darted a look, was an exploration of mankind's quantum physics findings over the ages.

"Closer," he said without missing a word of that obviously fascinating page of scientific research.

When I moved close enough that I could hear him breathing, he continued to read; but he also reached out with one of those sculpted arms, put it around the center of my back, and drew me even closer until my nonexistent six-pack melted into his immovable stone-like shoulder. The sleeve of his shirt hitched a bit and I could see the initials BR, in faded green, tattooed to the inside of his wrist. Alarms began to go off as I willed myself not to react—despite a rush that raced down my spine. I wanted to run a finger over that tattoo, and then ask him a million questions about what it meant. But I shouldn't. And I didn't.

He continued to read while reaching up until his calloused index finger gently touched my face and smoothed several strands of hair away. Neatly, he tucked the strays behind my ear and then gave my earlobe a little tug. Either the polar ice caps melted down my neck at that moment or it was sheer adrenalin. "You can't drive those pods if you can't see," he said, continuing to look down except now he had his hand on my upper back and he gave it a quick, surprisingly gentle rub like he was trying to calm my nerves. My mouth went dry. "Remind me to stay out of the library while you're navigating one," he said. "I've seen you swim. You have no sense of direction."

At that moment, he finally looked up.

"Feeling better?" he said.

He meant better than yesterday. Weakly, I smiled and nodded.

His smile went wide, and those full lips spread, illuminating the shadows and creases. "Now, get out of here. This is private," he said, hand back on the table, and nose back in his book.

He was done. *Finito.* But my heart was pounding so hard, and I knew there was only one way to get a real grip. It didn't involve thinking about how my skin jumped when he touched me or how it felt to use his chest as a raft in the water. I had to focus on school. School never made you feel like you just put your wet finger into an electrical socket.

"So you skipped gym. Walter wasn't happy. As for me, thanks for asking, I nearly died in a lake yesterday. Nearly died from baseball dodgeball today," I said. "In case you were wondering."

111

"I wasn't" he began, his eyes crinkling at the corners, but still reading. "Wondering, that is. Now go. Please."

"Did you know you can't die twice," I said and then smiled. "Got that lesson yesterday from some total idiot. What's on the agenda today? Haunting houses? How about some really freaky paranormal activity? I'm up for it. Can we walk through a wall or two?"

Nothing.

"Thanks, I will sit down for a minute," I blathered. "Long day. Eternity, you know. Exhausting."

Damn, but all I wanted to do was get lost in his gray eyes. And I did for a split-second as he glared at me until my common sense returned.

"So what are you doing?" I asked.

He began to gather his papers. "Leaving," he responded. "No privacy."

It was now or never. I looked down and saw that some of the papers he had gathered related to science; specifically, navigating different realms and intradimensional travel. "Portals and how to find them?" I remarked, fixated on what he had highlighted in one of the open books. He had written "45 minutes—max" across one of the papers and circled it three times in thick ink.

"Shhhh," he bit out. "Come on now."

"This is one hell of a science project . . . or something else entirely," I remarked.

He remained stealthy silent.

"A guy could get himself into trouble reading about these sorts of things," I said, noting that he had also checked out the complete *Twilight Zone* collection. "I like the one where those little guys walk on the wing of that plane."

Nothing. And then . . .

"Callaghan, quit while you're ahead," he said, and when his

112

head popped up from his pack-and-run act, it wasn't the flirting Daniel of five minutes ago, but a cold, hard stranger who was now giving me a dismissive stare. "Don't you have to write a report on your new life as a dead girl," he said in a curt voice.

Jerk.

"Don't you have to write your own report on asswipe guys who push girls into lakes as a way to welcome them to town?" I retorted.

"Leave this alone," he said in a hard voice. But he knew I wouldn't. And I knew it, too, which is why I said the words he least wanted to hear.

"So, are you planning on taking a trip?" I blurted.

CHAPTER 10

1.

That night mom and I went to the local grocery store, which was called the Piggly Wiggly as a tribute to the great grocery chain of the southern United States. It was all so normal and regular. We cruised the aisles and loaded up with tuna, Raisin Bran (although why we cared about bran anymore was beyond me), and a giant economy-sized box of Cap'n Crunch for me. They weren't even making Cap'n Crunch anymore back home, thanks to an enemy known as trans fats. Maybe the captain had retired to that great sugary-cereal planet in the sky and went back into business for himself out of boredom. I made a mental plan to pick out each one of the special, chemically coated crunch berries and eat them first. Mom didn't have any issue with me selecting five different ice creams either. When she put a package of Weight Watchers muffins in the cart, I looked at her quizzically.

"Really, Mom, live a little," I said, choosing eight-hundred-calorie muffins as big as giant cinnamon fists from the grocery-store bakery. They were even frosted with an inch of heavy icing. It was the thick kind that was one hundred percent butter and sugar.

I'm not sure what our bill came to that night. The checkout lady just smiled warmly and said, "I'll put it on your tab, ladies. Enjoy your time."

"What is the limit of our tab?" Mom asked in that defeated voice of someone who knew poverty.

"Infinity," said the nice lady.

Unlike our grocery store at home where you collected little stamps at the checkout counter in hopes of a free sparkling casserole dish, the nice lady pointed to a shelf and said, "Need anything? Just take it. Don't need it? Don't take it. Got it? Give it. It's all up to you."

"And . . ." she began.

"Enjoy your time," I finished it.

2.

Back home, Mom made a nutritious dinner of frozen pizza. We washed it down with a pint of Ben & Jerry's each; me opting for Chocolate Chip Cookie Dough and Mom digging into Chubby Hubby. It was by all accounts a glorious evening that we topped off with three *I Love Lucy* reruns including the one where Lucy and Ricky drive to Los Angeles, loading up eager Ethel and cheapskate Fred in the back, and together they meet all sorts of wackos along the way.

Mom drank half a bottle of vodka and she wasn't a drinker.

"I didn't believe it, but alcohol does nothing. I don't feel it at all," she said.

It was sort of like regular us—with booze. Somehow we were on this big trip that kept getting weirder by the minute. In a way this felt like the world's greatest Michigan vacation and, to that end, we left the back door open to enjoy the cool winter-spring breezes wafting into the kitchen, bringing with them the sweet, fragrant smell of the blooming cherry trees from our yard and those fragrant red roses.

By ten p.m., after watching reruns of *Raymond*, Mom grabbed her lower back and mentioned something about trying to find some aspirin and turning in. Seeing that she was in pain again I asked her about going to see a doctor because certainly there must be one who set up shop on Main Street. "Doctors don't exist up here," Mom replied, smiling at me and kissing my forehead before she did a worrisome hobble down the hallway.

What kind of place doesn't have doctors? Then it dawned on me. When you're invincible, you don't need doctors because you're never broken. *But why was my mother the one exception?*

Strangely, I had never felt better or more energetic. Even when I walked into the side of the couch, pinky-toe first, klutz that I am, it didn't hurt a bit. But I still swore—softly.

Before Mom walked into her bedroom, she offered up a quick parental, "Don't stay up all night, honey. You need your sleep . . . I think." Mom was wrapping it up for the day. Whatever was happening to us, at least we were here together, which made me beyond grateful.

Since my school didn't believe in homework or tests, I didn't know what I would actually do with my time. Everyone kept saying, "Enjoy your time." With no tests, no papers to write, or books that I had to read, I could really enjoy myself . . . by doing what? It's funny that when you're busy, you long for nothing to do, but when you have absolutely nothing to do, the hours seem endless.

I could hear my mother's voice in my head. *You can certainly find something to do, Walker.* So, I grabbed one of my zombie books and began to read the first chapter for what seemed like the zillionth time, allowing my mind to wander to what my friends were doing back in Chicago. Then I tried to focus on Letterman doing his monologue, but Dave was just background chatter as my mind took a proverbial U-turn.

What was Daniel doing tonight? With all his quantum physics know-how was he building a spaceship that would jettison him to another planet or even an alternate realm?

Camped out in the living room with my legs curled under me on our new leather recliner, I dozed off with thoughts of Daniel in his rocket ship doing the countdown *3, 2, 1, blast off.* My mind hit "play" and that old Elton John song drifted through my brain: "*Daniel is traveling tonight on a plane. God, it looks like Daniel, must be the clouds in my eyes.*" I could see Captain Fantastic sitting at his piano is his blinged-out jumpsuit singing it. "*Daniel, my brother . . .*" But my Daniel, not that he was *my* Daniel, didn't exactly inspire brotherly feelings in me. *Stop, Walker, stop,* I told myself. That was the last thing I needed. Life, or the lack of it, was complicated enough.

What I didn't notice were the two black eyes staring at me from outside the window. They were close together and focused. I couldn't know at that moment that those eyes had been on me from the moment we arrived—and had no intention of leaving.

3.

The knock on the door jolted me out of my sleep. *What time was it? Was it morning? If not, who could be making house calls in the middle of the night?* Glancing at our new grandfather clock with the swinging golden arm that made soft clicking noises, I saw that it was about two minutes until the witching hour of midnight. I don't know why, but I knew from this time onward, I would keep track of the day and time.

Grabbing my sweat jacket, I took a curious walk to the door, preparing to yell at whoever or whatever was on the other side because I knew they couldn't harm me. Then my city-girl instincts kicked in and I peered through the tiny glass window where a set of hard eyes met me head on. They weren't black, but gray and seriously annoyed. I could see Daniel was standing there in the dark, his black shit-kicker boots shifting from side to side in some sort of uncomfortable dance.

What the hell! Whipping open the door, I stepped outside to let him have it. "Are you crazy? It's midnight and my mom is sleeping," I whispered loudly, the fire in my eyes intense on his face, which was mired in dark shadows since our porch light wasn't on. Then it dawned on me, and I knew exactly why he was visiting me in the middle of the night.

In newspaper lingo, it's called damage control.

"It's that stuff I saw you reading," I said with a smirk and I knew I hit a nerve. What I didn't expect was his reaction. Before he answered, he grabbed both of my arms, swung me around, and stepped inside the house.

Nervy, I thought.

Second thought: *Get out. My mom is only two rooms away.*

Third thought: *Act cool. You do like him.*

Fourth thought: *Stop liking him.*

"Sure, why don't you just come in? I usually do most of my entertaining after midnight," I snapped, closing the door behind me when I was sure that he wasn't leaving anytime soon—and he wasn't.

I could see the determination. He was going to say whatever it was that he came to say and wouldn't let me interrupt him again, which was becoming my trademark up here.

"I'm here to ask you for a favor—a personal one," Daniel said, looking disgusted that he even had to ask. "Please, Callaghan, just shut up about this. Don't say anything to anyone—and don't ask me what I'm doing. That's it."

He froze to make sure no one was listening because he heard talking in the other room. "Oh, David Letterman," he added with a grim smile as the Top Ten list was being announced for the night. Walking over to the TV, I turned it up a little, praying my mother was sleeping and didn't know I had invited some strange guy into the house. Generally, she frowned on me doing this in any reality.

Mentally, I could write my own Top Ten list: Ladies and gentleman, here are the top ten reasons why you should never allow a lunatic into your home late at night. Number ten—he's taking off his worn leather coat. Number nine—wow, he really does have a lot of muscles under that black short-sleeved T-shirt. Number seven—he's staring at my zombie book, which is embarrassing. Number eight—what is with the half-dead, half-alive tree tat.

Cutting my countdown short, I blurted, "I don't really read that stuff. It must have belonged to a kid who lived here before me." Then I pulled my own sweat jacket off and purposely tossed it on top of my Teen Vogue. Even though my fashion sense was hopeless, he didn't need to know I was trying to impress anyone.

"Why is it that I shouldn't say anything?" I said, bringing us back to why he was making house calls in the middle of the night.

The tan leather couch seemed to wheeze when he plopped down and I couldn't help but notice how the stress of this situation, or whatever it was, had forced him to drop his head into his wide hands, as if he was exhausted just thinking about the whys.

"Callaghan, we don't really know each other, but you have to trust me when I tell you that it's not their business. It's nobody's business. It's my business."

He was going to have to do a whole lot better. "I'd be happy to keep my big mouth shut," I whispered, "but here is the deal. I'm a reporter—or I was five minutes ago. I was going to work for the *New York Times* someday, but now that's shot to shit."

"Anyway," I continued, "I have a naturally curious mind. But I do have a code of ethics. I will keep my trap shut, but first I'm wondering why someone like yourself is reading up about portals and quantum physics. And what's with the forty-five minutes—max? What do you need to do in forty-five minutes and what happens if it takes longer? And what's with the BR on your wrist? Are you part of some secret group of Baskin-Robbins lovers?"

With those last words, he was up like a dart, standing much too close and towering over me. I forgot he was well over six feet and imposing. "You don't know anything about BR!" he shouted. "And you damn well don't need to know anything about those forty-five minutes."

"Shut up," I hissed. "My mom is sleeping, idiot."

Now that I had his attention, I continued to whisper in a hard, clipped way that kept him quiet. "And if you say that you have your reasons for keeping this private, well then, I can't make you any promises about keeping your secret because I hate that answer. All reporters do."

"First off, I'm sick of you calling me an idiot," he retorted, moving closer to narrow the gap between us to mere inches. He went back to business. "And what if I warn you that you're only safe if you mind your own business—and not my business," he spit out.

"Yeah, like being safe is so important to me now . . . that I'm dead," I said, pointing at the door before shaking my head in disgust and insisting, "You know what? Get out. This being dead thing is trippy enough. I don't need complications either. Good night."

I said it in the most fake pleasant tone of voice, as if I was sending a group of children outdoors to play on a swing set on a hot summer day. Daniel didn't move so I actually walked toward the door; and when he didn't follow, I plopped down on a hand-carved bench near the front window. Staring up at him, it was clear that I had all night to sit in this spot, which technically I did. It was my house.

"It's a family matter," he said firmly.

"So, where are you going with the help of quantum physics and a portal for forty-five minutes? Miami? For some sun? San Francisco? For a trolley ride? I know, New York City. Catch a Yankees game. You can't be going to Chicago. The Cubs still suck," I said.

"You won't let it rest," he began to say, and loudly. "You'll never let it rest will you?"

"I'll never stop asking," I retorted, standing again, with my hands on my hips, because for the first time in a few days I really felt like myself again—and it felt great.

"Okay, Miss 'I'm a reporter' . . . you really want to know?" he demanded, skulking to the door.

"I really want to know," I repeated.

"Then, let's get out of here. Unless you have other plans. I can hang out in the living room all night if you need to check your schedule."

Suddenly, I wasn't so sure that I really wanted to know, but this train had left the station. In the silence of the late hour, I put up one finger to Daniel and dashed back to Mom's room to check on her. She looked peaceful for a moment. Then I heard her start muttering in a low, scary whisper.

Leaning in, I tried to make out her words, but they were muddled. "Can't leave," she sighed. "Won't do it. Don't want to do it."

I thought about waking her, but then she drifted off peacefully again with a happy murmur and began to snore.

What else could I do but grab my new black leather jacket and motion to the surly giant in my foyer that I would meet him outside, where a cool spring night had given way again to a freezing winter chill. I had all the time in the world, or at least until dawn, to hear what I hoped was a whopper of a story.

What I couldn't see were those black eyes in the bushes sinking lower until they were only a few inches away from the dirt. It would wait for me to return. It had all the time in the world, too.

4.

"Callaghan, you want to learn about rule breaking? I'm probably the best teacher up here," Daniel said, pointing to the black Harley at the end of my driveway.

"No one calls me Callaghan," I smirked. "And by the way, where do you live exactly? And is that your bike?"

Wordlessly, he pointed. Suddenly I was embarrassed because I was so obsessed with my own drama that I didn't notice he actually lived next door to me. So much for my reporter's eyes and my so-called nose for news.

"Sometimes you look so hard that you miss what's right in front of you," he said. He said it such a low, sexy voice that what was right in front of me was actually making me very nervous.

A light misty rain was falling and freezing the minute it hit the pavement, icing over the trees and the streets in a sparkling glaze. Ballerina that I am, I actually tripped down the first of my three front-porch stairs. Daniel reached out to grab my arm, but missed. Instead, his hand looped around my waist and pulled me too close—again. Our breath mingled in the wintry air.

"It's raining ice. No way am I getting on that bike," I said to him, stating the obvious while my heart pounded against my new leather coat that was extremely formfitting. I'm not sure who my stylist was here, but we needed to have a serious talk

because I was more the baggy-shirt, big-coat type. Releasing me, he just hooked his arm into my arm, which meant that my body was still several inches too close to him. It was a public service, I told myself; one more step onto that ice and I'd be face-first kissing the pavement.

"It's going to start snowing at any minute," Daniel said. "The ecosystem up here is a big bag of tricks. Did you know there is no surface more slippery than ice covered by snow? So, get on the Harley. Live a little."

"You're demented," I said, gazing up at him.

"That's better than being called an idiot," he said with a half-crazed smile. I tried not to think about how appealing it made him look.

"Get on the hog, Callaghan," he repeated.

"The roads will be like glass," I said and shook my head. "We won't make it off the block without wiping out."

I didn't think what I said registered. Then I realized that it did.

"No limits. Or at least that's the rumor. Want to give that idea a test run?" he said with another one of those grins that threw a spotlight on those sloping cheekbones and full mouth.

"Oh, I get it," I finally said, standing under those puffy storm clouds that were spitting cold mist at us. "No consequences, so we try to tempt fate. We jump off the skyscraper, if there were any in town—"

"Get on the bike—unless you're chickenshit," he interrupted, walking me down to the end of my driveway and almost slipping twice in his thick boots.

123

"I'm guessing that you don't believe in helmets here. Why worry about cracking your head open when it won't be cracked for long," I muttered.

Laughing like a half lunatic, I did the only thing I could do under the circumstances. I jumped on the back of the black hog and he slid onto the front. Compressing my body to his iron-tough backside not only had my skin jumping again, but I was also forced to wrap my arms around his chest.

I wondered if there was a reset button for a teenage heart attack. The way my pulse was hammering, I wasn't even sure if CPR or mouth-to-mouth would bring me back to this existence.

5.

He only knew one speed and it was ridiculously fast. We didn't talk at all because I was too busy screaming as Daniel slid down roads that twisted and turned like we were on some sort of insane racetrack made up of only hairpin turns and paper-thin ice. He careened through the town, almost wiping out several times, and then made a beeline straight for the thickest woods.

Screaming was pointless, but only natural. My shrilly yelps evaporated into white puffs in the frigid night air. With the moon bright and guiding us like a spotlight, Daniel pressed the gas down as far as it would go. Hard wind slapped me in the face and my hair was whipping everywhere, but at least I was still upright. For a moment, I relaxed and pressed my face into the small of his back, which was strangely comforting. The rest was like flying—the ice and the wind actually lifting us off the road and into the air where we were at the mercy of forward thrust.

Daniel narrowly avoided skidding into a large oak tree and the way we leaned over to the right was so extreme that we were suddenly parallel with the road. Touching the asphalt, my leather jacket instantly shredded, but my skin remained perfectly unharmed. "That jacket needed some character," he yelled.

Like a madman, Daniel seemed to have a destination in mind. When I could see where he was taking me, I screamed louder than I ever had before in my entire life, while he seemed to howl with delight. Racing at over 125 miles per hour toward a large construction sign that read DO NOT ENTER, I felt Daniel kick up the speed even higher.

"No!" It was my voice pleading with reason.

He was going to drive until he lost the road.

As the warning got closer, I closed my eyes and began to pray as he purposely crashed us through the sign, which crumbled like it was made out of toothpicks. Unsure of what was on the other side, I braced and closed my eyes.

I felt my face actually crash into the back of Daniel's head—hard enough to snap my neck; and then the reset kicked in. We raced past what was left of the sign, which was in smithereens. My eyes popped wide when Daniel skidded to a twisting stop an inch before plummeting us over the edge of what was a sheer drop-off.

"Let's live!" he said, punching it as we went over the first ledge. And then we were falling hundreds of feet into a rocky quarry that looked like our own personal Grand Canyon.

The reset took care of the rest. When my brain unscrambled, I saw that we were still on the bike and Daniel's black hair was slicked straight back off his frozen face that was a mixture of ice shards and some serious stubble. He whipped around and laughed like he was having the time of his death. "Had enough yet, little rule breaker?" Daniel taunted.

Then he touched the key. And the engine roared back to life.

Where I'm from there was no mistaking it. It was a dare of the highest quality. He was playing chicken with me, a game I loved to play. Bring it.

"Have I had enough?" I repeated, shocked that my lips formed actual words. Then in my most flippant tone, I added, "That's it? That's all you got?"

It was the equivalent of a double dog dare, obviously a game he loved to play.

"Let's do this!" he yelled.

That's when he punched it. And we went over another edge that took us even deeper into the abyss.

CHAPTER 11

1.

The reset button was infallible and I found myself six hundred feet below street level on the canyon floor, splayed on my back, laying upright on a large rock like it was a cushy lawn chair at some posh beach resort. Time stopped. Time started again. It happened in the span of a nanosecond.

Again, my hands went on a quick journey up and down my arms and legs as I felt for broken bones, rips, or tears. *Nothing. Not even a drop of blood. Not one ache. Not a hangnail.* All I had was a lovely view of the cloudy night sky and a six-foot-something boy-man relaxing next to me, but on his stomach. From our position on that rock, it was as if we were just hanging out in bed shooting the breeze. His head was propped up against his hand and I was tempted to ask him if he wanted a pillow.

But then I looked deeper. His eyes were intense and staring into mine in a way that made him look almost lethal in the dim light casting a glow from behind the clouds. "Callaghan, never ever double dog dare me again," he said, his eyes flashing a warning sign.

"Okay, let me get my notebook and write that one down," I mimicked him. "The rules according to Daniel Reid."

A soft light snow began to fall, and by the time it reached us down below it looked like sparkling pixie dust. Then after only a few minutes, the clouds parted to reveal a clear, starless sky.

"Here it is," he finally said, breaking the last few minutes of silence. "I'm going to tell you this story only once because it's not easy for me to tell it." I could see he was searching for a way to make me promise to never repeat what he was about to tell me. "Pinky swear you won't tell anyone else," he eventually said, invoking a childhood tradition that was drilled deeply into me in kindergarten.

"Pinky swear," I said reverently. This was no laughing matter. Where I'm from, this was better than a written contract. Since this was obviously of a high, serious nature, I took out my left pinky.

I swore.

Then I leaned up and quickly kissed him on the lips.

To seal the deal.

2.

True, he was shocked, but not as stunned as I was because I don't usually go around kissing people who are complete strangers. And I've never kissed a boy who drove me off a cliff into a canyon on his Harley-Davidson during an ice storm after nearly killing me by crashing into a construction sign. But obviously there are first times for everything under the moon and no stars.

"So, where is the reset button on that one," I joked, keeping my eyes firmly shut. Kissing was probably more risky than anything we had done so far.

Daniel didn't reply or even laugh at my lame attempt at humor. I could smell the fresh air on him and the faintest hint of evergreen trees with their forest-scented perfume lingering around us. *Focus on the trees*, I thought. *Focus on nature. Why were there no stars up here?* My eyes remained sealed shut. Daniel interrupted my own personal astronomy theories and newfound blindness, by putting his wide hand on the back of my neck and drawing me closer by lifting me upward.

Without any warning, he kissed me again, lingering—his soft, full lips moving slowly as if he had all the time in the world and meant to take this moment for the sheer joy of it. He kissed me softly, but deeply like he meant it, because he did. I was sure of it. It was the first time since I had arrived here that I felt truly alive again.

"There is no reset for that either," he said in a deep voice when it was over.

I opened my eyes and turned my face to the night sky, refusing to meet his gaze.

After a few moments of staring into the blackness I quietly said, "Just tell me. I won't tell anyone. I give you my word."

Without looking at him, I lifted my pinky again and gingerly he took it into his hand, drew it down, and kissed it.

Then he launched into the story of his life, which was also the story of his death and the death of almost his entire family. I listened as if we were a couple curled up on a cold winter night under the covers discussing important matters of the day.

Now, there was no turning back. We had bonded.

3.

Death Story: Daniel Reid
Age of Demise: 18

We were the Reid family of upscale Lake Forest, Illinois. My parents were Edward and Maureen Reid. They met in college at the University of Illinois's downstate campus. My father was from Ohio with political ambitions to study law at Northwestern University— old Eddie planned on becoming a senator and then perhaps president one day. My mom was a farm girl from rural Illinois studying to be a teacher. She had to work her way through school; scrimping and saving every penny to pay for her tuition, room, and board. She was gorgeous—blonde with the most beautiful sky-blue eyes; a stark contrast to Dad's black hair and cold gray stare. They met when she served him a large cheese pizza at the Pizzeria Uno on campus. She also worked in the library. Mom said, "He met me and was a goner." He despised her little trips down memory lane.

My father would always say that sentimentality is for the weak. I remember once, on their anniversary, when Mom was telling the story of how they met, Dad was crinkling his Wall Street Journal *as loudly as possible, as if turning the pages in such an obscene way would mute her.*

But I'm getting ahead of myself here, let me rewind a bit.

When they met, my dad was ambitious and full of himself. He swept Mom off her feet with glamorous downtown dinners and even a small diamond promise ring. He vowed he would become a millionaire before age thirty and take her with him on the ride of a lifetime. My mom didn't really care about money. She was in love.

After graduation at U of I, they got hitched in front of a justice of the peace. Then Dad went to Northwestern School of Law and later paid off some of his student loans by working for the City of Chicago in the public defender's office, which was the first step on his march to riches and glory, although it was a baby one.

Times were tough and Dad's hours were long and grueling, but Mom found work as a teacher and knew how to make ends meet. Meanwhile, Dad endlessly bitched about how they lived in a shitty apartment on the bad side of town. He promised her that their life would change and soon they would be living large. But she didn't really care. Mom was all about being with the people she loved, and for some reason she found the need to love him.

Two years went by and then a law firm that specialized in "difficult clients" came calling and offered my father the moon—two hundred and fifty thousand dollars a year to start, with bonuses galore in the offing. Of course, there was a major hitch.

My dad wasn't married to the mob, but he represented them. Defending scumbags paid a lot more than dealing with sad-sack clients who got hit by a city bus and couldn't really afford a lawyer.

My father became a vicious mouthpiece for some undesirable Chicago "businessmen" who were in and out of jail for stuff like laundering money and selling drugs. The money was flowing in, and he built himself a custom-made, ten-thousand-square-foot mansion in the most expensive suburb of Chicago. Lake Forest: Home of several-acre front lawns and polo matches. When you move there, your blood runs blue.

And Dad knew exactly how to morph into a rich person. He forced my mom to retire from teaching in order to focus on social events and starting a family. Not long after that, I was born. I was a big baby, which pleased Dad. It was like a badge of honor for him to have the most of anything.

I think day one of my life was the last day he was actually proud of me. He liked the idea of a big, strapping son to carry on the Reid *family name, although the joke was that my father was a skinny, short guy with these bony, but lethal, hands. I guess I took after my mother's side of the family or "pack mules" as Dad liked to call them.*

As I grew up, everything I did disappointed him. I grew big so quickly that he called it "abnormal." When Mom took me to play Little League sports, he flew into a rage and said, "My own father forbid team sports because, like he always said, teamwork is for the followers. Leaders don't need a team."

I guess old Gramps was a major head case, too, who used to toss young Edward around. The day Mom told me about Gramps hitting Dad as a young boy, I saw my father slap her. I was nine and lunged at him, hitting just the right spot on his knees that made him buckle forward onto his desk and split his lip. He seemed to fly across that desk, grabbed me by the neck, and flung me across the room. He said that if I ever even looked at him that way again that he would kill me. Mom picked up the letter opener from the desk and told him, "If you ever threaten him again, I'll use this on you."

The battle lines were drawn. And, unfortunately, I got to share the wealth of his parenting with the rest of the family.

Three years after I was born, Peter arrived. Luckily, Mom had another boy because I was already obviously disappointing my father. And girls seemed so useless to him, but Dad smiled for a picture in the Lake Forest Journal *when Mom gave birth two years later to Jenna; and then beamed for the press again when a surprise bundle named Andrea arrived twenty-three months later. At that point, Dad said we weren't farmers and that there were enough faces around his dining room table. But Mom was always full of surprises—except the one we all really wanted, which was for her to leave him. For some reason, she couldn't quite do it.*

Five years after Andy was born, her big surprise was another son. She named him Bobby, after her father, Robert.

Dad treated him like an unwanted dog. He had absolutely no

132

interest in yet another annoying child. To him, Bobby was just a screaming, wet, messy inconvenience. But the rest of us kids . . . we loved him from day one. We loved him hard. We called him Bobby the Great.

My dad didn't have time for babies because by now he had a much younger girlfriend who was being kept, not so secretly, in a fancy downtown high-rise. Her name was Betsy and she would meet him on his boat at Belmont Harbor for an afternoon quickie between his court dates. Basically, my father was a stranger to us who would arrive in Lake Forest from time to time to make an appearance at the family compound. His arrival always put us on edge because he was judgmental, quick to anger, and openly allowed Betsy to call the house; he didn't care how any of us felt about it, least of all his own wife.

Finally, he had to show up on a more regular basis. Mom put a crimp in his disappearing act—she died of stomach cancer when I was fifteen.

So now he was stuck with five motherless children who needed his guidance and support. He even had to pack a suitcase and leave his slutty girlfriend downtown. To keep up appearances, he had to actually live with us.

My father made a good show of mourning Mom for several weeks, including a well-placed photo op in the Chicago Sun-Times of the multimillionaire father of five roughing it alone at a local charity event with a cute, restless, crying three-year-old on his lap. But when the photographer walked away, he shoved Bobby back to the nanny and hissed, "Can't you teach that child some discipline? He's loud and obnoxious. I won't have a Reid acting that way!" The nanny dared to talk back and said, "He's three and just lost his mother, sir." Of course, Dad fired her on the spot and she was replaced that night. In Edward Reid's world, everyone was replaceable by just writing enough zeros on the check.

133

A year later, Dad had a new model. Officially. The new Mrs. Reid—Brittany—was only twenty-five years old, beautiful, stupid, stacked, and cared about two things: exfoliating and tanning. She also liked to spend money. Lots and lots of money.

She became accustomed to the finer things in life and made it clear she didn't "even sorta like" children. So she and my father spent the bulk of their time at their brand-new West Palm Beach mansion in sunny Florida.

Our new nanny, Mrs. Watson, was now living on the premises to help. But I became the official surrogate father. Dad was too busy traipsing all over the world with his new trophy wife.

Soon I was a champion high-school soccer player on my way to a scholarship at UCLA. Each week, I had received a new letter from a different college. Scouts from schools all over the country had already talked to my father about giving me a full ride.

Dad wasn't impressed. He told me, "Your shelf life is short in sports. Go do something real. Who is going to follow in my footsteps? My sweaty, just-average son who kicks a f-ing ball around in some pathetic field?"

The last thing I ever wanted to do was follow in his footsteps. I just had to bide my time. Just make it until the end of senior year. Then I would never have to take his crap again.

My senior year was brutal. Dad and I had a lot of screaming contests. Each one seemed to escalate to the point that someone might not survive it. I remember him ripping up the letter of congratulations for a full soccer ride to UCLA. It didn't matter because I had already filled out the paperwork and accepted on my own behalf.

One night he yelled, "Why don't you go find that farm your mother wandered off of when I found her? Maybe you could work a plow. You certainly have the body of one of those mules. A big, breeding farm animal like your mother."

I couldn't stop myself from flying across his expensive French desk and grabbing him by the neck. I was much bigger than he was. I trained every single day. I could have killed him with my bare hands. I felt myself applying just a little bit of pressure, which scared me. Then I pressed just a little harder.

"Don't you ever talk about my mother again," I warned him.

He wasn't even hurt. He was just powerless—and he detested it. He kept screaming at me in this raspy voice to stop, and that soon I would be banned from the house. He yelped, "You're done! You'll never see a dime!"

I told him to keep his blood money. Then I released his neck.

"My son, the pauper prince," he hissed back at me. "Go to UCLA next fall and stay there. Don't even think about coming back—ever."

I didn't need to be told twice—and I would have disappeared forever. But then it dawned on me that I couldn't leave like that. What about the kids? Dad didn't give a shit about any of them.

It was December and I had six more months to live with the bastard until I would move to Los Angeles—with the kids. I had to figure out some way to get them out of there and take all of them with me to California. If it was the last thing I ever did.

That fall, my bored father had taken flying lessons at the new Lake Forest Airport, which catered to wealthy businessmen with their own planes. Of course, he picked it up right away, at least in his mind. But reality was a far different story. My father's flight instructor, Ted, who he called "that grease monkey," was a decorated former military lieutenant who served two tours in Afghanistan flying copters into war zones. Ted insisted that the great Edward Reid needed at least another hundred hours of lessons before going on a solo flight.

My father wouldn't hear of it.

So he spent over a million dollars on his own ten-seat executive business jet. He planned to fly it on his own because he was boss. In Edward's world, money talked. He would do what he wanted. He fired Ted for his insubordination, which really meant he had refused to be another "yes man."

On December twenty-third, my father announced that we were going on a family winter break. This was his version of telling us that we were spending Christmas in Palm Beach—all of us, including the dazzling Brittany who had been sunning herself there for months. The idea was that we would fly in for one of those storybook holidays where it looks good on paper. With no notice, we were supposed to pack and gather downstairs. My father bellowed from the bottom of the winding staircase, "Get your things together and be ready in twenty minutes. That's an order!" He was like a general with no real army. Everyone wanted to go AWOL, but we didn't dare. And I didn't dare not go . . . and leave him alone with the kids.

Dad figured that he was technically required to spend a few days around Christmas with "the brats" even though it would be hell for him. But he certainly didn't need to spend it in the freezing cold going through the motions of a family holiday. We were more tolerable in a warm climate.

Silently, we piled into the black Escalade and drove to Lake Forest Airport, ignoring the weather forecast that called for a strange phenomenon called thunder-snow. It was rolling in as a powerful one-two punch that might mark the holiday storm of the decade. No one told Edward what to do . . . not even Mother Nature. On the ride to the airport, he kept ranting, "These weathercasters couldn't find their own asses, let alone a storm."

It was a freak storm that could potentially combine the power of a thunderstorm with hard, driving snow instead of rain. "If we leave early enough, we'll beat the storm," Dad had insisted. He loved being right and got off on defying the odds. So then came the lecture, "Weather never stops a Reid from getting where they want to go. Nothing stops us."

Ted happened to be at the airport that night doing a little paperwork. I remember him begging my father not to take off. "Mister Reid, please, you're just not ready to solo. You don't know enough about landing on your own. *A storm is rolling in, and you can't handle that kind of serious weather. Let's take her up a few more times after the holidays. You'll be good as gold."*

Irritated at being interrupted from his preflight inspection, my father barked, *"Ted, if I waited for when you think I'm ready, I'd be flying solo by the time I was ninety. I don't pay you to annoy me. In fact, I don't pay you at all. I fired you. Fuel up the plane. Do whatever it is that you do to make my life easier. Or I'll have you removed from this airport."*

Ted continued to plead with him, but Edward ignored him and filed his flight plan to West Palm Beach. He told us that we were only two hours away from a warm, muggy night and a pool. The five of us had no choice; we boarded the little jet. I remember Dad climbing into the pilot's seat and shouting back to me, *"Daniel, do something for once. Make sure everyone is buckled in and ready to go."*

Dad then went through the preflight motions while we settled into large leather seats complete with our own mini-TVs. Bobby asked if he could watch the SpongeBob SquarePants movie he brought, so I popped it into the video player. The kid deserved a little happiness in his life. *"Bobby the Great, enjoy the Pants,"* I told him.

Dad took off to the east, away from the storm front, but it only took a few minutes for him to become disorientated in the thick winter clouds. He began to curse the weather, as if that would help. I actually heard him say, *"Damn it. I can't see a thing."* I guess Mother Nature wasn't one of his mistresses because the jet started rocking. We were bouncing up and down, right and left. At one point, we were sucked so hard to the right that I thought the jet was going to rip in half.

The girls began to cry and my father actually took his focus off the plane. He started to yell at them to stop their bawling. *"When we get on the ground again, I'm cancelling Christmas,"* he shouted. This made Bobby burst into tears. *"Is he gonna fire Santa?"* Bobby asked.

The plane was really rattling by now, so I unbuckled my seatbelt and climbed into the absent copilot's seat. I saw that a light sweat had broken out on my father's neck. Suddenly, the man who stood in courtrooms with killers, mobsters, money launderers, and drug dealers was truly scared. I could see in his eyes that he didn't know what to do with that panel of instruments that were now all blinking red. It was as if he had never seen those buttons before. I yelled at him, "How many lessons, Edward? How many, damn it!"

His voice became suddenly meek and he said, "I didn't show up for all of them, but I know how to fly. I'm an excellent pilot."

I knew this wasn't the time to fight. I had to think of the kids. I took a deep breath and tried to keep my father focused. "Get your bearings. Climb out of these clouds and right the plane," I said calmly, even though my heart was pounding.

Nervously, his face ashen white, Edward answered, "Okay, but I don't know which way up is anymore. I'm starting to think that down is up and left is right." Sweat was now falling into his eyes, which he wiped it away with one hand. Then he pulled up on the yoke as the flight tower came over the radio telling him to turn around and land immediately. Wrestling with the throttle, he ignored the air traffic controller's instructions and turned the plane in what seemed like a downward direction.

The kids screamed when the plane plummeted several hundred feet.

A moment later, he righted the plane again, but was even more confused as the clouds seemed to swallow us whole. These weren't the light clouds that we had taken off into, but darker, turbulent ones that were almost black. When the lightening sizzled through them, it was like the brightest light on the darkest canvas. This freak of nature, thunder-snow, had arrived, and we were right in the middle of it, midair.

Without warning, the plane plummeted an additional five

hundred feet and then leveled with a loud bang as a sizzle of light raced through the cockpit. We had been hit by lightening, which wasn't uncommon. Planes were built to withstand lightening strikes.

I yelled for the kids to hang on. My dad started screaming that we were going back to the airport. He actually took a few seconds to blame us for taking too much time packing. "If you would have just moved your asses like I told you to, we would have beat this storm! You never do what I tell you to do! Why do I have to haul you miserable brats with me?"

Andy and Jenna were sobbing by now so Pete unbuckled himself and somehow, despite the hard bouncing, rolled over to them. He took one of their hands in each of his own and I could see that he was crying, too. Bobby was white-faced screaming, "Danny, come get me. I hate boomer storms!" Bolstered by his rage, Dad jumped on the radio and finally tried to communicate with the tower, but couldn't really tell them his position. Turning the plane in what seemed like endless circles, he wasn't even sure if he was level anymore. The constant jostling from the weather didn't help. At this point, my teeth were rattling so hard it seemed like they would crack out of my head.

Then my father told me he had no other choice, and began to descend—although toward what, he didn't know. He told me that he would do a visual, see the runway, and level out. He kept repeating like a madman that he was good at landing. He reminded us that he was good at everything. "A Reid never quits!" he shouted. He clutched the controls and told us, "This is Ted's fault. He never taught me how to fly properly, so he could keep making money off of me. All anyone wants is my money! All you kids want is my money!"

He continued yelling that this weather didn't matter. That he always won. He ranted that this would be no different because he was a lucky man. "This is ridiculous. Lucky men don't die at Christmas," he kept saying again and again.

The little plane began to shake violently. I climbed back to hold hands with Bobby who still had SpongeBob playing on the TV in front of him. I was praying we would land anywhere. I also vowed that if we got out of this alive, I was going to beat the shit out of my father and then go to court to get the kids taken away from him. I had plenty on Edward to shut him up in court. I could have probably sent him away to the state penitentiary.

As the storm clouds finally spit out the tiny plane, I looked out one of the semifrosted windows and all I could see was white—like a giant sheet of computer paper had covered the ground. For a moment, I heard Bing Crosby in my head singing, "I'm dreaming of a white Christmas." Funny what you think about when you're about to die.

I saw myself on a soccer field in a UCLA jersey, and I saw my mother cheering in the stands. Then I saw the white paper again, and it covered what seemed to be the entire earth. The quiet in my head was loud for some reason.

My rational self kicked back in and I wasn't sure if this really was the ground or just more clouds. Then another streak of lightening lit up the clouds above us as if God had flipped a light switch. I knew then that we were never landing in a way that mattered.

I closed my eyes, and I held Bobby's hand.

The plane crashed into a field next to the actual runway. The earth was like a giant cement wall when we dove, nose first, into the hard winter ground and then skidded, blinding white sparks flying, the length of two or three football fields until the plane finally exploded into a toasty fireball when it hit the first row of trees in the nearby woods.

My father wasn't in the pilot's seat at the end. He unbuckled, left the cockpit, and ran to the back of the plane—his only chance to survive. There was only room for one in the way back. He didn't say a word to us as he raced past.

The next thing I knew, I was flat on my back in the field, staring up at the snow, which was softly falling on my face in large, beautiful, lacy flakes. I kept feeling myself for broken bones or burned flesh, but there was nothing wrong with me. For a minute, I thought that maybe I was paralyzed, but then something inside told me, "Just stand up. Try your legs. See if they still work." So I did—and they did.

I walked over to check on Pete who looked like he wasn't breathing, but he was. He stood up. Jenna wasn't far from him and I could see that dried blood had crusted on her face. Little Andy was the worst. Her body was face up, perfectly placed in the fresh powder as if she was going to make a snow angel. The red outline around her was life rushing out of her. The girls eventually got their bearings and stood, shaking off the blood and dirt like it was a mere annoyance now.

Next to Jenna was a suitcase that had burst open. In the distance, both of the girls' green velvet Christmas dresses were now flying like flags from a tiny fence post. A headless Barbie doll was resting in peace in the gravel next to the runway.

I then heard my father yelling, "I'm fine. I'm totally fine. I knew it would be all right. Everybody get up. I'll go get the car. Hurry up. Damn it! You have five minutes."

Somehow Edward was thrust out the back of the plane during the skid, thanks to the fact that the entire tail broke off like a toy a child had snapped in half. I took one or two steps toward the direction of his voice, but then my legs seemed to freeze in place and I couldn't reach him.

It was almost as if there was some sort of force field that separated the two of us.

Before I blacked out, I heard Bobby cry out nearby, "Danny, where are you? It's dark. You always come get me when it's dark. And you said to never go anywhere without holding your hand."

As my world faded, I saw him—Bobby the Great—in the middle of that white field, his curls covered in snow, holding up his tiny, perfect hand.

4.

The sky held high, puffy clouds at dawn, with a round, silver-dollar moon in the distance. Daniel and I were still laying on that rock, face up, and staring at the misty tops of high cliff peaks. We didn't say a word after he finished his story, but his hand was shaking as he held mine. When a shy sun greeted us with a few weak rays, I knew it was time to go back even though all I wanted to do was stay here. We had to go to school. We had to start a new day. My mom would be frantic.

"Dad went to Lake Forest Hospital. They did twenty-four hours of observation, set his broken leg, and he was fine as wine. All of us, except Bobby, came here together like you did with your mom," Daniel said.

He cleared his throat and stared off into the trees. "That night was the last time I allowed anyone to call me Danny. I just can't . . ." His voice broke.

I found myself reaching out to smooth the top of his hair back as a morning breeze tossed it in my direction.

In a low voice that waivered, he told me, "I know Bobby is stuck at the crash site. It's my fault. I was always telling the kid that he had to wait to go places until I was holding his hand. I was always afraid of losing him in public places. He was such a squirmy kid. So, I'm the one who made the rule, 'Don't move, Bobby, until I have your hand.' He would say, 'I'll stay forever. I won't move a muscle.'"

For a long time, he didn't say a word.

"Certain spirits just get stuck. They're called earthbound spirits. Souls that are not ready to go. They die violently and quickly—and they're pissed or lost," he eventually said. "They don't come here—or go anywhere. For some reason, they're just trapped at the sight of their death. That's why I've been trying for years to go back to the crash site and get Bobby."

Daniel showed me his tattoo: BR—it made sense now. All of it made sense. Suddenly, I flashed back to Halloween in Chicago at my high school. There was a ghost hunter who came to visit to talk about the spirits who haunted O'Hare after that 1979 DC-10 crash. The residents near the field, many years later, still reported hearing voices in the middle of the night saying, "Have you seen my lost luggage" or "I have to hurry or I'll miss my next flight." These were voices with no bodies.

With great care, I rubbed my pinky finger across his tattoo. His eyes glistened, but he stopped himself from actual crying, which was probably a skill he had perfected in his father's house. "I have to get Bobby. He can't stay out there in that field alone for all eternity. Don't ask me how I know. I just know that he's there. Waiting."

At that moment, I knew why he was studying portals and physics: It was possible to go back. He just needed help figuring it out.

CHAPTER 12

1.

The time for crazy stunts and gunning it was over. Not exactly in the mood for any daring moves, Daniel knew where the access road was that would lead us up out of the quarry and back to our civilization. Biting back the tears that threatened to roll each time I thought about his family, I stuffed my emotions down my own personal rabbit hole.

I wanted to say something, anything, but there was nothing I could say. How could I tell him that his father was a rich jackass who killed his entire family and put an eighteen-year-old boy-man in charge—and quite possibly for eternity?

The black Harley easily reached the top of the quarry and swerved onto the main road. I could see that it wasn't the same entrance we had dramatically shot down to find our little perch down below. This morning we were on the other side of the giant hole, and in the early sunlight what I saw stunned me. My eyes glanced up into the sky where I gazed at what looked like a medieval guard tower with a giant searchlight piercing the milky-white dawn. Blinking a few times, I saw a massive and menacing fortress that extended into the sky similar to how the Academy pierced the clouds; but this new place wasn't at all welcoming and bright like my new school.

It was a forbidding stronghold of sorts, obviously built to be intimidating, which was why it was so expansive—three hundred yards across I guessed—and Gothic in its design, like the ultimate haunted castle. What made me gasp was the mere fact that it looked as if some monstrous force had reached out its giant claw and grabbed a large chunk out of what I would learn was the Black Mountain range—removed all rock and slammed this monstrosity into what was left of nature's wall. And then whoever or whatever did this apparently meant business because the jagged onyx rock of the mountain seemed to hold onto the building like a stalker who was finally able to grasp its prey and was now squeezing hard. One thing was clear: It was never letting go.

The end result was an enormous eight-story rock and glass structure hugged by a craggy ridge that was devoid of any other life. Above the roof of the building the mountain jutted so far skyward you couldn't see the top. But the real mind bender was that the front portion of this world within our world had nothing beneath it for support—the entire front length of the façade was defying gravity and dangling midair.

Was it my never-ending, overly active imagination that made me hear ghastly sighs and hopeless cries in the morning wind as we grew closer?

Shivering, I knew that somehow this place was being kept secret because whatever was slumbering inside wasn't to be wakened. For a moment, I allowed my rational mind to justify why I had never seen the building, even from a distance. That was because it was too far away from town and even when you got closer, it was hidden in tall trees and dark shadows.

"What the hell is that—over there?" I asked Daniel as the Harley's tires whispered across the wet pavement. "It looks like—"

Daniel didn't let me finish. "A maximum-security prison? A penitentiary?" he said, driving slowly so I could hear him above the roar of the cycle. "It basically is. It's a prison of sorts—called the Institute for Troubled Teens or ITT. Don't know if they told you this Callaghan, but we're not the only school up here. That place over there is where those who didn't follow all those annoying society rules go."

So, we were back to him calling me Callaghan. The intimacy of the night seemed to be evaporating by the minute. I had to just let it go . . . for now.

"So, it's the Big House? *Orange is the New Black*—in death?" I choked. "It's the juvie of the afterlife? Are you kidding me?"

"Teenage gangbangers go there, murderers, rapists, school shooters, bullies," he listed in a casual way, as if he was glad to have some "light" conversation now about local sites. "All the inmates, as we call them, were under nineteen years old when they died."

Then he stopped the bike on a desolate street, turned his head, and looked at me. "Knowing about the place is okay," he said. "Going there to check it out is frowned upon, so don't get any ideas, Miss Reporter. There are some real nasty guards at the entrance who will flog you for even trying. They're into old-school torture there. More fun, I guess."

"Uh huh," I nodded. "What do the kids do there? Just rot?"

"Reflection, remorse, redemption—the three Rs," he explained. "Many are being tortured physically and through other means. I heard that they played Britney's 'Oops! . . . I Did It Again' twenty-four hours a day, nonstop for a month until the inmates were begging for relief."

146

I had to laugh.

"Otherwise, they're supposed to be doing honest work like shoemaking, weaving, washing. At least some of them work. Most of them just sit in their dark cells all day and night. Grim is an understatement," he said.

"I'm still not over the Britney part," I said without a smile. Then I hit him with my real question. "How do you know so much about ITT?"

"In rare cases, you can get permission to go there for Academy school-related projects. They send some kids who like to study psychology at the Academy up there to do case studies—or they did until there was an unfortunate incident a few years ago. Now, they only send us up there in very special cases," he said.

"You know a lot about this," I retorted, and then it dawned on me. He was obviously interested in matters of the mind, but I didn't see him making a study out of being a shrink and asking people if something was troubling them. "I'm guessing that you need to go there," I demanded, my reporter genes kicking in again. "You don't impress me as the Sigmund Freud type, so spill it."

"They have some information that I need up there," Daniel said, his steely eyes focused on much more than the road. "Pretty soon, I'll be going back. For my studies."

He looked absolutely determined.

"To get Bobby," I stated.

"To get Bobby," he replied. "If there is anyone who knows how to break rules and get back to where they once didn't belong, it's someone in the fine student body at ITT."

2.

Luckily, I snuck into the house that morning while my mom was taking a shower. She didn't seem to have a clue that I was gone all night, which was probably a good thing. She did catch me at breakfast just staring off into space while I thought about Daniel placing his hand behind my neck and . . .

"Earth to Walker," my mom said with a laugh. I had to smile because Mom looked really pretty today in a brand-new lime-green skirt and white cashmere sweater. She didn't seem like she was in any pain at all and said that she planned to go get her hair done on Main Street at Vidal's Salon where he was going to give her some kind of chic, short do from that scary film *Rosemary's Baby*. I was only half listening when she told me about some delightful woman she met in town the day before named Joan who told funny jokes about marriage. "That's nice, Mom," I said.

"I think she's subbing for the drama teacher today," Mom said. And then she did something so un-Mom like by adopting a New York accent and saying under her breath, "Can we talk?"

"Talk about what, Mom?" I shuddered, thinking she was onto my late-night activities in nature.

"No, that's what my new friend Joan said," Mom answered, smiling like she was quite happy.

While I ate my chocolate Pop-Tart, I gazed out the window hoping to catch a glimpse of my neighbors the Reids, but all I saw were a few bikes leaning up against the side of their house. The motorcycle was gone.

A movement caught the corner of my eye, and for a split second it felt like something was watching me. Then it was gone.

3.

Given no other choice except a ride from Mom, which I turned down, I made the slow trek to the Academy on foot, all by myself, so I could think or try not to think. I walked through the deep-green forested streets while gazing up at the blanketed hills where the glistening snow looked like a lush magic carpet. I felt the mystery of this place more than ever because on the way home this morning, Daniel had told me there were several other schools hidden away in these woods. I wondered who decided your scholastic fate in the afterlife. Was it based on your permanent record . . . or something more vague?

It was a deceptively long walk to school, so I had plenty of solitude to remember and log in the details of last night. And when that seemed overwhelming, I forced myself to think about the facts Daniel shared with me about ITT before he dumped me at the end of my driveway and took off. Ironically, ITT was a safe subject for my mind, which was in overdrive.

The Institute for Troubled Teens's front entrance wasn't easy to find, which was the idea. There were no electrified or barbed-wire prison fences or even an obvious ominous sign as a tip-off. To get "in" there, first you pulled down a nondescript one-lane back road, the sort of road that signified you had lost your way. On either side of it, the overgrown grass was packed with thick weeds that sprouted everywhere. When you got closer, there were signs every few feet that read: No trespassing. At the end, the road just stopped basically due to the fact that the side of the mountain stopped it.

At the mountain base, a wall of burly guards met those who would be incarcerated or the few who had business inside. They looked like a pack of yellow-uniformed hornets swarming a black-bricked boxlike base camp that was the ground-level guardhouse.

Large pit bulls prowled the area making it clear that once you had a student ID at ITT, there were no field trips or days off until a Higher Authority (this realm's version of an intense school board) paroled you, which was quite uncommon.

If it was your fate to be escorted inside for any reason, the guards would usher you into the shack for a quick full-body scan for weapons, an uncomfortable pat down, and then your name would be punched into a machine that spit out that ID, plus shackles, and sometimes even a woolen full-face mask to conceal the identity of some of the more infamous inmates.

Once past the initial violation, a guard would take you back outside for a short, shackled hike around the side of the mountain where, with the move of a rock, a rather expansive silver panel emerged from the rugged mountain face. A code would then be punched in to reveal that the panel was actually a mammoth elevator door. The students called it the "Loading Dock" and supplies, along with human beings, were both loaded there. There were guards armed with AK-47s in front of it for one reason: It was the only way into ITT . . . or out if you were very lucky.

Once you stepped inside the elevator, it was as if the mountain swallowed you whole.

Inside, everything turned the color of nothing. Neglect had faded the walls, so now they cast a hue of puke. Black slate rock was the only view for the students with an interior cell that backed into the mountainside and never revealed sky or air again. And there was no prison yard. There was no world anymore. There was just ITT.

Of course, there was the occasional breakout attempt or wayward freedom plan that usually fell into ruin. You had to scale down a mountain infested with wild animals, including hungry mountain lions, flesh-eating spotted leopards with quick attack skills, and

150

wolves that hunted in packs and were always undernourished.

Last year, two eighteen-year-old gang members from Los Angeles's infamous Crips fashioned a rope out of stolen underwear from ITT's laundry. They lowered themselves several stories down the mountain before falling. The leopards were swift that night. At ITT, you couldn't die twice—but you could and did feel extreme pain. All intimates were strictly denied access to the reset.

Intense physical pain wasn't the only fate worse than death for ITT residents. Those with breakout plans or in need of an attitude adjustment often found themselves taking that one loading-dock elevator to a place not so lovingly called the Hole. This is where the punished were punished to another degree. The Hole was actually fifty stories deep past ground level, where there were special titanium capsule cells for those needing attitude adjustments. Most of those students who took a trip down returned to ground level without all of their marbles intact.

ITT's warden was not-so-affectionately dubbed the Godfather or GF, which he accepted because he loved to watch old movies—and Brando was his favorite force of nature while The Godfather was his favorite film of all time. The GF found his young charges absolutely unnerving and completely unredeemable, if not utterly annoying, which was why he saw himself as larger than life in every way that counted, from his overly stuffed gut to his street-honed and cruel guile.

He was here after doing his own several-decades-long rehabilitation for issues he always said "need not be discussed with lost souls." He would wax eloquently on his own time in solitary, or the Hole, when he was at ITT for the un-discussable. "They thought they could break me," he'd tell his guards and any visitors who would listen. "Nobody and nothing will ever break me—especially not these little sinners."

Suffice it to say, GF could think exactly like his surly young

151

inmates. And he certainly didn't believe in the theory of coddling kids to heal them. "Don't spare the rod," he always said. "The last thing we need up here is a riot."

At this instillation, there were over twenty thousand dangerous inmates. Someone new arrived just about every hour.

Upon arrival, the elevator was an express ride to the destination of someone else's choice. The first level was processing; second level, administration; third level, kitchen, chow hall, and laundry; fourth level, recreation facilities and medical; fifth level, A Block and the library; sixth level, B Block; seventh level, C Block; eighth level, D Block and then a few stairs leading to a small rocky ledge above the building. The thin precipice was embedded in rock and there were no footholds to climb upward. If you made it to the ledge, you sat on your perch until a guard fetched you. Escape upward was impossible and even the wildest dreamers knew it. The mountain jutted up into the sky over ten thousand feet high, and in this case everyone knew what was up there: a wildlife preserve that made Jurassic Park look like a petting zoo.

Each prison block contained endless rows of one-person, smallish, unbreakable glass "rooms" that were really cells because they were locked from the outside all day . . . and all night. The faces peering out of those clear cells were grim, and belonged to kids who never got a chance or others who just went very wrong. There were mean-looking mugs and others with bright eyes that were a little screwed up at best or glowering devilish red at worst. Some eyes were vacant like no one ever lived there.

The school was an unregulated animal shelter depending on survival of the fittest. The biggest dog usually lasted the longest.

Block A housed the students who were certainly troubled like your school bullies, young arsonists, and other inhospitable, surly types and generic bad apples. They were well on their way to rehab and perhaps could even earn temporary probation and a slot at

152

another school. GF frequently complained that all the talk therapy higher authorities insisted on for these kids was entirely a waste of time.

The B and C blocks at ITT were for your more creative criminal minds including gangbangers, drug dealers, ex-cons, common thieves, not-so-special sociopaths, low-grade criminal masterminds, and hard-core tormentors.

The D Block was for the real crazies including school shooters, rapists, and murderers. No one ventured near the D Block unless it was absolutely necessary and the core staff was armed with semiautomatic rifles at all times.

Internships to ITT were strictly frowned upon. A few years ago, an Academy student named Simon, who was sixteen and from Atlanta, got permission to travel to ITT to do a series of psyche reports. He never came back.

"No one has a clue. He is just gone-gone," Warden GF had told Principal King at the Academy. Of course, Dr. King demanded a full investigation, which cemented the fact that Dr. King was a major pain in the GF's wide behind. Simon was known for his full face of freckles, love of cats, and obsession with Tori Spelling, whom he insisted had been reincarnated from aliens. The fast-talking GF insisted that Simon must have just "gone Up or Down." These youngsters did move on. It happened all the time. But Principal King wasn't convinced. He knew something must have happened to him at ITT. The case remained open.

At ITT, there were two things that made the inmates get up in the morning. The first was a possible rehab and ticket outta there. The second was sports—specifically the annual hockey season and the eventual championships that usually included ITT's team because hockey was such a brutal sport. Who was better at body slamming, punching, and general surliness than someone whose jersey had a big fat "I" on it.

Three larger, lower-IQ specimens from Cellblock C were the stars of the institute's hockey team.

They were the Wargo brothers of Booneville, Alabama, who were royalty at ITT because they committed heinous crimes and excelled at inflicting afterlife bodily harm. Each exactly one year apart, the brothers were eighteen, seventeen, and sixteen years of age. They were all a shade over six feet tall and each weighed around three hundred pounds of blubber-coated muscle.

The eldest was Eddie Wargo, who removed all the stop signs from the intersection smack dab in the center of his small town and killed ten people in the process when a gas truck hit a Greyhound bus packed with senior citizens on a trip to the state fair in Mobile. The 300-pounder with a fat, wobbling bottom lip, permanent snarl, and deep-set brown eyes that made him look like a squinting human raccoon called it "a fun prank gone real bad." Then there was Daryl Wargo, 275 pounds and usually smelling like rotten fish thanks to a mouth full of buckteeth that had never seen a dentist. He couldn't read past a second-grade level, but knew about cars. One night in Mississippi, he decided steal a vintage Mustang, evade the local cops at 125 miles per hour, and then wipe out a family of five in a crosswalk. He refused to stop until the police got close enough to shoot out his tires. Even then he ran for miles before they picked him up near the county line. Daryl was just sitting in a ditch waiting for the inevitable, figuring jail meant at least three squares a day.

Finally, there was Billy Wargo—the string-bean baby of the family at 265 pounds—a not-so-sweet sixteen with dirty-blonde Tom Petty–style hair. With one brown eye and the other bright blue, he earned the nickname Two Tone. The most progressive Wargo, he was thinking about his future one day and decided to hold up several of the town's PTA members at gunpoint in order to finance his own personal move out of town. His last victim only had five dollars in her pocketbook and a heart condition.

Billy insisted that he was "just havin' a bit of fun with her." He certainly didn't expect her to keel over and die on the sidewalk. "Not my fault that she got a broken ticker," he told the cops who handcuffed him and threw him into the local jail, aka, the Wargos' home away from home.

Back in Alabama, the Wargos were even banned from their high school's football team even though their brawn was needed to win state championships. They played dirty and spent more time than not with their backsides on the bench, from racking up dozens of penalties at every game for infractions like spitting, biting, and illegal punches to the gut.

Their father, Frank Wargo, bitched half a fit about "his boys being denied their God-given right to put those other damn players in the freakin' hospital." Papa Wargo, a trucker who spent most of his life swimming out of a bottle, was mostly too drunk to remember the games the next day. He didn't care about much except his next trucking run and if his cooler was stocked with cold Buds. The boys' mama couldn't take it and just disappeared one night never to be seen again. "Now that's white trash," Papa Wargo said from the front step of their old family farmhouse. The farm had seen much better days, and the Wargo brothers were the only livestock still residing there.

Hungry when their daddy was on the road and without a cent to their names, the Wargos would camp out behind the magnolia trees in the Winn-Dixie parking lot and grab grocery bags off the very young and those clanking along in walkers as they made the slow crawl back to their cars. A good night meant the boys ate both dinner and breakfast.

Frank didn't even intervene when the boys were suspended from school for constant bullying. They had put a freshman in an arm cast after tossing him out a third-floor school window. The poor kid's crime? Breathing.

"Pancake!" the Wargos would yell and crush whoever or whatever was in their vicinity by body smashing their victim from the front and back.

It was like these boys were wild dogs unleashed on the world. No one was surprised when they died together drag racing a semi on the interstate.

There was no question where the boys were being sent.

The Institute for Troubled Teens had three spots waiting for them since birth.

4.

Sadly, during my walk, I didn't run into Daniel or his brother and sisters. I refused to admit—for at least thirty seconds—that I wanted to see Daniel badly; but he had simply evaporated. What I couldn't guess was that this would mark a long period of time when I wouldn't see much of him. On this lonely, windy morning, I would have to be content with the majesty of the sun-bathed trees as I continued my long hike alone in the woods.

A few times I stopped because I heard footsteps behind me.

And I whipped around.

Something was following me, but nothing was there. When I turned around, there was an eerie silence punctuated by the cruel winds hissing through the trees like little stolen whispers.

CHAPTER 13

1.

After three Daniel-less weeks of adjusting to my new "life" at the Academy, I was thrust into my first-ever drama class, which was odd because I was not the "audition for the school play, join the freaking glee club" type. My teacher was a young man, maybe twenty-six or twenty-seven at best, with a wild mop of unruly blonde hair.

He wore extremely played-out jeans and a faded red hoodie, plus black combat boots that looked as if they had been rode hard. "He used them in the movie," whispered my two new drama girlfriends, Gracie and Tosh, who were actually becoming genuine friends because we had so many classes together and were all scorned by Demanda and her popular, cheerleader cohorts. After her big death confession, Demanda had shunned any future talk. I guess I didn't fit into her group. Even in the afterlife, the cliques still ruled the world, or at least the hallways and the lunchroom of this school, leaving us mere peons to band together. The more things changed, the more they remained generic high school.

"Hey, I'm Heath," said the drama teacher, introducing himself to me, but he really needed no introduction. He knew that I knew. How could you not know? Looking down at his boots, he said, "We'll try out a few exercises. See if this is your thing."

I nodded, assuring him that even if it wasn't my thing, I would try to make it my thing because how often did I get to hang out with someone who was a real movie star! The focus here was on the "was." Heath was the best Joker with all due respect to Mr. Jack Nicholson who still wasn't here. Funny, how a guy like Health got his lifetime walking papers early, while someone who pushed all the limits like Jack was still there, as in There. But who was I to judge?

Heath was so low-key that you couldn't help but like him even if he still had a nasty smoking habit and was always puffing away.

"Walker Callaghan from Chicago," he said, smiling up at me. Yes, he was ready for his close-up. Sadly, he wasn't a star anymore, but a drama teacher. This was his choice. No one worked at the Academy, I was told, without requesting the assignment. "I made a little movie in Chicago, once upon a moon ago," he said, pushing a hand through his unruly mop of hair.

"I know," I said, blushing to beat the band.

"One night, I saw the Batmobile, or the one you used in the movie, parked in the Arby's parking lot by my mom's house," I blurted. With a twinkle in his eyes, Heath put a finger to his lips like this was all one giant secret. But his smile didn't fade. "You won an Oscar," I whispered to him. "After . . . well, after you left town . . . maybe you know."

"Oh, we get CNN up here. And *Entertainment Tonight*," he said. "But, thanks for telling me. My daughter keeps it in her room and I visit her regularly, so I get to see it—and her." His smile morphed into a grin as my eyes bugged out a little bit bigger. It made me sad that his little girl never really got to know him. I knew that feeling.

"Acting 101," he announced to the class. "You don't have to overthink it. Just be it. Walker, I want you to step onto the stage. Amanda, please join her."

For the next fifteen minutes, I pretended to do a "scene" where Demanda and I were lifelong best friends. By all accounts, it was the best acting job of my entire life. Where was *my* Oscar?

When we finished, Heath introduced our special guest speaker. I would have known him anywhere. I realized it was him I saw in the park that first morning, but now he was closer—and it was clear.

"Robin, thanks man, for joining us," Heath said.

Suddenly, my favorite man from Ork, in jeans and a sweater, was standing a few inches in front of me making puppets out of his fingers and acting out the entire first hour of *The Breakfast Club*. In life, I had never laughed harder, but not harder then him. He threw his head back joyously, laughing like he ruled the universe.

Don't you forget about me, indeed.

2.

By fourth period—and yet another morning with no sign of Daniel and just a wave from little Jenna in the hallway—I was getting seriously perturbed. Daniel had missed all of our classes together the past few weeks, leaving me to sit by myself at those solitary back tables. Occasionally, I did catch him in the hallways, where he looked distracted, even when he much-too-politely stopped to see "how I was doing" for less than a minute. He barely made eye contact before insisting with a quick arm squeeze that he was really crazy-busy and had to go. It didn't help when I went to dress for gym class and Demanda and her friend Jasmine were shimmying into their too-tight T-shirts with a giant A on them. I wondered if it was possible for each of them to develop actual whiplash from flipping their long, grown-down-past-their-rear-ends, blonde hair back over and over again. They did so with the kind of wild abandon usually saved for shampoo commercials.

When Demanda saw that I was looking at her in the mirror, she frowned and bit out, "What do you think you're looking at, 'I Need a Walker'?"

"Nothing," I said, cursing myself for my previous question because of course they couldn't get whiplash here. These hair-flipping queens must have been in heaven or at least thought they were in some sort of prom-queen nirvana.

It wasn't long before the bell rang and a bunch of us girls filed out of the locker room into the gymnasium. Our teacher, Walter, was waiting impatiently with his big whistle around his muscular neck and a clipboard in his hands.

Ignoring him, my eyes did a quick scan around the gym, but except for Arnie, who had his nose stuck in a contraband science book, and Tosh, who was busy stretching and doing backbends on the wooden bleachers. There was no one else I knew in the room despite the fact that I had been in this place for several weeks now. I didn't see Walter approach me, but when I looked up his dark eyes were focused on my face like two lasers.

"Hi, Mr. Pay—" I began, but he interrupted me.

"Hi, yourself," he said with a quick, friendly smile. "Walker, it's come to my attention that you haven't picked an extracurricular sport yet and since you're new here you will need to do so immediately."

"I don't do sports," I said, looking up at him sheepishly while

160

running a hand through my nonspectacular, straight brown hair.

When he didn't speak, I repeated, "Ask anyone. I'm the biggest klutz. I don't do sports."

"Well, you will *do* sports here because teamwork, plus a healthy body, equals a healthy outlook and positive journey. You'll also enjoy your time on the playing field," he said, shoving a piece of paper in my hand. "I'm shocked that your guidance counselor hasn't discussed this nonnegotiable with you. Who is your guidance counselor?"

All I could do was look at him quizzically while shrugging my shoulders. No one had exactly mentioned the need to go see a counselor except Daniel on my first day, but that's when I wasn't taking advice from anyone. "Let me guess?" Walter said, "You don't do guidance either?"

I laughed and said, "No, sir. I like guidance."

"Read the paper. Make a choice. Tell your guidance counselor, whoever that might be, what sport you've chosen. Do it today," he commanded. Then he turned to the class and said, "Line up everyone. We're going to go do laps outside. I don't want to hear your moaning. You could do a hundred laps here and not even break a sweat, which is exactly my plan. I want you to do a hundred laps. No back talk."

Shoving the piece of paper he handed me into my pocket, I stood behind Tosh whose eyes laughed with me. "Walter is right. Running is cool here. You can run forever," she said. "The only thing he did forget to tell you is that the wind does still wreck your hair."

I nodded.

It was tough being a girl . . . here, there, or anywhere.

3.

At lunch that day, I ate my tuna noodle casserole with Tosh and Gracie. We didn't really talk about all that much until they got to the one topic that I truly wanted to avoid. "So, what's the deal with you and the unfriendly one," Gracie said with a big, goofy smile on her face. "We've seen you guys together a bunch of times now. Please don't tell us that you have a crush on the Academy's nonliving, yet breathing bad boy."

"Is he even really eighteen? He looks like he's twenty-four," Tosh said, eating her cake. The "yum" she tossed out might have not been for the cream cheese frosting.

I laughed and rolled my eyes. Sometimes no answer was the best answer.

Of course, Daniel wasn't at lunch although I saw Peter, Jenna, and Andy eating homemade peanut butter and jelly sandwiches together and waved to them. Out of sheer boredom, just like at my Chicago high school, I began to fidget for something to do when it dawned on me that I had transferred the paper Walter had given me into my new beige leather saddlebag.

"This should be rich," I thought, opening the folded page and looking at my options for extracurricular activities.

The paper indicated that all of these sports were for both boys and girls who would play them at all times together because the Academy did not discriminate based on race, creed, sex, or previous ability.

My choices were as follows: football. I had to stop reading right there. *Football!*

Was he insane? That's just what I needed . . . to be on a field where bigger guys were trying to mow me down. Scanning the list, I noticed some of my other options were soccer, archery, and gymnastics. I could barely do a forward roll when I was a kid in summer camp. Gymnastics was strictly out of the question for the embarrassment factor. Forget soccer because I had absolutely no hand-eye, big-white-ball coordination. I knew that archery meant I'd probably shoot myself.

The last choice caught my eye and it sounded like the least of my bad options: air hockey. For a moment, I thought back to a party I went to in eighth grade in Madison's basement. Her brother Seth, who was seventeen going on twelve, had one of those dumb air-hockey games where you just stood there and pushed little plastic paddles around to smack a puck back and forth across a table. Someone threw a minipuck the size of a bird turd in the middle and the fighting began.

Smiling, I knew I had found my sport. It didn't require a drop of sweat or any exertion at all. I figured that the only danger was a broken nail.

Air hockey would be my extracurricular whatever.

I confirmed this later with my so-called guidance counselor who had summoned me to her office several times, but the notes kept going to the wrong locker. Feeling like I had done something terribly wrong by ignoring her requests, I went to her office where I promptly kept my eyes focused on the lavish Oriental rug. When I looked up half an inch, I could see a stunning black antique desk and a pair of white Chanel high heels that were perched on it.

Miss Elizabeth was round, womanly, and smelled delicious. She had the most stunning almost-grape-colored eyes, which she hid behind bifocals. Her inky black hair fell loosely on her face. Plum-sized, sparkling diamonds weighed down three of her fingers. These weren't rocks; they were boulders.

My gaze was drawn back to those intoxicating eyes that were

the color of spring violets. I wasn't sure how old she was, but guessed that she was in her late fifties. I had been told that teachers could pick the age they wanted to be when they arrived here, and I wondered why she didn't choose her early twenties when her beauty was heart stopping. On this day, she was still stunning in a chic purple dress and an elegant purple-and-gold striped silk scarf around her neck.

Her accent was strange, as in old Hollywood mixed with a little southern charm. Her words were not as potent as the fire in those eyes.

"Good afternoon, Miss Walker. You can call me Miss Elizabeth," she said, introducing herself in the softest female drawl. She answered before I asked. "I would never want to go back to my younger self. Age means wisdom—and now I know something about everything, especially men. Well, maybe I don't know all that much. Do we ever?" She laughed and I continued to gaze in awe.

Awkwardly, I handed her my extracurricular form, which I had completely filled out by now.

"Air hockey," she said, smiling in a way that looked like she did it for a living. "I'm impressed, Walker. It's the hardest and most dangerous sport we have at the Academy."

How could that possibly be true? You just stand there. What was dangerous about standing and playing a table game? Would I be horrifyingly demoralized when I let the other person score?

"Guts and guile," she said, gazing at me in a way that seemed like she actually respected me. "Those two things will serve you very well during your journey at the Academy and beyond. Now, let's sit down and look at your class schedule," she purred. "I have an opening in health education taught by two lovely young men who have learned their life lessons. You can call them Mr. Belushi and Mr. Farley, but I call them frick and frack."

4.

It was Friday afternoon and a long weekend was looming. As hard as I tried, I couldn't seem to purposely run into Daniel Reid although the other Reid kids were always outside riding bikes or playing street ball or tagging each other screaming, "You're it." For a few minutes, I went outside and played with them, thinking that it would be only natural for their oldest brother to join in. But he never joined us, making me the one who wanted to scream . . . out of frustration. The only thing worse than seeing someone who drove you absolutely nuts on every level was not seeing them at all.

My mother had reestablished her love of baking, and delicious smells were wafting out of our kitchen at almost every hour. She made raisin cinnamon scones in the morning, apple pie in the afternoon, and fudge nut-chunk brownies for dinner as a side dish. Although it was feeble, I couldn't take not really talking to Daniel anymore and brought a big plate of chocolate-chip cookies over to the Reids that evening. It was so 1960s of me.

My face sunk when little Jenna answered, stepped outside, and gave me a big hug around the midsection. "Thanks, Walker," she said. "Hope you have a good weekend. We're just hanging out, but we're not allowed to invite anyone in. Big bro is not home." Without saying much more, she waved and went right back into the house, closing the door as quickly as she had opened it.

I didn't even have time to ask where her brother was these days—or whom with. Was he with that Angelina from Perks. Jealousy was obviously still alive in me.

Finally, while I was helping Mom on Saturday morning plant some cheerful, red geraniums I heard the Harley fire up in his

165

garage. Quickly, I stood up from my backbreaking (although, not really) squat in front of my next victim, a pot of azaleas. He peeled out of there without even a wave. I don't think he saw me—or maybe he did. I don't think he saw anything but the quest in front of him.

This time I did muffle a scream by yelling into a bag of potting soil.

"Honey, gardening is supposed to be de-stressing," Mom instructed.

"I find it very unnerving," I answered, staring down the road and plunging my hands into thick, warm dirt.

CHAPTER 14

1.

The following Monday, I made my way to hockey practice, which I thought was the most ridiculous thing in the entire world. How was my brain and body going to get in shape playing a stupid game that at most required standing or moving a little bit from side to side in front of something that said Hasbro on it? Of course, I scanned the particulars of hockey and guessed "practice" would be in the school cafeteria in the late afternoon after they moved the lunch tables away. Maybe there would be leftovers as a snack before we played, which sounded so good because working out was always better when accompanied by a bowl of rocky road or a giant chocolate-chip cookie.

I had just done my nails on Sunday night after watching *Mad Men* reruns with my mother who I think had a mad crush on the Don Draper character. Mom was feeling really great, and her back had officially stopped hurting, which was a major relief. Who cared about some troubled guy next door when I had my mom back in working order? We were "two peas in a pod," like my dad used to call us.

We had a wonderful time just making dinner and curling up in the living room to watch shows and talk about the good old days when we were alive. It felt so much like our regular life back home, except I had new friends and a new school that wasn't really bad at all. *Teens don't want to leave their regular life. They think the afterlife will be boring,* I mused. *It's not that boring.*

Of course, I was furious with myself when my eyes kept drifting to the living room picture window to scan for any movement at the Reid house. The side of our house had another amazing, floor-to-ceiling window in the little den, perfect for my spy mission. At Casa de Reid, the lights were on inside, but as far as I was concerned, no one was home.

I wondered what Daniel did all weekend long—and I had plenty of time to think about it as I trudged through town over some fresh snowfall on my way to the actual hockey practice, which I guess was mandatory and wasn't located in the cafeteria. The bad thing about this school was you couldn't even fake a stomachache.

Kindly administrator Miss Travis had set me straight. "Oh dear, we don't play hockey in the cafeteria. How silly! We play at the stadium. Wear warm clothes and comfortable shoes for your hike over there. The stadium is out of this world, but it's also very chilly inside," she cautioned in her Mary Poppins voice, and then nodded a good-bye on a rush to meet with three new students who were victims of a weekend drinking-while-boating tragedy. I couldn't ask her my first question, which was simply, "Why would anyone play a garage game in a real stadium?"

With the address of this stadium in my hand, I kept crunching over the new layer of snow on that dusky afternoon. The sun had slipped behind the clouds and the late-day sky had taken on a dark purple-black cast that made it look like a giant bruise. My mind wandered back to Daniel who had literally disappeared from my life after the night in the quarry. How could he share something so private and then just vanish into thin air?

There wasn't time to answer because as I rounded a corner, I could see him walking at a fast clip about half a block ahead of me, carrying what looked like a load. He had on a big blue jersey with a "C" on the right shoulder and a large A in the middle. His jam-packed backpack was slung over one large shoulder. He didn't hear me when I called out for him. *Great, tell someone you don't even know your sad story, kiss her a few times, and then check out. Typical!*

Tall and powerfully built, he took strategic strides and soon disappeared into an enormous oval building that was stark white against the dark sky. It had to be exactly where I was headed, and suddenly hockey was looking like a great choice. It was obvious that Daniel Reid, although athletic looking, preferred to play kid's table games, too.

But why were we playing in an arena that looked like the 20,000-seat United Center in Chicago?

A few minutes later, I trudged up to the back door of the stadium and was surprised that there was a warning sign for all patrons and athletes. It read: Attention: This building enjoys what can best be described as a strange gravity. Be prepared for an uplifting experience once you enter the actual rink.

With one hand on the outside door, I cautiously walked inside and nothing at all seemed strange in this dank backstage hallway that smelled appropriately of musty basement. It was just a small area with worn-out, blood-red carpeting and cement-gray walls. So, I took a few steps to another larger metal door where I would enter the actual stadium. Taking a deep breath, I pulled the handle, but it wouldn't budge. So, I pulled harder.

Nothing could have prepared me for what I experienced inside.

2.

With my first step inside the stadium, my entire body levitated approximately six feet upward.

Whoa, Nelly! I rushed through the sky and then stopped as if some otherworldly force had literally slammed on the brakes.

Immediately, I put my hands out like I was going to fall either backward or forward, but my balance wasn't impaired in the least. I was absolutely upright and simply floating, feet down, balance intact, but in the air like a bird. So was everyone else.

In the distance, I could see my gym teacher, Walter, floating, too. Daniel was racing around with a large hockey stick in one hand and his "C" captain shirt blowing in what seemed like a real wind. There were other students I recognized in big blue jerseys on the "ice." There was Izayah from my chemistry class and Ben from English. The only thing was . . . it wasn't ice at all that was our playing surface. It was just slick air that seemed to have the consistency of real ice, so you moved—fast.

Ferrari fast. Lamborghini fast. Supersonic fast.

Like Bambi, I took a wobbly first step, but that didn't feel right. My eyes darted to the right and I could see my lunch-buddy Tosh doing pirouettes in the air.

"Glide," Tosh said, racing past me like she had ice skates on her feet, but the truth was she was in what looked like funky white athletic shoes. I tried it in my new black boots and it worked just fine, too. *One foot in front of the other and then let go.* It was like I had instantly become an Olympian speed skater because in a nanosecond my feet were in the groove and gliding rocket fast.

One thought: *Oh my God, how do you stop?*

As I continued to do my first lap around the outer perimeter of what was a regulation hockey rink, I could see Daniel throwing down a black puck and then slapping it hard with his stick until it jettisoned into the goalie's net. Slowing down my glide by turning in my right toes (something I found entirely by accident when I almost tripped), I made my way to the outer wall of the rink to slide into the shadows. Finally, I stopped by crashing hips-first into the waist-high wall. The reset kicked in a minute later and I was completely fine.

Daniel saw me at that point and had a quizzical look on his face.

"Coach, Callaghan over there isn't ready for hockey. She'll get hurt. Real hurt," Daniel called out. For a moment, my heart did a little flip because it felt good that he was actually worried about the one person who didn't even know how to stop gliding, let alone play hockey.

A bigger girl, perched in the goalie net, shouted back to him, "Sexist! I bet Walker can hold her own. It doesn't matter if she gets hurt—unless you just can't stand to watch it. Plus, it's not like she'll get the chance to play, since she's just the backup."

Shaking his head at Daniel as if his words were utterly ridiculous, Walter caught me out of the corner of his bifocals. He couldn't wait to glide over to where I was checking my hips for signs of permanent damage, but of course, there was none.

"Welcome to air hockey," Walter said with a hearty laugh, stopping midair on a dime. When my mouth dropped open, he added, "I guess you do sports now, Walker. Welcome to the team. You're an Academy Ace now."

3.

Walter must have sensed my confusion, which is why he turned into a one-man recruiter and information specialist for the new sport of human air hockey and gave me the rundown.

The Academy Aces regularly practiced in that massive arena bathed in fluorescent lights. Spectators were told to read the list of rules on the back of their tickets on game days when the Academy played air hockey—just like the icy sport, but midair—against the other schools in the vicinity including ITT and another place called the Frederick Reardon Establishment of Academics and Kinetics. Kids around here called it by the initials and it took me a minute to figure it out: Freak U.

"Freak U is for teens with oddities," Walter informed me. "You might never know it from looking at them, but something is rather peculiar and they possess it."

I had to let that bit of information slide for now—no pun intended. There were other priorities including the rules of the game and this strange place.

The spectator rules included the following: Absolutely no standing. Stay in your seats at all times. Spectators also enjoyed the odd gravity of the room. Ushers escorted fans to their seats. Just like on a rollercoaster ride, a harness came down over them to keep them seated and in place. They were also advised to buckle up. No one needed a spectator floating onto the rink. Or hitting the ceiling.

Daniel, as our captain, led the Aces. He didn't make the rules, which demanded that each game was a coed experience. Of the six members of each hockey team, the rules stated that two must be female including the hard-core rule that the goalie must be a girl.

"Walker, here's the deal," Walter told me in plain language. "We have Daniel and three other guys including Ben, Jack, and Izayah. Tosh was a prima ballerina back in her day. She's amazing. Thanks to her dance background, she can leap and do all sorts of twists and turns. Our goalie's name is Zea—she's from Iowa. She's used to run her daddy's farm until an unfortunate tractor-trailer incident. But she grew up playing every sport. Her father wanted a boy."

I was confused. Why was I even here?

"Just stand there," Walter said in a firm voice. "Your job is just to stand there on the sidelines. You're the backup girl. I doubt that you'll ever play, but there must be one backup male and one backup female just in case. A kid from one of my gym classes is the male backup and the female backup is . . . you."

I'll never play? It was the best news I had ever heard in my afterlife.

4.

For weeks, I just stood there. It was my job to show up to practice three times a week where I basically stood there looking disgusted while the Aces went through the motions I didn't really understand.

Vaguely, I knew the rules of hockey. A bunch of guys usually rushed around chasing a tiny puck and then body slammed each other into the wall to have little mini side-dramas and brawls. The goalie hung out in that little netlike thing trying to stop the puck. It wasn't exactly brain surgery.

Human air hockey did have a few special particulars. The first involved our bright-blue uniforms that were made up of large jerseys and matching pants, plus special white shoes that were greased up on the bottom with Vaseline to ensure maximum air glide. The puck was the same size as regulation hockey and so were the sticks. No one wore pads or helmets because it wasn't exactly like you could get hurt. If you did get banged up, the reset kicked in and everything went back to normal—if you could call any of this normal.

On Saturdays, we played games against the other schools and I was allowed to sit on the bench. When no one was looking, I'd sneak a book out from under my jersey and read until Walter gave me dirty looks. Occasionally, I made a good show out of standing up and cheering for my team. I'd smile at Daniel when we won and rush out onto the rink to slap palms when the game was over. Eventually, I learned to stop on my own instead of crashing into the nearest wall, which was just downright embarrassing.

A few more weeks passed and we were in a dead heat with the Institute for Troubled Teens for the league championship. As usual, Walter spent each practice giving us words of wisdom like "Winners never quit and quitters never win."

I tried to pretend like I was interested while I just stood around, trying to avoid any action. "Winners, they, uh, never cry," I repeated.

"That's quit," Walter said.

"Uh huh," I replied.

"Walker, you're not playing, but for the ten millionth time, I don't want you sitting," Walter said. "Come out onto the rink and stand there or practice your basic movements."

When I wasn't standing, I attempted to glide around with a hockey stick in one hand. The first time, I dropped the stick, tripped over it, and landed face-first on the slick "air ice." But I bounced back up, the reset kicked in, and the only thing I died of was shame. A concerned Daniel was right there in my face asking, "You okay?"

"Superior," I said, shaking my head. "Love hockey. Love sports."

Once or twice, I could see Daniel chuckling like it was obviously ridiculous I was even on the team. Why did they even need a backup girl and backup boy in a place where no one ever got sick and nothing could happen to you? But my consistent inquiry here always got me the same answer: "Walker, less questions, more standing," Walter barked.

Daniel was friendly on the rink, but standoffish in other ways. At school he gave me more of his annoyingly polite greetings, and a few times we even walked home together, but we didn't talk about anything much more important than the weather or how Arnie was blowing himself up again in science class.

After revealing so many personal details, it hurt that he wouldn't open up again. When I asked about his "mission," he gave me a silencing look and bit out, "Just leave it alone." Then his face softened and he said, "I've done all the research I can at school. I need to go on that field trip."

I knew what that meant. He needed to go to ITT and find the rest of the information. "When hockey season is over," he said, "going home is my full-time priority."

Why he waited so long became obvious during a short conversation we had on one of those walks home. "I've read that you must go back on the exact day that you died. That's the only time a portal will open up for you. It's your only shot. I have until it's two days before Christmas," he said.

It was a lot of time . . . and no time at all. If he couldn't figure out how to go back now, he would have to wait an entire living year back on Earth to try it again. Even though there weren't any calendars here, most everyone still counted sunrise to sundown as one day and kept track of the months. We made makeshift calendars and tacked them on the fridge. Again, old habits dying hard. Plus, for what Daniel was doing, he needed to know the "when's."

Prior to the championship game that fall, we had a team meeting where Walter gave us the ultimate pep talk about our collective mission. "We're playing ITT on Saturday for the championship. I hate ITT. I hate them with every bone in my body. I'd play them if I could—and stomp on every bone," he said. "There is no such thing as second place. See you on Saturday for the big win. Don't disappointment me."

Despite all this rah-rah "we can do it" bravado, I still didn't give a flip about sports, except for one particular. I was beyond curious to see these ITT hooligans up close and personal. Would they be scary? Would they look like teen felons? I tried to make myself focus on my own team, although it was laughable that I had one. Maybe I could sit on the bench and do a few crossword puzzles before high-fiving everyone at the end of the "big game" and then kiss the trophy. Since my uniform was pretty cool, I asked the one person to attend who I knew would be shocked to see me "sort of" not really playing a sport.

My mother was thrilled when I handed her a ticket. When she read the back of it, she came into my room and sat down on my bed to ask the big question, "What do they mean by saying I will levitate?" she asked. "Do I have to wear special clothing?"

"We're not in Kansas anymore," I replied with a laugh, before adding, "I'd bring a sweater. You can never go wrong with a sweater."

5.

On the Saturday of the big game, there was a hint of an ice storm in the air—dark clouds hanging low into the sky. Mom and I piled into the Honda with all my equipment and I gave her directions to the stadium.

"Remember Mom, it's not a regular place. You levitate the moment you step into the actual stadium. It's really weird at first—like you're flying. So you have to sit down in your seat, put on your seat belt, and watch for a harness to come down over your head like being at an amusement park ride."

"I don't know what's more odd," Mom said. "The idea of having to strap myself into a seat or you playing sports, honey."

"I don't play," I reminded her, laughing. "I stand."

We laughed all the way to the stadium and today the place smelled like hot dogs and popcorn, with the faint smell of cotton candy hanging in the air. The crowd filing in the empty seats consisted of mostly teenagers and their teachers. I saw Heath in the stands and he gave me a quick, shy wave. Kurt was there in his basic flannel shirt and ripped jeans. Principal King sat in the press box, way up on top; a giant white sweatshirt that read The Academy replaced his typical black suit. Score one for school spirit.

He sat next to a giant of a man with a scowl on his face. I heard someone call him the GF, and I stared at the man that Daniel had described so perfectly. He had a bowling-ball round, bald head, which looked unceremoniously plopped on a doughy, mountain-sized body—fitting for a man who ruled a school embedded into a mountain.

"Oh my!" Mom exclaimed when she entered the actual stands, making her way to her seat in section 110, row 13, seat 6. Swiftly, her body was airborne several feet, but a kindly usher helped to drag her back down by her legs and into her seat. After getting Mom harnessed in, I asked another usher to give me a yank down, gave her a quick kiss on the cheek, and took off for the locker room. But halfway there, I decided to glance onto the rink where the ITT team was doing a few practice laps.

It was hard to stop my heart from pounding. Six monsters were swirling around with savage looks in their eyes and I knew they would destroy us.

177

Tosh popped up next to me to explain the particulars. "Their goalie is a girl from New York named Bertha. She's about three hundred and fifty pounds," she said, while I gazed at Bertha's 'fro that had an actual green comb purposely stuck in it. Daniel had given me her twisted tale when he told me about the fine residents of ITT, but seeing her in the flesh turned what seemed like fiction into fact. She had lush lips and kept smacking them as if she were a wolf just waiting to eat the opposing team alive. "Female gangbanger who was murdered in juvie. Don't look into her eyes," Tosh said. "She has crazy peepers."

"Of course, she's reformed," Tosh added, rolling her eyes. "Or *supposedly* reformed, which is why she gets to play. But you know how it goes with sports. The coach just wanted her on the team."

With the back of her bare hand, Bertha casually slapped a puck away like she was swatting away a fly. She hit that puck so hard, I imagined that it landed in oblivion. Afterward, she released a self-satisfied grin and licked her lips again before shouting, "Now, *that's* what I'm talking 'bout!"

Three large tanks began to roar around the rink, and they were so gross and disgusting that my eyes diverted for a moment. "The Wargos," said Tosh with another eye roll. "Eddie, Daryl, and Billy. They're redneck legends."

"Legends who look like they need a good shower," I told her, looking closely at each one while holding my breath because they were taller, rounder, and more disheveled than how Daniel had described them. Mentally, I tried to calculate the last time any of them had actually used a comb. Obviously, deodorant wasn't a welcome commodity at ITT.

"Just when you thought there were no hot guys here," Tosh joked. "The Wargos are probably free on Friday nights, Saturday nights . . . all nights."

"Well, maybe there are one or two hot guys here," I interjected, glancing at Daniel warming up.

"Yeah, what spell did you put on him? He actually looks at you. He's never looked at anyone," Tosh began.

I could feel my face start to flame red.

"A lot of us females have tried, you know. When I first got here, I even made him a digital mix tape with a lot of vintage Justin Timberlake. *Mor-tify-ing*, I know. But the point is, now Daniel and I are just friends. I think. He barely talks to anyone. Does he actually talk to you about anything real?"

"Later," I said, winking at her as we laughingly made our way toward the locker room. Out of the corner of my eye, I could see that the Wargos were whaling on *each other*. Eddie shoved Billy into the wall and Daryl roared up behind him and punched both of his brothers in the face. Hard. Billy reared up, raising one knee and clipping his brother in the jaw. The refs stood around watching and laughing. They didn't move to break it up because obviously they found it so entertaining. "Now, Walker, you don't want to mess with the Wargos. First thing to know: Anything goes in team play and they don't play nice," Tosh said. "It's a good thing that I'm much faster than either of them. They live to pulverize other players. Their favorite move is something they call the 'Pancake.'"

Shuddering, I knew we had to pass them to get to our own locker room. For a split second, Eddie Wargo stopped pummeling his brother and looked me up and down slowly like he had never seen a women in his life, then gave me a half-sneering smile.

At eighteen, the guy could haunt a house with a face that looked like a side of beef with two dark sunken slits for eyes. "Hey, baby. New around here? Wanna visit my cellblock tonight?" Eddie shouted with a sneer that made me want to toss the contents of my stomach. *Wanna visit my cellblock tonight? Was that dating at ITT?*

"You're a scrawny one . . . less meat on your bones than a starving pigeon," Billy taunted me.

Where I'm from, it's better to face a bully than offer your back as a target. So, I stopped, turned, and looked at their meat-faces.

"You're so dead," Daryl jeered, warning me that no one said a word to the Wargos.

"Why don't you geniuses tell me something I don't already know?" I said with a sarcastic sneer.

"Are you sayin' I'm stupid," Daryl countered.

"The engine's running, but nobody's driving," I replied.

"Say what?" Daryl responded, clouds in his narrow eyes. "What do cars have to do with this?"

Eddie took one sausage-sized finger and poked his brother right in the eye. "Told off by a skinny runt of a girl," he taunted. "Pussy!"

What followed was a stream of words I couldn't even repeat.

Entering the locker room, I could hear Daniel and Walter in a heated argument. "You absolutely can't do it. It's ITT out there," Daniel yelled, to which Walter gave him a look that could stop your blood from flowing. After being a Hall of Fame running back in the NFL, Walter didn't take crap from anyone.

"You don't make the rules, son, despite the fact that you're the captain!" Walter countered just as loudly. "And we don't have a choice. It's either do it or we forfeit the league championship. You're out of your mind if you think I'm forfeiting."

Gliding up to Daniel, I purposely allowed myself to stop (a skill I now possessed) just inches in front of him. "What can't Walter do?" I asked in a laughing voice, but the hard look in Daniel's eyes stopped me cold.

"Walker," Walter began, "I have a problem. Zea didn't show up today. I don't know what's wrong or where she is. I tried calling her room at school about a hundred times. No answer. I sent someone back to school to find her. It's like she vanished." Daniel and Walter gave each other a knowing look.

"I need you to go in," Walter finally said.

"Go where?" I replied because I didn't understand what in the world he was saying.

"*In*," said Walter. "As in . . . in the game. As goalie."

"I don't do sports," I repeated in a half-hysterical tone. "The whole agreement we made was that I just show up. I'm here. I glide around a few times at practice. I give high fives. That's it! Mostly, I stand there."

"We can't find Zea and we need a goalie," Walter said, the look on his face indicating that he was as sick to his stomach about this as anyone else was, which was pretty much everyone else on the team. "Go get dressed. As of today, you do play sports. Get ready."

CHAPTER 15

1.

For a moment, I just stood there, jaw sinking, not moving, and barely breathing. Somehow this had to be a bad joke and any moment Zea would race breathlessly through that door screaming, *"Put me in coach. I'm ready to play."*

That moment never came even though I hung back long enough to allow it to happen. That old song floated through my mind: *Wishing . . . and hoping . . . and dreaming.*

This was obviously going to go down as one of those lessons where all the wishing in the entire world doesn't make it so.

I had to go in.

Of course, there were other alternatives. I could go AWOL. For a minute, I thought about turning tail and racing out of the building, running as fast as I could until I hit regular gravity. Once I sunk back to ground zero, I would run home and hide out in my new bedroom, which would be my safety zone with my lucky rabbit's foot. I wasn't sure if anyone or any force would actually stop me.

Nah. That seemed so chickenshit.

Instead of running, I went to my locker and suited up in bright Academy blue, a color that did go very well with my coloring. Then I made a slow trek back into the stadium, levitated, turned sharply, and stepped in the direction of the rink until there were no more steps left and I was actually *on* the rink.

It warmed my heart when I saw my entire team of Academy Aces applauding, hands overhead, like I was their favorite rock star. I was Pink!

Around me was my band. There was Tosh who was our right winger. Ben was on left wing, Jack on defense, and big, bad Izayah backing him on defense. Allowing my gaze to sweep to the middle, I spotted Daniel, our captain, who was now racing up the centerline to meet me just as I found and entered what was obviously the net. *Was he kidding? After freezing me out for weeks, he chooses now for a private moment in front of a room of fifteen thousand fans and classmates?*

"Callaghan," Daniel said in a deep, serious voice, his frown cutting unhappy slashes throughout his tense-looking face, "first of all, I don't want you to do this today."

"What is your name again? You look so familiar," I said, flippantly.

He had much more on his mind.

"You could just say no. You could bolt. Maybe that's actually the best course because this ain't gonna be pretty. We're playing against convicted felons. These aren't the boys next door. Just get out of here. Just say no."

"No," I stated, looking into his kind and concerned gray eyes and wanting to drown in them.

"Good," he said with a sigh, dropping his head.

"No way I'm saying no. I'm in," I insisted and his face jolted.

"That's what I figured," he uttered with a deeper sigh, gliding a little closer and placing his warm hand on my shoulder. Daniel leaned in until we were just millimeters apart to almost-whisper into my ear, "You can actually do this, you know. Please don't look at me like I'm nuts. Please, just don't look at me at all. You can do this, Callaghan."

He said it basing it on the only two things we actually had on our side tonight, which were adrenalin and foolish, youthful dreams. *Yeah, we could do this. Sort of like how they thought they could put a man on the moon before actually inventing rocket ships. It was a good idea in theory, but it was an insane one in reality.*

A man of strong convictions, I could see that Daniel was trying to convince himself just as much as he was trying to convince me. Suddenly, he sounded older, wiser, and a little bit nervous.

This wasn't a movie or some TV show where the inexperienced girl who never played hockey in her life saved the day and won the big game. This was real life with real thugs who were here to give us a real ass whupping. We couldn't die from it, but it sure was scary to think about these spitting, sweating, snorting ITTers slamming their bodies into whatever stood in their way of this championship. The reset didn't eliminate your need to flinch and your desire not to play chicken with rage-a-holics. And this game was the only thing these lifers at ITT had to look forward to in their otherwise bleak, incarcerated existences.

I put my hand on the goalie stick and moved it around a bit to get acquainted with my weapon, which was thick on the bottom and flat. A garish white spotlight seared down on the rink and I had to squint to see who—or what—I was up against. I couldn't be sure, but I thought I locked eyes with their captain, snort-man Eddie Wargo.

No, he didn't.

Yes, he did. Blow me a kiss, that is.

Then he gave me a quick middle finger.

"I have faith in you," Daniel whispered, his back to Eddie so he was clueless when it came to our little exchange. "And we'll keep the puck away. Izayah and Jack will flank you and play great defense. The Wargos won't even get near you. That's crucial. Stay away from them. They're like rabid dogs. All you need to do is stand there. Just freakin' stand there."

Then, after a brief pause, he added, "On second thought, try to block if it comes to it. If you think you're going to get hurt then just glide away. I know you can move fast. I've seen you mad. Remember when I shoved you into that frozen lake? You didn't even have this gravity, and you moved pretty fast. For a girl."

"Don't get romantic on me now," I said with the smile of the condemned.

He didn't say another word, but glided a little closer, cupping his hand over my ear. A shiver ran from the top of my head to my toes when he gave me a peck on my earlobe. For good luck.

I was sure this wasn't in the official rule book—and I didn't give a damn either.

2.

Our fearless coach, Walter, was the next one to glide by me before the game officially started. "Do I get a mask and pads?" I asked him.

"What do you think this is, Walker, the NHL?" he said with a grim smile. "Remember, the reset will help you. Just stand there. And one more thing."

"What thing would that be?" I asked him, humming a few bars of "Stairway to Heaven." *There's a feeling I get when I look to the west.* "Are we looking west?" I asked.

The coach ignored that one.

"Walker, you enjoy certain privileges as a member of the Academy, which is thanks to the honorable and perhaps even outstanding way you lived your life when you were alive. In other words, you were an upstanding citizen," Walter said. "The kids at ITT haven't earned the reset, meaning they *can* get hurt. And they *will* feel pain. Their bones break. They will bleed. They could lose an eye and not get it back again—if you know what I mean, and I know you do. You're a sharp one," Walter said. "I'm not saying that you could or should get rough, but I *am* saying an eye for an eye. Meaning—"

"If they whale on me, I whale on them," I finished.

"No whaling. What do you weigh? A hundred pounds soaking wet? Those boys are three hundred pounds plus a few greasy chicken dinners. That girl Bertha is close to four hundred pounds. So, just freakin' stand there," he repeated.

"I already heard that advice," I said, shivering although I wasn't cold.

"I'm telling you this because it will get rough and messy and bloody as the periods—and remember, there are three of them—progress," Walter concluded.

"Don't play their game and engage them. Don't antagonize them either. Just evade them," Walter said. With those words, he glided away intent on doing some final morale boosting for the rest of the team before the starting horn was blasted.

Back on ITT's side, I could see their coach, Maurice "The Rocket" Richard (pronounced Ree-chard), a former NHL player whose stare was known to frighten his opponents. He was giving his team a little pep talk. The Wargos actually respected The Rocket, as did the other ITT players including Bertha, who filled up the entire goal with legs that were wide like the trunks of ancient redwoods. I wasn't even sure if a puck could actually fit in there. Eddie Wargo was the team captain and center; Billy was the right-winger while Daryl was the left-winger. A brother-sister convenience-store-robbing duo filled out the rest of the motley pack.

Bonnie Phillips played defense as did her brother, Clyde— no relation to the real bank-robbing legends Bonnie and Clyde Parker, although their ex-con mother thought it would be cute to name her twins after two people she truly admired—two felons. She gave birth to her kids in jail and like many of the ITT kids, they bounced around the foster-care system.

"Do start fights and then finish them," The Rocket told his team. "Eddie, send your brothers in to do all the crushing and punching. The girl they just put in as goalie looks petrified. Confirm her worst fears. Make them real. You finish it up. Daryl and Billy, remember the Pancake. Bertha, you're the muscle. Eddie, you're the hustle."

"Do something you're good at," The Rocket concluded, adding the entire team. "Massacre them."

3.

"Welcome to the league championship. The Academy versus ITT," bellowed the sports announcer, Dan Fanatic or Dan Fan for short. "We're in for one hell of a game coming at you live from Dick Clark Arena. Let me turn this over to the broadcasting legend who made New Year's Eve's so rockin'. . . Dick."

"Thanks, Dan," said Dick Clark who couldn't resist hosting an event. *Any event.* That's why he chose to come here after departing

Earth. The mike with his name on it was waiting. "Today, it's the boys and girls from a totally too cool school called the Academy versus the brawn at the school ITT. Go, Academy, go!"

Dan took back the mike. "Not that Dick is partial or anything," he said with a laugh.

"May the best school win," Dick said, swiveling his body so it looked like he was busting an actual dance move. Without the jail cell of his stroke, and with his body healed now in the afterlife, Dick couldn't stop dancing—and no one dared deny him the beat inside his head. When he mentioned that a close friend named Casey would be joining him soon, no one was surprised.

4.

The horn was loud and garish. There was no mistaking the message it carried: Game on!

Daniel skated over to center ice for the face-off with Eddie Wargo. In the moments before the puck was dropped, Eddie thought they might enjoy a brief conversation about world events. "What kind of kissy-faced crap was that over there?" barked Eddie, his upper lip lifted like it needed to make room for white foam to slosh out of it. Then he pointed in the direction of the Academy's goal.

"Had to give your sweet girlie friend a little talk? Where did you pick that one up? The chess club at your candy-ass school? Better get a good look at her before we rearrange her face," Eddie taunted, wiping the juice he kept spitting out of his mouth on his black ITT jersey. After a school vote, they had decided they would be the ITT Idiots. Their school mascot was a cockeyed monster with the word "Duh" on his forehead. Everyone at ITT seemed proud of it.

Killing Eddie on the spot was an option; but Daniel refrained, figuring they could settle this on the rink. He had gone toe-to-toe with Eddie Wargo at the beginning of the season, and it was never good. ITT won that game in overtime, and Daniel carried a major grudge. But there was no time to dwell on the past because the ref was dropping the puck, which sank quickly to the bottom of the air at their feet.

It was game on! Daniel sliced at the puck hard, mustering up all the rage he felt for Eddie Wargo in one neat slap shot. What he couldn't see was Billy and Daryl Wargo flying up to him like bats out of hell.

Billy raced hard from the right while Daryl pounded up from the left. Before he could move, they sandwiched Daniel, each throwing three hundred pounds to crush a specific side of his rib cage. Stuck in their trap, Daniel was momentarily paralyzed while Eddie Wargo raced at him from the middle. About an inch away from Daniel, Eddie took his stick and jabbed it hard into Daniel's stomach until the Academy's team captain folded like an accordion.

All of the air forced out of his lungs, Daniel collapsed, and his large body hit the bottom air of the rink's floor. "Just stand there, pretty boy," Eddie taunted, obviously mocking what Daniel told his goalie. "Now that you're down, it's time to pay your little girlfriend a visit."

5.

I blinked and the reset was kicking in. As Daniel slowly got to his feet, the Wargos enjoyed this little extra time on the air without our captain upright. It was no wonder they came barreling toward me like a freak summer storm. Tosh tried, in vain, to flip around them to get the puck back, but Bonnie of ITT caught her midair with a hard elbow to her face. Tosh was also down for the count.

We were playing a physical school where no rules were the rules.

I was doomed.

As fast as a tornado racing down a farmer's field, Eddie was suddenly upon me, the two destructors known as his brothers at his side. Doing what I was told, I stood there, holding my ground, spastically moving my stick as I tried to block, but my adrenalin was pumping so hard that I couldn't even focus. With a ferocious roar, Eddie slammed at the puck and shot it hard at me.

It was only natural. Only human. I closed my stupid eyes.

"ITT Scores!" Dick yelled, his trademark, *We're going rockin', we're going rockin' today* blaring in the background while most of the stadium emitted a loud hissing boo. "Kids, remember good sportsmanship and to use Clearasil if you're spending eternity at ITT—where apparently there is no reset for zits," Dick said in his sleek voice, but the booing only got louder.

The crowd was almost all Academy students because the kids at ITT were generally too dangerous to attend a public event. Just one section was occupied with ITT kids on the road to parole, but it only contained about fifteen kids in their trademark black school shirts and matching pants. The Idiot logo was prominently displayed.

190

After he scored, Eddie Wargo sailed up close enough to me where I could smell the fishy stink of his breath. "Candy ass," he yelled in my face. A fine mist of tuna-scented spit flew at me, putting an exclamation mark over his score.

His crazy-eyed brother Daryl had even more to say to me before he took off for the centerline. "This here is gonna get to be a lot more fun, girlie," he said. "A lot more fun than move-in day at the trailer park, yessir. You just wait and see."

"Hillbilly," I muttered under my breath.

Daryl stopped cold, did a one-eighty, and whipped around to face me. "What did you call me?" he demanded.

"I said, 'You better go get your brother Billy,'" I lied and I could see his three brain cells were not really comprehending, although they seemed to be working overtime.

"I don't think y'all wanna get nasty with us, girlie. We don't put up with no shit from girlies, as a rule. We'll knock you into next week," Daryl explained, as if he was shining a light on his secret code of hillbilly honor.

"Duly noted," I said under my breath as he began to glide away. He stopped again and turned around hard.

"It's not like I'm dang stupid," he bit out.

"Is dang stupid a level down from real stupid?" I retorted under my breath.

His ratlike almost-black eyes became even narrower slits in his otherwise slab of a face. Then he gave me his worst version of a threat. "It's on like Donkey Kong with you now. You're gonna have real fun," he chided, finally racing up to the above-mentioned Billy for support.

I know he heard me when I yelled after him, "Fun! If things get any better, I may have to hire someone to help me enjoy it."

Both faced me from across the rink looking dumbfounded and then they did a curious thing with their rough gorilla hands.

191

They kept turning their hands over to the sides and with each flip continued to press their paws together hard.

"Pancake! Pancake!" the small ITT crowd began to chant.

I got it—even if I didn't want to get it.

"This will jar your preserves, little lady," Billy yelled, flipping his hands in double time.

6.

Now that he was fully recovered, humiliated, and totally pissed off, Captain Daniel Reid was ready for the next face-off with Eddie Wargo. The minute the puck hit the air, Daniel cut right, pivoted sharply, and slapped the puck to Ben, his left-winger. Flying around the goal where Bertha was perched, Daniel whipped around and was at the exact right spot when Ben passed the puck back. Giving the puck a hard whack that had the crowd cheering, Daniel sent the little black disc flying like a missile toward ITT's goal.

Bertha caught it in her massive tangle of hair, which was that thick and dense.

"No score," shouted the referee, and I actually swore under my breath.

The ref dropped another puck and Billy snaked it in, rushing with Daryl down the rink, where I was "just standing there" a little bit outside the goal. Izayah and Jack were flanking me, playing defense, when the thugs arrived. Almost sensing blood, Billy allowed the puck to slip from his grasp.

What I couldn't know is he did it on purpose, so Izayah and Jack would chase it and slam it back to Daniel at center rink.

I was still out of the goal. But with my defense gone, I was alone.

Billy reared his ugly head first, bearing down on me from one side of the net while Daryl came from the exact opposite side. They yelled one word that made my blood freeze in my veins: "Pancake!"

The impact knocked my teeth into my head and made my insides flatten. Their assault was like being pulverized to death. I was literally one of those old cars at the wrecking yard that was being crushed out of existence by two pieces of steel that slammed together until there was no space between them.

I'm not sure what happened after I saw stars and hit the deck with a thud. Still levitating, I was floating facedown like I was sleeping on a cloud.

Then I blinked hard and could see Eddie racing up from the middle with the puck. When I finally stood up, Eddie flew into my face with his whole body weight while the brothers squashed me from both sides again with all of their muscle and blubber.

Then Eddie took his shot.

I couldn't get back to the goal.

When the reset kicked back in, I floated to my feet to hear the ref yell, "No goal! No goal!"

Apparently in all the confusion, I actually fell hard on the puck before it could go into the net. It wasn't exactly expert net minding, but it got the job done.

Shaking it off, I went back into the goalie's net as Daniel came racing up and slammed his fist right into Eddie's face, hard. When Eddie reeled backward, Daniel gave him a right to the gut that buckled his knees. Before the referees could even bother to interfere, Izayah shoved Billy and Tosh did her best to trip Bonnie and then shove her skinny rump into the wall.

Eddie didn't take lightly the fact that his nose was bleeding, and swung for Daniel who moved easily right to miss the hit. With both of Eddie's hands ripping at his jersey, Daniel still managed to jam him back into the wall. Eddie actually fell over his brother

Daryl who was just standing there, which was like a declaration of another war. The brothers started pushing and throwing punches at *each other.*

Walter started going ballistic. "Play within the rules!" he shouted at the refs.

"We are playing within the rules," said one of the refs who actually jammed himself into the middle of the mayhem and told both teams to "break it up and break it up now or I'll break you." I could have sworn I saw him wave a stun gun at the Wargos.

"Well, that concludes the first period," said Dick Clark, with a merry little laugh. "It's one nothing, ITT leading over the Academy. We'll take a short break where Casey will count down the top ten songs at Perks and then we'll return, I hope, in a much better mood." Dick didn't know his microphone was still on when he said, to no one in particular, "This is like New Year's Rockin' Eve on steroids."

7.

Back in the locker room, a vengeance-seeking, seething Daniel punched one of the lockers so hard that he made a huge dent in the metal. "We have to try to score!" he told Tosh who just shrugged because she was trying her best and having him go batshit wasn't helping.

"That Bertha is so big that her fat rolls will stop any puck," she said dryly.

"Defense, good job, but you have to stick by Callaghan. They know she's green," Daniel said. "Those Wargos are going to play even dirtier as this goes on. Who knows what they have up their sleeves."

"A bag of Doritos? Beef jerky? Deep-fried pig's ears," Tosh suggested and then received Daniel's glare.

Totally ignored, I sat on a bench, sipping water, completely stunned that I played an actual period of championship hockey.

"I'm done. Can I go home now?" I asked, waiting for someone to give me any sign to take off my jersey and call it a day.

"You did it for one period. You can do it for two more. We just need to score," said Daniel, slamming his water bottle into the garbage. All I saw was his rigid back as he started to glide back out onto the rink without uttering another word.

8.

The second period was an exact duplicate, except I stood there and actually worked on blocking. Mostly, it was Izayah and Jack who played hard defense and kept the Wargos out of shooting range. Every few minutes, it got nasty and punches were thrown. Billy Wargo, who found himself energized in the midst of violence, tripped Tosh and cross-checked her. Izayah made sure to slam him into the boards and then shot the puck back to Daniel who went in to score, but the puck easily bounced off of Bertha's big stomach.

"Ouch," she said, rubbing her actually sore ribs.

"No score," said the referee.

With so many Academy players on defense to protect me, it only left Tosh and Daniel to try to score, which meant they were seriously outmanned. Daniel tried his best to get shots on goal, but to no avail. Each time, he hit another of Bertha's massive body parts including her booty. It turns out that simply turning around in the net was one of Bertha's best plays.

The Academy became weary and the Wargos seemed to get energized as if this kind of warfare was their meat and potatoes. As the clock ticked, they appeared to get stronger and continued to slam pucks at me that were blocked by my warriors.

The third period continued on now and I could see Walter was worried. It was still one-nothing.

With less than a minute to play, Walter called a time-out. He could see that Izayah and Jack were getting tired because shots were starting to get through them. "Push yourself!" he yelled. "I know you have a little more in you! The shots are missing Walker and landing just wide of the net, and we still have to hold them." Then he turned to Daniel and yelled, "And we have to score, dammit!"

"I want Izayah and Jack to join offense," Walter continued, turning to me before he announced, "Walker you're on your own now. We're either going to lose this thing two to nothing or tie it up."

Freaking out doesn't begin to describe my response. "I can't do it alone! They'll flatten me!" I exclaimed, searching the stands, but I couldn't see my mom in her seat. Maybe she could . . . write me a note. But she was nowhere to be found, which made me think, *What a great time for her to be escorted to the hot dog stand.*

"Walker, buck up," Walter said, moving away from me to draw up a play.

Buck up! Is this what you tell someone in the middle of a giant battle against fire-breathing monsters? Buck the heck up?

The horn sounded and it was time for the last play.

9.

Daniel and Eddie met at the centerline for the last face-off. Eddie balled up a fist and pushed it hard into Daniel's right shoulder as he sought to separate the muscle from the bone. Daniel returned the favor by shoving him back and then putting his fist into Eddie's marshmallow chest that was all-parts blubber. "We can settle this another time. Let's just play hockey," Daniel said before Eddie could speak. That was a challenge for ITT's finest and Eddie shouted in his unmistakable twang, "So, you're leaving your little precious girlie friend open. Maybe I'll give her one last kiss that she'll never forget."

In the net, my heart exploded in my rib cage, pounding so hard I was sure that the entire room could hear it.

Glancing across the rink, I could see Eddie was once again in Daniel's face. "You gonna punch me again?" he taunted.

"You have no idea what I'm going to do to you," Daniel said in a quietly lethal voice, as the ref dropped the puck. Eddie was busy thinking up something to say when Daniel slashed madly at it, passing to Jack who sliced it back to Daniel who then whipped it to Tosh.

Tosh eluded Billy Wargo's defense when she launched into a few fast-spinning pirouettes around the net, which mesmerized poor Bertha whose limbs were probably falling asleep from just sitting inside the goal. It was odd that Bertha appeared to be smiling, as if she was actually enjoying Tosh's elegant air dance.

As Bertha continued to smile and look up, Tosh slid the puck under Billy's legs as Bonnie and Clyde crashed into the boards.

The clock wound down. *Ten, nine, eight, seven, six . . .*

The crowd couldn't stand, so they raised their fists in the air and began to shout, "Shoot! Shoot! For God's sake, shoooooooooooooot!"

Looking as if he was flying, Daniel cut in from the back, snagged the puck, and pivoted to face the net. Bertha moved just a tiny bit to the right as if she was searching to see what that ballerina girl was doing now, her right leg shifting just a few micromillimeters to allow a better view of the lovely show. It was obvious that she didn't have a lot of grace in her life.

At that moment, Daniel slapped the puck with all his might. He was used to kicking soccer balls to speeds that exceeded sixty-five miles per hour.

He shot. And he meant it.

He scored!

Three seconds were left on the clock. The wild crowd transformed into an electrified mass of spirit humanity. "I've never seen anything like that in my life!" Dick said, shouting into the mike, "We have a tie. It's one-one. Now what? We go home? Maybe there's a dance."

"Oh Dick, you need to stick to the music. This is hockey. It's not over," Sportscaster Dan Fan said. "We're going to be forced to go into a shoot-out."

10.

It was just as bad as it sounded. A shoot-out meant each side chose three players who would start at their own goal, glide up to the center, and then it really was on like Donkey Kong. Each player would skate as hard as possible until they reached the opposing team's goalie and then shoot hard. "The first team that has the most points after three shots wins. If there is a tie, we go into an extra shoot-out," said the ref.

Daniel and Eddie flipped a coin. The Academy won the first shot.

Walter glided over to give me a few tips.

"Walker, just do . . . whatever you can do," he mumbled.

I could see that he had absolutely no faith that I could do freaking anything except stand there and lose.

Eddie wasn't going to be silenced. Absolutely disgusted that it was a tie game, he took out his wrath on his teammate Bertha. "You big, fat, worthless dumb ass! I'm going to kill you," he yelled across the rink. "This is all your fault! You best not let them score! Each point they get is a punch you get!"

On her knees in the net with her fat draping over her sides like rolled blankets, Bertha looked utterly and entirely demoralized.

My heart began to break for this poor girl as I remembered what Daniel had told me about her bleak life one night when we walked home from practice.

Death Story: Bertha Jackson
Age of Demise: 16

She had been homeless her entire life. Her mama gave her up at age four when she just dropped her off at the hospital where she was born and simply said, "I want to make a return."

The kindly nurse said, "Miss, you can't return a child." But Bertha's mama just said, "Here's your receipt" and then she handed her birth certificate over and walked away without a good-bye. Bertha never saw her mama again. After that, she bounced around various foster homes where she was mostly unwanted and ignored. Food was her only friend, but it was also her enemy.

No one adopted the little fat girl and the other kids in those foster homes were vicious about her weight issues. "Don't go near her. She'll squash you," they taunted, pointing at her and laughing. There was always another kid saying, "I don't want to share a room with the fatty. If she pees in the bed, I'll drown."

Eventually, at age fifteen, Bertha joined the Hood Barbies, a New York girl gang, but she never did anything too bad. All Bertha wanted was a family and she figured the gang could be her own. These girls were tough and rough, but at least they had each other. They laughed when Bertha refused to learn how to use a handgun, but they didn't push it. The girl gang knew that Bertha was the muscle they needed by the sheer size of her.

When they wanted her to rob a fancy house in the suburbs, Bertha tried to talk them out of it. In the end, she lost that argument, but she couldn't abandon her family. So, she went with the other girls and stood outside on the curb while they conducted their first break-in. She never even set foot inside the actual house.

The cops arrested all of them and Bertha was sent to juvenile hall, where one night a young felon named Sal broke free and ran for the exit. Bertha was simply in his way. Too stunned to move and too large for him to maneuver around, he took out the knife he stole from the kitchen and stabbed her dead.

She woke up at ITT and was housed in Building A. "Absolutely, this girl can be rehabbed," insisted her counselor, Amy, who signed her up for a myriad of different activities, including hockey, to prove to the Higher Authority that she didn't belong there.

Now at the championship game, her other family—her team—couldn't see the tears that were threatening to run, although it was obvious she was desperately trying to stop them.

Eddie continued to release a vile stream of words at Bertha.

"What's the matter Eddie? Getting a little tired? Picking on women now—women other than your brothers?" Daniel taunted.

Eddie gave Daniel a Bronx cheer while Tosh took her place at the Academy's net, gearing up to make the first shot. Gliding like she was an Olympic figure skater, Tosh took her time, doing a few fast spins as she gracefully made her way down the rink. From the shimmer of her tears, Bertha watched with absolute admiration.

As she made her way closer to ITT's goal, Tosh did the one thing that Bertha never expected. Jumping as high as possible, Tosh executed a "perfect ten" midair split, both of her legs parallel to the ground, her toes pointed. The crowd burst into wild applause and my eyes got huge when I actually saw Bertha begin to silently clap her hands in applause. There was just one tiny burst of joyous emotion, but it was unmistakable.

Tosh easily scored when Bertha left a tiny opening where her hands were once resting.

The crowd erupted into even louder cheers as Eddie Wargo fell to his knees in a manic rage. "Get that fat ass out of our goal," he screamed at The Rocket. "She's mentally irregular now! I'm going to kill that bitch!"

The Rocket just ignored him. "Billy, make me proud. You're up," the stone-faced coach said.

11.

I stood like a statue as Billy Wargo launched himself toward me, gliding absolutely straight like a human arrow that was shot out of a cannon. As he got closer, I could see his face was a contorted combination of a half-toothless mouth, a nose that had been broken too many times, and eyes that were as hard as granite.

Billy stopped cold about ten inches in front of my net. He looked to his left and then spit a big loogie into the air directed at my face. There was no reset for a spit spray dripping down your jersey that made you sick to your stomach. There was no time to dwell on it either. Billy locked eyes on me and slapped the puck hard.

He was so grossly intimidating that I flinched for a split second, but diverting my eyes was my downfall.

Billy Wargo easily scored and did a little victory cheer that included his own personal crazy dance where he fell on his back in the air and kicked his feet up toward the sky like a crazed donkey.

He wasn't near finished. As he made his way off the rink, the drooling convict made sure to sail inches in front of me. At the exact moment we passed each other, he turned toward me and spit, this time hitting my face. Disgusting bits of greenish ooze melted on my cheeks and rained into my eyes.

A feeling of utter defeat swept over me and out of the corner of one blurry eye I could see Walter running a hand over his forehead like he had just broken out into a spontaneous fever. Daniel was holding onto one of the boards, his face mirrored in the shadows and his fist clenched.

"Daniel, stand down—I'm not playing here! Izayah, you're next," Walter said, hoping that his big, bad playa from Los Angeles would prove his mettle.

Starting at the centerline, Izayah made sure to wiggle his behind just a little bit as he glided toward big Bertha. When he was close enough for her to hear him, he reached deep down for his best Denzel Washington inspiration and said in a low tone, "Hey Bertie, baby. You're looking real pretty sitting there. Nothing bad about you."

Bertha cried, "I am good. I didn't really rob that house."

She gave Izayah the most heartwarming smile he had probably ever seen in his life, and for a moment he looked like he felt bad, real bad, about what he had to do to her because she was obviously a little smitten with him. But he had no choice, except to glide right up to her, almost stop, toss her a dazzling smile, and then shoot the heck out of the puck, which flew right under her armpit and into the net.

"The Academy scores!" yelled the ref while the Wargos went ballistic. Eddie grabbed Billy in a headlock while Daryl let out a stream of choice backwoods cusswords that even had Casey upset.

"What are you thinking, you fat piece of . . ." Eddie screamed. "He doesn't like you! He doesn't care about you! Nobody cares about you!" Those last words were the same four Bertha had heard from her mama before she gave her away.

12.

What could be said about Daryl Wargo except the score was 2–1 and this plague on humanity, alive or dead, was up next. I risked a long glance across the rink and I could see him lurking at the center line just staring me down like he was X-raying my bones.

There was no mistaking that it was Daryl—a poster teen for bad dental hygiene, and I use the h-word loosely. He had big brownish buckteeth and, combined with his long face, he looked like a barnyard donkey. In a yard, he would be one of the bigger animals, yet he was surprisingly agile as he kicked his right leg behind him to push off hard.

All I could see was that donkey face coming at me and I couldn't help but say one word aloud: "Jackass." I knew he heard me because he lifted that top lip impossibly higher to show even more teeth, and I could swear I saw little puffs of steam fly out of his toxic piehole. It made sense that middle-child Daryl had his issues with the opposite sex, and knew what girls thought of him.

Strangely, he embraced his peculiarities, and even took it upon himself to take a giant yellow highlighter to his own life.

"Hee-haw! Hee-haw!" he brayed like a donkey as he slammed his wide load toward me, continuing to pick up speed with every thudding, thundering glide. His feet moved in some sort of lumbering double-time that was beyond transfixing. It was actually hypnotic.

Daryl didn't have to announce his arrival.

When this Wargo mutt was close enough for me to smell that rotten tuna breath, he brayed again tossing his head back and slamming those teeth together hard. Forcing myself to focus on the puck, I could see him jam his stick back high for an inevitable slap slot.

"Hee-haw, girlie!" he taunted and I braced for the impact of a fast puck that he would certainly slam forward with all of his might.

What happened next shocked everyone.

Daryl wound up, but only tapped the top of the puck like he was giving it a little kiss. In hockey terms, it's known as a whiff. As I continued to brace for a fast one, the puck moved at a reduced speed as if it was being filmed in some sort of black-and-white, artistic slow motion. That little black disc slid closer . . . and then closer, until it grazed the side of my left kneepad like it was a nosy neighbor knocking once just before entering.

"Score! ITT!" Dick bellowed.

That's when Daryl Wargo turned around hard, moved closer, and hissed at me, "Who's the jackass now, little girl?"

That made the score 2–2 with two players left to shoot. Daniel started the next series at the centerline. By now, Bertha was bewildered and you could tell that her lackluster expression didn't sit well with him. Bertha's look seemed to say, "I'm emotionally spent. Done-done."

Daniel easily scored because Bertha wasn't even trying. It was 3-2 with one shot left.

He made his way off the rink the long way by skating right past me and stopping for a quick second.

"Callaghan, it's up to you," Daniel said in a low voice. "You stop this one and we win. Just stand there. Try to block it. You can do it—or not. Just try."

Eddie Wargo figured he would deal with Bertha later. Right now, he had a job to do, which was to tie up this shoot-out and go into another one. He decided to start by Bertha at his own team's goal because that way he could gain maximum glide speed as he thundered down the rink. In the second before he started, he turned to his goalie, who sat in a lump on the bottom of the airy floor.

"You're mine," he said to Bertha, and then looked down the rink. "After I'm done with her."

13.

The horn blared and Eddie was off, one foot in front of the other, barreling at me like a charging bull that had fire spurting out of its wide nostrils. I gasped as the skin on his face billowed back from the sheer velocity of his speed. A mountain of a beast with loose skin convulsing in waves, he roared loudly as he got closer, the tiny puck seemingly stuck to his weapon.

In my mind, the stadium went stealth quiet.

He was going to hit the damn thing as hard as he could. I could see that he was aiming right for me because a tie score wasn't his only goal. He wanted me to go down. He wanted me as messed up as possible. He wanted the puck to actually *go through me* if possible.

Just stand there. Try to block it. That's what Daniel said. I couldn't move anyway. It was like I was standing on railroad tracks calmly watching a screaming runaway locomotive that was about to run right through me.

What happened next was a blur. My eyes fluttered closed. My hand lifted to protect my face. Eddie shot. I screamed at the top of my lungs.

I felt a whoosh of air smack me in the face.

I felt something else, too.

The puck landed square in the middle of my hand. At first it stung like fire but then I felt its smooth roundness and leathery solidness, so I closed my fingers, hanging onto the weight of it. Then I lifted my hand skyward.

"No goal! The Academy wins the league championship!" Dick shouted as the entire crowd roared their approval.

On the sidelines, a dejected Eddie kicked his brother Billy, who slapped Daryl. As they began their standard Stooges routine, I held onto the puck and remained in the net, though I dropped my stick and had to grab the side of the goal to keep myself upright.

The next thing I knew, Daniel was grabbing me and twirling me around hard before lifting me up and tossing me over his left shoulder so I hung in the air with his strong arms banding around me. I could see Walter grinning like a happy fool. He shouted loudly, "Walker Callaghan, we told you that all you had to do was just stand there! And you did! In the end, you *could* play sports, young lady!"

"I don't do sports," I said in a weak, but happy voice as I scanned the crowd for my mother. I was sure she was the second most shocked person in the arena, if not the universe. What a good laugh we would have over this one later tonight. And tomorrow. And the tomorrow after that.

14.

Back in the locker room, Walter got his congratulations from Dr. King who told him the news. "Zea, your former goalie, wasn't here for a reason," he said. "She went Up."

I wasn't exactly sure what that meant, but I knew it had to do with leaving the Academy and going off to the next realm. I wasn't so sure where that was. Going Up was an unpredictable type of thing, sort of like life and death. You just never knew what day would be the travel day.

I thought it was a good thing.

Daniel eventually came over to give my shoulder a little tap. "For the record, Callaghan, you're okay for a rookie and a girl goalie," he said with a smile, holding the largest silver trophy I had ever seen in my life. A second later, he began to say something and looked absolutely flustered. "You maybe want to hang out tonight? The whole team is going out for pizza at Carmines on Main Street to celebrate. You don't have to go if you're busy, but if you weren't it would be nice. Real nice," he said, looking everywhere but exactly at me.

Really? Really.

I did want to celebrate, but first I had to find my mom. "Yeah, I'll probably be there later," I teased, pleased that he looked a little disappointed. Ignoring him was a tactic I hadn't yet tried, but clearly it was working. "I'll just go tell my mom I'm considering pizza. I know she wouldn't have left without me."

"What type of pizza? Thick crust or thin? Pepperoni or sausage? How do they make the pizza? How many people will be there?" Daniel began to rattle off a list of questions in a high-pitched voice, and I knew he was gently mocking me. "I just have these one hundred little inquiries . . ."

"Nice," I said. "Who will be there? And I don't do anchovies. For the record."

He laughed in a way that warmed his entire face and then he allowed his fingers to linger on my forearm. "Okay, for the record, I'll save you a seat next to . . . the non-anchovy contingent."

"Do you do fishes on pizza?" I smiled at him while asking.

"That, you will have to find out for yourself," he smiled back.

Dr. King had left the room only a few minutes earlier, but was now back and walking directly toward me. For a minute, I wondered if he would be included in this student pizza party. From the look on his face, I thought that maybe he was upset they let me play. Being a rookie and all. "Walker, I need to see you for a moment in private," he said with a grave look on his face. My victory joy slowly evaporated.

"Did I do something wrong?" I asked. Maybe I shouldn't have called that boy a hillbilly. I hated a bully, but there were times when you had to defend what was right.

"No, dear," he began, and then he said three words I would never forget. "It's your mother."

I stopped breathing.

"Is she sick again?" I asked in an anxious voice. "Can you take me to her? Did she get help? Is it her back again?"

"Walker, I need to talk to you in private," Dr. King repeated, but I waved my hands quickly and shook my head.

"I don't want to wait for private. Just tell me," I insisted, knowing that waiting was usually worse than the actual news you waited to hear.

I could see Walter looking at his toes. The rest of the team seemed to disappear from the room.

"Walker, this isn't the place—and I can't think of worse timing,"

Dr. King said. "But, I'll tell it to you straight. Your mother went back."

"Back home? To our house. Okay, I'll run home and see if she needs me," I said, confused. *Sure, it was a little weird, but why were they making such a big deal out of my mom leaving the stupid hockey game early and going home to rest? It wasn't a tragedy. I could just tell her about it later. These people made such a big deal out of freakin' hockey.*

"She didn't go to your home here," Dr. King said. "She went home. To Chicago. To life. For good."

His words didn't even register. "Didn't you ever wonder why your mother felt pain when no one else here does? She talked in her sleep about not leaving, like she was having a conversation with someone, didn't she?"

"Just tell me," I begged.

"Walker, your mother came here with you to help you transition. She was never dead. She was in a coma for several months. Now, she's not. She just woke up at Michael Reese Hospital in Chicago where she's expected to make a full recovery."

CHAPTER 16

1.

"My mother is at home," I stated in a strangely calm voice. What in the world did this stranger know about what my mother would do? He doesn't know her. I do.

Dr. King put his hand on my shoulder, looked hard into my eyes, and said, "Exactly. Your mother has returned home. To Chicago. To her life."

"My mother is *at home*," I repeated. "She's here. At our house."

Dr. King punctuated his announcement by doing the worst thing possible. He didn't say another word. Turning my back to him as if it would erase the last five minutes or several weeks, I didn't care if I was being rude to the highest authority figure I had met since I arrived. His words were threatening to change everything.

My body went into some sort of programmed overdrive. Kicking off those white hockey shoes, I pivoted and started running as fast as I could in the regular gravity of the locker room. Before I could burst through the large metal doors of the stadium, sanity returned for a minute and I went back to grab my new Nikes courtesy of some afterlife athletic shoe foundation that left them in the hall closet of the house that I *would* continue to share with my mother. *My mother was at home. No matter what world we were in she was there. Always. These people didn't know us. They didn't know how much she loved me. Loves me.* I wasn't certain of many things in life or death, but I knew she would never leave me.

I burst through the outside doors, which is when my legs went into some frenzied hyperdrive. Still in my hockey jersey and pants, I pumped my legs hard, sprinting at top speed through the blue-greenish late-afternoon mist that had risen from the ground like it wanted to gobble me whole. The mist was odd. It was almost as if all the colors of those early spring flowers had evaporated into a strange pastel fog that rose from some underground artist's palate. It lingered waist high and enticed you to wade into it.

Maybe the mist was a sign. As I ran, the blue, green, and yellow melted together into what became an ugly, colorless gray.

Finally, I could see my house in the near distance. It only took another minute until I flew past the Reid home with skates, balls, toys, and even a small plastic pool on the front porch.

Blasting through our front door, I yelled out for her just like it was any other day. I kept my tone as normal as possible as if a normal voice would mean a normal life.

"Mom, I'm home," I said, but it came out like a croaky little whisper. "We won the big game. I have to tell you all about it."

"Mom?"

The only answer I got was a clock ticking garishly loud from the living room where the air seemed heavy and solid. *Tick-tock, tick-tock,* that stupid clock seemed to scream, reminding me how time was evaporating into that ugly mist.

211

Stop. Walker. Think.

But my mind wouldn't stop.

I struck out with my right hand to slap open the white wooden kitchen doors and then dodged them easily when they tried to smack me back. *There!* I could see my mother's cable-knit white cardigan draped nicely over the kitchen chair. She never went anywhere without that damn sweater. Her house keys were on the table, too. So was her purse. That settled it. She must be here.

Tripping over a few magazines she had piled neatly in the hallway for recycling (yes, she insisted that you still had to take care of the environment—even here), I barreled down the hallway, ducking my head into my own bedroom, which was just as quiet, and messy, as I had left it that morning when I rolled out of bed, barely said a word, and raced off to my hockey game. My pink comforter was in a ball on the floor and a pair of mismatched socks was in a trail to a bathroom that could have been condemned by the Board of Health if there was one up here.

The hallway bathroom was neat and clean, which was a sign that my mother had cleaned it because we shared this space. A new tube of toothpaste was unopened on the counter with a white washcloth next to it. Two unopened bottles of shampoo and a neatly folded towel sat on a shelf. It was almost as if she had stocked up on supplies.

Quickly, I returned to the hall, but stopped in front of my mother's bedroom door, which was closed. It was the only room I hadn't checked. If she wasn't there . . . she wasn't here.

Nervously, I placed my trembling hand on the knob and didn't make a move. I didn't want to turn it because it was always easier to avoid major answers. My mind flashed to that game show where the contestant had to say, "Final answer." This room was my final answer. Slowly, I twisted the little piece of brass, which protested only slightly, and then I stepped into my mother's room with great caution. It was my last chance.

Our last chance.

The moment I stepped inside, I saw her. Smiling.

It was her favorite picture of the two of us from when I was ten and she was happy. Her head was touching mine. Her smile was wide and brilliant. We had our whole lives in front of us.

The rest of the room felt oddly as if it didn't belong to her anymore. It was as if a professional clean-up crew had already gone through their motions. The bed was stripped, with fresh sheets folded in a neat pile mocking me from the end of the naked mattress. Her green comforter was gone and her pillows were missing cases. There was no bodily imprint in the bed or a stray amber hair. The closet door was open and inside it was empty. There wasn't a speck of dust in the room. The smell of Shalimar perfume, her favorite, had already evaporated. Nothing in here even smelled like her anymore.

There was nothing to do but fall face down on the bed before I fell down onto the floor.

I thought about the day we took that photo—a warm spring day in Chicago when she had insisted we go down to a farmers' market and buy fresh tomatoes. I remember not wanting to go to some dumb farm thing with my health-conscious mom. I had movies to watch and books to read. I didn't want to go on some time consuming vegetable-buying spree with Miss Vegan. Grasping that picture to my chest, it was suddenly everything I had to my name. It was the sun, the city, and the sweetness of the only person who had ever truly loved me.

What happened in the next minute horrified me. Suddenly, my new world made complete sense as the truth washed over me. My mother was gone. My mother was alive—and I was not.

It was almost as if I floated outside of my body and heard myself weeping, a deep, desperate wail that started from the farthest reaches of my soul. Even though I was exhausted, I just couldn't stop. At one point while struggling for breath, I'm pretty sure I turned blue and passed out. When I returned to consciousness, he was there.

His big, strong arms were holding me tightly. Daniel was lying on the floor next to me, hugging me tightly with every ounce of his being. His arms wrapped around my arms; his legs tangled over my legs; his face was buried in my hair. I felt his breath like a warm wind on the back of my neck. He mumbled something about running all the way home behind me and it was true. He was still in his hockey jersey, too.

By the time I could focus on what was actually happening, he had gently lifted me into the air and was carrying me down that dark hallway and out the front door, past the tulips she planted and the strawberry bushes she nurtured, and across the front lawn that was cheerful green under a thin layer of icy snow. With the toe of his black boot, Daniel kicked open his front door and I buried my wet face into his neck. I was still lost in all that flesh and muscle when a fresh crop of tears fell from my eyes, running down his neck. He never brushed them away.

We were in his kitchen and I heard three chair scrapes on a tile floor. I heard Jenna begin to remove the Nintendo games from one of the chairs. Then she picked up a cloth and started wiping at a feverish pace. From the corner of my eye, I could see that the Reid house looked like a tornado had permanently blown into it. A dirt bike was actually leaning against the sink. What must have been about twenty Barbie dolls were reclining half-naked near the stove. Pete's skateboard was hanging out on the counter with bread and peanut butter tossed carelessly on top of it.

Andy started crying and she rubbed my silky pant leg. "I'll make cookies," she said. Then she stopped and touched my hand. "Walker, you don't really want cookies do you?" she asked.

"No, stupid, she doesn't want your cookies. Nobody wants

them," taunted Pete who looked completely embarrassed and at a loss for what to say to me. "She needs a root-beer float. That's what she needs—and I'm all over it," he said, going to the fridge and getting out a new carton of ice cream. From my quick glance into the freezer from my perch in Daniel's arms, I could see that ice cream was one of their staple foods.

"You guys, just chill out," Daniel said with an appreciative smile. "I'm going to put Callaghan to bed."

2.

My dreams that night left spaces open for my mother. I was walking around Chicago frantically looking for her, and then I'd see a woman with amber hair and a white sweater. Confident that I'd found her, I would touch her shoulder. But when she turned around, it wasn't my mother. It was just a woman in a white sweater looking confused as to why I would dare lay hands on her because she was a stranger.

The rest of it was a big, fat blur. I remember Andy making pancakes the next morning and flipping them recklessly like she worked at a pizza parlor and wanted to hit the ceiling with her doughy concoctions. Even when I shook my head and refused to eat, she put one on my plate and took my fork and knife away. Without asking me, she cut my food and began to feed me as if I was the little girl. It was so sweet because I was certainly old enough to eat my three bites by myself. Our roles were suddenly reversed. When I slowly chewed, Jenna sat down on the other side of me and put her smaller hand over mine.

Who knew the afterlife could be so cruel and so kind at the same time. Daniel sat across from us at the small wooden table, sipping his black coffee and looking concerned and helpless. Almost afraid that I would slide off my seat from nerves, he wrapped his legs around mine under the table as if he was anchoring me in place. It was almost like I was weightless and would ascend without his steadiness keeping me firmly at ground level.

After breakfast, I went back to bed. I'm not so sure how I got there and maybe crawling was involved, but probably not. When I woke up ten hours later, Jenna was sitting on a cushy chair by the bed working her iPad. When Daniel entered the room, she seemed to disappear like a wispy cloud on a windy spring morning.

I saw his body fill most of the doorframe; the concern on his face taking up the rest of the space.

It was around midnight when I drifted back to sleep. This time, with Daniel holding me the same way he had after finding me on the floor of my mother's bedroom—fully clothed with his arms and legs wrapped tightly around me in a cloak of protection.

3.

We fell into some sort of familiar family-like routine. We didn't go to school that next week. All of us stayed home because it seemed important and necessary. The Reid kids quietly played board games or read or watched TV turned way down low. When he wasn't keeping an eye on me, Daniel had his head buried in books about portals, wormholes, and time travel. Slowly, I began to eat again and Daniel monitored my bites. Without asking, he must have gone next door to pack a bag of my clothes because they were suddenly in the bedroom I was sharing with him.

Each night, Andy drew me a hot bath and poured half a bottle of bubble bath in the steamy water; so each day, I walked around smelling like new gardenias and fresh tears.

One late night when I was missing my mom terribly, I paced the floors and stumbled upon an unopened bottle of vodka in the kitchen pantry. Taking it out, I opened the seal and then fished around for a red Solo cup because the Reids didn't believe in real glassware.

This was teenage afterlife . . . no limits, right? The one thing I hadn't really tried was getting rip-roaring drunk.

While I was pouring, Daniel padded into the kitchen in his socks, shorts, and an Academy T-shirt that fit tight across his chest. With his voice groggy and his black hair going every which way, he glanced in my direction and then said in a nonjudgmental voice, "That doesn't have any effect on us here. I know. I tried it. It's like drinking water. But you can certainly try it."

Without asking me, he took out the OJ and poured me a glass. Then he grabbed the vodka and took a big swig as I stared at the sinewy lines that ran up his arms. With a shrug, he said, "See. Nothing. Nada."

Damn it. I couldn't find any of that kind of relief from the pain.

So I just went about my days playing checkers with Pete and letting him win because the kid wanted it so badly. During those days, I'd braid Andy's hair and even painted some pink streaks into Jenna's locks, which she clearly adored. "We should do Daniel next," she joked, and her biggest brother grabbed her in a mock headlock and then flipped her up in the air and caught her as if her body weight was like catching a feather.

One night, I saw Daniel rocking Andy back to sleep after a nightmare woke her and I paused outside the room to hear him tell her, "Nothing can touch you, baby. I'm on it. No monsters under the bed, but I can check again."

217

When he walked out of the room, he wasn't so shocked to see me standing there. A hint of a smile playing on his lips, he walked me back to our room and then did something so touching that I almost burst into tears. He actually tucked me into bed, making sure the covers were snug around my shoulders and then kissed my forehead.

Without knowing how it happened, we were slowly becoming a family. At night, I brushed Jenna's hair, played Xbox with Peter, and dressed Andy's Barbies in the latest spring fashions. I even cleaned the house. Without ever talking about it, Daniel and I would retire to the bedroom we had been sharing since I arrived. It was Daniel's room. Each night he stayed in his day clothes, or some mismatched T-shirt and shorts combo, and cuddled me until I fell asleep. If I woke up in the middle of the night with a fretful dream where another woman's face wasn't my mother, he would run a few fingers up and down my cheeks softly until I drifted off again. We usually woke up in a spooning position, but Daniel never pressed it any further, although I knew that his body wanted him to take action. I'm not so sure I would have resisted anything or could have said no.

Dr. King called several times to inquire about how I was doing and to inform us that a room was waiting for me at the Academy. He suggested that I move into the school and become Tosh's new roommate. "Is it a suggestion or an order?" I bluntly asked him. Quite frankly, I didn't have anything to lose now.

"Walker, I'm going to let you decide," Dr. King answered, adding, "You know there are no rules on this, although I do believe you should move to school."

"I'll let you know," I said. "And thank you."

Of course, it was an option. Everything here was an option. But now I wasn't the strange girl living with her mom. I was just one of those kids stuck here with no family, which sort of made me an afterlife orphan.

But that wasn't strictly true. I had four people who took me in like a stray puppy. Without any paperwork or a real ceremony, I had been adopted as a Reid.

Officially.

4.

During that week off from school, we had others come visit me including my famous guidance counselor, Miss Elizabeth. She smelled like she walked around with a personal and permanent cloud of the strongest perfume known to womankind relentlessly following her.

"Darling, I would suggest that you move into a dorm room at the Academy because you don't need any further complications in your life or people talking about any unorthodox living situation," she said, staring at Daniel who was busy spreading fast-food hot dogs from Foxy's on Main Street onto plates. He didn't even glance up as he divvied up the fries and onion rings.

"Of course, Doctor King will tell you that it's obviously your choice, but it's wise to grieve with the help of professionals available to you twenty-four seven," she said. "And no complications." Each time she said that word, she used those gorgeous violet eyes as laser weapons to drill imaginary holes into Daniel's skull. I saw him stop squirting mustard long enough to give her the look. By now, I knew that his narrowed eyes and slight head tilt meant that he was not impressed.

Jenna bounced in at that moment, gazing at me in an adoring way while shooting Elizabeth her own death-ray stares. "We don't want her to go, Miss Elizabeth," she pleaded. "It's like having a big sister. We're a real family now."

"Jenna, darling, I completely understand, but it's not your choice," Elizabeth said, staring at Daniel again. "What I meant is that Walker doesn't need to complicate her life with any entanglements. Take it from me. I was married quite a few times and know what I'm talking about here when it comes to the obvious distractions." Her violets shifted to the largest distraction in the room for the umpteenth time. He sipped a Mountain Dew and kept his head down.

Knowing he was in her cross hairs, Daniel finally looked up, a jar of pickles in one hand and a frown on his face. The Distraction was a bit pissed off. "Lady, I've been called a lot of things. I'll take that last one as a compliment," he said.

"Mister Reid, the last thing I need from you is attitude," Elizabeth smarted, her usual purring demeanor hard and cold like the massive diamond rings that covered almost every finger.

"Oh, all Daniel is . . . is attitude," smirked Pete who returned the conversation to what was really important now by asking his brother, "Did you get me extra-large fries with my dog?"

"Who is your guidance counselor?" she demanded as the chef here continued his plating work.

Now it was Daniel's turn to mess with her again. With a large grin covering his handsome mug, he said, "Mr. Carlin. You might have heard of him. He has a fondness for foul language—and we really understand each other. Great, great guy."

"I should have known," she huffed. "George. Figures."

Defeated, Elizabeth rose and pushed a button that summoned the black town car that had driven her to the house and would be returning her to the Academy. A driver in a crisp black suit peeled up to the driveway and stood outside the gleaming automobile as if he was waiting for the biggest movie star of all time to materialize from the modest sea-blue Craftsman house. "We'll revisit this later, Walker," she said. And then before leaving, she turned to Daniel and in a clipped voice said, "Mister Reid, I'd watch myself."

"Why?" Daniel said. "So many of you are watching me. Have been for years. Isn't that enough watching?"

Elizabeth sighed in disgust and waltzed out the door like the Queen of Sheba—or, maybe more appropriately, Cleopatra.

Back in the land of commoners, Daniel passed me a white paper plate and said, "I hope you like green relish on your dogs. If not, you're stuck with it—sort of like how you're stuck with us now."

"It's good," I said with a smirk. "It's all good."

Wait, when did I start smirking again?

Two days later, a black Escalade pulled up the driveway. Dr. Marvin King drove himself over to check on my progress. He also came with an update and explanation that began with him requesting that the kids and Daniel leave the room. The kids fled the kitchen in record time, but Daniel tried to linger. "Mister Reid, I'm asking for a moment of privacy for Miss Callaghan and myself," he said in his regal, no-nonsense tone. When Daniel didn't move, he added, "In other words, get your ass out of here because I'm not really asking, son—and I'm certainly not going to ask you for a third time."

Reluctantly, Daniel walked into the living room, which was Dr. King's cue to take a seat at the head of the kitchen table and then motion me to join him in the hard wooden chair that faced him. I didn't really know we would be having a boardroom meeting about my future.

"Walker, I'm sure you're full of questions. Why was your mother here? Why did she have to leave? I'm going to try to give you the simple version if you want to listen to it," he said in a soft voice. "I'd like you to find some peace here."

All I could do was sit across from him at the kitchen table and sip coffee that had no effect.

"As you know, your mother was in that horrific accident that killed you," he began. "You'll learn more about that over due time. You never know when it's truly someone's time to move on. It wasn't her time even though she was severely injured in the crash. The thing is, you never know about the human spirit. It will surprise you. Just when you're sure that life has no more surprises in its bag of tricks, well, there's a little more, a reserve, a moment of faith, a stunning surprise that some people call a miracle."

"Your mother's body was crushed in several places, but it wanted to mend. Her spirit wasn't ready to go," he continued. "She was badly injured and knew you were gone. That's why she allowed herself to slip across to the Other Side to be with you. It was a mother's instinct. A mother's love. There remains tremendous guilt over the accident. She feels as if she killed her only child. She desperately tried to stay here with you, but her spirit wouldn't allow it. Her body fought the coma just as hard as she tried to fight going back. She was what we call a lingerer. Obviously, there was still some business for her to finish up back in life. That's not her call. It's not any of our calls. It just is."

Nodding, I tried to blink back the tears that were forming. "Did you ever wonder why your mother was in so much pain when she was here?" he added.

"She always had a bad back," I replied. "She was constantly lifting Aunt Ginny after she had fallen and broke her hip. Aunt Ginny got better; Mom's back never did."

"No one is in pain once they've truly passed. Disease? Gone. Crippled legs—fixed. Deformities—a thing of the past. Can't walk on Earth? You can now. Blind? You can see the light and the details. Deaf? Crank up the volume because you've got a lot of rock 'n' roll to catch up on here," Dr. King explained. "It's a pretty good deal," he added with a laugh. "Just look at me. Diabetic my whole life. Had my foot amputated when I was forty-five. They chopped off the left one at the knee because I wouldn't listen and ate way too much sugar. Figured, I'd beat the disease, but it beat me. Took away a piece of me."

For a moment, I didn't focus on my pain anymore, but felt badly for Dr. King.

"The day of that school shooting, I walked up to the shooter as fast as I could, but I was never too fast on my feet with the artificial leg."

Rolling up his pant leg, he said, "Look at me now."

Sure that I didn't believe him, he rolled up the other one.

All I could do was stare at two perfectly whole legs: flesh, knees, and all the rest were in perfect working order. Of course he was fine. I always saw him racing around the Academy to his appointments. To illustrate, Dr. King stood up and ran in place quicker than a teenage Olympian. "Bet I could outrun the wind now," he said without gasping for air, which was odd because he looked older than all of the adults up here.

"Now, you're thinking, 'But he's too old to run like a wolf.' But old isn't a disease here. Old is just older. It doesn't mean slower. It doesn't mean feeble. I bet I could challenge that strapping young man in there, Mister Reid, to a little flag football and you'd never know who would win."

Sniffing and wiping my eyes, I looked at Dr. King in a way that said my admiration of him was boundless.

"Sir, my money is on you," I said.

"Who do you think practices air hockey with the faculty?" he posed. "I love new teachers because I always bet them I can get more goals. The youngsters lose their cherry-pie slices to me every single time. Hell, I even whipped Walter's skinny ass."

I had to laugh at that one.

Dr. King took that moment to put his hand over mine.

"Walker, I want you to know that your mother is a miraculous woman. She came to my office many times to talk while you were at school. I tried to tell her that she might be summoned back, but she insisted that she would refuse to because of you. Again, not her choice, although she felt terribly guilty about your accident," he said.

"I told her that you would be more than fine up here alone. You're one of the smartest young ladies here or anywhere," he said. "I know these types of things, and I wanted to put her mind at ease.

"And one more thing," he added. "I've been keeping tabs on her back at your home in Chicago and she's making an amazing recovery. She left the hospital a couple days ago and she's walking with the help of a walker, your Aunt Ginny, and the nurses at a rehab center. Of course, it's going to be a long recovery process. It isn't easy emotionally either. Your mom really misses you. And, like I said, she blames herself. Only time can eventually heal those wounds."

"Doctor King, can I send her a message or write her a note?" I begged, allowing tears to finally roll down my cheeks. "Something that tells her that it's fine. I'm fine. I want to tell her I don't blame her for the accident—whatever happened. And I want her to go on with her life. If I could just tell her she doesn't have to worry about me, I could rest easy. Can I just go back, see her one more time, and tell her?"

"Walker, what did I tell you about going back?" he replied in a serious tone. "There is no going back. Ever. I want you to take that more seriously than anything you have ever been serious about in your life or in your death. Going back is not an option. It's not even possible to go back."

"My mom went back," I said in a quiet tone.

"Because she was alive—and you're not," Dr. King stated.

All I could do was sit there stone-faced.

"You can send your mother loving thoughts and I promise you

that she will feel that energy. In the coming years, I will teach you other ways to contact her, but not now," he suggested.

I shook my head. "I've watched all that psychic BS on TV, sir," I said. "These psychics tell those poor people that their dead relatives love them. Blah. Blah. Blah. I don't want to just tell her that I love her. I want to tell her that it's not her fault. Like you said. If it was my time, then it was my time."

"I can't help you there," Dr. King said, firmly. "It's best you just let this idea go because it's futile. As you kids like to say, delete it."

I nodded like any other teenager who is listening to some adult give her directives knowing full well that she's going to do the exact opposite of what's being told.

"By the way, I can't tell you not to play house, but I do expect you—all of you—back at school next week," Dr. King said, scraping his chair and standing up. He said this loudly as if he knew they were all listening outside the door, which they definitely were. He focused on me again. "It's time to concentrate on something other than your grief. School will be a great healer. You will be able to throw yourself into your studies and other matters."

Oh, I was concentrating.

And I knew what those "other matters" would be.

I just had to tell someone else about it.

5.

The Sunday before we had to go back to school "officially," Daniel waited until the kids were out of earshot and said in a grave voice, "Two things, Callaghan. One, maybe I should sleep on the couch, although I don't really want to sleep there. It's tough to just sleep

225

next to you. Your call. Two, do you know how to cook anything real? That's not a prerequisite for living here, but it sure would be nice to eat something that didn't come out of a white bag or from a can. I can't face another box of mac-and-cheese or a takeout burger," he said with a warm glance sent my way.

I looked at him leaning over the counter in his tight jeans and no shirt. Yes, he was doing laundry and was out of everything. That's why he was wearing . . . nothing. Which was so distracting.

But I had to focus.

"Two things," I repeated back to him. "One, the sleeping conditions are fine except for the fact that you do snore. Loudly. And you hog the bed." His mouth opened, but I didn't let him speak. "Don't argue with me. It's a medical and architectural fact. Two, I know how to make Chicken Parmesan with a side of pencil-point pasta in a light marinara sauce. Have you ever heard of a foreign substance known as fresh tomatoes?"

"I guess we still have a few things to discover about each other," he said with a stunned, sexy glance that melted me.

"A few," I repeated.

Sometimes, it's best to let a moment pass, which I did. But it wasn't easy. He had a wide sculpted chest that tapered to a slimmer waist. My eyes traced the muscles that ran like a road map near those defined ribs and—

"Callaghan, stick with me here," he interrupted my reverie, grabbing a navy sweater out of the dryer, which was conveniently located in a closet off the kitchen. His voice was muffled as he swung it over his head.

"Can you please make us a real dinner? I will get down on my knees and beg if that's what it takes," he pleaded. "I hate cafeteria food at school, and I haven't had a home-cooked meal since I was twelve."

Glancing out the window and across the yard was painful, but it was time for me to face it. "My mom has the recipe in her recipe box in our kitchen. She also has all the real cooking stuff that most humans might have heard about like bowls, casserole dishes, and pans. I don't know if you've ever seen an actual spaghetti strainer, one of the better inventions of modern mankind. All you have here is ketchup packets and paper plates," I reminded him.

"We also have mayo packets and coleslaw so old that it's growing an actual garden in the fridge," he corrected with an almost boyish, hopeful face.

Instead of allowing my heart to skip a beat, I gazed out the window again until a general uneasiness gripped me. "I don't know about this," I finally said. "I haven't been in the house since the day you carried me out of there."

"I'll go with you," he said with certainty. "We'll only be in there a few minutes. Come on . . . don't make me beg here. My culinary future is on the line."

Whoever said the shortest distance between two points is a direct line was crazy. It seemed to take forever for my feet to walk the twenty-odd steps across the lawn because of the dread flowing through my veins. The last thing I needed was to see her things or to remember opening the door and having her there.

Daniel gently took my hand as we walked up the three wooden porch steps. When he swung open the door and stepped inside with me, it felt like a tomb. I was so chilly cold inside the house that I instinctively wrapped both of my arms around myself. "The heat is set at eighty," he said, but he didn't finish. He knew better. He also didn't have a chance to say another word.

A noise jolted us.

We both heard it at the same time.

It was a loud crash that seemed to come from the kitchen followed by sharp nails racing across the kitchen floor. "Stay here," Daniel mouthed, grabbing a knife that was in his pocket.

Frozen in place in my own foyer, my eyes darted into the living room and then down the dark hallway. What I couldn't see was the thing had silently crawled in a low crouch from the hard kitchen tile onto the soft carpeting of the living room. Tired of standing in place, I made my way to the couch and sat down with a thud, not really caring if some force had arrived to gobble me alive.

Wet nostrils that were set below a pair of black eyes inhaled my smell from behind the couch. Crawling on all fours, it slid to the side of the overstuffed furniture. Meanwhile, I closed my eyes from exhaustion, allowing my hand to fall carelessly off the arm of the upholstery to the side of the couch. That's when I felt it. The sensation could only be described as warm air breathing into my fingers.

Before I could scream or stand, it made its move. Darting out in front of my legs, a large black mass of fear and frenzy reared up on its back legs until we were eye to eye.

What happened next made me scream as loudly as I had ever screamed to date. The black eyes widened as did mine. Tossing its weight back, it lurched on top of me with a force so mighty that I flew back, losing the wind in my lungs as I gasped for air. Before I could know what was happening, my eye caught the steely flint of Daniel's knife, which he raised high in the air ready to strike.

"No, no, Daniel, don't!" I screamed like a banshee as the creature pinned me to the couch.

Daniel stopped midair and held the knife in the sky, ready to strike. But then he stopped holding it in a kill position. He stopped cold.

In an amazed silence, he watched my hundred-pound Labrador, Jake, whose tail was wagging furiously, lick me from the top of my head, down my neck, and to my kneecaps. Not satisfied that I was completely covered in dog saliva, he decided to start from my toes and work his way up again.

"Callaghan, are you okay under there," Daniel said with a mix of concern and glee.

"Did I ever tell you that I'm a dog person?" I said, kissing Jake again and again on the nose as he dive-bombed onto his back on the floor, so I could kiss his belly. "This is actually my dog and best friend, Jake. He has big ears, so we used to say he looked like a Jackalope, which is why sometimes I called him the Jake-a-lope. I just can't believe it's him and he's *here*. Do you like dogs?"

"We don't get many dogs here. They go somewhere else at first," Daniel informed me, putting a hand out so Jake could smell it and then slobber it with dog spit. "Hey, boy," Daniel said. "It sure is nice to see one of your kind around these parts."

Then it dawned on me. "He died when he was two. Run over by a truck when the building super left the front door open. My heart was broken," I said, as Jake sat down in front of me and produced his trademark dog smile. "If there are seven dog years for every human year then he died at age fourteen."

"Just what we need. Another wandering teenage soul," Daniel said with a sigh.

For the first time in a week, I really smiled.

"I thought all dogs go to heaven," I said between licks.

"I bet he went somewhere pretty cool first and then smelled you here . . . not that you smell anything but good. Anyway, he obviously has unresolved issues," Daniel said, patting Jake's head, which made him wag so hard that his tail hitting the floor sounded like he was the drummer for Pearl Jam.

"You just better be house trained because Pete barely is," Daniel said, trying to sound commanding.

"He loves chicken parm," I added, throwing my arms around my dog and hugging him hard.

"I wonder why he didn't show himself when my mom was here?" I asked, knowing it was one of the first times I had admitted to myself that Mom was indeed gone now.

"Did your mom and the dog have issues?" Daniel asked, scratching Jake under the chin.

"Sort of. She loved him, but kept saying we had to give him away. We couldn't afford to keep him. Each time she talked about relocating him, he would hide out from her—or I'd try to hide him," I said, petting Jake and leaning down to whisper into his ear, "I'm never giving you away. You and me, boy. You and me."

After gathering up everything I needed, including two big bowls for Jake, the three of us headed back to the Reid home. The reaction there was totally predictable. "A dog!" Peter yelled before he did a happy dance around the door. "Our family has a dog! This is the happiest day of my entire life!" Jenna and Andy went bonkers, too, when they saw him, which was enough for Jake to drown both of them in a drool bath as they fought over who would pet him next.

It was funny how quickly he was assimilated, how quickly I was assimilated.

"Since I got here, I always felt as if something was watching me. You know that feeling you have that something or someone is always looking at you," I said while putting the cheese on top of the chicken.

With a smirk, Jenna teased, "Personally, I don't know that feeling. In your case, that someone who is always looking at you . . . that's our brother." Peter and Andy burst into convulsive laughter while their big brother gave them silencing looks.

"Don't the three of you ever have something to do?" he half begged. "Why don't you act like the first kids in the neighborhood to run around a yard with a dog in a long time—because you *are* the only kids with a dog."

A few minutes later, Jake was racing down the street with Pete. We didn't need a leash and I didn't even flinch when a Toyota almost hit him. I knew it was the same thing with dogs: You can't die twice.

"That dog sensed you were on his side of the road now," Daniel said in an admiring voice. "It didn't matter where he was hanging out before you got here. Real love doesn't go away. It finds you."

Putting down a box of noodles, I knew what needed to come next—and it had nothing to do with my own feelings.

"Daniel, I'll help you find your brother," I said in a quiet voice. "I'm not just talking about the research part and figuring out how to get back. I want to go with you. You're going to be transported exactly where I need to go. I have a little bit of unfinished business back there, too."

CHAPTER 17

1.

"Why?"

One little word was all he uttered and it was a loaded one. He even stopped cutting vegetables for a foreign substance to the Reid family known as a green salad.

"Going back is the most dangerous thing you could ever do," Daniel said. "You might never make it back here. And what would be left of you . . . well, let's not go there now. But it's something we have to discuss."

I didn't care about the consequences. My silence was the end result of that epiphany.

"Why?" he repeated. "You have no real stake in me finding my little brother."

That last comment stung because I was beginning to feel as if I did have some stake in the Reid family dynamic and an even bigger stake when it came to the young man staring at me.

"I'm not afraid, if that's what you want to hear," I said. "The truth of it is I have nothing to lose anymore. I'm the perfect travel companion—someone who has no one. And you need someone smart to help figure things out once you get back there. That's where I come in."

Was it possible that he looked slightly bothered by my dismissive words?

"Plus, our school can't afford to have our best air-hockey player lost in the cosmos," I added, trying to keep it light.

But his dark hair was falling into his eyes now and his mood was suddenly dark, too.

"Do you really have any clue how to even start looking for a portal or wormhole or whatever it is that takes us back?" I asked and the quick twitch in his left eye confirmed that he really didn't have much of a clue.

He looked like one of those guys who studied extra hard for the test and still got a B. At the mere mention of his inadequacies as a time traveler, Daniel stopped chopping and pointed his salad-tossing fork—courtesy of my mother, the gadget queen—at me.

"Callaghan, you're out of your freakin' mind," he said. "I don't want to hear you even talk about going back. You don't even know the half of it." He pointed a cutting knife at me now to make another point. "I'm sure you have no idea how you can be trapped back there in a worse limbo."

"So enlighten me about the dangers and the clues," I taunted. "From what I guess, your crack team of researchers on how to get back consists of just one person—you. Frankly, I've seen you do homework. Your study habits—not so good. I'm sure it's not a cinch trying to figure out what souls have been dying to know for centuries, which is how to bring the dead back to life."

And then I added, because it was the truth, "This might require math skills. Science. Maybe even some physics. Subjects I know you avoid like the plague."

"What do you want me to tell you about my C-grade-level research?" Daniel snapped in a surprisingly savage voice. "Here it is! I don't exactly know how to get back—yet. But I'm working on it. I'm getting closer every single day. I've been working on this for years. Each year passes and nothing! Nothing!" He slammed his knife down on the chopping block on the counter, stabbing it hard.

Figuring I pushed it plenty hard enough, I stopped to listen.

"What you need to know is the risk," he hissed. "It's not just that the school forbids us from going back because it annoys them. It's fatal on a soul level for us. There are forces waiting. These demons want you to come. They will hunt you. For the hell of it. You could be what is known as extinguished, which isn't a joke. That means gone. Blasted from ever existing. Your soul could fragment and just disappear. Go outside and grab a little dry dirt. Blow hard on it until it's gone. That will be you."

"And even if you get lucky and escape that part of it—if you did get back here by some sort of miracle, although unlikely at best—you'll be arrested by Doctor King for even trying to go back," he continued. "Did your big buddy Doctor King tell you that's a one-way ticket to incarceration at ITT? The sentence is eternity with no chance of parole. On Earth, killing is the worst crime. Here, going back is the equivalent because you're killing your soul. It's soul suicide."

My eyes went wide. The truth was I really had no idea of the exact consequences of going back and now it made sense why the school took such a hard line against it.

"Now, are you still interested in pushing the one limit the good doctor warned you never to push?" he demanded.

"You're right. I take it all back," I replied in a low voice, stirring the spaghetti sauce and watching a slow relief began to spread over Daniel's face. Knowing I should enjoy it for a moment, I savored his gaze, which I knew wouldn't last long.

To prolong this lovely time, I cut a tomato in slow motion.

"Actually, there is only one part that I take back. I do have something to lose, so if I'm extinguished, please make sure Peter takes care of my dog. He likes a nice meatloaf once a week and lots of ice cubes as treats. A walk once a day would be good for his spirits, or should I say spirit, too," I said as my sassy voice returned to its regular glory.

Daniel's stunned look said it all.

"You should be at ITT," he said, slamming the fridge door shut. "You're insane."

"One thing," I said. "I want to see my mother when we go. One last time. I never got to say good-bye to her."

Proud of myself for not bursting into tears or losing it, I added, "That part is nonnegotiable because my services aren't free. That's the price of my realm-traveling research skills. From where you stand, it's a win-win. You get my brains. I get a bodyguard and a travel companion."

He slammed a pot onto the stove, but then picked it up again to make noodles; it was obvious he had no clue because he put the pasta in the pot without any water.

"By the way, salad doesn't belong near the stove. The lettuce might be extinguished. And try some water in that pot. You're going to burn the noodles," I taunted as he stalked out of the room, broad shoulders sulking and faded jeans moving fast down the hallway, to rage it out on his own.

2.

Daniel returned thirty minutes later to find the chicken baking and the pasta boiling. By all accounts, it smelled divine, and the hint of fresh garlic bread in the oven made the house seem like a fine Italian restaurant.

He just looked at me and nodded. It was a deal. Officially.

He sealed it the way we did at the quarry. He stuck out his pinky finger. We swore on it like little kids.

"When this delicious dinner is done and the kids are asleep," I began, "I need you to tell me everything you know about going back."

Another nod.

Then he grabbed me by the hips until I was face to chest, so I was forced to look up into his gray eyes. When he lifted me off the ground, I gasped. "You're really going to do this?" Daniel asked, looking at me hard. "What if I don't want you to do it? What if I forbid you? The last thing I need right now is to worry about you once I get there."

"First of all, you can't forbid me to do anything. And you won't have to worry," I insisted, secretly pleased that he cared that much. My surprised body pressed into his furious one.

"You and I are going to spend the next few weeks going over everything you've learned. We're going to leave nothing to chance. We're going to become scholars of time travel, but my way. We become experts by trying to answer every question," I said, my feet still off the ground.

"We're taking a really desperate, not to mention audacious, chance; but then everything in life and death is a desperate and audacious chance," he said, softening his grip, lowering my feet to the ground, and holding me close.

"Then let's be audacious together," I said, glancing out the window where the kids and the dog were falling onto fresh snow mounds on the front lawn, thanks to an afternoon storm that seemed to represent the blank slate we needed to start anew.

Perhaps my period of desperate mourning was over, although the pain was still there and the wound was fresh. Daniel seemed to know it was also time to move on and he made that clear when he put his fingers under my chin, tilted my head up, and pressed his lips to mine in a hard kiss.

"Callaghan, chances are we'll never make it back here," he said into my ear as he held me. The beating of his heart told me a different story.

"I don't like those chances, so let's kick them in the ass," I said.

3.

"So take a look at this," Daniel said, spreading out a series of papers with maps and diagrams on them on our bed later that night when the girls were sleeping and Peter was still bonding with Jake in his room. "It shouldn't be this complicated, but it is travel to a different realm of existence. Maybe it should be complicated."

"I'm not a sci-fi aficionado or even a Trekkie," I cautioned him. "For now, this better be a case of Keep It Simple Stupid."

"Callaghan, you're the smartest person I know," he said with real admiration. Reclining on his side, he had his head resting on his elbow as the rest of him took up most of the bed. His face was stubble with a warm glow beneath. "Well, maybe Steve at school is smarter, but you're right up there."

Pleased beyond belief, I did what anyone would do under the circumstances. I shimmied closer to him in the bed where I was sitting with my legs crossed. Trying to play it cool, I said, in my most seductive voice, "So, explain the whole portal thing to me again. Portals are so sexy."

Warning bells went off in my head as Daniel explained what needed to be done to go back. When he needed to illustrate how far A was from B, he took his finger and ran it over my arm as if it were a computer screen. Chills ran up and down my spine. Apparently, all realms in both life and death had portals to different times, places, and dimensions. He said that much was pure fact. In this case, we would need to find the exact spot that was our portal here and it would send us back to a mortal, breathing world otherwise known as the living realm. Somewhere, we would have to cross the threshold between life and death.

Daniel told me we wouldn't go back as living beings, which was fortunate because this was a spy mission all the way. We would go back as spirits no one living could see, which would make it easier. I liked that he described it that way because I couldn't wrap my head around the g-word. As spirits, we could accomplish the mission: Get in. Get the kid. Say hello to my mom. Get back—before we were extinguished. But I wasn't sure who or what was doing the extinguishing.

It was just that simple and just that utterly complex.

"I've read that there are forces there that will come out in droves to stop us," Daniel warned me. "All the books agree on that fact." As bigger goose bumps formed on my arms, he jumped out of bed to grab a book that was so thick he had to muscle it from under ten other books where it was hiding. It was *The Universal Guide to Death* complete with every theory ever known about the logistics of hovering between the worlds of life and death.

"I've read this entire book three times," Daniel said, "and from what I've studied, the forces that will try to stop us are a case of Ka. Ever heard of it?"

"Ka-na-na," I joked.

"This is serious. This is about your immortal soul," he said, grinning, and then tapped me on the nose before he opened the book. "Pay attention. Be a beautiful reporter for a moment."

Beautiful?

Really? Really.

Focus. Nodding, I stopped goofing around and decided to listen. The minute he began to explain, my formerly warm mojo was gone and a cold feeling of dread shot up my spine.

"The Egyptians had a belief that human beings were made up of several components or several souls in one being. All those souls together make up your Ka," Daniel said. "When you die, the good parts ascend to a better place, like here, and keep ascending as you pass through different levels upward, which is what we call going Up. The bad parts—the nasty you, the jealous you, the vengeful you, the hateful you—stay behind. Everyone has those sides. The good news is that upon death you've literally shed them like a second skin and they're not happy about being stuck in the living realm for eternity without a living host."

"So they're really pissed off," I said.

"They sense your return back almost immediately and attack. They want the good part of your soul extinguished permanently, so they can win this epic battle between the good and evil that exists in each of us. Believe me when I tell you that they attack hard."

"So, it's the classic case of good versus evil, but you're actually fighting forces that are you," I said, beginning to understand.

"I guess you can hide for a little while when you return, but then they start to hunt you like a savage pack constantly stalking," Daniel said. "Remember how Jake smelled you and sensed you. He's just a dog. These forces have many other powers. And they're not exact versions of you, but distorted versions of your former self."

"Is there any confirmation of this happening? Any case studies?" I asked.

"Supposedly there is a kid from the Academy who tested it out. He went back. And now he's paying the ultimate price for doing it successfully," Daniel whispered in awe. "The rumor is that he was only back for less than an hour when his Ka went to work to extinguish him. He was lucky to get out in one piece."

"And then Doctor King and the Higher Authority sentenced him to ITT?" I asked, my jaw agape. "For eternity?"

"Like I said earlier, if the Ka doesn't get you then the forces here go to work," Daniel answered. "That's why this is the most dangerous thing we could ever do. For me, there isn't a choice. You don't know my little brother."

"But I will," I promised him.

That night, we curled up together in our clothes and fell asleep in each other's arms. I'm not sure if it was hours or minutes later when the chase began. A sudden flash of blinding light indicated that it was on. My chest heaving, I was running at top speed trying to get away from something that was much stronger than I was. I ran through a grassy field, tripping over tree branches and overgrown weeds because it was deadly dark and I couldn't see a thing. I could feel the forces descending on me.

I was racing through stalks of corn now and the forces stalked me, cornering me from the right, left, and from up above. They wouldn't stop the chase. I could barely pause long enough to squint as I tried to identify who or what was descending.

Stifling a scream, I saw it was my greedy self, my envious self, and my jealous self; and each were contorted to look like a freak-show version of me with oddly shaped faces. One had a mug that was half-melted off and the other didn't have a nose or a mouth, but just shriveled flesh where they were supposed to be located. Each kept descending and I tried hard to shove them away, but they wouldn't allow me to run any longer. They were too powerful and suddenly they were on top of me. Suffocating me. Dancing on my aching, melting bones and ripped flesh.

Each time I looked hard, it seemed like five more had materialized to join their cohorts. They danced hard on top of me until my body began to splinter and every particle that was my good soul shattered into a million pieces. Then Envy blew hard and the good pieces dispersed into the wind, swirling into the cornstalks while Jealousy seemed to conjure up a quick rainstorm to wash the rest of me away. What was good about me could not ascend with Daniel to any other levels. I was eternally gone.

I was extinguished.

CHAPTER 18

1.

I never told Daniel about the dream. It plagued the dark corners of my mind as we dragged our sorry behinds to school the next day. The kids were excited to see their friends and we were fearful to let the teachers see us. We were worried that they would be able to read our minds, know what we were doing, and send us straight to ITT for even thinking about it. We had done more than think about it. We were busy hatching a plan. The scary part is cracking the egg open with even a hairline break. Our egg was cracked and that break was about to get wider.

Of course, school was the ultimate distraction and as we reached the grounds, I could hear what sounded like a school fight brewing in the side rose garden. One person I didn't miss since I took a little grief vacation was rah-rah Demanda and her nasty cheerleader girlfriends who, for some reason, had formed a circle outside near the white, sweet-smelling oleander flowers that were suddenly in full bloom. One of her lackeys was shouting a stream of curse words at someone and another pointed her foot toward whoever was trapped in the middle of the circle. She then jabbed her target in the chest with one of her mile-high stiletto heels.

"Go back to where you belong, tub of crap!" Demanda yelled. "The last thing we need around here is some lowlife thug. This isn't the school for your type."

A supermodel-tall, obviously starving cheerleader wearing thigh-high designer boots, kicked at the ground as hard as possible until a fine mist of gravel flew in the face of their victim, causing a million little stings and a cry of pain that was guttural.

Another pep-squad princess reached inside her purse and produced what looked like a curling iron. "You see this? You want some of this?" she taunted. "It's still burning hot and I don't think you're immune from pain yet," she taunted. "At the Academy we don't wait for your kind to strike. We strike first up here." I watched as she jammed the thing into her captive's leg. This time there was a scream of pain along with burning flesh.

At six foot two, Daniel could easily see above the cheerleaders and into the pit they had created in the middle of their huddle. What he saw made him stop short. It was a familiar face that was experiencing her first day of school here, but not as a new arrival. She had been around these parts for years. Yet, she was crying. Big dollops of tears raced down both of her round cheeks.

For all her good work a week ago at the hockey championship, Bertha had been pardoned from ITT and the Higher Authority transferred her to the Academy. It didn't happen often—but it did happen.

This was her welcoming committee.

"Amanda, knock off the shit," Daniel said, shoving past her into the middle of the girls where all four hundred pounds of Bertha was bullied to the point she was hovering on the cold, hard ground, her face protected with her now muddy hands. When she saw Daniel, she didn't move or say a word. She was like a dog that was beaten into submission for years. She sat there just like she sat in that goal. Bertha looked sad, but resigned to her fate. She just took it.

"Bertha, stand up," Daniel said, pushing past the cheer bullies and holding out a hand to her. "Let's go, darlin. They aren't worth it!"

Tossing him her best flirty smile, Demanda cooed, "Dan, we should really get together and talk about this. I think you've gotten the wrong idea here. Maybe we could eat lunch together. I could explain. She fell. We were just helping her get to class."

I was ready to get into the mix now as I moved closer to stand by Daniel's side. He wasn't done with Demanda and said, "We're done talking and soon you'll be cheering for Miss Bertha at our hockey games, so cut the crap. Nod if you're understanding any of this."

Demanda did her best hair-flip-nod. It was the universal airhead signal of confirmation.

With her palm shaking, Bertha took Daniel's outstretched hand and allowed him to pull her upright, which wasn't easy despite his strength. She blinked hard, once and then twice. No one gave her anything let alone a hand up.

"Meet our next winning goalie," I said as Demanda shape-shifted away from flirty-cheerleader mode to her regular hateful self with that permanent hard face. Obviously, her nasty soul had ascended up here for some reason that I couldn't explain.

After Bertha was standing, I put my arm around her—or as much of her as I could. "Come with us," I said. "We'll show you around. Luckily, they're not all like her. In fact, most of the people here are very nice."

When her tears stopped, Daniel asked the million-dollar

question. "Why not just flatten one of those anorexic bitches?" he asked her.

Bertha sniffed hard, clearly embarrassed at her outburst. Handing her a few tissues I had been carrying around since my mom left, she spoke in a wee voice that was East Coast mixed with a little girl's whispers. "Parole, baby boy. One infraction and I get a one-way, life ticket back to ITT," she murmured. I could see that she was trying so hard. Now, her new black skirt was caked in mud and leaves. Her only shirt, that had been clean and starchy white, was crumpled and creased. Both were covered in blood, sweat, mud, and tears.

"Maybe I should just go back to ITT," she cried. "That's where I probably belong."

"No way," I said. "I hung out with the kids from your old school for one afternoon. It was more than enough."

"And you kicked our asses," Bertha said with a little smile.

"Coming from a kick-ass goalie, I'll take that as a compliment," I said. Then I told her, "You're going to love it here. I'll take you to the office, so you can get your schedule together and then we'll go to the bathroom and clean you up a bit. A little soap and water and you'll be as good as new to meet Doctor King."

Smiling, Daniel gave her a quick wave and then did something unexpected. He leaned over and gave me a quick kiss on the lips.

"Lucky girl," Bertha murmured. "He is so fine. Is he your boyfriend or something?"

"Or something," I said, watching him walk away.

2.

Bertha was a tough fit in many ways including practical ones. She required a bigger than normal desk in almost every class, which elicited stares, laughter, and whispers. When her chair actually broke in English class, I hoped she could ignore the uproarious laughter. I knew I'd never forget her splayed out on the floor, humiliated. I tried to help her as much as possible because we were in this together. That's what my friends in life never understood. They were so splintered that no one seemed in it even remotely together.

In music class Kurt was busy noodling around on his guitar, his long blonde hair falling into his thin face and his piercing blue eyes flashing. He stopped to tell us a story about being on tour. "Court was pitching a fit," he said. "And we were staying at the Mercer Hotel in New York City. I ordered five hot fudge sundaes to make myself feel better. Had the room-service guy bring them, one after another, so nothing melted. Gave him a hundred dollar tip with each one."

Then he looked directly at Bertha who was sitting on the floor in the back because none of the stools in the music room would contain her. "Sometimes, you just need a little something sweet in your life," he said. Bertha smiled and Kurt walked over to her, guitar in hand, to play her a few bars of "Smells Like Teen Spirit." He had never done it in class. People in the living realm would have paid anything to hear the acoustic version.

"*Here we are now, entertain us. I feel stupid and contagious. Here we are now, entertain us,*" he sang, slowing it down so every word became its own poetry.

When it was over, Bertha clapped first, loud and long, and the rest of us couldn't help but join in. In fact, we even stood to give him a standing O. Sometimes you really do need something sweet.

We were so busy cheering for an embarrassed Kurt that we didn't really notice when a large black man—and I mean large, as in the size of a building—walked in wearing what looked like a long black robe with sequins racing down the front from his chin to his toes. He carried a gold sax with him and a wide smile. "Clarence is in the house. He's going to sit in unless there are any objections," Kurt muttered.

Of course, there were none.

The same thing happened when Arnie dared to ask for a picture with both of them, quickly whipping out his camera phone for the ultimate selfie times three. "Come on, let's give the finger!" Kurt shouted before posing.

3.

One of the great benefits of the Academy was that you could study whatever you wanted . . . whenever you wanted to study it. That fact informed the plan Daniel and I made knowing it might disturb only the sharpest minds at school. It fell into our hands that we were required to do a yearly project, a research paper, on one topic that piqued our curiosity. We had decided that the psychology of the criminal mind would become our new obsession and eventual paper, even though we didn't really think about it before or really care beyond a few great episodes of *CSI*. Now, it would serve us well in our quest.

The only thing we had to do now was sign up for Criminology

101 taught by one of the Academy's most controversial professors on campus who was actually just a visiting teacher doing a little penance for his past deeds on Earth. His name was Johnnie.

He was an American lawyer known for being one of the outspoken members of the defense team that successfully acquitted some football player of killing his ex-wife and some other guy. Of course, now everyone knew that the football guy did it. Johnnie's most famous line that got this jock off the hook (at least the first time) involved outerwear. He said, "If the glove doesn't fit, you must acquit." That football player got off, although he eventually did time for something else. Johnnie kicked the bucket later thanks to an aggressive brain tumor. In the end, maybe it was justice. Maybe it was karma.

Daniel and I tried to be natural about our newfound interest in criminal motives, which was hard because his classroom wasn't exactly packed. Johnnie was known as a loud, rhyming, boisterous visiting professor, but the subject matter was daunting. Just three other students joined us and one was going to drop it because the class was—in his own words—"too emotionally draining."

"Miss Callaghan, can you please tell me why you're so interested in the criminal mind," Johnnie grilled me as if I was on the witness stand. He wore a serious black suit and had a little mustache and round specs on his face.

Of course, I had already figured out that answer, plus I was real good on the fly. "Sir, I would like to work toward a better crime-free world and I wish to understand why there is so much chaos," I said.

Even Daniel looked impressed.

"And I'm even more curious to see you in here, Mister Reid," he said, turning to Daniel. "I heard from Doctor King that your only interests are brooding and Miss Callaghan."

"Well," Daniel began, clearing his throat at this obvious

248

intrusion into his personal life. "I think it's time for me to explore different aspects of the mind, which I've always found fascinating."

We rehearsed that one while brushing our teeth that morning, and Daniel was doing us proud. "I want to study why someone would become a school shooter," Daniel said without pause. "When I was alive that was a real issue, and I want to help figure out why these shooters are so prevalent now, so the living can be prepared and protected."

Johnnie was enthralled. But not convinced.

"I'm a big believer in the fact that life is about preparation, preparation, preparation," Cochran ranted. The way he spoke, it was almost as if we were at some kind of church revival meeting.

As planned, we stayed after class to discuss with him our all-important independent study project. "Both of us want to help the living with the school-shooting problem," I bluffed. Of course, we cared about it, but we didn't really want to get that involved. But self-obsessed Johnnie didn't need to know the truth.

If the lie fits, you will outwit. That's what I say.

"We want to figure out what makes a seemingly normal teenager snap," I said, pretending like I had a twig in one hand. I did an imaginary air snapping of the nonexisting wood as if working with faux props would prove our point.

"How else can you prevent violence unless you understand violence?" Daniel added just like he was coached.

Johnnie considered our project for a moment. "We've got to be judged by how we do in times of crisis," he preached. "And there is no bigger crisis than kids shootin' kids. In fact, I've been looking for a few students to do some research on this matter, but it's dangerous."

"We're from Chicago. We know dangerous," I shot out.

Johnnie seemed amused at my bravado. "I'll need to ask you to do something distasteful," he said, pacing the length of the chalkboard. "But both of you are on the hockey team, correct? You've already had dealings with the fine students at ITT."

My heart was pounding because this was going better than expected, but I forced myself to look bored and uninterested. "Yes, we know several students from ITT from the games," I said in a casual tone.

"The two of you might find there is safety in numbers, which is what you'll need if I send you to ITT for a few days to interview the baby-faced school shooter who still lives there in D Block. I think the other trigger-happy troublemakers have gone Down, as they say," he informed us. "This is one who is still working on his rehabilitation—although it seems doubtful. He hasn't spoken much since the actual shooting. So this might be an impossible task, although I think it's worth it all these years later to try to interview him and figure out his motivations."

"But," he cautioned, "he won't talk to adults, therapists, or counselors. Maybe he would talk to his peers, although doubtful. Actually, he hates his peers, which brings me back to the idea that this might be risky."

"Would we be safe at ITT?" I asked, feigning concern because I figured that we had the edge.

"Of course you would be safe. He would be behind unbreakable glass. There is no way this prisoner—I mean student—could hurt you," Johnnie said.

"It's DOA *Silence of the Lambs*," said Daniel.

"What he means to say is it's perfect. When do we start?" I asked.

"Let me see about getting you clearances," said Johnnie. "Until then, please keep this highly unorthodox idea strictly under wraps. I'll have to convince Doctor King. *That* won't be easy."

"The shooter," Johnnie added, "is Just Shoot First Jackie Silver. I'm going to use lawyer-student confidentially here when I tell you something. You'll need to take an oath of silence."

If he only knew that we were social outcasts.

We nodded, with me wondering if such a thing as lawyer-student privilege actually existed.

"Jackie's the kid who killed Doctor King. Shot up the cafeteria with his Daddy's gun. Doctor King is a good man. The best. He charged head first into the action, but never walked out of it. So, let's just say that this will be personal to Doctor King. Highly personal."

4.

Even though it was also highly unorthodox, Daniel and I made a quick visit to our favorite computer expert Steve, the fruit appreciation teacher, who helped us download all the files about Jackie Silver without asking many questions. The great thing about Steve was he didn't pry because he believed in following hunches and dreams. It was his trademark. We went home with a thick file of Jackie Silver paperwork to read after dinner was over, although after a mouthful of salad I was wild to dig into the particulars.

Family life meant we had to cook meatloaf, feed the kids, clean the kitchen, play with the dog, insist the kids shower, fight with them to brush their teeth, and then deal with any emotional dramas that came up along the way.

I walked Jake. Jenna was in a particularly sensitive mood after some boy at school shunned her friendship, which meant her big brother Daniel not only tried to nudge her out of her funk, but eventually lifted her up and ran through the house for a game of high-speed tag. The rest of us let them win, including the dog.

Watching him tuck his little sister in made my heart skip a little beat. He was so tender with her, making gross faces and telling endless bad jokes that it made me smile.

When everyone was finally tucked in, including the dog, we sat down at the kitchen table and spread out the file on Jackie. We started out not really caring about him, pegging him as our ticket into ITT. "There really isn't much more here than what Doctor King told me," I informed Daniel. "He was a kid whose mother left him and the dad raised him. They were doing fine until the recession came knocking and they had to move into their SUV. Home sweet car."

"Each day the dad drove Jackie to school in a Chevy Tahoe that was crammed with so many of their belongings that Jackie got the brunt of his situation in the school yard," I told him reading from the files in a whisper. "They called him Jack Rabbit, Junkyard Jackie. The kids bullied and taunted him. He wore clothes from the Salvation Army and got super skinny from eating just one meal a day, which was basically his state-approved school lunch. The dad kept a gun to protect them because they were sleeping on the streets of Detroit in that car. I guess one day Jackie just snapped and brought the gun to school," I said in a sad voice.

Daniel raked a hand through his hair and pushed back on his chair. The air he was holding in his lungs was slowly exhaled. "Welcome to modern high-school life where you might not live through third period," he said.

"Callaghan," he remarked to get my attention. "We can't focus on this kid. We have to keep our eye on the prize, which involves that other kid at ITT who went back. He isn't a school shooter, but he's somewhere on the same D Block. He's a science nerd. Some kind of visionary. And once upon a time ago, he found the portal. The portal back."

"Well, we have to find him and learn how he did it. One talk with him could save us months, hell, years of trying to figure it out ourselves—if we ever could figure it out. The big if," I said.

5.

Three weeks passed and within that time we celebrated a family Thanksgiving. I tried not to think about my mom at home eating with Aunt Ginny and without me. I wondered if she even celebrated at all. To get my mind off of her, I made cookies with Andy and had to laugh as Daniel tried to cut the bird that I actually cooked for us. He wasn't much with carving and turned it into actually hacking the bird. He was amazed that I could make stuffing from scratch, although I slid the cranberry gel right out the can just like we did at home. When it came to the wishbone, Daniel snatched it and motioned to me to break it with him.

He won.

I knew his wish.

After the last dish was washed and the last overstuffed kid was asleep, we watched *It's a Wonderful Life* on TV, which was a bit ironic. When it was over, I was laying on Daniel's lap on the couch, half-asleep, which seemed like a natural thing to do. When I sat up to get some water, he moved his hand around my back and turned me around. He leaned down and kissed me slowly and tenderly.

"Happy Thanksgiving, Callaghan," he said, kissing me again as his hands rested at the bottom of my ribcage. "We shouldn't make it any happier."

"I know," I said, wrapping my arms around his waist and kissing him back in a way that made it seem like the room had suddenly overheated.

We stopped before we went upstairs because it seemed like we should, although I'm not exactly sure whose rules we were following anymore. Maybe these rules were our own. For the first time in a long time, getting into bed as roomies seemed a little awkward. When I came out of the bathroom in my red-plaid short-shorts and white lace tank top, Daniel looked up from the Stephen King novel he was reading and allowed the book to slip from his hands onto the floor. It landed with a thud.

The air in the room seemed sweet, but suddenly heavy when I slid into bed. Instead of turning the other way, Daniel cleared his throat and propped himself up on one elbow, and stared at me. Really stared at me. Without warning, he ran a finger from the indent on the bottom of my neck down to my belly button. He did it slowly. "Did you always have little freckles?" he asked, twisting his fingers through my hair. "I wish there were pictures of you as a little girl. Bet you were cute, but not as cute as now."

I brushed a finger over the faint scar on his square jaw. "And the Indiana Jones scar? Beating off prehistoric monsters in another life?" I inquired.

"Something like that," he said with a full-face smile. "You want the truth? It's from a bad fight with my old man."

"Brutal. But it adds character," I said. "Or is it that you are a character? I'm still not so sure."

"Callaghan," he grumbled, hitting the lights off, plunging the room into absolute darkness, "I'm turning over. Now. Because if I stay in this direction even one more second, then I won't turn over. And I . . . I think we need to focus."

"Nighty night," I said with a big smile that he couldn't see, but I guess he felt.

"Don't do that," he grumbled. "Don't try not to look cute in the dark. And flip over. Stay on your side. I mean it. I feel your butt touching me. Don't do that either. Don't do anything. Stay far away. You're the North Pole. I'm the South Pole."

"Yes, boss," I teased. "Don't want to lose your . . ."

I allowed my voice to trail off.

"Focus," I finally said, turning over, but what I really meant to say was, "heart." For a moment, I hated the whole idea that we could do anything we wanted up here, which wasn't really true because we still had the limits of the past echoing in our minds.

6.

It was only eighteen days until the anniversary of Daniel's death. Cursing under my breath as I walked to school with fresh snow falling on my cheeks, I knew that we had to resort to a measure I didn't want to try because I don't like using people. There was no choice.

On that blustery Friday, with the threat of a major snowstorm on TV, Johnnie, our lawyer-teacher, only added to my internal dilemma when he told us that Dr. King had finally cleared us to visit ITT for our school-shooter term paper, but not for two weeks. That was cutting it way too close. I knew what I had to do. We had to get the lay of the land at ITT. There was only one person who was slowly becoming a friend and who knew ITT—inside and out.

"We have to shake down Bertha," I told Daniel while we walked to class. "She was there a long time. Maybe she's heard rumors about this science geek who went back to life. She might even know the kid. You know, put in a good word for us. 'I have some friends who need to realm travel . . . where do you hook up with your nearest portal? Just wondering.'"

"No way," Daniel whispered in a hard tone. "We can't show our hand. We don't really know her that well. What if she told someone like Doctor King? She could get some brownie points here for ratting us out. Remember, she's on probation."

"You need to trust me," I begged him. "I know how to do this so she won't even know what she's telling us. Journalism 101."

"I don't like it," Daniel grumbled. "The more people who have even an inkling about what I'm doing, the higher the chances are it will get royally screwed up."

"The more people who know about what *we're* doing," I corrected him. Then I smiled at him and announced, "Suck it up, Reid. And pay attention, because I'm going to teach you how to really get information out of people. Information is power."

7.

I needed time to think. We talked to Bertha regularly at school and watched out for her, but she still eyed us suspiciously because trust wasn't exactly her middle name. She looked at everyone at school as a potential enemy and kept her distance. The only one who ever got a real smile out of her was Kurt, who was always playing songs for her to check out. These were new songs from his own personal vault and it seemed like Bertha was now serving as his muse of sorts for a new album he was writing, too.

It took a couple days to figure out a plan.

Then I spotted him sitting alone and knew he was Bertha's Kryptonite.

"Izayah," I said, spying my handsome hockey buddy who was dressed in dapper black slacks and a matching designer sweater that molded to every last muscle. If you looked hard enough, you could probably see his spleen outlined by cashmere. He looked like he just stepped out of a GQ ad, six-pack and all.

"Long time, no see, goalie," he said. "How's it going?"

Then he stopped midsentence.

"Jeez, Walker," he said, motioning me to sit down. "What am I thinking? I'm really sorry to hear about your mom. I should have come over and talked to you about it earlier. I'm not ashamed to admit that I miss my parents every single day."

"Thanks," I said, a sudden pain stabbing me deep in the pit of my stomach. I couldn't go there, wouldn't go there, but I was getting better about blocking it all out and just going about with the chores of the day. It was time to focus on someone else for a change.

"Iz, can you do me a favor?" I asked him. "Can you come over and have lunch with Daniel and me, plus a surprise guest visitor."

"A girl? Someone hot?" he asked with a grin. "I am single— and very available."

"Oh, she's very cute and very alone," I said. "It's Bertha from ITT's hockey team. Remember her?" I said it praying that he could see the real Bertha and would look deeply enough to get past what most boys would probably shun. "She has a very gentle soul and a wonderful sense of humor," I told him. It dawned on me that I was sounding like a used-car salesman or some lame matchmaker on the Internet.

"Walker," Izayah said with great hesitation in his voice. "I'd love to help you, but . . . this is weird because I did that move on the rink at the championship game that made her miss the puck. All I could think of was distracting her. You know what I mean. And now I'm sure she doesn't want to see me or have anything to do with me."

"I'm sure you're wrong," I said. "She would probably love to see you."

I spent the next several minutes explaining how Demanda and her crew had bullied poor Bertha on her first day of school. Izayah was nothing if not compassionate. "She could really use a few genuine friends," I said. "Come on, Iz. For the team. Go Academy! Rah, rah, rah!"

"All right, all right, all right. You wore me down. I'd love to have lunch with Bertha and you. Daniel's the one who annoys the crap out of me." Without further hesitation or tempting fate, I grabbed his tray and said, "Let's go!"

Daniel had just recruited Bertha in a similar way by telling her that I needed some girlfriends now that my mom had moved on. She was overjoyed at the invitation. The truth was she mostly ate alone, so she could go back for seconds and thirds without any commentary. I could see her careful brown eyes watching me as I came closer with Izayah who touched her arm and said, "Now, this is a nice surprise."

It was almost her undoing.

She pulled the pink comb from her hair while her other hand was busy straightening her starchy white shirt. There was no time to do anything more in the way of self-improvement projects. I could see that she was flustered, flattered, and about to fly off into orbit.

"Bertha, you remember Izayah?" I said in a breezy voice. "He plays hockey with us. Now, we're all on the same team. Imagine that."

Izayah didn't miss much and he continued to smile at Bertha as he planted his tray right next to hers. Without even asking, he took two of her French fries. "Now, don't tell me that you're gonna be stingy and not share some of those with me? We're friends, right? No hard feelings," he teased Bertha whose face began to beam.

It didn't take long until we all began to hang out with each other as much as possible. Bertha was shy around Izayah, which

258

was pretty adorable. Iz even picked her as his cooking-class partner and they laughed when she nearly blew up the stove making some hot-pepper appetizer that literally blew the roof of your mouth off, too. This was one of those times when the reset was a snacker's best friend.

As Bertha opened up and began to trust me, I asked her a little bit about ITT and how she survived it. She told me some sketchy details about her past and confessed, "I just got involved with the wrong people. I'm lucky to have found some real friends when it counts the most, which is now."

She told me about the beatings at ITT. Some were courtesy of the other inmates, including the infamous Wargos, and then there were the guards who also had a heavy hand with the kids there. She told me how Eddie Wargo ruled the place with an iron fist, although he got his fare share of beatings from their warden, the Godfather, who used Eddie to do his bidding. Eddie seemed to get special privileges and acted as the GF's errand boy and muscle-man intern of sorts. He would bring in the GF's lunch deliveries, fetch the daily newspaper, and even escort other inmates into the inner sanctuary of his fearless leader. Apparently, the GF gave Eddie free rein to manhandle all he wanted as he moved an inmate from point A to point B. Other times, the GF just wanted a little company and invited Eddie, of all people, to sit in his office and watch shoot-'em-up mob movies. Apparently, both of them could recite almost every single line from every episode of the *Sopranos*, a boxed set that Eddie kept at the ready to pop into the GF's DVD player. Any request from the GF denied on Eddie's watch? Fuggeddaboutit.

When I asked how she got along with this GF, her head fell. A minute later when she finally looked up, her face was covered in a mask so fearful that I didn't ask any other questions about this man who apparently did not believe in sparing the rod and who beat Bertha several times for infractions as simple as speaking too slowly or losing a hockey game.

259

"What happened to you after you lost to the Academy in the championship," I had to ask her.

"Don't want to ever talk about that, Walk-*her*," she said, involuntarily rubbing a scarred spot on her upper arm. But she did talk about daily life at that hellhole.

It was almost as if Bertha talking about her time served at ITT made her seem lighter. I felt bad about the fact I was using her to get information about the place, but it was without much success over the last week or so. And, as usual, I was running out of time.

"Tell me about the kids on D Block," I asked her one afternoon as we walked through the campus on another tepid day with full cloud cover above and snow covering the ground outside the school gates. The wind should have stung like a hard slap, but instead it caressed our faces in a fast, frantic way.

"Walk-*her*, come on. What's with all the questions?" Bertha asked me as we made our way into English class where some humor writer named Erma was lecturing about how to get your grass really green. It was cute how Bertha sort of butchered my name and made it sound street cool. "You're not thinkin' about doin' something stupid up here that will get you sent there for reals, are you Walk-*her*?" she asked in her breathless intonation, which was low and controlled.

"You're nothin' but a little thing," she said. "You'd never get through a day at ITT. Eddie would destroy you. He's the meanest to the pretty girls. He stopped aging at age eighteen. He has a lot of hormones going on . . . I know."

I let that last comment sink in, but didn't want to push her. Not today. "Thanks B, for the concern," I said and dropped the rest. Later, we walked to computer class where Steve was going to recite his famous graduation speech that was supposed to be inspiring. I was excited to hear it in person although I read the transcript when I was alive. On one of his laptops.

"Walk-*her*," Bertha said as we trudged down the hallway. "Don't be so smart that you're actually stupid." Then her eyes filled with tears, which stopped me in my tracks. We were standing in the ornate third-floor school hallway where Picassos hung on the walls beside student projects. "I haven't had a girlfriend in a long time and I needs one like you. You know what I mean, Walk-*her*?" Bertha said.

I'm not sure why, but I threw my arms around Bertha and ignored the three tears that she allowed to roll down her pillow-like cheeks.

"I haven't had a close girlfriend in forever either and I like having you around," I said and then added, "I forgot, but I was supposed to invite you over to the house for dinner tonight."

I felt as big as a bug. I really liked Bertha and inviting her to dinner to pry information out of her now seemed like such a low-life thing to do. But I was desperate.

It was now Monday, December nineteenth—four days away from the night Daniel died and the day before our first visit to ITT. I had no choice because we were no closer to finding that portal.

"Who's doing the cooking?" Bertha asked. "I hope it's not you Walk-*her*. No offense. But all hundred pounds of you don't look like no real cook to me."

"Daniel's cooking," I told her. "But don't expect anything like Julia whips up for you in cooking class. His idea of gourmet is not burning the burgers on the Weber grill."

"One more thing," she said with a wide smile. "How's it that the two of you are living together?" she asked.

"We're friends," I said.

"I ain't stupid either," Bertha said, slapping me on the back in a way that I almost fell over. "I see the way that boy looks at you."

261

"Like how?" I said, suddenly quite pleased.

"Like our teacher Kurt told," she said. "He looks at you like you're his hot-fudge sundae."

CHAPTER 19

1.

It turns out Daniel wasn't in the mood for ice cream that night. "We're having a dinner guest?" he moaned like this was the worst news he had ever heard. "I have a lot of research to do and I hate being social. You know I don't do small talk."

Sometimes in relationships, if that's what this was, you just have to humor the other party because your needs are really his needs—he just doesn't realize it.

"Yes, we're having a guest, so please put on your faux happy face," I said. "Our passes into ITT start tomorrow morning and we only have till Friday to find that portal. We really need a full briefing from Bertha because the clock is a-ticking. We need to get her away from school, give her a hot meal, and some relaxation. Then we find out a few things we need to know. It's not like we can waltz into ITT tomorrow, look into the eyes of the crazy school shooter and say to him, 'Hey, school shooter, in addition to telling us what made you snap and kill our principal—really bad move, by the way—we really need to find some other wacko kid here who knows where there is a portal back to life. Any clues? Can you help us out? Got a cell-block address?' I don't think so," I said, setting the table by placing the forks down on the wood as hard as possible. Our collective needs were starting to really piss me off now.

Daniel slammed down a few spoons. "And in the weeks you've been friends with Bertha with secret plans to interrogate her, you've found out . . . exactly nothing," he reminded me. "We need to think of something else."

I slapped down some knives and said, "Bertha was at ITT for six years. She's smart. She might have heard something about this other kid. She might know if this person really exists, if he is still at ITT, in this realm, or if all of this portal lore is just a figment of someone's imagination."

That was the unspoken fear that neither of us wanted to confront. What if the time traveler had gone on, Up or Down, and worse yet, what if he never really existed at all and was just an afterlife urban legend?

"So start grilling those steaks and act like a host, even if it kills you," I implored, pointing to my cheeks. "I'll go wash up, so I can interrogate my new friend and try to produce better results."

My snarkiness might have not been welcome, but it did grab his attention. And it made him reconsider the bigger picture.

"If you strike out, I think I should go alone to ITT tomorrow," Daniel announced, but before I could argue that one the doorbell rang. "Let me welcome the guest with my manufactured charm, which will certainly make her confess all," he suggested.

2.

By all accounts, it was a perfectly pleasant dinner. Jenna and Andy adored Bertha from the moment she walked into the house with a tin of fresh peanut-butter cookies she made in cooking class. Pete couldn't contain his shock when she went outside with him after dinner to toss some tennis balls to the dog. Bertha loved dogs and told us about pets she used to know, mostly strays like herself, when she lived in New York. By the look on Jake's furry face, the feeling of love was mutual, and dogs are always great judges. When she slipped him a few cookies, it was love with a commitment of total adoration. The belly rubs didn't hurt either.

"Ok, Ace," Daniel said, while Bertha was still playing with Jake, "it's almost nine o'clock and she'll have to go back to the Academy soon. It is a school night. So, it's now or never because all we've learned tonight is that she makes pretty good cookies—and that's not going to make any headlines or help us."

I just glared at him, but felt my own stress levels rise. *What if I did strike out?* There really was no tomorrow to find out what we needed to know.

When Bertha came back inside, she sat down and I poured her a cold Coke, which was her eighth of the night. There were no horrible-tasting diet products up here because you really couldn't gain more weight, so we all enjoyed the sugar taste without the rush. Sitting across from our friend at our little wooden kitchen table, I downed a few sips of cola for courage and began.

"B," I said, using the pet name I had been calling her all week, "I gotta ask you something crazy. It's about a rumor I heard at school."

"That Izayah might ask me out?" she asked hopefully and we laughed.

"I think you should ask him out," Daniel said. "He's really a cool guy and a great hockey player. You two have a lot in common."

For the next ten minutes, Daniel went on about hockey at the Academy and I could have screamed because the clock was ticking. "Hey, B," Daniel finally said. "Here's the thing, and I hope you can keep a secret."

For a crazy moment, my heart actually stopped, but it didn't matter because I was already dead. Still. Was he going to tell her our plan to go back?

"Bertha, Callaghan and I are doing a little independent study project at ITT on school shooters. We're going there with permission tomorrow to interview a kid named Jackie Silver. That's why we've been sort of grilling you about the place," Daniel said. "I know Callaghan has been asking about the people and the layout and the crazy stuff you know about the inmates."

"For example, what's the craziest thing you've ever heard about one of them—and how he landed at ITT? He or she, I mean," I interjected in my sweetest voice. The inquiry was almost a dare to come up with something mind-blowing. This wasn't a patented move, as it can work for almost anyone. Just ask; most people will try to knock your socks off.

Bertha told me alright. She told me good.

"I gotta pee," she said, standing up. The scrape of her chair was deafening. I was too busy looking at my "friend" Daniel across the table to notice that she bypassed our downstairs powder room and was actually lumbering up the back staircase to find the so-called ladies' room up there.

"I'm so sorry," I whispered to Daniel, tears of frustration building. "I thought I could get all kinds of information from her. It's not fair to her—or to you. I just suck at this."

266

Daniel put his hand over mine and allowed both to rest on the surface of the table. When I could finally look at him, I saw his warm gray eyes caressing my face with a look so inviting I wanted to wrap myself up in it.

I was falling in love with him.

It was as clear as knowing my name. Staring at the mound of dirty dishes in the sink and feeling hopeless about our situation, I knew was in love with him, although I didn't know if the feeling was mutual.

"I love you for trying," Daniel said.

It was such an awkward moment—I love you *for trying?*—that I could only conjure up words that anyone would say under these circumstances. "Where the hell is Bertha?" I asked. "She's been in the bathroom forever. What is she doing? Having a kidney transplant?"

It turns out that Bertha wasn't only in the upstairs bathroom. She had also done a quick canvas of our bedroom, including the nightstand where Daniel kept a few notes about his favorite subject of wormholes and portals. We hadn't hid anything away because ever since I moved in, the kids had been absolutely respectful and never entered the bedroom zone.

Lumbering heavily down the stairs, Bertha didn't look like Bertha anymore. She was surprisingly fast and agile when she was furious. Before we could speak, she was back at the kitchen table hissing, "I just knew it! You liars best tell me the truth!" Then she turned to me and said, "Walk-*her*, I thought you were my friend. Why did you grill me steak tonight? Why are you really going to ITT?"

"The way you're going Walk-*her*," she continued to rant, "you're going to be at ITT for all eternity. You best remember what I told you earlier. Your skinny ass will never survive even one day there. Not one hour!"

"B, don't be silly—" I began until Daniel interrupted me.

"Bertha, let's cut to the chase," he said. "I need some information about ITT because I have a family emergency on my hands. A nine-one-one moment. I can't tell you everything because it would make you an accessory after the fact and that could land your ass back at ITT forever—and I don't think *you* would survive an hour of it now that you're one of us. If you really want to help us, you won't ask us even one thing about what we're doing. But you can tell us one thing about ITT, and it doesn't have to do with a school shooter or procedures or dipshit Eddie Wargo."

Bertha was still angry, but she sat back down at the table and sipped her Coke in large gulps. I poured her another one.

"Please just tell us about the one kid who went back to life," Daniel asked. "Who is he? Where is he? Is he real?"

"Please," he implored her again, proving that he wasn't too proud to beg. "It's for a good cause. I promise you that much. This isn't some vanity thing or a lark. It's a family emergency, and nothing means as much to me as my family."

Bertha began to twist her hands as if they were towels that she was rolling up to put into a cabinet. She chug-a-lugged that Coke, and motioned for me to open another like she was an alcoholic at a bar needing some liquid courage.

"Yeah, I heard those rumors," she began in a slow voice. "But I hate to tell you this Dan-*yell*, but the boy time traveler don't near exist. He's a figment of a lot of imaginations. He's, at best, fiction."

"No sirree, no," she said. "It's just a wise tale. What you call a mythology. A prank. We had to tell stories at ITT. We'd go crazy if there wasn't a story about someone who got out or did something 'tacular. So, someone made up the story of the guy who busted out and returned to life. A big whopper of a story, if you ask me. We kept adding onto it, telling it longer each time. My favorite part is how he opened a door to his past world and just took a walk back home. D-R-A-M-A, yes sirree, drama."

"So, he's just urban legend like Bigfoot or the boogeyman?" I asked, my heart sinking fast. All our planning and studying was for absolutely nothing. I almost couldn't deal with it. I could only imagine how much worse the pain was for Daniel.

"Yep, total mythological mumbo jumbo," said Bertha, "and that's all I'm gonna say about that."

In that next instant, I knew.

She was lying.

It was written all over her sweet, trusting face. She had a kisser that absolutely couldn't tell even a small fib. Despite the years of abuse, she still had an open heart and a protective nature. It was no wonder she played goalie. Right now, she was trying to stop us by blocking and dodging and grabbing at anything to save the day, the same way she did on the rink.

"Bertha, please tell us the truth," I said in a quiet voice. "You're lying because you don't want us to get hurt or get in trouble, but we're going to find him with or without you. If we have to wander all over ITT looking for him, we could get hurt. Real hurt."

Bertha kept it up for several long minutes. Then she released that melon-like head and allowed it to sink low as if her neck was refusing to work. I thought Bertha looked like a human weeping willow tree.

"I'm asking you to help us," I said in almost a whisper, "as a friend."

"Why do I always get caught up in something bad," Bertha began to weep into her hands. "Why is it that I can't just be normal with no bad caught in the middle?"

"This isn't bad. It's just something that needs to be done," Daniel said. "Please, Bertha."

"I don't nearly know nothing," Bertha said, trying to compose herself. Then finally, she opened the gates just a bit. "What if I tell

269

you that there *is* such a kid," she said, slowly. "That he did it—went back to life—only one time and it landed him in ITT for breaking the most sacred rule up here. . . . And then he did something worse."

"What could be worse than breaking the sacred rule of not ever trying to go back to life?" I asked.

"He was planning to do it again," Bertha whispered. "He put an ad in the school paper at ITT the minute he got there to serve his time. The paper is made for students by students and the guards and officers don't ever want to read about 'the crazies,' but somehow the powers found out. The GF found out."

"The kid had guts!" she continued. "He actually put an ad in the ITT paper asking for others to break out and then go back to the living realm with him. He wrote that it was too dangerous to go back there alone. He needed what's called some backup. He asked the others who might volunteer to bring weapons with them. The ad was beyond creepy. He wrote that your safety was not a for sure. He didn't explain exactly who or what made it so dangerous to go back to the life realm."

"So, he advertised, got caught, and was sent to the Hole and then back to D Block at ITT," she concluded with a shudder. "I talked to him one time when I saw him in medical. I was always in medical. He told me his only choice was to advertise because he needed bigger kids to help him once he got there. He needed kids who could fight. Even kill for him. He said when you go back, there are forces that try to destroy you."

"We need a name," Daniel said.

"It might just be a tall tale," Bertha bluffed. "Like in a movie. Maybe this little loony was making the whole thing up to pass the time."

"Please give us the name," I begged, but Bertha began to cry again and insisted that she didn't know anything more about the

270

guy who skipped back to life. She had no idea why he came back to this realm or if he was forced back.

In that instant, I knew what we had to do at ITT. "We have to make it to their school library and find the actual advertisement so we can find him. Find the ad, find the otherworldly traveler," I announced.

"Do you know the approximate date this kid got sentenced to ITT?"

She shook her head. "It would be easy to find out," Bertha insisted. "I hears that only two or three kids have ever got switched from the Academy to ITT. If you find out those dates and then look at ITT's school paper that same week of the switches you might be in the knowledge."

"That time-traveling kid had conviction. We have to give him that much," I said.

"You haven't been there," Bertha said under her breath. "Anyone stuck at ITT would do anything to get out, including slipping through some magical portal to another dimension. It sure beats another day of beatings at ITT."

3.

After Daniel swore her to secrecy and made her take an oath over our last Coke and cookie, he walked her back to school. Later, we tucked in the kids and I put out clean clothes for Jenna and Andy, which had become a habit. I had become their big-sister stylist who each night smoothed out a fresh pair of jeans or skirt and the perfect matching sweater. It was kind of fun coordinating their outfits and it was making me spruce up my act, too.

Daniel stripped off his shirt before getting into bed, which meant he was only wearing black sweatpants and his naked six-pack. For some reason, I also abandoned my sweatshirt and bounced into bed in a pink tank top and just my undies. Maybe it was the excitement of finding out something real that had me in a reckless mood—or maybe it was something far more dangerous.

"Wow . . . um . . . oh . . . hi, Callaghan," Daniel stammered when I entered the room. It was exactly the reaction that I needed. Nervously, he tried to immerse himself in the information displayed on his laptop where he was reading a long e-mail from Steve, who practically lived on his own laptop. I swear, you could e-mail the guy at two in the morning and he would answer at 2:01 a.m.

"I e-mailed Steve—and, uh, look, he answered," Daniel said in an unusually husky voice that made it sound like he had a chest cold, although that was impossible now.

"He did?" I said, sliding into bed and sitting right next to him.

I watched as he put his two large hands under the covers and shoved me several inches away. "You stay. Over there. So I can concentrate," he demanded. "And don't talk either. It's distracting."

The sound of his voice played on all of my nerve endings, too. "Did you put on perfume?" he fumed. Then he imitated Bertha when he said, "Give me a break, Call-*a-han*."

"What did our big buddy Steve tell us?" I inquired in the most innocent way as I swung my long hair forward.

"I . . . uh . . . what?" Daniel said.

"Steve. The wealth of knowledge. The computer genius," I reminded him. Then I asked, "Are you okay? You look feverish."

"Right, Steve," he said and cleared his throat. "It seems that Bertha was right. In the history of the Academy only three students have ever been expelled from our school and sent to ITT. Two of them have moved on, so they're not around here anymore. A kid named A.E. with no last name remains."

"He left the Academy on June tenth, two thousand eleven," Daniel continued. "So we have to find a way into ITT's school library and look through back issues of their school paper, appropriately called *The Rant*. Hopefully we can find that ad if the school hasn't destroyed the issue. I'm sure once they noticed the ad, all the issues were burned, but we might get lucky if all the newspapers are scanned in and everyone forgot about the computer archives."

"Yes, you might just get lucky," I said in a seductive voice I didn't know I possessed.

"I'm going to prison in the morning. I need my sleep," Daniel said. Then he turned off the computer, placed it on his nightstand, and rolled away from me.

"Good night," I said in a chipper voice, speaking to his muscular back.

"Nothing good about it," he mumbled.

CHAPTER 20

1.

It was midmorning on December twentieth and our little field trip began after a lengthy session with one worried and furious Dr. Marvin King who summoned us to his office at the crack of dawn. The idea of not showing up was not an option. "What the hell do you kids want with ITT?" he demanded. "We've already lost one student to that hellhole. I'm not ready to lose two more of you." He even curtly dismissed Miss Travis who valiantly tried to wander in with tea and cookies.

Dr. King wore a gray sweater and black slacks. He looked younger than the age on his driver's license and the shots of gray through his black hair gave him an air of ultimate authority, although his mood was dark and forbidding today. He paced the length of a beautiful handwoven rug, and I caught him muttering, "Damn research projects. Suspend all the rules, my ass." Then I heard him sigh and say, "What about the good old days when we told kids what to do—when we told them NO?"

Over breakfast, I had coached Daniel to sit there and just take it.

"I'm not entirely against your project," he stated in a clipped tone that told us this had been a tormenting decision. "I didn't want to put the old kibosh on it for my own very personal reasons."

"Doctor King, we're so sorry about—" I began.

"Leave it alone, Walker," he insisted.

I couldn't even begin to imagine how he felt about us interrogating the kid who killed him. The weight of the mission suddenly felt very heavy, too heavy for words. I couldn't help but think about my mom at home alone in Chicago. What would she think about me putting myself in so much danger? She didn't ever want me walking home late in the afternoon, especially on dank winter days when the sky turned dark so early. "Lunatics are lurking," Mom would insist. Now, I was going to put myself into a den of insane people, deadly crazies my own age, so I could help a guy I was now living with find his dead brother. In a crazy way, it all made absolute, perfect sense.

What could they do to me? What wouldn't they do to me?

"Sir, we just want to study," Daniel interrupted Dr. King, who was reading us a list of warnings.

Our vigilant principal glared at me when he read one about not wandering anywhere at ITT. "You have a wandering soul. Contain it!" snapped Dr. King. "I know the criminal mind." He pivoted and looked at Daniel hard and said, "Funny, but you were never so interested in the criminal mind before now. I am only allowing a maximum of three visits conducted this week and never again. If I hear of any dangers there, then I will pull the plug on this project immediately."

"I'm going to give you tracking devices to put on your bodies," he continued. "This way I can monitor you at all times." Motioning

275

us to come to the desk, he produced what looked like a stapler and asked us to turn our backs to him. He touched the upper fleshy part of both of our arms. Quickly, he shot into both of us what looked like a tiny microchip. It didn't really hurt and Dr. King said our bodies would eventually expel it like a wooden sliver. "You can get it wet. Just obviously don't try to mess with it," he said.

My skin was actually crawling because I wanted to get started, but obviously Dr. King wasn't done reinforcing his list of rules. "You will just visit Mister Silver's cell—and go nowhere else while you're at those premises," he said. "Now, get out of here. You have your phones. Call Harold if you need him. He's ex-CIA. He might look old, but he can still take care of business like none other."

I didn't leave his desk area for what seemed like a long minute. "Sir," I began in a slow voice. "Is there anything you particularly want or need to know . . . when we interview Mister Silver?"

"Absolutely nothing," said Dr. King as in the case was closed in his mind. Slamming the book he was holding onto his desk, he tried to mask his worry with anger. "Get on with you. Get out of here. And be safe over there or you'll have to deal with me when you get back."

The way he said it worried me because his tone indicated he wasn't so sure if we'd ever be back.

2.

There was no skimping at the Academy. The school car was a silver Bentley, and it was gassed and ready to go. After Dr. King's lecture, we were driven to ITT by kindly, pie-loving Harold, the gate guard at the Academy, part-time chauffeur, and—stop the presses—former

CIA agent. Normally, my mind would race with questions to ask Harold, but not today. After we settled into the cushy, navy-blue leather backseat, he informed us that he had explicit instructions to stay in the car and wait for us at the mountain's bottom at ITT in case we needed to make an ultra-hasty getaway. If we weren't out of there by six sharp, or when the dinner bell struck in the main hall of the Academy, he was instructed to call Dr. King who would personally arrive at ITT with repercussions—whatever that meant.

Safe in the backseat of the car, I whispered to Daniel, "So we're doing this! Just a nice day hanging out with a bunch of creeps and murderers."

"What did you kids say back there about murderers?" Harold inquired, driving for what seemed like a slow-motion long time before eventually swerving off to that back road with the bricked guardhouse. It marked the entrance to ITT.

As we neared, the AK-47s came into view and were pointed in the direction of the car as I heard what sounded like two packs of dogs growling—and this was probably the safest place at ITT. I could barely contain my excitement. Harold whipped around to inform us, "Just say the word, kids, and I'll have you back at the Academy in a jiffy. Maybe we stop for a little breakfast first on Main Street. A little eggs and bacon, extra crispy. What do you kids need with this element?"

"We need—" Daniel started, but I finished it.

"To do this."

By all accounts, it wasn't a lie.

3.

Two guards with black police caps covering their massive foreheads greeted us. They looked like human versions of pit bulls. Of course, pit bulls can be lovely dogs if they're raised right. So can humans. You could almost immediately tell that these two had been raised in the pound or on the streets.

One of the guards, with a cigarette dangling from his lips, began to hassle Harold about incomplete paperwork while blowing smoke right at us into the car. The other guy was built like a Mack Truck and was more interested in poking his palooka face into the Bentley to see who or what he was dealing with as visitors. There weren't many visitors to ITT, so this was what was known as An Occasion. "Just some punk and a skinny girl," Palooka Number Two said with a sneer.

"Get right into the guard house for your visitor's passes and name tags. Don't pass go. Don't collect two hundred dollars. Don't blink an eye until you got yourself one of those passes," said Palooka One. "We'd hate to confuse you with one of the inmates and give you a toasty new glass cell that would be unbreakable for eternity—just in case you were wondering what *could* happen to you here."

Palooka Two fired up his own cigarette and suddenly his face was obscured in a cloud of fresh smoke. I could see his name tag, which read: Roy. "What the hell are you two virgins doing at ITT?" he asked. A north wind blew hard into the car as I answered, "Research. We're here to do psych research. For a paper."

"Little Missy, we got plenty of psychos here. But here's what my research tells me," said Palooka Two. "Stay in your car, back

278

up, turn around, and go back to your candy-ass little school on the hill where they tuck you in at night with some warm milk and cookies."

"Nobody wants you here," added Palooka One. "The last thing I need is to crack some skulls so your sorry butts can race back to your fancy car in one piece."

Even though he was old, Harold kicked into high gear. "There is no need to be rude," he admonished the first Palooka who just shrugged like he could care less.

We didn't take more than two steps out of the car before two different armed guards grabbed us by the flesh of our upper arms, near our trackers, and all but ripped us off our feet as they escorted us into the guardhouse. "Good luck," Harold called after us. "Call me."

4.

The grounds at the base of ITT didn't look like a typical prison entrance. Tall weeds spiked waist-high while brown scrubby grass on the side of the narrow dirt road marked our pathway to the actual rock at the bottom of the mountain. The guards manhandled us the hundred feet or so it took to get there and I noted that even the natural elements around this place lacked any life-affirming green. It was all just wilted death.

It was still morning, but a murkiness had turned the sky dishrag gray. The guards shoved Daniel, who worked hard not to react, toward a large silver panel emerging from the side of the mountain. It was the elevator to the inside.

As we waited to enter the bowels of ITT, I thought about

bolting. Daniel stood next to me staring straight ahead despite the AK-47 that poked into his back. *Definitely out of our comfort zone.* At that moment, I remembered something my dad used to say to me: "Your comfort zone is a bad neighborhood. Step outside of it."

Just then, the entire realm started to weep. Sheets of mist dampened us with an ominous greeting while water-weighted clouds hung heavily in the air. Fat drops of rain announced their arrival by stinging our faces and matting the scrubby dust at our feet into pits of mud. It seemed like the elevator would never come, which was fitting. Anyone's last moment on the outside should linger.

Just minutes before this, a set of guards had checked us in during our scan and pat-down inside the brick house. They even made visitor passes on those lame little white, "Hello My Name Is" tags you find at office supply stores.

"Don't get too many lookers," a skinny guard had said, carrying an automatic rifle with a scope on it as he lingered during my pat-down. I could see Daniel automatically react and lurch forward, but then he checked himself. There was nothing he could do but watch as the guard decided he would do a second pat-down in my case—just to be sure. His gun looked like it weighed more than the guard did and although it would have no effect on us, who knew what *else* they were capable of here? Again and again, the missing boy, Simon, popped into my mind, as did their punishment chamber called the Hole. Handing us the tags, the guard chuckled and we could see that half of his teeth were missing. "At least the inmates will know you by name now, which I'm not so sure is a good thing, dolly," he said. Then he asked my name and I told him.

"Walker?" he stopped and asked before he wrote it down with a Sharpie.

"It's a family name," I said in my monotone voice while Daniel looked at him with disgust. "Okay, Texas Ranger and Daniel

280

Boone, here are your tags," he said. "Have fun in the chaos."

Our long wait at the mountain base ended when the elevator finally announced itself with a metal-on-metal grinding sound that made the hairs on your arm stand up. Slowly sliding open with the screech of a tortured cat, the elevator door beckoned us, and I knew it was our last chance to turn around. Instead, we took a breath and stepped inside.

Two more armed guards were permanently positioned inside the elevator since it was the only way in and the only way out. After a series of codes were punched into a keypad inside the elevator door, we rose up, then were spit out inside ITT's core, which looked like the outer-space installation in some futuristic sci-fi movie. Each wide corridor we walked through came with a steel door that opened from the ceiling and then shut tight behind us by slamming into the solid titanium floors and then locking in place with a click that made the finality of it known to anyone without a hearing problem.

We bypassed processing, which meant our first stop was the administrative floor where we were met by an information officer named Ken who looked like a former pro wrestler. He had shoulders twice the size of Daniel's build, which made him freakishly wide. His head was almost square with a short dark buzz cut on top. He kept a toothpick permanently dangling from his full lips. "Okay, let's start with the rules, adventurers," he said, staring down at us because his six-foot-six frame made him also look a little like Lurch from *The Addams Family*. "Here are the particulars. Walk in here at your own risk. And listen to me or I'll feed you to the inmates," he said, laughing like it was the first time he told his bad joke.

He took us back to that elevator and punched it to reach Cellblock A. When we stepped onto the block floor, my eyes went wide. Past a flanking of guards, this floor housed thousands of unbreakable glass cells that measured about six feet by nine feet. They seemed to be suspended in air in neat rows like large children's blocks. Peering into the lower cells, I could see that each contained what looked like a clear glass bed, a clear toilet and an almost translucent desk. The only thing of prominence in these cells was the human fleshly spirits trapped within.

As we passed the first-floor cells, a few of the kids waved like we were visitors at a zoo and the inmates were happy to see fresh blood. It was strange because they could have been kids sitting next to us in chemistry class or in music appreciation. Many of their faces had just a glimmer of hope and youth.

Ken was a good tour guide and gave us a few particulars. "She busted into her school's computer system and gave the entire senior class A's. Then she tried to hack into the White House's mainframe with a bomb threat," he said, pointing to a redhead girl with her nose buried in a book. His index finger jabbed in another direction where a boy who looked vaguely bored was playing solitaire on one of those strange desks. "He didn't pull a trigger during a home invasion that went wrong, but he did drive the getaway car. Little bastard was high on his mom's prescription pills."

As we passed him, the boy sneered at us trying to look as dangerous as possible. It didn't take long before hundreds of young faces were pressed against their glass outer walls to see the new specimens. "Girl up there to the left?" Ken said. "Tried to poison her baby brother with bug spray. The kid just got a good case of the runs. She tried to do it again by giving him floor cleaner to drink. That landed him in the hospital."

Some of the kids who were ready for some kind of rehab or parole had perks like colorful shelves in their cells filled with chessboards and various schoolbooks. "How you're treated in here depends on the infraction," Ken said, watching my eyes take their silent inventory. "Some of the kids who behave and didn't do anything too heinous when they were alive get to lift weights, do yoga, read books, or shoot hoops. Others never get to leave their cells and have nothing inside the cell except for the basics: a bed and a john."

"The idea here is to lay low and stay out of trouble," Ken continued. "We even allowed one kid on A Block a pet lizard he found in the rec area. He collects bugs for it in the prison laundry, but not too many bugs hang out here. Even they don't like the vibe."

"Over there," Ken said, pointing past the cells down a hallway to a large glass door with a small white plaque, "is the school library. Only Cellblock A students get the privilege to use it. It's a big deal because books are the only way to feel like you're on the outside—at least in your mind."

The ITT library.

It was the ultimate tease and our eyes were fixed upon it. There just wasn't any reason we could think of at the moment for a short pit stop at the library. It was almost painful when Ken walked us right past the clear multicelled room where that advertisement was lurking in some old school newspaper—we hoped. I thought about breaking away from Ken and Daniel, but it was hopeless. It was just the three of us right now and we were obviously under a microscope.

A quick elevator ride later, and Ken took us upstairs to the Cellblock B floor where the inmates had slightly worse infractions. "Drug dealer, junior gang banger, serious bullying," he rattled off as we passed by all the grim faces in their cells.

By the time we got to Cellblock C, he had us on the back of what looked like an industrial-sized golf cart so the mayhem would go by quickly. It took four steel doors that lifted and lowered until we finally made our way onto Block C where kidnappers, rapists, and those with manslaughter charges dwelled. But they still weren't the worst of the worst.

As we neared the deepest recesses of the floor and the cells embedded into mountain rock, Ken shouted back to us, "Welcome to Wargo-ville." I imagined Jimmy Buffet writing the theme song.

There they were in their three respective glass cells. Daryl Wargo was picking his nose while Billy Wargo was shooting wads of paper into the toilet. Eddie was punching the pancake-flat pillow on his bed. Ken even slowed down for a minute and said to us, "I assume since they play hockey against your school, you're well acquainted with the Wargo boys. Maybe you want to say hello before we bring them to the delousing room to hose them down for the week. Strangely, they're usually pretty clean. Even the parasites in here avoid them."

Pressing an intercom button inside his cell, Eddie Wargo flipped us the double bird and yelled, "Welcome to the jungle. Hope to see you around." To me, he added, "Around and alone, sweet cheeks." Then he licked his lips. Slowly. Eddie's face had a way of melting off the human features and making him look like a feral animal. To Daniel, he shouted, "So you finally landed your sorry ass in here. I'd be happy to show you the ropes or find a rope and hang you with it."

I could see that Daniel's fists were tightly clenched.

"Thanks, Edward," Ken said, gunning the gas on the golf cart. "Always delightful."

Zigging past a group of guards on patrol, we finally reached the heavy elevator door that led to our ultimate destination.

"I'll take you right upstairs to the D Block if you're still sure that you want to go there," Ken said. We nodded in unison as he tried a feeble attempt at humor.

"Am I sure *I* want to go there?" he joked.

5.

On our elevator ride up, Ken filled us in on Cellblock D. It contained only twenty-five cells and, instead of glass, each one had a soundproof electric force field in front of it that was "managed" by devices that protected the guards, but nearly burned prisoners alive if they tried to take even one step out of their cells. And there wasn't any delousing room. Once a week, water poured down from the ceiling for three or four minutes. It was the weekly shower. All other contact with the outside world was strictly limited. The bottom line was once you were in a D Block cell, you were never getting a new address or an upgraded one. The only way out was a serious medical issue, the Hole, or a circumstance beyond anyone's imagination like going Down. Way down.

Inside D Block, where the most heinous dead high-school murderers, serial killers, and other rabid souls were housed, it didn't come as a shock to us that there were armed guards posted every few feet. As we walked up to the door leading to the cells, Daniel grabbed my elbow, almost holding me still so I wouldn't wander even an inch away from him.

Ken gave instructions to three no-neck guards at the door. "These kids have clearance for a project. Don't hassle them," he said. Without another word, one of the guards pushed a large handle down and the thick steel door, the type you might see in a bank vault, began to move. Grinding metal begrudgingly heaved its way open to what looked like a dark, damp cave.

Once inside, the steel door sealed tightly shut behind us, which signaled that there was no turning back. There was no choice, but to walk down a small hallway that ended at a set of wide double doors. Ken unlocked them and we entered the cellblock. We stared down the neat row of twenty-five glass cells in a long line.

Almost in slow motion, Ken walked us past the first cell. I jumped back a foot when, from a dark recess of nothingness, a girl who looked around fifteen hurled her body at the glass, bouncing off of it and hitting the floor hard, face-first. She flipped over and looked like a large cockroach turned upside down with her arms and feet whipping wildly in the air.

The next cell housed what looked like a seventeen-year-old boy sitting in bed in a prayer pose. Was he the one who placed the ad? Or was it his next-door "neighbor" who opened his jaw and kept snapping his teeth at us as we passed. He looked like a human raptor. Whatever he was screaming was drowned out by the invisible soundproof cell walls. "His intercom was revoked," Ken said.

Every once in awhile it was almost as if there was some kind of power surge and you could hear the electric current sizzle. With a loud snap, a spark would fly off of the invisible shield in front of the cells. Was it a malfunction . . . or just a warning?

On we walked past each and every cell until we reached the end, knowing that the boy we really wanted to grill was in one of the cages we had just passed. *Was it the redhead? Or the baldie? Or the boy who had ripped out half his hair? Or the one making bite marks into his own arm?*

We were told that our interview subject would be placed in a special locked room way at the end of the block and that our location would be in an adjoining room where we could talk on a phone through an unbreakable glass partition. "Why can't we just talk to him through the intercom of his cell?" I asked Ken, thinking that maybe we could wander a few cells down and check out his fellow inmates.

"He doesn't have an intercom," Ken said. "Also, it's best not to start a ruckus in here."

"What starts a ruckus?" I asked him.

"A pin dropping," he said.

6.

Jackie Silver wasn't what we expected. He had a mass of dark hair and thick bushy eyebrows that shaded piercing hazel eyes. Ugly, black large-framed glasses wrapped around his ears and there was white tape in the middle from an obvious break. He had a young, sad, and serious face all at the same time. In another world, he could have been a stick-skinny prep school student. His shoulders were close set and withered now. There was no way this kid could carry the weight of the world. He was just too puny.

Ken had left us to our work when two guards led Jackie into his private discussion room across from us. Not once did he look up at us as they guided him in shackles and chains to a folding metal chair that didn't look all that comfortable. I could guess that Jackie hadn't seen creature comforts in a long time. His nails were long, jagged, and dirty and his ITT jumpsuit was stained in front from some sort of juice or blood.

In front of us was his file, which I had already thumbed through while we had waited. The most shocking line in the file was what trigger-happy Jackie said before he began mowing down the student body. "It sure beats the hell out of algebra, doesn't it," he yelled.

Daniel left the interview process to me, opting to sit by my side for protection and moral support. "Jackie," I said, picking up my phone, which was piped to him via an intercom speaker in his room, "I'm Walker and this is Daniel. We go to the Academy down

287

the road. Daniel's here thanks to a plane crash. I'm here because . . . well, it's a long story. You know how that goes."

I knew why Jackie was here, but he wasn't talking. He was sitting and looking at his hands. Holding the phone to my ear I told him, "We're here to work on a paper because everyone wants—needs—to understand why you did what you did. Maybe if you could help us out a bit."

The icebreaker of explaining our deaths didn't work and neither did some mindless chitchat about afterlife on the outside. Jackie Silver was like a walking coma. He was breathing and sometimes blinking, but he refused to utter even a grunt. Even though he wasn't our main objective here, I decided that while we had the time with him, we could certainly make the most of it. Maybe we really could find out something about school shooters. "Jackie, it says here in your file that you and your dad were going through real hard times," I said. "I know. I've been there. My mom and I had to deal with our house being foreclosed on."

Jackie didn't look a bit sympathetic, but Daniel looked shocked. It was true that I had skated around certain parts of my past including the fact that we were dirt poor most of the time and had to live with my Aunt Ginny. I wasn't sure how that would sit with one of the Reids of posh Lake Forest, Illinois.

"Anyway, Jackie, you know our principal is Marvin King," I said. "He was your assistant principal. He's a very nice man, but he didn't send us here. In fact, he just wants to close the book on what happened to him."

At the mention of Dr. King's name, Jackie lifted his head a bit and gnawed on the side of his parched lip until it began to bleed. But just as quickly, he lowered his face all the way to the table allowing his forehead to smack into the steel.

"The guy is catatonic," Daniel said under his breath.

An hour passed. Eventually my hand hurt, so I put the phone back down.

"So, what's the game plan?" Daniel asked. "We can't just sit here all day long." When Ken popped his head in to check on us and I gave him the thumbs up that we would keep going.

Another hour passed and now Jackie was awake and staring straight at us, but not saying a word. I tried countless times, asking him about the happier parts of his life, his school, and his father. I reminded him of the time he played the oldest boy in his school's version of *The Sound of Music*. I told him that his best friend Ben finally graduated. He just stared into the air when he wasn't picking at his right ear as if it hurt to hear someone talking to him.

Flipping to the back of his file, I read aloud the last pages of that fateful day when he mowed down Dr. King and his fellow students. "And then you shot yourself," I said, expecting an explosive reaction. But he just revved up the ear picking while opening his mouth into a wide O. No sound came out.

Almost three hours into our nothingness, Ken ducked his head back in and asked how it was going. "Oh, it's going, but he hasn't said anything," I said.

"Just like I thought," Ken replied, shrugging. "He almost never speaks and if he does, it's just some rambling gibberish that no one can translate."

"I'll give you a few more minutes and then you kids should take a break," he said. "Maybe you could go to the guard's room and have a quick snack and then come back and try again. We can leave Jackie in here. He's perfectly safe unless he strangles himself with the phone cord. He can feel pain, but he can't die twice. So who really cares if he hurts himself? I don't care, especially since it's lasagna for the staff. Do you kids like lasagna?"

Jackie sat perfectly still without an emotion floating across what could have been a handsome face.

Ken walked out of the room, which was Daniel's cue to stand up. Rubbing my aching back, I rose and glanced at Jackie one more time. What I saw surprised me. His arms were unfolded and he was flexing his right fingers convulsively. When he reached for the phone, I raced for ours. I knew he was about to say something I could bring back to Dr. King, and I considered that my secondary mission.

"Jackie," I said in a frantic tone, listening into the receiver as my heart raced.

"Waaaaa," he moaned, sounding like an abused animal.

"Do you have something to say to us?" I almost whispered.

He did—and suddenly his words were clear as a bell. "Aren't you dead yet? Didn't I kill you already?" he inquired. "Bang, bang! Everyone dies today. Hahahahahahahahahaha."

"Guard," Daniel yelled, taking my hand and pulling me into the hallway. Clearly, he had enough, and wanted to get as far away from this confused, troubled specimen as possible. Ken returned with lightening speed. "I told you it was pointless," he said.

"We can't go back with nothing," I said.

"You tried," Ken said. "No one can make that kid talk. At least he talked a little bit to you. That will probably hold him for a whole year."

"But we still have to write our report," Daniel picked it up from there. "We can't write nothing."

Looking bewildered, Ken told us, "I wish there was something I could do, but I can't do anything. I'm not a shrink."

"If only we could look in your school library for some other case studies like this one. Then we'll come back here and try to talk to Jackie again," I said. "The library might help us understand what famous psychiatrists say about these kinds of kids."

It was a shot in the dark that hit the target like a bull's-eye.

I knew it was past lunchtime and stashing us in the library seemed like a good way for Ken to get to his lasagna. "I don't see why you can't go in the library since it's in Block A where it's much

290

safer," Ken said, picking up his cell. "Let me just make sure that the place is empty because I don't want you to have to deal with the other inmates. If the library is free, you can chill out for an hour in there and I can get back to my office to finish some paperwork and eat my lunch."

It was just that easy.

CHAPTER 21

1.

We got lucky because the ITT school library only contained one person: an ancient librarian who liked to rob banks. So she was working off her past indiscretions by helping promote education at ITT. They called her Ma Polly and she was as bony as she was friendly, although when she spoke she hissed a bit. Two missing front teeth will do that to a librarian.

Ma Polly could have cared less about our school project. She was obviously bored when it came to teenage children, though she tried to be momentarily helpful. When we told her we needed anything she had on the mind of a teenage killer or school shooter, she muttered something about "checking the stacks" and then got back to reading her *People* magazine. While she was busy searching the issue for any news about her favorite star, Richard Gere, Daniel posed an innocent question. "Does ITT have . . . you know . . . a school paper?"

Ma said, "Yeah, the kids in Block A put it out weekly. *The Rant*. It sucks. I let my cat pee on the back issues."

"Must be nice to have a cat," he said.

"She came with me. She was my accomplice," said Ma, slapping her knee. "She minds her pees and cues. Get it?"

Nodding as if he didn't only get it, but loved it, Daniel forced a laugh. Praying hard, I asked her the next question that would decide our future, "I'd love to know more about the place. Do you scan the school papers into some computer file, so there's a record? You know, for the archives?"

At first, Ma just ignored me while I held my breath. Then I saw it. Movement. Ma nodded and blew her nose into some brown-looking rag. "Love to scan stuff. It's fun," she said. "I scan that rotten school paper, recipes, pictures of Russell Crowe looking hot like he did in that movie where he played a mental patient."

She didn't mind when I jumped on one of the three other computers in the room and began searching those newspaper archives. As long as she didn't have to expend the energy, Ma would probably let you dance naked on one of those computers.

It turns out Ma was a woman of detail, which is probably how she figured out how to pop bank safes. Each issue of that newspaper for the last fifteen years was scanned into several computer files including the fateful week of June 10, 2011. That was when a certain roamer named A.E. was shipped directly from the Academy into the maximum-security prison's Cellblock D for his attempts at traveling between the living and death realms.

I scanned quickly in case Ken returned to fetch us. My entire system was on high alert, hoping that one of the days wasn't deleted. But Ma was good. In fact, she was great. She got the whole week in—and somehow, higher-up ITT authority figures forgot to ask her to remove the offending material.

I found the ad tucked between a classified from one of the

guards selling a vintage Chevy and another ad from someone looking for a chess partner in Cellblock A. It was only a few lines, but the impact was staggering.

Wanted: Volunteers to go back to life with me. This is not a joke. Number 17, Cellblock D. Find a way to come talk to me. When we go back, you must bring your own ancient weapons. Guns don't work. Your safety is at best questionable. You'll be paid if we get back. PS: I have only done this once before. PPS: They will never stop me. I will do it again and again and again.

2.

It was 2:45 p.m. when an annoyed, preoccupied Ken walked us back to Cellblock D. The guards recognized him immediately, nodded, and lifted the gates. It was as if we had an all-access pass to the loonies in their cages as it was clear Ken wanted to just dump us up here, and retrieve us later before he called it a day. Quickly, we passed through the main entry door on our way to the last row of cells where Jackie Silver was still waiting with his nonanswers. Ken dropped us in our adjoining cell, and I made a mental note of the code he punched on his way out: 97712. He punched it slowly like he could barely remember it. Mom used to say I had a photographic mind—and she was right. This was a piece of cake.

And then we were alone . . . just the three of us.

We didn't care about Jackie, who was just a ruse for us. With no intention of talking to him again, Daniel and I kept our eye on the prize. When the coast seemed clear, we looked as far down the hallway as possible and nothing. Slowly, I stood up, praying that I wasn't being watched on an overhead camera. I punched in the code and our door opened.

Suddenly, it was just the two of us, walking the dank hallway of D Block.

It was easy to count the cells down. We passed a screwball who thought he was Spider-man and was hanging upside down from his bed, and a girl spinning in circles by her toilet. Cells flashed by us quickly. We counted 20, 19, 18 . . . and then there was Cell17.

He was waiting inside.

He was . . . a kid?

A.E. was a pimpled-faced young boy sitting on his cot, engrossed in a book. He looked thirteen years old, which was a surprise because we thought our realm traveler would be older and wiser, and maybe seventeen or eighteen. This was just . . . a wide-eyed, zit-faced little prepster.

Pictures of his mom and dad, plus a little sister, lined the walls. A newspaper article from the Bangor Daily News in Maine was also taped to the left wall as close as possible to the electrified field that sealed him inside. It was as if the clipping was his calling card. And the article told his story, which was short and sad. Apparently, he was playing hide-and-go-seek with his little sister. He always hid in the attic, but that evening his sister, Taylor, decided to pull the ultimate trick on him. To trap him, she pulled the attic latch closed on the outside of the door. And then she locked it before going to play. Later, she would sob to her parents that she forgot it was locked.

The article said that his parents thought he was sleeping over at Timmy White's house that night and had already left. That's why they didn't question the fact that A.E. was missing at dinner. At two a.m., a fire broke out in the house. It supposedly started in his father's downstairs workshop, a place A.E. loved to spend time in with his pop. They were a tight-knit family who did almost everything together. His father was an inventor who was always tinkering as he thought up "something really big" while his mother, though she loved her husband dearly, always insisted that someday his "wacky ideas were going to blow up the house."

She wasn't one hundred percent right. The house didn't blow, but a space heater in the workshop room sparked and caused a throw rug to burst into several tiny flames. It wasn't much of a science experiment, as the rest was predictable. The flames licked the ancient wood of the floors, and then began a slow climb up a winding front staircase to the bedrooms upstairs where the family slept. It was Taylor who smelled something funny, and raced out of bed screaming. She burst into her parents' room where she was carried outside by her frantic father and hysterical mother. A.E.'s father told the fireman, "Yes, sir, everyone is out. My son is sleeping at a friend's house."

A moment later, Taylor looked up in horrifying slow motion as she saw A.E.'s face in the attic widow, his fists pounding on the hot glass. His face was contorted in a scream, and his mother fainted when she saw the tall flames leap from behind and engulf him. It was way beyond too late.

The newspaper article concluded with a quote from A.E.'s father saying, "My son was a kind and brilliant young man. It was a dreadful accident and we miss him desperately. He was only fourteen. I know my boy wanted to help me invent the next big thing. We were going to save the world."

It was no wonder A.E. tried to get back to his family. I figured that it wasn't so much to save the world, but that he missed them all terribly and was a kid who just wanted to go home. He looked so sad and alone in his glass jail cell, which did contain several books. I could see that he was reading about the Civil War.

At first, I stood there reading his article and he didn't look up, although I knew he saw me. Maybe he gave new people a few minutes to get acquainted with him. When he finally glanced my way and popped off the bed like a bouncing ball, Daniel and I were just standing there staring at him, not unlike his sister did on that horrible night. Again, he was trapped. Turning on his intercom, we heard him speak in a way that was crystal clear and with a child's nasal New England twang.

"Really! Really!" he said in an excited voice. "I never get people. Who are you? Are you for real or am I dreamin'?"

"Listen kid, we're not exactly visitors," Daniel said. "We're seekers of information."

"I'm Walker. Very nice to meet you. We read your ad," I interrupted him. *This was a boy, and we needed to win him over. The only thing we had to offer him was friendship and new faces.*

"We need to go back, too," Daniel said, cutting right to the proverbial chase and I winced. "By the way, I'm Daniel. Sorry, but we don't really have time to chat. We don't know how long we have to talk to you." I could see him scanning the long, dark hallway for guards. In the distance, I heard the sickening sound of metal clanking, which could mean anything.

A.E.'s face had a dusting of freckles across his nose. He wore his thin blonde hair in long bangs and his entire body weighed no more than ninety pounds. His big blue eyes suddenly filled with tears.

"They took away my books—at least the ones that mattered like the science and math books. Left me with history books, which at least is something. But they can't take away my dreams. I go back all the time in my dreams to my real house. I miss my mom. Her name is Pauline."

Leaning close to the intercom, I said in a low voice, "My mom is Madeleine. I miss her, too. I miss the smell of her perfume and the way she would crinkle her nose at me when I said something weird."

"My dad, you know what he does?" A.E. countered in an excited voice. "He invents stuff, and when he has a really good

297

idea, his entire face turns bright red 'cause he's so excited."

"Callaghan, you're killing me," Daniel whispered.

"Is he your boyfriend? He's really big," A.E. muttered. "But I'm probably smarter. And way less rude."

"You know what? I want to talk longer with you about your mom and dad—and who is smarter," I said, gently. "But right now, we really need your help. Daniel's brother is stuck. He's only six years old and he's stuck at a plane crash site. All alone. In the snow and the cold. We need to go back and get him because he doesn't have a mom or dad there. He's all by himself. Can you imagine?" I pleaded. "We need your help."

Biting his bottom lip like he wasn't sure, A.E. considered it and then shrugged.

"Please, help us," I begged, trying to push the hysteria out of my voice. It was only a matter of minutes before they found us.

"Well, why would I do that – help, I mean? I don't even know you. You're strangers," he said in a little boy's voice. "I don't really talk to strangers. My mom said if you're not family or friends then you're strangers."

"Please," Daniel pleaded, "if you feel alone being here imagine being only six years old and trapped somewhere alone. In-between. All by yourself. Or with strangers."

A.E. considered it. His eyes filled this time.

He provided his only disclaimer. "Those weren't just tears. They were brave tears. I'm good at brave tears. It's okay to cry them because if you're being brave, you're allowed just four brave tears. That's what my mom says."

"Your mom is a smart lady," I said.

Daniel moved closer and tried to reason with him. "Bobby, my little brother, was a lot like you. Brave. Daring. He had scabbed knees all the time and liked to play catch. He would pretend his bike was a pony. And he loved to watch the Bob."

"SpongeBob," A.E. said, brightening. "Wow, I loved that sponge. They don't have the Bob here. They have old DVDs, but they make us watch bad stuff that you know you're gonna hate like sitcoms with the stars of *Friends* after *Friends* was over."

"Torture," I said.

He paused and then lifted his eyes to ask, "Why are you dead? Drugs? Car crash? Acting like an imbecile? My mama would say, 'A.E., don't be an imbecile.' I'd say, 'Mama, that's not really possible because I have a genius IQ.' I do, you know. Have a genius IQ. We did tests."

Daniel answered him in a low voice. "I died because my dad thought he could be a pilot and he didn't have a genius IQ. Crashed us right into the middle of a field."

A.E. seemed unmoved by that bit of information and then his face lit up as if the most brilliant idea had just crossed his mind. He posed, switching subjects again, "So, I was thinking. If I even talk to you—a big if—then what do I get?"

How could we make a kid in D Block happy?

"Well," I said. "You could just be happy that you helped a little boy. And us. We'd be grateful and you could sleep well tonight knowing you helped a lost little kid find his family."

"I never sleep well in here," he said, shivering hard despite the fact that it wasn't that cold.

I couldn't help but see that A.E. looked frightened now. Then he was quiet for an excruciatingly long minute. This was followed by the terms of his deal with us.

"You'll be lucky to get back whole and you won't have time to buy me any Legos, which is all I would really want. I'd also like a few comic books, but they won't allow me Spider-man in here. Some shrink says it too stimulating. Might give my highly scientific mind ideas," he said with crooked grin.

I knew our time was ticking away, and I couldn't admit to

Daniel that I wanted to break this kid out, give him a good hot meal, hide him from the powers here, and then ask him a million questions. A sad-sick feeling consumed me. He was only fourteen. I did the math in my head, which I had always been good at doing. He lived for only 168 months. That was it. Could he be accountable for eternity for his actions? Wasn't it possible to find leniency on your first offence?

There wasn't time for any real answers.

"We'll do anything if you help us. What do you want? " I implored.

"Anything?" he shouted, putting his index finger to his brain as if he was deep in thought. "Tick tack, no take backs?"

He actually thought about it for another painful minute, where my heart raced and I kept an eye peeled for the guards who would surely notice we were not at our post. For some reason, luck was on our side for once as the guards seemed to be preoccupied with something else down by Cell 1.

"I want a report. A written report," A.E. finally said in a brisk voice, sounding like an English teacher handing out an assignment. "Honest bones, I don't even know if it's even possible to stay there longer than just a few minutes. I only lasted back there about forty-five minutes before . . . well, before 'They' came to get me and I was booted, but still intact."

"Who came to get you? Who is 'They?'" Daniel asked in a rushed voice, while keeping one eye down the hall.

A.E.'s eyes became glazed like he was slipping into a trance. "Oh, it's easy enough to get back. Stupid easy," he said. "But that's when 'They' start tracking you. They can sense your presence and it doesn't take long before they're actually upon you. . . because they know everything about you. They will hunt you."

"They?" I repeated.

"I don't like to use the other d-word," A.E. said. Then he

whispered loudly, "Demons. Don't make me remember."

Demons. They will hunt you.

"That's why you need old-school weapons. For some reason, bullets do nothing. But knives and fire work." He added in a creepy singsong voice, "Sticks and stones will break their bones, but an Uzi will never hurt them." With that he doubled over in convulsive laughter.

"Why don't guns work? Make me understand - quickly," I implored.

"'Cause, in the end, it won't be about nukes and missiles and guns. It will be a primitive fight," he said, sounding suddenly scholarly and much older than his years. "A primitive fight requires primitive weapons like fists and sticks and stones."

Standing there, I forced myself to memorize every single word this strange boy was saying to me.

"Like I said, the weapons should be ancient ones. The older the better. Primitive ones are the best. And if you're not good at fighting, you must run like you have never run before, and when you just can't run anymore because your breath is gone, you must find a way to . . ." His voice trailed off and his finger quickly pointed to the ceiling.

Without warning, a red light began to flash above us in the forward corridor. I knew it was some kind of alarm system and we were the ones tripping it. By now, I also knew in my heart that we had been spotted on some monitor and we'd be lucky to have a minute left with this wacko kid before they came to haul us away.

"Find a way to do what?" I demanded in a breathless voice.

"Find a way to kill them. Kill them all!" he said, all traces of little boy gone, and suddenly sounding like he had the vocal timber of a much older man.

"A.E., here's what's in it for you: You love to read. I will write a long report. I was a reporter for the *Charger* newspaper in Chicago.

I love to write. It will be full of details. I'll leave absolutely nothing out and you have my word. You have my sacred promise," I assured him.

"Neat with no bad spelling," he said so slowly that I wanted to rip the words out of his throat with my bare hands. His little-boy voice was back now.

"Typed and double spaced. I swear," I pleaded. "Please tell us how to start. Where is the portal or the wormhole or whatever the hell it's called? We don't have much time left."

That's when I heard the hideous sound of metal sliding nearby and knew the guards had made it through the first barrier gate. We only had seconds left, and would probably never see this crazy genius again.

"You don't have to type it. Just use neat penmanship. You do write neatly, don't you?" A.E. asked. "And I do want all the details— if you make it. Oh, don't make any spelling mistakes. I hate bad spelling. It's just plain rude."

"All details. No misspelling. For heaven's sake, we'll probably be sharing a cell next to you after we try it, so we can also talk about it for all eternity," I ranted, moving my face closer to the thick, glass barrier so he could see the desperation in my eyes. "How do we start?" I begged, as Daniel grasped my shoulder. When I turned my head, I could see five guards in uniform with clubs at their sides starting a fast-clipped run toward us. A.E. saw them, too, but his face remained youthful and expressionless. He did have all the time in the world.

Slowly, he craned his neck slightly closer to the barrier and whispered, "Here's how you do it. The portal is here. It's at ITT, of course. Just go to the scariest place at *this* school. Go to a place where no kid ever goes. I mean, no kid EVER goes there. In fact, a place that will make you puke, puke, puke."

"The nurse's office?" I implored.

"No way!" he said with glee.

302

As the guards began to march toward us with clubs drawn, A.E. added, "Hey! One more thing you need to know. There's a gate guard at the portal. A real-life monster. He killed a lot of kids and buried 'em in his basement. They put him here to repent. But there's not enough time in the universe to repent. Not for what he did."

"Some of the boys and a few girls were never found," he continued, his eyes trancelike now. "They put him in charge of the portal to scare us shitless. The portal is now his to hide because no one would dare try to scrape past him. He smells kids. Smells them coming. Like a starving dog smells fresh meat."

"Where is the portal?" I whispered so curtly that my voice broke and it came out like a sick pant.

"It's a place where no kid ever goes at any school filled with things no kid ever uses." He paused before speaking again. "One more thing: Once inside, if you make it that far, just remember that old song and turn, turn, turn."

"Won't you just tell us?" I begged. Then I knew I needed to say three words that could determine if we ever got back. "What old song?"

I was never someone who was into the oldies, but instantly I recognized this tune.

"My mom used to love that song. You know," A.E. said and then he began to sing in the high-pitched voice of a prepubescent boy, "To everything—turn, turn, turn. There is a season—turn, turn, turn. And a time to every purpose under heaven."

I didn't get a chance to ask him again what he meant. A guard spun me around hard and smashed my body headfirst into the rocky wall opposite the cells. Another raised his club to Daniel, hit him hard in the head, and then cuffed him before cuffing me. "Don't hurt her!" Daniel yelled, struggling now. "She had nothing to do with this!"

"We'll see what our warden thinks about all these shenanigans," said the tallest guard in the group.

As we walked away, I could hear the faint voice of A.E. still singing with his boyish rasp, "A time to be born, a time to die. A time to plant, a time to reap. A time to kill, a time to heal. A time to laugh, a time to weep."

3.

The road to the GFs office wasn't paved with good intentions. It was filled with narrow corridors, which led to several pit stops as we waited for normal prison activities to commence. Quickly, we were shoved into that cargo elevator where a guard punched buttons leading to the administrative floor. Once out of the elevator, we found that the hallways on this floor were crowded with guards and their charges. Even though Daniel tried his best to slip his hands out of his cuffs, it was pointless since we picked up an entourage of three additional guards on our trek and they flanked him like a solid wall of authority.

"Don't want you kids goin' missing unless we're told to lose you," one burly type hissed at me, tightening his grip on the fleshy part of my upper arm. It didn't hurt because of the reset, but the pressure of it made me believe that he was tearing into my flesh. And the nearness of his pockmarked face made me sick to my stomach.

"Heads up! Stop 'em here, Doug," the lead guard spit out.

I wasn't sure why we were pausing as they led us down another dank hallway, but soon it became evident.

The delay this time was a group of six kids with giant "As"

on their chests, signifying that they were in A Block. They were about twenty feet in front of us in what looked like a fire-drill line from elementary school. None of the inmates were talking; most were just staring straight ahead like zombies. In fact, they were the walking dead.

"Just keep walking. Keep walking. One foot in front of the other," their guard shouted at them although he was gawking at us. I could see that he was leading his little prison campers to an all-purpose glass-walled room at the end of the hallway.

In a strange way, it was fascinating to watch them go through their paces and I wondered where their little field trip would end up. What was in this large glass room? When I looked harder, I could see that their destination looked like a school cafeteria complete with several industrial-sized tables. "It ain't a food court," said my guard. When my eyes focused on the far wall, I could see a sign that read: Visitation.

From watching a million movies, I knew that this was their little meeting room with the outside world, obviously a benefit given to A Blockers, which still begged the question: Exactly who visited dead, incarcerated teenagers?

The answer wasn't obvious although I saw older, shadowy figures waiting on what looked like long glass benches. Some stood and paced. A few were smoking and the plumes of smoke even stunk up where we were standing. My eyes were transfixed on one of the teens already in the room with a visitor today. It was none other than C Blocker Eddie Wargo. It made sense since Bertha had told us that he was granted the perks of prison life.

Somehow Eddie compressed his belly fat enough to sit on the metal bench attached to one of the long tables. On the other side facing him was a man who was extremely tall in stature even when he was sitting down. I figured he was about six foot four with close-cropped, greasy-looking black hair and a bone-thin frame leading up to a face devoid of cheeks. His mug was all bone and sunken hollows. When the man stood up to tower over Eddie, I could see he had hands that looked like old, worn gloves. The way his mouth was moving, extra fast, I knew that he was yelling, although I couldn't hear a thing. The other Wargo brothers were nowhere in sight.

The guards shoved us into motion and we made it most of the way down the hallway before we were forced to wait again, right outside the visitation room, for a different group of A Blockers to be led inside. When I was jostled close to the glass and stared harder inside, I watched transfixed as the thin man took one bony hand and slapped Eddie hard across the face. ITT's favorite hockey player looked like his big melon head would roll off his head, but quickly he righted his face again. The man took that as a sign to slap him again—and much harder. A trickle of blood ran from Eddie's top lip, slid over his teeth, and stopped mid-chin.

Maybe it was pride or this routine was a common one. Eddie didn't make a move to mop up the blood with his hand, and there were no tissues or napkins. He just stood there dripping and I could almost feel sorry for him. Almost.

"Whadda you looking at?" the guard asked me, shoving me with all his might until my head actually bounced off the glass front of the visitation cell.

Eddie looked up. And so did the thin man.

It was the older man who slowly, step-by-step, approached the glass and began to stare at me as if we knew each other. Upon closer view, I noted that his eyes were almost black and his face was so long that it looked garish. My guard was preoccupied now with his walkie-talkie, but firmly held me in place with my face just centimeters from the thin man, separated only by glass. I jumped when he tapped the glass with his gnarled, long finger. He tapped low. For a moment, I thought he was a perv because he picked a spot on my chest, but then it dawned on me. I had my name tag on. Obviously, this was yet another person questioning why I had a strange first name. Why did he care? In that split second, I stared up into his dead eyes.

As we walked away, I couldn't help but glance back for a second.

I wasn't much of a lip reader and I could no longer feel cold, but it chilled me to the bone when the thin man clearly mouthed my name.

4.

The Godfather or GF, had just finished a late lunch and was smoking a cigar in his office when the guards threw us roughly into the front of his massive wooden desk. We landed with two loud thuds that confirmed he had a special delivery. Since my hands were still cuffed behind my back, I couldn't help but fly onto the hard oaken desktop, my face stopping inches from the amber glow of his ashes.

For a moment, he seemed amused in a sick sort of way. When one of the guards grabbed Daniel and smashed his face into the wall, the GF held up one of his meaty hands with bloody cuticles on it. "Please, you'll ruin my artwork," he said in a slow, Southern drawl, as a poorly hung oil painting rumbled on the wall.

"Just how I wanted to start my week—with company," he said, putting up his other chubby fingers to stop his guard from inflicting more damage. Then he rolled his sagging desk chair back and rearranged the massive fat roll around his stomach, so it hung over his beige polyester pants. He did this in order to stand up.

There was a lot to him.

He wasn't a tall man at six feet, but he was extra wide, and it made him seem imposing, like a brick wall that could fit around a city block. Then there was that dome, a head that was extra large like the biggest watermelon at the state fair. It was also shining and completely bald. His eyes were movie-star blue and bright, although not big enough for that face. There were nasty sweat stains under the armpits of his white work shirt and he smelled like a combination of old body odor and barbecue sauce. I could see that his hands were wide like catchers' mitts while his knuckles were freshly bloody from some sort of altercation.

"Can't send 'em back bruised and battered, although I guess we could try. But they don't bruise, damn it all to hell, and I mean all the way to hell," GF said to his lead guard. When he spoke, a tiny wheezing sound punctuated his words. "Still, old Doctor King wouldn't be amused, especially after one of their little classmates lost his head here, so to speak. Doctor King keeps harping on what happened to this Simon kid, where did we last see him, and all sorts of other annoying questions."

He also spoke in a slow, eerily pleasant way, punctuated with a loud boom when he wanted to make a point.

"Sit down?" he boomed as if we had a choice. On knees that were quaking, somehow I found the will to place myself into a hard wooden chair that was in the middle of the room.

GF paced by one of his large windows that overlooked the entire valley because, of course, he had a beautiful view. Perhaps it reminded him of what he was keeping his inmates from destroying.

"Now, let me ask you lovely joy suckers a question. Don't you think I have enough to do here, kids? Rapists. Murderers. Gangbangers. Now I have two little assholes running around this place like you're freaking Walter Cronkites trying to interview as many crazy kids as possible and stir up some news. Isn't that what this is really about? Some school project for journalism? I know you, little missy, are a reporter type. Looked you up in the file I grabbed when I visited the Higher Authority. You know about them, don't you? Anyway, you were editor of your school paper before you kicked the bucket. Boo hootie hoo. Sorry, but we don't do sensitive here," he sneered.

And he wasn't finished. "Kudos to your old lady for surviving it. What a bitch. The situation—not your mother. Excuse me for any rudeness, Miss Callaghan. But your poor ma is now home alone and tormented by the idea that she shut the lights out on her only kid. Ah, tragedy, you gotta embrace it," he said with a laugh.

It was hate at first sight when it came to this man.

"Did Walter Cronkite, the old coot, actually put you up to this? Is he at your school lecturing?" GF said. "Walter always loved a free vacation away from his wife. Puts the good kids up to all sorts of mischief in the name of journalism education."

I didn't say a word, which was probably lucky.

The GF lumbered over to me. I had righted myself and turned to face Daniel who was obscured by the man's girth. "Insolent teenagers. You're the worst species on earth. But now, here you are. Interrupting my day. Don't I have enough on my plate?!" He screamed the last line into my face in a tone that made the water glass on his desk start to rumble. For a split second, I thought that this was a man who could actually cause earthquakes.

Daniel lurched forward, but he was quickly checked when the GF smashed his forearm into the younger man's Adam's apple. I could hear Daniel chocking for a second, and then the reset kicked in.

I wanted to run to Daniel, but I didn't.

I knew I would never make even a few steps.

I also knew that I couldn't appear afraid.

All I could do was look at the GF's empty lunch plate, which was mostly covered in the cleaned bones from a meal that was once-upon-a-time-ago baby back ribs. "Sir, you have nothing on your plate," I said. "Lunch must have been very good."

The GF almost laughed, ignoring Daniel now to tower over me. "Oh, you have guts," he said. "But I don't really like guts too much, so don't be too pleased with yourself. And I hate girls with guts because I hate girls in general."

I winced.

"Let me explain something to you before I lose my temper," GF said, the smile completely wiped off his fleshy face that was covered in afternoon shadow. "No one said you could just roam around here and interview every psycho under my roof. You can't stroll around D Block like you're at a church picnic making new friends. You might get yourselves very hurt. In fact, I only allowed this today to prove to Doctor King that the two of you would return in one piece, which is still debatable at this moment."

I could feel Daniel seething next to me as the GF continued in his pronounced Southern twang.

"Now, I believe you have done enough damage here for today," he said. "I agreed to three visits over one week. You lost one visit thanks to your antics with that little dirtbag A.E. I will allow only one more visit, so plan on wrapping it up Friday, which is in three days. And it's also just a day before Christmas Eve, so you can bring me a nice present. Or little missy can cook me a goose. After Friday, you can go back to that kiss-ass school of yours with happy little smiles. If I ever hear about a news report or article in your school paper about anything else regarding ITT, I will personally visit you there late at night where things might get somewhat . . . uncomfortable."

And then he added in a low whisper, "You can't die again. You can't feel pain. But you can disappear here. I'm good at magic tricks where kids are suddenly gone—*poof!*—like a rabbit who never gets

310

pulled out of that hat because they've sunk down into the Hole."

He wasn't done. Not by a long shot.

"We won't tell your Doctor King how you might have made an error in judgment today. Old A.E. is a trip. Jackie is a cold-blooded killer and dangerous," he continued. "The less that self-righteous bastard Doctor King knows about what happened here today the better."

Walking slowly over to his bookshelf, he grabbed what looked like the Bible and for a minute I thought he would start to quote verse. "Heed this warning," he yelled like some demented preacher. Instead of praying for us, he took the book and slammed Daniel as hard as possible in the face with it. I felt it down to my toes, but had no recourse. Of course, after he stood up again, the only pain Daniel felt was humiliation combined with rage. He looked like he wanted to rip this fat bastard in two with his bare hands.

"By the way, that was for the hockey loss," he said. "I hate to lose a good sports competition, especially to my enemy, your Doctor King."

"But back to today's activities," he continued. "This place isn't a playground. It's not a resort." At that point, he pulled out an actual map and drew a red circle over the interview room in Cellblock D. "Anywhere else but here is off limits. You don't move from that cell. If you have to take a piss, take a piss in your pants for all I care. You could get very lost in here—as in forever," he reminded us. "Do you understand?"

Before we could answer, he pushed a red button. "In fact, I'm going to have my favorite intern personally escort you and guard you on Friday. In other words, he will be sticking to you like glue on a rat's ass."

A back door opened slowly and Eddie Wargo himself sauntered in. I could see that his right cheek was still burning red from where the man had slapped him, but Eddie didn't seem to dwell on his pain. Instead, he looked shocked to see us standing there and his eyes darted from me to Daniel. When he focused back on me, I swear I saw a look that I could only describe as remorse float across his meaty mug, followed by the glistening in his eyes of what appeared to be an actual tear forming. Maybe he was still hurting from the slap. Maybe he was embarrassed about what I saw in the visitation room.

"Edward, how nice of you to join us. I assume your visit with your father was a pleasant one," goaded the GF. "Go fetch me the TV remote. I left it on the conference table. And put this file back on my desk."

He handed him my file.

That was Eddie's father! Why was he here?

"Yes, boss," Eddie said. "Thank you much for my visit. Daddy set me straight on some things."

One thing about Eddie: Battered and bruised, he still knew how to serve his master and walked the three paces that the GF refused to walk in order to fetch the remote control and toss the file onto a file cabinet. Just like a trained poodle, he was back in a quick second and handing what he retrieved to the one in charge.

"You be nice to my boy. My poor boy Eddie recently suffered a terrible loss, if you could call the demise of his daddy, Frank, a terrible loss," the GF announced.

"He kicked the can a few months ago," Eddie muttered and, without asking, handed the GF a cold Coke from the minifridge.

"Keep up this kind of service, boy, and I'll let you watch the Super Bowl this year with your daddy," the GF complimented Eddie who kept his head hung low until the GF slapped him hard on the shoulder. It was strange that they seemed to enjoy a more fatherly relationship than Eddie and his newly departed next of kin.

Emboldened with the support of his mentor, Eddie became

the regular Eddie again and began to let his eyes do a slow walk from my head to my toes. I could see what he was doing, and as my face flamed red, I noticed that he stopped somewhere in the middle and hung his head low again.

"If Miss Callaghan takes matters into her own hands in here again, I'll give her to you. Like a pet," chuckled the GF.

Shifting his gaze, the GF locked eyes with Daniel and this time he didn't look away.

"Not an idle threat, son," the GF promised. "Not a someday promise. There are seven days in a week and someday isn't one of them. If you screw around, these little threats will take place on Friday."

His attention was now directed at his own.

"Edward, I have two guests who need protection for a visit on Friday and I know you're the man for it," GF said. "Write it down on your 'To Do' list."

"Boss, you've got to be shitting me," Eddie said, his gaze shifting between the two of us.

"Edward, this language is not the way to make our guests feel safe and welcome at ITT," GF said.

"I mean, sir, you've got to be shitting me," Eddie replied, in his unique attempt at having actual manners.

"Your first assignment: Uncuff them," GF barked.

CHAPTER 22

1.

That night for dinner, it was another Reid family special of burgers, fries, and chocolate shakes, which thrilled the kids. Peter was the great mood booster and I laughed when he grabbed a handful of fries off my plate despite the cease-and-desist look on his big brother's face.

"Hey," Peter said to Daniel as Coldplay wept on the stereo behind us. "I can steal her fries. She's one of us now, you dork."

Jenna looked at me adoringly, her big blue eyes swimming with happiness, as she told us about her latest boy crush.

Andy brought out a six-pack of Orange Crush. It was a family dinner. Simple as that. Daniel grabbed a beer and took a swig. He liked the taste of it.

When he wasn't looking, I took a sip. Peter tried, but Daniel slugged him in the arm. Peter was only fifteen and it was the equivalent of him being carded.

"Shitballs!" Peter exploded and then was told to watch his big mouth.

Something funny caught in my throat. *What if we never made it back to them? What would become of these kids? Who would take care of them if we couldn't come back? Ever?* I glanced at Daniel whose face was melancholy and grim. It's one thing to make a plan, but quite another to execute it. What I saw on his face was a mix of adrenalin, worry, and excitement because we were getting close.

When the kids wandered off to do their own thing, we moved to the den and spread out the map conveniently given to us by the head honcho of Hell Pit. Daniel was sitting on the couch and I had my head in his lap while the map was spread out on my stomach. My flannel shirt flapped open and the white tank top I wore underneath wasn't much. I was trying to keep our minds on business, which wasn't easy. "The portal," I reminded him, trying to refocus, though not really wanting to, as his hand brushed along my side. Accidentally, I thought.

"A.E. told us the portal was a place that was scary, but no kid ever went there. We have to pay attention to his exact wording," I said.

In jeans and a white cable-knit sweater, that made his shoulders look even broader and his dark features stand out like there was a spotlight was on them, I looked up from my spot and could see Daniel gazing down at me with, dare I even think, admiration? My mind was racing and it wasn't all that sugar in the Orange Crush.

Gently, he took my finger and placed it on the administration level. "Okay, let's narrow it down. What's a place that no kid goes at ITT? GF's office? That was a party and a half in there. Teacher's lounge for a smoke?" he posed and then answered his own questions. "But we know there are students in GF's office. I bet they wander into the teacher's lounge, too."

"Let's think outside the box here," I said. "What about the

315

boiler room? It would be a scary place that's dark and steamy. No kid goes there."

But the problem with that idea was that there were several boiler rooms at ITT and it would be impossible to go through each one trying to find a secret portal. Maybe we could explore one or two before we'd be caught, but we didn't have time to conduct an endless investigation of all the nooks and crannies in the school's basement levels.

"I have a hunch that the portal is in D Block," Daniel said. "The place has the most security so there is no chance any of those inmates could break out and go looking for it there—and no one could get into D Block without permission."

"How awful for A.E. I bet that portal is only a few hundred feet away from him. His ticket home is so near, but so far. . . . Okay, let's rule out places in D Block," I insisted. "There's the guard's workroom, but I don't think that's it. No big fear factor there. There is no public bathroom."

There was a small chapel on each block, which seemed like a strange place for a portal, plus kids could ask to go there to atone for their past sins, which might even be encouraged depending on the sin.

"A chapel isn't scary," I said, pointing to it on the map. "It's comforting. Even if you were locked in this hellhole for eternity, it would be the one place you could find a little solace."

Daniel lifted his finger, and in that moment the world went quiet for me. Just like any nagging question, the answer was so obvious that it almost called out to us, daring us and tempting us to look in its direction.

This spot was definitely a place at any school where no kid ever ventures into filled with what A.E. called "things kids never use." Suddenly, I didn't care if the school was in New York City or the depths of Alaska.

"The jan—" I began.

"The janitor's closet," Daniel interrupted, reading my mind again. "It's a place where no kid ever goes filled with things no kid ever uses—or would want to use. What kid ever touched a cleaning supply at school?"

"Bingo," I said in a giddy voice, putting a big red X on the spot. For some reason I felt light-headed for a second, which I knew was a sign that we had figured it out. What didn't make sense was his second comment about how once inside you must *turn, turn, turn.* We would worry about that once we were there.

"But who is the gate guard in a stupid janitor's closet?" Daniel questioned.

"A.E. said that the portal was guarded by someone who smelled kids coming," I reminded him. "He was a killer of kids back in the living realm."

"I don't think we're going to know it all—until we really know," Daniel answered ominously.

CHAPTER 23

1.

B ack at school the next morning, we had a mission to complete and it had to be done today. We would, of course, have to be stealth about it. Normalcy was key.

I even stopped to talk to Tosh who was sitting on one of the front stoops at the Academy admiring how the sunflowers had blossomed into bursts of vibrant yellow the size of dinner plates. She invited me to see her room before our first class. I couldn't focus during her tour, although I noted how plush and comfortable the dorms were if you could figure out the twisting maze of narrow hallways that led to the sleeping quarters. It was a good thing I lived off campus or I'd be wandering these hallways for hours each day.

Each dorm room came with lavish white comforters that looked like big puffy clouds hovering slightly above each bed. There was an abundance of antique chests and dressers, plus famous oil paintings on the walls, and exquisite plush rugs on the shiny mahogany floors.

I noted that some kids were in common areas watching MTV, laughing at those stupid baby-mama dramas and playing Wii with gusto, while others were listening to Eddie Vedder on the radio. I was never sure where the broadcast was coming from, and I didn't ask. Maybe these DJs were intergalactic.

Daniel spent the morning with our teacher Steve on his personal souped-up computer, which wasn't restricted the way our laptops were at home. Steve's computer was an all-access pass to just about anything you ever wanted to know about anything you were curious about in that moment.

Again, Steve didn't ask too many questions, but actually encouraged us to do whatever harebrained thing we were working on. "As I always like to say," he said, "take chances. Be a little bit crazy, but use your seat belt."

"How long should you wait to take big chances?" Daniel asked him.

"Don't wait," Steve said wistfully. "Right now is the oldest you've ever been and the youngest you'll ever be again. So what are you waiting for . . . an invitation?"

Bolstered by his words, Daniel began looking up what we needed in order to go back because A.E. had also warned us to bring weapons, but not just any kind. They had to be ancient ones. For some reason, Daniel's pocketknife wasn't going to cover it.

Of course, Steve blocked a mechanism where Daniel could make contact with other realms because he knew it might prove too tempting to send some rather interesting emails. When Steve went to lunch, he left Daniel alone in there, which spoke volumes about the trust between the two of them.

It turns out that Daniel wasn't the only one wanting to jump on Steve's desktop.

319

A man walked in with a full head of light brown hair and a warm smile. Daniel glanced down at the monogrammed leather day planner he was carrying; it was tattered and the middle initial was worn off. You could only see the first and third initials: JK.

"Son, do you think you'll be much longer," asked the handsome man who had A.E.'s type of New England twang.

"No, Mr. President. I'm almost finished," Daniel replied. "But I can jump off now and come back later." He stood up immediately and started to push away from the desk.

"No, I see that old Steve has a rocking chair over there. I'll just relax for a few minutes until you're done," he said. "I do love a good rocking chair."

While the man sat humming and rocking a few feet away from him, Daniel sat back down and thought about it for a moment. Later, he would tell me that the pull was strong to never leave this place of wonder, but duty still called to him. So he typed in the key phrase he needed and the exact website he wanted popped right up: Extreme Badass Ancient Weapons.

Let's just say it didn't disappoint because the word badass didn't even begin to cover it.

2.

During a midmorning huddle in our school library where we were pretending to start our criminology paper, Daniel explained a few of the choices to me like we were ordering pizza toppings. "We could order up one of these babies called a culverin, which is a medieval cannon. I guess that's too complicated to get or make today," he said in a low, sexy voice, which wasn't really necessary because his chair was half an inch away from mine. Not that I was complaining.

"Make?" I repeated. "What are we? An ammunitions plant?"

"Callaghan," he said. "We're going to have a sudden interest in shop class because we have to make weapons in the next *two* days. We can't just pop into Al's Hardware and say, 'Got any ancient weapons in the back? We need to go badass on something or someone, but we don't know exactly who or what.' So, we're stuck making them in shop class. The class where you actually make things out of wood and metal? You can't get more ancient than those two substances."

Looking at a picture he copied of a culverin, I said, "I don't think you and I can melt metal and make an ancient cannon to take with us. Plus, it won't fit in our backpacks. What's next?"

He took out the next picture, which was called a caltrop. It was a weapon made up of two or more sharp nails or spines arranged so one of them always points upward from a stable base like a wood stick. Basically, the thing looked like a large, deadly jack from a game of ball and jacks, but all the points were extremely sharp little knives. "Now, this would come in handy during a mugging in downtown Chicago," I retorted.

His face only breathing-distance away, he gave me his trademark half smile and then moved on. "Ancient people would throw boiling oil at enemies, which is good to know," he said. "We could bring a small canister of oil."

"Easy enough. We could even bring more than three ounces. We aren't going back through any airport, so we don't have to worry about a TSA guy shaking us down," I said, grabbing his paperwork and stifling a chuckle. "A Greek flamethrower? I don't think so. That's not exactly convenient to carry across realms."

"Next," I prompted him to continue.

"Have you ever heard of a Hunga Munga?" Daniel asked.

321

"Yes, I do the Hunga Munga all the time," I answered. "We're going to kill evil spiritual forces by doing some crazy dance?"

"Baby, it's actually a hook-like device with a handle. Think of Captain Hook's hand, but as a weapon. It's easy, small, and powerful," he said. "Every realm traveler should have one and I'm making us a few in shop today."

I read the paperwork and it said that the Munga was an African weapon so powerful that your enemies didn't have a chance. If you dared to throw one at your enemy and actually hit the bull's-eye, it would create a deep, penetrating wound.

"Then we have a morning star," Daniel explained like he was selling this stuff on a late-night infomercial. "This is truly going medieval on someone. It's a club with one or more sharp spikes sticking out of it. You could have big spikes, but we can't pack anything too big in our backpacks, so I'll make us small ones," he said, reading the description to me. "These weapons are most effective when you hit someone on the head with them. The English army in the sixteenth century made them all the time and they were a favorite of King John of Bohemia, who was blind. He would just sit on his horse and swing away until he hit one of the bad guys where it counted."

When he paused, I took a mental inventory and began to make a list for packing. *We would bring a few of these weapons, a change of clothes, and our toothbrushes?*

"Well, I think that's enough to fill two industrial-sized backpacks," I said in a businesslike voice.

"Let's get to shop class and pretend we're into metalwork," Daniel said.

"I do love heavy metal," I said.

As we started to pack up and head for shop class, the ultimate weapon was upon us. Dr. King was doing a slow loop around the library where he was intent on minding everyone else's business.

Daniel didn't flinch or move to sweep up the papers when the good doctor stopped right in front of us. The fact that a page labeled "Badass Ancient Weapons" was on the table in plain sight wasn't lost on us. Surely, it was not lost on our ultracurious school principal.

"Planning to arm yourself for your next visit to ITT?" he said to me in particular. Then Dr. King narrowed his eyes and allowed them to slowly sweep across our entire table. One thing about him is he didn't miss anything. It was like his brain was doing a mental scan of exactly what we were reading, so he could figure out our future motives.

"It's fascinating how people protected themselves during ancient times," I blurted out, hoping he would actually believe that we were just innocently studying the history of weapons. The truth was the only weapon either of us had ever used was a steak knife in the cafeteria.

"Um, you know how it is, Doctor King," I stammered. "Mankind couldn't exist without protecting itself against bad forces." Why I had to use the word forces instead of bad guys was beyond me.

I was sure he could smell my guilt.

"Existence is a funny thing, Miss Callaghan," Dr. King said in a mysterious voice as he towered above us. "Of course, you do know that existence doesn't just depend on defending yourself with weapons. The best weapon we have is our minds. Our existence is based on figuring out a great many things that seem impossible until we put our minds to it. I believe that whatever we can imagine, we can do," he said.

Then he flipped it around.

"Why would we be able to imagine it if we couldn't do it?" he asked.

For a quick second, I thought he knew *exactly* what we were doing. Then I noticed a DVD in his hand and it was one of the classics: *20,000 Leagues Under the Sea.*

"Just think," said Dr. King, noticing my glance. "When they made that film, it didn't seem even remotely possible to visit the ocean floor. And now? It seems quite tame to think about it." He paused a moment to smile. "Pure imagination." Then, like a curtain falling on his angled face, he allowed that smile to instantly fade into a forbidding frown. "However, pure imagination can be dangerous thing. You have to harness that energy and weigh the consequences of what your mind tells you that you can do—and decide if that is what you should do."

"Absolutely, sir," I said, rising up from my chair with Daniel following suit after quickly gathering up our suspicious paperwork.

"Be very careful," Dr. King said, and it wasn't a suggestion. It sounded more like a warning. Then he diverted his attention to Kurt who was passing by our little impromptu meeting.

Dr. King turned his back on our follies. "Excuse me, Cobain," said Dr. King, his focus mercifully off us now. "I was just wondering if you're ever going to wash that hair. You might note that this school does have a hygiene code. This school does not do grunge."

3.

The shop teacher, a guy named Chuck who used to fly planes, was busy smoking a cigarette in a back room. There were absolutely no students in his class, and you got the idea that Chuck liked it that way. "I guess kids don't want to make stuff anymore," he grumbled, sipping coffee out of a giant Thermos cup. "Don't know why the school stocks up the shelves with materials like we're going to build the Taj Mahal in here. Kids just aren't interested in creating structures—maybe because their existence now has such little structure."

"Knock yourselves out and use any of the stuff you want," he said, motioning us to step away from his TV set where he was watching some classic movie channel. "Got *Braveheart* on in ten minutes. If you have an accident with a saw just mop up the blood, put the cut-off limb on ice until it reattaches, and don't bug me about it."

We didn't. Cut off anything important that is.

Of course, I was hopeless when it came to building weapons.

For some reason, Daniel was a natural.

It was easy finding any raw materials or tools we needed in the overstocked shop. My best effort was a clunky, but wicked-looking morning star. It started with a smooth wooden handle I happened upon that fit perfectly in my hands. After that I found a roundish hunk of metal and gathered the longest, thickest nails I could find to weld onto it . . . well, for Daniel to weld onto it. I wasn't in the mood to watch my fingers melt off then coagulate back together over and over and over again.

We spent the rest of that school day and part of the next forging our arsenal. Our collection was crude, but looked effective. In addition to the exotic ancient weapons, we threw in a couple of small axes, a pick, and some stakes. At the end of the second day, when I saw Daniel's stockpile, I couldn't believe that we had enough to go to war—or at least a small battle. I just had one question.

"What are we going back as? Ninjas?" I inquired.

"Exactly," he said with one of those smiles that made his eyes crinkle and my heart do backflips at the sight of his joy.

4.

Daniel might have sounded like he had it all under control, but his nerves had a way of making themselves known. Late that night, back at the house, he was nearly burrowing his way back to life from the hole he was wearing in the carpet from his pacing. This was after he had ditched the kids and spent part of the evening upstairs in a locked bedroom packing two large backpacks for tomorrow, one for each of us. When he was done, he repacked them again.

Tomorrow was December twenty-third. The anniversary of his death.

It begged the question: What exactly do you need for a realm-travel trip? I had ducked my head into the room after he unlocked the door because I knew there were two things I had to put into my backpack—that picture of my mother and me at the farmers' market and my lucky green rabbit's foot. You just never knew when you would need a little extra luck.

I thought about taking Jake, but that was impossible. For some strange reason, it was as if the dog knew something was wrong. While Daniel was doing his postpacking pacing, the hound was at his heels nipping and barking.

At nine p.m., Daniel wrote the note he would leave for the kids. We had already told Bertha and Izayah we were taking off for a few days. I knew that they thought this was a romantic trip. They agreed to babysit, and Daniel told them we would leave them a few instructions that would be waiting for them when they came to the house after school.

"Have fun, you guys," Izayah had said with a wink. If he only knew.

Iz and Bertha would make dinner for the kids tomorrow night and be there when the note was read. It was simple, short, and sweet:

Dear Jenna, Andy, and Peter:
We knew this day would come. And it has. So please don't be sad because you being hopeful is my fuel. Part is not a whole. I'm going off to find the missing part. If I screw it up, please, please don't go looking for us. In the end, we know that distance, no matter how far or even close, doesn't matter. We are all in the Midst. Of what? We don't know. But we're here together. Somewhere.
So, please walk the dog. Check in on Bertha. Go to Izayah if there is trouble. And if anyone asks, you have no idea. You must never ever tell. If the worst happens, wipe away the tears because the time for mourning is long since over. Make it all stand for something. Every. Single. Day. Take your stand.
Eternally your brother, Daniel

I wanted to add something meaningful to the note, but my heart was in my throat. All I could write to them was:

From Walker—Thank you for the love and care -- when I needed it the most. I will never forget. Your friend and sister forever.

At ten p.m., the pacing resumed. I couldn't take it anymore.

327

I knew that keeping busy would take our minds off things, so I took it upon myself to cross one of the more disgusting tasks off our prep list. I pulled a small all-purpose knife from the kitchen drawer. Running it under the hottest water for a minute, I handed it to Daniel and closed my eyes hard when he dug in gently and removed my tracker. Handing me back the knife, I did the same for him, although I think it caused me more pain. He did wince, but only when I kept closing my eyes. "Callaghan, pay attention. Before you remove something important," he said. Once Daniel had safely placed our trackers in his backpack, I knew he'd get back to the relentless pacing.

"Why don't we just go there now? Break into ITT and find the portal while the rest of them are sleeping," I suggested, knowing it was futile.

"What?" he asked.

"Never mind."

Daniel looked confused.

"Why don't we just get out of here," he blurted.

Now it was my turn.

"And go where?" I said. "Hawaii? LA? Australia might be nice at this time of the year."

I was all ears.

"Tonight, we're going to do the one thing we've never done before—at least not together," Daniel said.

"Deep-sea diving?"

"We're going on a date," Daniel said.

"You're serious?" I asked him.

And suddenly I got it. Even with only a few hours left, he was going to make it stand for something. Every. Single. Minute.

CHAPTER 24

1.

Jumping on the back of the Harley, I heard the engine roar to life. Almost instinctually, I put my arms around Daniel's chest and before he hit the gas he grabbed my hand for a quick squeeze. I began shivering, and not because the night was cold. That didn't mean anything to us anymore.

The time frame hit me hard. It was officially that time of year when holiday magic was in the air. With the trip looming, we hadn't done anything in the way of getting ready for Christmas, but as we whizzed past the rows of houses, I could see twinkling red-and-green seasonal lights winking at us as the bright, illuminated evergreens dotting the lawns went by in a blur. On one of the lawns sat three fat plastic reindeer. Rudolph's nose didn't quite work right, but it was the idea that mattered. At several of those identical Craftsman houses, the teenagers inside had lit their fireplaces and the thin evening air took on the delicious smell of natural burning wood mixed with the fresh pines.

In a reckless mood, Daniel didn't even wear his helmet tonight, but let his hair whip around in the blustery wind and I did the same thing. He felt strong and solid when I wrapped my arms even tighter across his wide chest. Feeling bold, I allowed my fingers to wander inside the sheepskin collar of his leather jacket. He had a small speaker attached to the front of the bike and he punched a few arrows to crank one of his favorite tunes.

Tonight

We are young

So, let's set the world on fire

We can burn brighter

Than the sun.

I wondered if we could just stop time right now, remain in the moment, and feel hopeful about the future we didn't really know we had anymore. For some reason, I still felt a sense of giddy anticipation. Why was it that the night before any journey was the best part? There is nothing on the table then except pure adrenalin and anticipation. In my case here and now, it might have been nerves or worry, but I felt light-headed, silly, and excited.

He punched it and we began our breathless race through the twisting, turning, desolate roads that were slick from a thin coating of winter ice. Tiny sparkling snowflakes came alive as if someone had flipped a switch and activated them so they could dance in our headlights. In some strange way, the growling engine was comforting as we rejoiced in the freedom of flying.

After one of the sharper turns, I let go of Daniel and threw both of my bare hands way up into the sky and embraced the wind. With my head tossed all the way back, I let out a loud scream of joy mixed with fear.

This very well could be our last night of existence.

Tonight.

We are young.

2.

I'm not sure when it finally dawned on me that we were helplessly lost. But Daniel didn't seem to mind. In fact, he purposely took a different route that had us ascending up a twisting mountain road with enough hairpin turns that I started to close my eyes every few seconds so I wouldn't watch us plunge over a ledge. When I peeked, I couldn't help but gasp hard as he leaned us slow and low into some dramatic dipping turns that had us hovering so close to the pavement that I could have collected spare rocks. Instead, I had my fingers well under the collar of his leather jacket and found myself gripping the flesh of his chest, which was as hard as rock.

He didn't seem to mind.

There was a certain recklessness in his driving that took us off the main road and eventually spit us out on a dirt path that was nothing more than a wide animal trail. The moment we entered what looked like a forest preserve, my entire body went slack, my grip relaxed, and I let go as my nose filled with the strong, sharp smell of Christmas greenery thanks to the ever-surviving cover of trees. The icy winter air felt wonderful as its frosty chill gently caressed my reddened cheeks.

I could see a night owl sitting high in one of the trees while two of his chocolate-colored deer friends were a little deeper in the woods looking for a little R & R and maybe a bit of dinner. Daniel continued his drive up, up, and up until the trail finally ran out and we lost the road again. Abruptly, he slowed us down and then hit the brakes, jumping off the bike and steadying it until

I could swing my leg off. Then he held out his hand. There was nothing else to do but leave the bike behind and start to hoof it as we climbed even higher toward the night sky.

"We'll have to walk the rest of the way," Daniel said, holding my hand tightly in his own. In a different scenario, this would have been nothing more than a boy on a date walking his girl onto the dance floor. We didn't have music or fancy lighting, but we did have the romance of the unknown.

Clearly, Daniel had a plan in mind as I happily took his hand and walked off the path with him, allowing the trees to engulf us like protective, generous giants.

As we walked through the pungent evergreens I was half tempted to find some tinsel and decorate one of them. The air was still and I watched Daniel's breath forming wispy white clouds that casually lingered and then evaporated into the night.

"Baby, it's just a few more minutes," Daniel promised, and we continued to walk up a small trail that led us straight to the upper reaches of the sky. Little snowflakes fell into my eyes now, which blurred the world for a moment. When they cleared, I could see that the flakes looked like millions of cascading diamonds. In the distance, I could hear a loud rushing noise that put all of nature on mute. On our hands and knees, we climbed and then scampered over several large rocks that took us closer to the highest peak. The moment we got there, I knew. I knew exactly why he had brought me here.

We stood on a small, smooth ledge that looked as if it were made out of polished black glass. When I peered over the ledge, I knew we were at least several hundred feet up in the air on a precipice. In front of us was something far greater than either of us. Millions of gallons of crystal-clear water blasted from a point even higher than we were and rushed in front of us with a force so strong that it almost took my breath away.

In the dark, I could see that inside the white foaming torrent of water were large chunks of broken ice that carried with them almost every color in the rainbow. Sparkling greens, pristine pinks, and vibrant yellows, along with frigid blues, rushed hard and fell fast like they were very late to some pressing appointment.

I knew we weren't here on a sightseeing trip.

"Callaghan," Daniel shouted over the roar of the waterfall. "I've been meaning to do this with you for a long, long time."

"Who knows if we will have another chance," he said. I looked into a face that was so solid, so loving, and so magnetic that I would have followed him anywhere. He just didn't need to know that—at least not yet.

I wasn't going to make it that easy. "What are we chancing now?" I yelled back, already knowing and dreading his answer, but also knowing my own.

"I'm proposing that we jump the Falls," he yelled, putting out his hand again like a man who was about to propose something else to a woman. So what if he couldn't offer marriage and all that "'til death do us part" stuff. He could only offer water, forest, and whatever came between heaven and Earth.

"Seriously?" I yelled.

"Seriously, yes," he said.

No restrictions.

No consequences.

I took a small step back away from the water, careful not to slip off the ledge. Daniel frowned because he thought that was a "no" answer.

"Turn around!" I screamed at Daniel who, with the waterfall to his back, looked as forceful and majestic as the mountain holding us up.

He turned to face the Falls.

No risks.

No returns.

No rules.

Remembering my ten almost-failed lessons at Miss Fern's School of Dance in Chicago, I sashayed back, put my hands on his shoulders, and leapt as gracefully as possible onto his back. Daniel's arms locked around my arms, now implanted into his chest, as he inched toward the edge. Suddenly, I wasn't afraid. Feeling a hard spray of water in my face, I whispered, "Forever."

Daniel couldn't hear one word I was saying. I was sure of that much. The water was blasting past us and the roar was like a fever consuming us both.

"For us!" Daniel yelled and then counted it down. "One, two, thr . . ." And then we fell forward into the rush.

3.

We were falling and tumbling, together and entwined—and then alone, but not lonely. I wasn't sure where we would land, but I didn't care because I was flying in absolute silence now. My arms flew up and my legs stayed down in an arrow-straight pose as the cold water rushed over every molecule that was me. At one point, I even did a cartwheel of sorts and started flying upside down as my brain shut off and in its place was a dizzy jolt of wonder and awe.

What goes up must come down. Daniel landed hard into the freezing river waiting below. The waterfall spit me out just a little bit in front of him and I was amazed that I didn't just shatter into millions broken pieces like a crystal goblet dropped off a mountain peak. At first, it seemed as if I was submerged all the way to the river's floor as my hands touched the bottom of something, but quickly, I popped up and swam to the side, no worse for wear. The river was calm, but deadly cold. A light misty fog lingered over the water's surface and through the white shadows I saw Daniel raising both fists in the air and then yowling with pure pleasure.

Swimming up to him wasn't hard because he grabbed my arm and hoisted me toward him until my legs were locked tightly around his waist and my arms wrapped firmly around his neck. He devoured me with a kiss that was as forceful and powerful as the rush of the water that brought us here.

He tasted like fresh love and pure determination. When my fingers raced through his hair, I felt unleashed.

It was probably twenty degrees outside and I was sweating.

4.

Eventually, we rose from the water, clomped out of the river, and sat down on a big old rock in the middle of a desolate cove of tall evergreen trees. Several inches of snow had fallen over the dead winter grass and it seemed so inviting. I'm not sure how he knew, but Daniel could actually rub sticks together until we had a small fire crackling to the side of us. When sitting became uncomfortable, we decided to lie down, face-to-face, on the snowy surface. Nature was our hotel and in our "room" the snow was like a warm, cushioned blanket.

"I'm living with a Boy Scout," I announced.

"I was a Boy Scout," he said. "Troop Seventy-Six. Lake Forest division."

"Girl Scout," I replied. "I sell a mean box of Thin Mints."

"I don't see you as the selling cookies type. Tell me something else I don't know about you. Who were you, Callaghan when you were alive? I want to know everything."

"What do you mean?" I asked, jittery nerves returning.

"I mean, food you would never touch."

"Brussels sprouts. Green onions."

"What were you on your last Halloween?" I asked, wanting to cram in every little fact.

"A cheerleader," he said in a dejected voice. "The kids made me do it—blonde wig and a bra." He cupped some nonexistent breasts on himself. "I stuffed them with oranges."

"Worst parental offense?" he asked.

"Biked to Madison's at three a.m. in the winter because she had just broken up with her boyfriend. Technically speaking, it wasn't safe. But it was necessary. Also, in seventh grade I roller-skated through the kitchen holding a glass of milk. My mom walked in, startled me, and the glass flew out of my hands. The milk hit the ceiling and I was grounded for a week," I told him. "It was raining milk all over that ugly blue tile."

His grin was ear to ear. Then he spoke.

"Okay, so I took the old man's Ferrari and accidentally drove into a farmer's field for a little bit of racing around between the cornstalks. What I didn't know is the farmer actually planted soybeans. And he had just irrigated the entire thing and the car sunk like it was in quicksand. The farmer came out with a shotgun and told me he was going to hold me there or shoot me or both. He told me to call Edward. But of course, he was out of town. So he finally let me go. Edward has so many cars that he didn't even notice for months until he finally said, 'Where is my blue Ferrari?' I just shrugged. I think that car is still in the soybean field or there is a farmer in Illinois with a really cool ride."

"In my entire life, I've never drank Doctor Pepper," I blurted. "It's not that I'm feeling denied, but still. No growing all the way up. No college. No marriage. No kids. No growing old. No Doctor Pepper. It doesn't seem fair now does it? But then why do we think it's all supposed to be so fair? Who promised us fair?"

He stroked my cheek tenderly.

"I don't know," he said in a somber voice.

A minute or two passed. Then he spoke again.

"Maybe we were lucky to get what we got. When my mom died, the best thing someone said to me was, 'At least you had her for fifteen years, which is more than some people have with their mother.' At least we were there for seventeen years. That's more than some people get."

I tried to catch stray snowflakes in my open palm.

Holding my face in his warm hands, he asked in a sweet voice, "First kiss?"

"A boy named Obie. Second grade. He was a dork and I kissed him. It was a dare from another girl at YMCA camp. Obie also had spaghetti breath."

"Last kiss?" he asked, pressing his lips to mine.

"Some guy who took me swimming . . ." I murmured, but he didn't let me continue.

"Mmmm, let's do that again," he said.

Leaning down, he kissed me sweetly and urgently and when my breath mixed with his and the cold night air caressed my skin, all the questions stopped.

He brought it back to the beginning.

"It's been extremely tough to be your Boy Scout, night after night."

"After night," I added, allowing my thumb and forefinger to explore those striking cheekbones until I wandered down to the two-day stubble that had grown across his cheeks.

The world was beautiful here. It was a winter-white spectacle with soft snow all around us. The air was so sweet and calm.

"People are so afraid of dying," I said, turning my head to stare up at the black night sky. I wondered if my view was home. Or maybe home was below us. My perspective was slightly askew now.

"It's not so bad being here," he said, turning my face back to his, and then wrapping his arms around me. Unlike the other nights, Daniel wasn't turning away in the other direction. When we kissed again it was slow, and building to something deeper. I felt light-headed and knew that soon there would be no turning back. And I didn't want to turn in any direction but his.

This was life. After death.

The kissing was our oxygen. It was rebellion and redemption.

Daniel attempted to pull back for a moment, but I checked his move and pulled him even closer until we rolled—me over him and then me under him. In the fresh snow, his hands unbuttoned my wet sweater and began to stroke the velvety skin on my stomach. It didn't take long before his shirt was tossed aside by the fire, which was burning liquid gold.

"You make me want to embrace the vole," Daniel said, kissing my earlobe.

He leaned in to kiss me on the lips, but I moved my head out of reach. "Embrace the what?" I murmured, shivering and not because of the temperature or the snow that was falling harder now.

"The vole!" he said, laughing and running his calloused hand gently down my neck. "I made that one up when I played soccer, but it's solid for you language-arts types. Embrace the vole means to risk everything in the hope of great rewards."

"Embrace the . . ." I repeated.

"Vole," he whispered, tracing a figure eight on the snow falling on my bare stomach and I began to laugh because it tickled.

That's when Daniel said in a serious voice, "Baby, something is bothering me. If it comes down to it, you and Bobby need to save yourselves. Promise me. In case it becomes a choice—and we know it's all about choices."

We were back to reality. Our reality.

"If you save yourselves it will be worth it to me. You promise me," he demanded.

So many questions raced through my mind: *Can we do this? Can we call it off? Can we get back?* For once in my life, I didn't care about the answers. All I could do was lean up and kiss him with all that I was in that moment and all that I might never be again.

Sometime later, he fell asleep in my arms.

CHAPTER 25

1.

"Harold," I said, "You're the best of the best. You didn't have to bring us doughnuts for breakfast *and* pick us up at home."

I said those words through a thick veil of tears as I stood waiting by the Bentley in the driveway the next morning. Daniel was still on the front porch hugging his little sisters while Jake ran toward the car barking furiously like he knew. "Boy, go back. Back!" I shouted, but he kept coming until he had jumped up on me, paws on both of my shoulders. Snout to nose, it was almost as if he was warning me with all his canine instincts not to do what I was about to do.

"Pete, call him," I said, kissing the dog's head. "See you sometime, boy," I whispered and the dog winced. Dogs always know.

The good-byes were gut-wrenching, although the kids had

no clue what was going to happen except that we were spending another day at ITT. "Be careful," Andy said. "I only have one cool big sister."

"I'll see you for dinner," said Jenna, trying to leave the house as slowly as possible. Again, it was like they knew. Children always know.

"What's for dinner?" Andy demanded. "What time exactly will you be home?" She had never been that specific before, and I dodged her questions. I couldn't tell her that her brother's note was dinner and might affect all the dinners after that one.

For some reason, I couldn't lie to her. I had no idea how the kids would react when Bertha and Izayah were there at the end of the school day with some lame explanation that Daniel and I were . . . what? Out of town? How many school days would they have to cover for us? All of them?

I grabbed my backpack, which was resting on the grass, kissed the dog again, and forced myself to get into the car without saying another word. I couldn't kiss the kids because they would know something was wrong. Daniel looked so bleak and serious that I knew he was having second thoughts. But he quickly slid his backpack next to mine in the backseat, insisting that Harold didn't grab it and toss it into the trunk. "It's really heavy," Daniel said.

Badass ancient weapons weighed quite a lot and tended to clank around.

"Got lots of books in there? Harold asked in his nosy, but good-natured way. If he only knew that we had blades and nails and spikes and sticks plus one green lucky rabbit's foot, because you never knew. "Well, it's a good thing I brought you breakfast," Harold said. "You kids look like you spent the night out in the woods."

Old people. They always know.

"Don't take this the wrong way, Miss Walker, but you look like you hardly got any sleep last night," Harold said. I swear I saw him glare in the rearview mirror at Daniel.

With a nervous laugh, I said, "Oh, Harold, maybe we could use some music to wake us up."

"Have you heard of this cool band called the Bee Gees?" he asked. "Brothers Gibb from Australia. Met a couple of them during a lecture here last month. Two are with us now teaching dance. Disco. Two things survive the ages. Cockroaches and disco."

He put on the opening strains of "Jive Talking" and Daniel sunk deeply into the plush leather seats. "You're killing me, Harold," he said. "Killing me."

"Are you sure they're not the Gibb sisters?" I joked with him.

"Shut up, eat your doughnuts, and suck up a little culture," Harold said, hitting a button until a song called "Staying Alive" blasted through the car speakers. Looking at Daniel, I had to smile and say, "At least it's appropriate in a weird way."

2.

The skies were dreary gray and drizzling over the monstrosity known as ITT. Quickly, we ducked out of the car and walked up to the guardhouse for our day pass into hell. I walked up to that beefy bigmouth named Roy who looked at me curiously before laughing in my face. "Back for more fun in the sun, sweetie?" he said in a mocking tone. "You must be a sadist or you just can't get enough of me."

When I didn't answer, Roy glared at our stuffed backpacks and I said a silent prayer that he wouldn't search them. Luckily, this place wasn't like post-September-eleventh life in America. These guards really didn't care if the prisoners or the visitors got hurt. Roy's only real job was to make sure no one escaped from Alcatraz, so to speak, or it would be his head in a noose. Literally.

Instead of passing us off to another guard or two, Roy walked us around the side of the mountain himself. Daniel walked in front of me and somehow his pack looked much smaller on his expansive back. He was muttering something under his breath, which caught pinhead Roy's attention. "Few more hours and we blow this place," Daniel said. "Ditch this shit-hole."

"I hear you, son," Roy said, walking toward two guards posted by the rocky exterior that would soon become the doorway to our destiny "Don't we all wish we could ditch this shit-hole. Me? Stuck here another twenty-six years unless I get parole. It's their idea of a work-release program."

"What did you do?" I asked.

"Murdered some kids," he growled, and I wasn't sure if he was just saying that to make me nervous.

With that needless personal information shared with two uninterested parties, he nodded to one of the guards, who pushed a code into a keypad, which would open the elevator door.

"I would say have a nice day," Roy bit out. "But that's not possible here."

"Well, now you only have twenty-five years and seventeen hours left, Roy," I said. "See how time flies when you're having fun?" He didn't say a word, turned, and walked back toward his post.

After our antics that had landed us in the GF's office, this visit would be strictly supervised. A grim-faced Ken, our favorite administrator, met us at the elevator on level two.

"Today will be strictly by the books. I don't need to take any more shit for your shenanigans," Ken said and then he launched right into business. "First, I'm wondering if you found anything interesting the other day in that hovel we call a library?" he asked me as a greeting. "Ma told me that you were searching old school newspapers. Why would you do that? It's not like we allow the school shooters to write about their past exploits. I repeat: Why were you looking through those newspapers? The GF would like to know. And don't give me more of that 'searching for past case studies' crap."

Ken was an obvious lightweight if he thought I'd buckle under pressure.

"I thought that maybe we'd find an interview or two with a few previous school shooters—not reflecting on what they did, but the remorse they felt for doing it. I'm sure you realize that their words could be an important tool in understanding their motivations," I said in a direct tone that clearly annoyed him because he was supposed to be in charge. "Do you think we could go back there again today for more research? It's not such a bad library and Ma is certainly entertaining," I said, knowing the answer would be an absolute no.

"Absolutely not, Miss Callaghan," Ken said in a clipped tone. "This isn't some free-for-all field trip. You're not at Disneyland. I have orders from the higher ups—or should I say the highest up. You're to be accompanied at all times and no wandering. In fact, we have to wait for your escort to get out of the john and join us."

I couldn't believe the GF was actually going through with it! But I knew I had to believe it when on such a joyless day, during the happiest time of the living year, the least joyful person in any realm came walking up with a slight limp and a glint in his muddy-brown, embedded eyes.

"Danny boy . . . and hot cheeks. How's it hangin'?" said Eddie Wargo, moving close like some monster in a nightmare. "Hot cheeks, you look tired. If you couldn't sleep last night, why didn't you come visit me in my cell?"

I had already convinced Daniel not to react to anything in here today, especially any taunting from Wargos. With one of his large, swollen hands Eddie reached out to grab my backpack and I recoiled. Daniel stepped between us and shoved Eddie back a few inches. So much for not reacting. But Eddie didn't fight back. "Down boy! Just trying to help the lady," he said. "Just being neighborly as we say down South."

"We're not in the South," Daniel growled.

I would have wrestled him to the ground if it was necessary to keep my backpack, but I didn't want to draw that kind of attention. "I can take care of it myself, Edward," I said, purposely using his formal name so he would know I meant business.

He was no Edward.

"Back off," Daniel warned, stepping into Eddie's space, but curiously the big bruiser bully backed right off again. He just gestured toward the open elevator door and said to me, "Welcome to the jungle. Ladies first—so that means Daniel goes before us."

"Eddie, let's not start," Ken said.

"I try to show some southern hospitality and this is what it gets me," he mumbled. "I even showered for today. I'm a professional."

"A professional what?" I whispered to Daniel as we walked inside the elevator and headed up to D Block prepared for our last stand.

3.

We took our death march down all-star row where the best of the worst were housed and salivating for visitors. Once again, the inmates decided to put on a show including screaming at the top of their lungs. We couldn't hear them, but saw their mouths contorted into giant, howling ovals. A few flipped on their intercoms and begged us to stop and talk to them, but we didn't slow our pace.

A blur of young criminal faces flashed before my eyes and all I could pinpoint was an eye, a nose that was broken, or a scar that would never be right. It was almost as if I was driving past them in slow motion and the landscape was too ghastly to ignore. A.E. was the first familiar face we encountered when we passed Cell 17. He looked up from his Civil War book, waved, and then glanced at our stuffed backpacks. A.E. didn't miss much either and remembered that on our first visit our packs were pretty light. He knew. I caught his "hand in the cookie jar" smile, which went from one ear to the next.

He lifted one hand, palm up, and made a writing motion on it with his other hand. I got it. His report. He knew where we were going later if we could get there, which wasn't seeming likely given our situation, where our every move would be watched and monitored.

I had planned a few distractions that I didn't share with Daniel. When we were just a step past A.E.'s cell, I clutched my stomach and stopped cold.

"I'm so sorry everybody. I think I'm going to be sick," I said, folding over and contorting my face while covering my mouth as if an eruption of breakfast was eminent. Daniel actually looked concerned, which was my plan. "If you toss your cookies, I ain't cleaning it up," Eddie grumbled. "No one said anything about barf duty. I do have my limits."

"Where's the janitor's closet in case we need a mop?" I muttered, still clenched over and faking a little bit of a gag. I was so convincing that I actually felt nauseous for a moment and my stomach did a quick backflip that almost landed in my throat. It was method faking at its best.

I could see from the corner of my eye that A.E. was giving me a thumbs-up sign. He knew that we figured it out. "Yeah, we got janitors. This place ain't the town dump," Eddie said. "Janitor's room is through those double doors at the front end of the cellblock. It's all the way down there." He pointed vaguely into the distance past the first cell. "Just don't ralph on me. I can't stand the smell of puke and I'm not going to the closet to fetch the mop."

Standing up and taking a few deep, cleansing breaths, I said, "Okay, I feel much better now. Just give me a moment." The truth was I didn't really feel that much better because my nerves were kicking in.

"Let's go," Daniel said, grabbing my elbow.

On this day, Detroit school shooter and lifer Jackie Silver was not in the mood for visitors. He sat in his straight metal chair, which looked like the most uncomfortable piece of furniture in the world, and then strategically placed his back to us. He stared hard into outer space. Daniel made a good show out of trying to ask him a few questions about "why he did it." Eddie just snorted and paced around before saying, "Kid is out of his freaking gourd. Why don't you ask him how he got to be such a good shot? Did his daddy take him hunting? Our daddy took us hunting all the time. We ate what we caught, plus those deer were so stupid. They deserved to die. Ever shoot a deer?" They stop and let you kill them."

"Eddie, please," I said. "Can you go get me some water? I'm feeling a little queasy again."

"What am I, freaking seven-eleven?" he muttered and then said, "No water. No john. No nothing. Piss in your pants. I can't leave you alone. Not for a minute."

We continued with the sham interview, my skin crawling because I now knew exactly where the janitor's closet was located and it was just one hard sprint from where we were. We were so close to our return trip and the life we once knew—but it seemed continents away. Breaking away from Eddie wasn't an option. Neither was any privacy. The worst Wargo remained the wall in front of us and now he was staring at me hard while Daniel talked in a hushed tone to the catatonic Jackie. I could see Eddie look at my ass in my new jeans, so I whipped around in my stomping boots to face him. Then he looked away with this real guilty expression of his face. It was revolting, but I had to stand there next to him and let it happen.

Daniel didn't have a much better fate. He was stuck with the shooter boy who wasn't going to make this easy.

Jackie's response to another day of questioning was to shoot spitballs in the air while Daniel just stared past him in the direction of those double doors. Eddie and I hung back a bit in the shadowy corners to give them a little bit of private confessional time. It also gave Daniel a chance to slip our trackers out of his backpack and quietly place them behind him on the chair.

"Eddie," I finally said in a hushed tone, shifting from foot to foot, because we had been standing there for over an hour now and he was looking at me like I had killed his dog or he had killed mine. "What is your problem? Just say it. What?" I whispered. "Why do you keep looking at me that way?"

I was pretty sure Eddie wasn't exactly a master at getting in touch with his innermost emotions, but perhaps he needed a soft ear to listen to what was bothering him. "You have a weird name," he said. "What kind of name is Walker Callaghan?"

"This is about my name? Really? Do we need to do this now?"

"Wait, I know how you got the name. I read your file. It was on the GFs desk. I do his filing," he stammered, adding, "I don't actually put the files back in the drawers. I just take the files across the room. Someone else does all that alphabetical stuff."

"You read my file?" I demanded. "What gives you the right to—?"

"Don't talk to her," Daniel hissed without even turning around to which Eddie flipped him the bird, firing it at the back of his leather jacket. Daniel's travel outfit was jeans, a black sweater, and that jacket. I was in jeans, those boots, and a warm, black winter cashmere, looking tougher than I had ever looked in my living years.

"Why do you even care about my name or what is in my files?" I said, staring up into his blank, but pained face. "If you really cared, you'd go get me a soda. Coke Zero. Seven Up. Sprite. You know, a little true hospitality for someone who is about to ralph on your shoes wouldn't kill you." Under normal circumstances, I would have grilled him about invading my privacy, but what was the point now? My job was to get rid of him—even if I wanted to ring his neck.

"It's not that I care about your life, Walker," Eddie said, continuing his eye lock on my face. He had to look down because he was a good six or seven inches taller. When his voice broke on the last word—life—I had to look his way because it was just too odd. For a second, he looked actually human.

Eddie Wargo, baddest badass at ITT, looked as if he was about to burst into tears.

And then the dam broke.

"If I told you something, it might make him feel better because he really does feel shitty about it," Eddie blurted.

"I told him I didn't care about his problems, but then he hit me," Eddie blathered on. "Smacked the crap out of me. And he told me as the oldest, it was my job to set it right. He can't rest until it's set right. He's done a lot of bad that can't be set right. But this can."

I had absolutely no idea what he was talking about—or whom.

"Who feels bad?" I said, impatient for him to just spit it out. "I didn't even know you were capable of feeling anything."

"I said it's *not* me," he said. "It's him."

"Him who?" I asked. "Just say it."

"You're Walker Callaghan from Chicago. I read about how you were some writer girl and did newspaper stuff. And your daddy died when you were just a young baby. Cancer. And your mama couldn't pay the bills. We couldn't pay the bills either. See, we're sorta the same," Eddie rambled. "That's why daddy feels bad about it. If you were some rich snooty girl with her nose up in the air, he might not evenst care."

"That file is private," I fumed. "You had no right.

"Oh, I read about all your fancy, falutin' awards for being so smart, which is why you feel like you're so much better than me," Eddie said, his regular self now returning. "But you're dead like me. So what does it all matter anyways? I know you died this year. Your mama, well, they thought she was roadkill, too, but that wasn't near true."

"Don't talk about my mother," I shot out.

"Get off your high horse! I know about feelin' bad! Our daddy isn't exactly shopping for a new double-wide. He's dead, too," Eddie spit out.

"I'm sorry your daddy died . . . but what does this have to do with me?" I snapped. The only person I cared about here was sitting with his back to me trying to interrogate some crazy kid. Another lunatic was standing next to me trying to tell me his life story and some sad-sack saga about his creepy father, which was typical. People were always trying to tell me their life stories. That's a reporter's life, and apparently afterlife. We had a portal to find, and the last thing I cared about tonight was the Wargo family tree and who just fell off of it.

"Walker, he's, um, sorry. Real sorry about it. Our daddy, I mean," Eddie blurted.

"Sorry about what?"

"It was one of those weird fate things. The night you died,

our daddy was on the road, too. Milwaukee Road. In the Chicago suburbs. Around eight p of m."

I couldn't speak.

"Driving in his eighteen-wheeler truck. Wargo hauling," Eddie rambled on. "He was doing one of his runs from Mississippi to Colorado but had to do a quick drop off first in Chicago at the stockyards."

All I could do was blankly stare at him.

"It was September, remember?" Eddie ranted in a loud whisper. "He said he ran into some freak polar bear thing. You know, when it gets real cold and then it snows, but nobody is 'specting it."

"A polar vortex—freak cold and then heavy snow," I said as my words came out like I was in some sort of a trance.

"It was a bad storm. Real bad. Nobody thought it would snow in September, least of all those weather dumbasses. He was on the highway, a two-lane one, smoking cigarettes, eating candy, and talking on the CB. Normal stuff for a trucker. He never expected to drive right into Mother's Nature's idea of a white wedding," Eddie said.

Breathing suddenly became an actual job.

"What are you saying, Eddie?" Daniel demanded. I never even noticed him approaching, but now he was standing by my side, holding both of my shoulders in his hands to keep me steady and upright. He slid one arm around my waist when my legs wobbled.

And then all three of us were jettisoned into stunned silence.

Not content to miss out on the drama, Jackie Silver took it upon himself to spring back to life. His ear-piercing, cackling laughter, animalistic and high-pitched like a wounded beast, pierced my eardrums. "He's sowwy. So very sowwy!" Jackie ranted. "I not sowwy. So not very sowwy. So not very sowwy. Bang, bang! You're dead."

"Shut up, freak," Eddie screamed.

351

Jackie ignored him and despite the chains attaching him to his chair, he began to rise. When that didn't work, he started to violently toss his head back like he was trying to snap it off. Everything was futile for him, but Jackie continued to flail and buck and scream until he exhausted himself. Finally, he slumped back into his catatonic state.

At the moment of Jackie's attack, my mind became a split screen. On one side, I saw the baby-faced killer of our principal. On the other, I remembered a white truck and all of that hard snow on the road the night I died.

Eddie continued when Jackie was quiet again. "Your ma and my daddy couldn't see each other coming. And Daddy said there was all those woods by the side of the road. The deer came out that night. In his headlights, Daddy could see their glinty eyes peeking out from the trees. Most of them stopped walkin' when they felt the dirt give way to the road. It was almost like they were lining up, but knew not to cross that line onto the asphalt. One deer broke from the pack. There's always one. The rebel. It walked slowly into the middle of the road. Both your mama and my Daddy hit the brakes. There was the snow and the black ice under them. The deer just stood there until all three of them met in the middle with a loud bang."

"Bang, bang, you're dead," said Jackie Silver in a wee voice.

"I guess . . . I mean, I hear that your old lady lived, which is nice and all," Eddie stammered. "Daddy is sorry. About you. He says you flew like a bird out of the car into the woods. And after, the rest of the deer just stood there staring at you until the ambulance came. But you were dead. Your mama was half-dead. Daddy saw it all. Then the other day, he saw your name tag and it broke him up inside. Daddy got real upset. He doesn't much care about himself. But he feels bad about killing a kid . . . and a girl."

Daniel's hand gripped me tighter when I asked, "What happened to your father?"

"The wallop of the crash made his cab roll onto its front. His head was cut clear off."

"But it's back on now," Eddie continued. "His head, in case you were wondering."

I was worried about my mother who was home right now blaming herself. My mind flashed back to the night of the accident and I remembered my mother saying to me, "*It's going to be a brutal winter. Snow in September. Who expected it? I'm sure that Milwaukee Road is safer than the highway.*" Then she turned on the car radio, and I heard some deep-voiced DJ warn, "Watch out for the black ice under the snow. The rain from earlier this evening is freezing. It's turning the city into a virtual skating rink."

"It wasn't his fault. It was no one's fault. Not Daddy's. Not your Ma. You can't put a blame here. You just gotsta accept it," Eddie insisted.

I'm not sure how I began to speak again at that moment, but I heard myself say actual words. "My mom still thinks she crashed us into someone. She still thinks it's her fault—and she has to live with that for the next forty or fifty years of her now unnatural, daughterless life until I can tell her," I said in a robotic voice.

"Well, that's your problem," an embarrassed Eddie responded. He looked so far down at his toes that his chin hit his chest. "But what I read . . . well, I didn't read it. I did have Rat in the GF's outer office, you know the skinny guard guy, actually read your file to me . . . and what he said was that twenty-three people died that night on the roads 'round there. But your ma didn't. So them's the breaks."

"Nobody knew to salt the road in September," I said, remembering more. "It was seventy-five degrees the week before the freak storm. There was so much black ice on that road. She couldn't see it coming."

When I involuntarily swayed backward, Daniel was a solid

wall behind me. Immovable. Granite. He leaned down to whisper into my ear, "Baby, just go home today. I got this. I'll go alone. Let's call it."

For a moment, I thought I really might throw up, and I prayed that I wouldn't do that in front of him. It was like a quick fever was rushing from my chest, up my neck, and to my head. When I swayed back for a second time, Daniel caught me, taking my full weight like it was nothing.

"You're going home. I'm calling Harold," he insisted, taking a finger and wiping a tiny bit of drool that came out of my mouth involuntarily. I didn't even have the strength to be mortified when he wiped my chin as if he was taking care of a child. Wiping his hands on his pants, he did a second round and then kissed me gingerly on the nose. "Let's call Harold," he insisted.

That's when I heard my mother's words in my still-fuzzy brain.

"*Your word is your promise,*" Mom was fond of saying. "*You can never break your word.*"

In that moment, I knew exactly what we would do. I wouldn't think about any of this right now or dare process it. That was for another day.

I was calm.

I was collected.

My gut was churning.

But no one would ever know it because I also had iron in there. My father, Sam, was a steelworker.

"Eddie," I said in a deadpan voice because mostly *I was focused.* I easily recalled the clear picture of the ITT map in my mind's eye. "Does this place have a chapel? Because I would love to say a prayer for your father. He deserves some absolution, too, which means we're going to make forgiving him official."

"We don't have to do anything that crazy," Eddie said. "Just say you're lettin' him off the hook, and I'll tell him next time on parents' day. We don't need to go to church. Wargos and church don't really mix up well."

"Yes, we do need to go to church," I said in a sure voice. "We have to make this right. You brought the confession to me. That was the first step. The church will bring the forgiveness. You can't have real forgiveness until it's official," I reminded him, staring up into his confused eyes that were mulling it over. I saw a spark in them. "Do this—for your daddy," I said in an impassioned voice. "To make it right."

"Well, that's mighty genius of you," Eddie finally said, because he couldn't really find the word "generous" in his limited vocabulary. Yet, he didn't move a muscle.

"Frank, I mean, Daddy, could use any of the redeeming he can get, but we can't go to the chapel now. It's not allowed. And it's all the way down the hall. By that janitor's closet," Eddie rambled. "I guess both places are for cleanin' up messes."

Gazing over at Daniel, I gave him a nod that could only be measured in a fraction. I could see he was apprehensive and eager at the same time. *It's by the janitor's closet.*

"Eddie, I need a few minutes in the chapel," I pleaded. "To come to terms. This isn't just about you. I'm the one who lost her life."

"Yeah, that part sucks for you, but I'm supposed to keep you right here. The GF is probably watching on some screen," Eddie fretted. "He'd beat me bloody for taking you all around like you're at Mall of America or something. This would be like him saying to stay in the food court and us going to Big Lots."

"Eddie, it's almost noon," I said in the same monotone voice. "I'm sure he has his fat face in a plate of ribs and chicken. Does he watch monitors when he shovels it in? I bet he just looks at the grub in front of him and watches mobster movies while he's chowing down."

"He does like his ribs and Jimmy Cagney. Sends the guards

355

over to Barry's because he loves their Cajun extra-spicy sauce," Eddie said, proving again he was a fountain of useless information. "He also watches mixed martial arts shows or *Pawn Wars*. Or maybe *River Monsters*. He loves the one about that big furry man-beast walking out of the lake in Arkansas or maybe it's Mississippi. I forget."

"Ed . . . Edward," I interrupted him. "I'm sure he won't be watching, and nobody ever minds a prayer. Nobody. We can't say the prayer here. It's just not right in front of this poor, deranged boy."

"I don't know," Eddie pondered. "But you do have a point. My daddy could use some church praying. Maybe we could go to the chapel. For just a minute or two. Then we come right back here and we never tell anyone. Promise? I mean really swear to me that you won't tell. I can't go to the Hole again. I'll lose all my marbles for sure this time."

All I could fixate on was the fact that on the map the chapel was only about five giant steps past the janitor's closet. I could see that Daniel was on board with my plan when he picked up the two backpacks and stood at the door of the room looking worried.

Eddie stopped.

"Danny boy, you're not goin'. This gotta be just me and Walker. No funny stuff, I mean it. We don't need you to pray for my daddy," Eddie whispered as he looked around for guards.

"You're not going anywhere with my girlfriend," Daniel grumbled.

Even that was lost on me in my current state. And just when I thought the two of them might punch it out over who would be field tripping now, an exhausted-looking Eddie just gave up.

"Okay, shut up! Let's all go. Frank needs all the help he can get," Eddie hissed.

He led us out of Jackie's interview room and back into the main dank corridor. The clock on the wall boasted that it was noon, and maybe the impending lunch deliveries were why there weren't any guards to be seen. We did a speed walk past the other prisoners, and by the time we reached the double doors, I knew that there was no turning back.

Almost like magic, and with the help of Eddie's fat fingers gingerly working one of his keys into the lock, the double doors at the end of the hallway near Cell 1 swung open.

We took two steps through those doors and Eddie grabbed them so they wouldn't make noise while he gently closed and locked them again.

We were so close.

But to what?

Inside this front hallway of D Block, it looked like any school hallway, but with jagged rock walls, and even a bulletin board hanging and touting a fire-drill plan. This was a small passage with only four white, and quite regular, doors to it like each was an individual office. Each was closed, and there wasn't another person in sight.

We walked past the first white door that read: Janitor. I refused to focus on it—not yet. *Poker face. Do not dare give it away.* We were headed to another white door that simply read: Chapel. This door was slightly ajar and I said a silent prayer that no one else was in need of religion this morning. Without any hesitation, I walked into the chapel first and said a silent thank you for the fact that it was completely empty. Then I said a prayer hoping that we wouldn't get caught. Eddie stood behind me thinking that these prayers were for Frank. He stood close to me as if he could somehow inhale a bit of the absolution he was sure I was sending directly to his father.

Looming larger and more ominous than ever, Daniel lingered behind Eddie adopting a pose that said he didn't want to get involved in Frank Wargo's future soul saving.

"Join me, Eddie," I said, motioning for him to kneel next to me by one of the benches. I held out my hand, and Eddie placed his calloused fingers in mine.

Not completely immune from church activities, Eddie got down on his knees in prayer and quickly lowered his head. "My mama would take me to church on Sundays. Every Sunday. Well, at least the major holidays," he whispered, remembering aloud. "She would tell me that the Lord works in mysterious ways and it's true. Look at you and me, Walker. We're tied forever now. Your ma brought you into this world and my daddy took you out. I don't know what it means, but it means something big."

I ignored the shivers running down my spine. *Focus. There was time later. All the time in the heavens remained to sit with this information. Not now.*

"She was right, Eddie," I said, distracting him enough that he didn't hear Daniel quietly opening one of the backpacks and pulling out the oblong metal object with a spiked nail top. For a split second, I felt a sadness that dug into my bones. Even with everything he had been and done to me in the past, it didn't seem fair that Eddie would have to take another beating.

But there was no choice. Daniel lifted the bat-like object behind him and he swung for the fences at the back of Eddie's head. The blunt handle of the weapon connected with his thick skull.

He never saw it coming.

"Good night, you son of a bitch," Daniel said.

CHAPTER 26

1.

"Callaghan, are you sure?" Daniel asked in a hurried rush as he grabbed my hand and we jettisoned out the chapel door on feet that seemed propelled by rocket fuel. Five giant steps back and we were turning the handle of the janitor's closet. In my case, no answer was an answer. I just looked into those gray eyes and I knew that I wouldn't let him do something this epic alone. I was going home.

"We got this," I whispered.

I was sure enough to be the first one to grab the handle of the janitor's closet door and twist it hard. A scream of frustration formed in my throat, but I caught it before it could be set loose. The door was locked.

"Son of a bee!" I whispered loudly. "We didn't grab Eddie's keys."

"We actually borrowed them," Daniel said, and I heard the

jingling, which sounded like beautiful music. A second later, Daniel turned the key in the door and we were inside.

2.

The janitor's closet in D Block was no bigger than two bathroom stalls without a wall in the middle. Slipping inside, it was like someone shut off our world as we ventured into complete blackness and the foulest of stenches. I wondered if this was the portal, but nothing felt that different as my eyes adjusted to the inky darkness. Daniel was feeling his way down a nondescript, dirty white wall and hit pay dirt when he flipped a tiny light switch. As a bulb flickered like it was on its last gasp, my eyes adjusted for a moment and then focused on a charcoal-gray industrial-strength sink.

Portal? It was almost laughable.

How could we be this wrong?

This was no rabbit hole to another existence or magic chute back to life. It was simply a stinky janitor's closet complete with foul-smelling, molding mop buckets on plastic wheels. These buckets contained the thick cotton strands of filthy gray mop heads. Ducking my head closer for a peek, I could see each mop head was coated in dirt, grime, and, far worse—bodily fluids. On a makeshift shelf in the corner were rows of generic toilet paper, or sandpaper as we always called it at my old school. And there was no need to worry about the mirrors shining in this place: There were many cans of Gleme glass cleaner at the ready.

A strange, yet familiar, odor drifted into my nose. I knew it was that hideous orange sawdust that the janitor sprinkled on the floor to clean up fresh vomit. Just the smell of it made me want to toss my breakfast, but somehow I kept it down. Again.

Twisting my face into my favorite tortured look, I glanced at the large-sized leather tool belt hanging on a nail in the corner. I could see it was on the last notch indicating that the actual janitor had a bit of a stomach on him. Or her. Who knew in this place?

The room was a closet with medium-gray walls and light-ivory linoleum with veins of darker brown running through it. Lifting my hands in the "now what" pose, Daniel just shrugged. It was probably obvious by now that we had gone missing and I knew ITT certainly had a search party of guards looking for us. Eddie would soon wake up and tell them exactly what happened to him, which would make it even worse. Our little moment of peace with him would clearly be over.

My stomach sinking, I glanced at that putrid sawdust again thinking, *We might actually need that in a few minutes.*

"We're missing something. Something basic. I know this isn't complicated," Daniel whispered, frantically looking around the room and then pulling open the two small cabinets on the right wall. They didn't lead to new worlds, but instead were packed with standard-issue janitor gear including light bulbs, rat traps, and a few extra packs of cigarettes, which were carefully hidden way in the back.

"I guess our janitor isn't afraid of lung cancer," I whispered, glancing up at the ceiling because maybe the way out of here was up. Taking one of the mops, I poked gently at our little roof, which was made of stucco that was hard as a rock and didn't move. Another dead end.

Against the back wall was a small coat closet that looked as if it was a last-minute addition because it was made from some cheap laminate kit where you build a closet with instructions in Chinese. We moved toward it with some trepidation, inching the latch open slowly. The door opened with a tiny wail. Could it be possible?

Absolutely not. The closet didn't transport us, but instead filled our noses with the stale sweat smell of two janitor uniforms that were well past a good washing, and a mossy green parka that had seen better days. The inside of a skullcap was covered in old dandruff.

"How could we be so damn stupid?" Daniel whispered harshly. "Maybe the portal *is* in the boiler room."

I knew that he was wrong. Then A.E.'s words rang clearly in my mind: *"Once inside, if you make it that far, just remember that old song. Turn, turn, turn."*

There was no choice. I returned to the position I was in when we first walked through the door. Then it was time to turn—starting to the left, I made three turns. I ended up facing the right wall and saw the supply cupboards. I opened them, rifled through some of the contents, then closed them again. Still nothing. So I went back to my starting position, but this time made my first turn to the right and, logically, my third turn ended up facing the left wall. Just like the others, it was made of a sick-colored yellowing cinder block. Moving closer toward it, I looked as closely as possible but it was just a wall with a mop and bucket leaning up against it along with a bunch of brooms. Moving closer, I ran my hand across the cold cinder blocks. That's when I felt it. And it would have been so easy to miss.

About four feet high and in the middle of the wall was something hard that was hidden in a pool of blackness. If it weren't for the small clear knob, we would have easily missed it. I pushed aside the mop and brooms. Then I put my hand on the knob and it turned. In slow motion, Daniel walked up to it with his backpack on. He placed mine on my back. We were ready. Almost ready.

Slowly, I continued turning the knob. A door creaked open.

Daniel placed his hand on my arm like he wanted to be ready to pull me back. But he was paralyzed because neither of us was even remotely prepared for what we saw inside.

3.

It was a makeshift bedroom and he was in it. The janitor slumbered on what appeared to be a small child's bed. He was on one of his massive sides and looked like the human equivalent of an enormous grizzly bear. When you got past his girth, sweat, and overall stink of rotten fish, what remained was an actual hulk of a man who seemed like he was hibernating for a long winter nap. It was a wonder the tiny bed didn't just collapse from his weight.

He was Caucasian, weeks beyond a good shower and wearing what was once a beige uniform, but now it was beige-black. Fat rolls hung off the side of him like they were creating their own mountain ranges. His lopsided haircut was a home job. It made what was left of his oily, middle-aged, black hair strike out in every which way.

His eyes were two closed slits and above his upper lip was the hint of a small black mustache. His name tag read: John.

His snoring had that monstrous growl of a lawn mower just starting up, sputtering out, and then roaring up again.

Quietly, we stepped into his lair and closed the door behind us. The room wasn't much bigger than the actual janitor's closet, but the air inside of it was still and dead. My heart began to pound and it wasn't so much from the man, but what surrounded him.

There were clowns—hundreds, maybe thousands of clowns around him. There were clowns in every shape or form. Fat clowns, thin clowns, and clowns that were sickly happy were here. Most of the clowns looked demented and evil, as if they knew a universal secret that children for centuries had always felt deep in their bones. Despite their white faces, red noses, and smiles, these seeming jokesters contained black hearts because everyone knows there is nothing scarier than a clown. I remembered an old quote: "Who loves a clown? No one . . . except other clowns."

These clowns weren't real; they were in statue and picture form. But John didn't just want to erect a monument to clowns. He was also one of them.

On a hanger, attached to a hook on the wall next to his bed, was his crimson clown suit with red, white, and blue fuzzy balls attached to the front of it. The side was detailed with red-and-white stripes and a large swirly rainbow collar attached to the gaping hole that made up the neckline.

The nightstand was crammed with clown statues made of both plastic and glass and another small table held his half-used tubes of face paint. A small, framed picture served as his makeup guide and the face staring back at us sent ice up my spine. He had printed his clown name on a piece of paper under the photo. Written in a child's scribble, it read: Pogo.

Looking at the photo, there was nothing extraordinary about the white paint on his skin, the big sky-blue triangles for eyes outlined in thick black, or the garish red mouth that extended from his thin lips down to the crease on his chin. His eyes were the most chilling part. Those orbs looked lethal in clown face. And the smile wasn't a happy one—his lips were pursed in a demented pose that made it seem like he could eat you whole. He drew sharp corners for the lips, not the rounded ones that mellowed most clowns so children didn't run away shrieking in horror.

Several more framed pictures of John in full clown face were hung on three of the ugly gray walls. I saw that he was sneering in most of them. His white face extended up and over his bald head that was a cap over his hair. A little red square hat with a black pom-pom in the middle didn't soften him a bit.

"Don't wake him," Daniel whispered as John grunted then

drooled a thin line of saliva out of his mouth and onto his pillow. I could see a bottle of sleeping pills on his night table, and I hoped he downed enough of them for a nice long nap. Allowing myself to breathe, my gaze shifted upward and I saw something that made my blood run cold. On a small shelf above his bed, he had the embroidered name tags of several young men, torn from their prison uniforms and some covered with dried blood. They were lined up side by side like monuments. It was like he was collecting them. When I moved closer, I could see that one tag wasn't like the others. It was a visitor's pass that read: Simon. *The missing boy from the Academy.*

I could hear A.E. saying, "*He can smell children.*" Looking down at the slumbering bear, I saw his nostrils flare wide open.

I knew we had to leave. Now.

"There is no portal here," I whispered, backing up a bit to stand near the one and only wall that didn't feature any paintings, portraits, or clown memorabilia. Maybe he didn't get to that wall yet. Or, perhaps it was a work in progress. But when I looked closer in the dim light, I could see that something actually *was* there.

The entire wall was a clown's face drawn lightly with a pencil. Obviously, it was his unfinished masterpiece.

"Callaghan," Daniel mouthed, pointing to the door we came in. "Let's get out of here."

I shook my head. I wasn't leaving that way.

Something drew me, almost hypnotically, closer to the unfinished wall. I don't know exactly why, but I took my index finger and followed along the lines of penciled-in clown's face.

And then I realized—it wasn't *my* death anniversary. Praying my hunch was right, I grabbed Daniel's hand and brushed it over the clown's roughly penciled eyebrows.

The heat from his body was transformative. The pencil drawing immediately mutated into thicker black lines from just the simple touch of his fingers. He was painting the face. Daniel quickly raised his other hand to continue the metamorphosis. When he touched the cheeks, white paint from behind the wall rushed forward to completely fill in the entire face and forehead. He hurriedly traced his fingers over the nose, which soon burned bright with bloody red paint.

The mouth—it was the only thing left. We touched it together and the red spilled forth, slathering the space like a child had just painted it. Extra red poured down at our feet as if the clown was actually bleeding now. We took a step back, but it was too late as the wall seemed to come alive. Our feet stopped moving. What we saw next was horrifying and fascinating at the same time.

The mouth opened.

Fanged teeth rose as high as the ceiling and as low as the floor until all that was left was just a large chasm into the jowls.

"Close your eyes, baby," Daniel said, grabbing my hand.

And we walked through the portal and back to life.

CHAPTER 27

1.

The darkness swallowed me.

The only sound I could hear was the shattering of glass punctuated by sparks bursting high in the black night sky. Somehow our mere presence in this new form caused a neat row of tall highway lights to explode instantly when we entered the realm. The glass covering the lights cracked open and the light bulbs inside detonated into tiny airborne flashes of gold.

Later, I'm sure the living would just chalk it up to some Christmastime power surge or the Commonwealth Edison power company having a snafu. They would never know the truth.

Talk about making an entrance.

Why we ended up in a ditch on the side of the busy 94 highway completely baffled me. The six-lane speedway that linked the Chicago suburbs with the actual city was crowded with cars exceeding the speed limit as last-minute shoppers raced to get home with boxes, bags, and holiday dreams.

We landed with a thud in the muck of a highway ditch that was a mixture of frozen winter grass, dead-elm much, and debris that included several old McDonald's bags that I slapped away from my face. The ditch backed up to dense woods, which smelled like pine and life.

"Daniel," I moaned.

I have never been much of a whiner, but it hurt like hell. Landing, that is. I fell in that ditch face up, back and butt down. In other words, I hit the living realm like a mountain crashing onto a postage stamp. My arrival sounded like a thunderclap and the impact was just as staggering on my body.

First rule of returning to this place: The cloak of pain protection we enjoyed at the Academy was gone, baby, gone. Biting my lip, I stifled a cry because of the white-hot flash of pain moving from my left knee up my leg, which felt like it was on fire.

This pain wasn't the only unusual sensation. Quickly, I felt something I hadn't experienced in a long, long time. My teeth began to chatter because I was freezing cold in a way that made my bones ache. I never even wore my coat when it was snowing outside the Academy. Now, I couldn't understand why my blood wasn't just freezing hard in my veins because the temperatures were well below zero. I was sure of that much.

"Daniel!" I cried.

Where was he? The answer came when I heard him cry out in agony. He landed standing completely straight up. It was a pose an Olympic gymnast would have envied as he "stuck it" in a perfect landing. Again, the human body isn't supposed to fly through realms and land feet up. The explosive jolt had him using just about every curse word in his vocabulary and a few in foreign languages. If we had one of those swearing jars on us, I would have been a billionaire by now.

"Callaghan!" he shouted. "Baby, where are you? Tell me where you are!"

But I didn't need to say anything.

In that instant, he saw me sitting by the side of the highway like some kind of philosopher who was just hanging out, staring at the full moon, and thinking deep thoughts. I pasted on a fake smile to let him know I was "alive," sort of, and then gave him a little wave. My arm felt a rush of new ache.

Throwing his head back, I could see Daniel sigh although I couldn't see his breath in the winter air. I guess it didn't work that way anymore. A few feet away, he waved back, his black hair flying off his face courtesy of a brisk north wind that acted like a whip.

Before I could answer him, he launched into another stream of swear words ending with a defiant "Son of a bitch!" Then he went practically Weather Channel on me and announced to no one in particular, "I forgot how cold it is here and I'm freezing my ass off already."

Welcome to a freezing-cold Lake Forest, Illinois.

"Glad to be home?" I asked him, standing up and finding my feet.

"Yeah, Merry freaking Christmas," he mumbled.

2.

In the distance, I could see a bank sign that read it was minus four degrees at 8:30 p.m. on December twenty-third. It was too early for Santa and too late for sanity on our parts. *We actually did this! We were back in the living realm!* This was despite the odds and the warnings from Dr. King, although I wasn't exactly sure what we had done and why it was so dangerous. So far, it was just nasty cold and slightly painful.

It was also a little confusing.

Just inches to the right of me, cars were racing by on the highway doing seventy, eighty, ninety miles per hour. I could see a few of the drivers were a little drunk because they didn't exactly whiz by in a straight line.

A faceless man in a red Corvette must have had a few because he seemed to think that all three lanes of the highway were his own personal racetrack. He was approaching speeds that were well over a hundred miles per hour.

Narrowly missing a white SUV, he was like a guy playing bumper cars in a seventy-thousand-dollar toy. Before I could scream, I saw a slap of rocks flying in the air as the Vette veered right into the ditch where I was still trying to get my footing in the murky muck. A loud wail launched from my chest into the night sky as the Vette man cut the front wheel to point the car in my direction. The last thing I remember before closing my eyes was the car driving right into me as he crashed into the ditch.

Then the world went black.

3.

When I opened my eyes again, I knew it wasn't the reset button that had kicked in. He drove right through me. Like I was Casper the freaking teen ghost.

"Call-a-ghan!" Daniel was screaming, but it sounded like he was under water and yelling in slow motion. I could see him moving. Running. Flinging himself in my direction with his legs flying. Then he was grabbing me. Moving his hands all over my face, arms, and legs. I was a hundred percent. "Oh baby," he said, burying his face in my neck. "I thought that was it. This can't be it."

For the second time that night, Daniel let out a sigh that was more like a howl.

The drunk driver kicked open his demolished door, although he didn't look much worse for wear. Slumping down into the ditch just a foot away from us, but not seeing us at all, he put his head into his hands for a reflective moment. Then he thought better of it and raced back to the car to pull out two empty bottles of vodka, which he flung hard into the trees. A police car pulled up as he was getting rid of the evidence. Neither of the two cops seemed sympathetic as they shoved him chest first into their cop car and asked the fateful question, "Have you been drinking?"

"No sirree, I haven't touched a drop," the drunk slurred and then tripped over his own feet as he tried to walk a straight line. The smaller of the two cops cuffed him. "Christmastime drunks," the officer said. "Gotta love it."

During this welcome-back show, Daniel was sitting behind me, cradling me between his knees. I had never felt more safe and secure with his arms banded around me and his breath warm in my ear. This whole scene was fascinating in an odd way. We could see them—the living—but they couldn't see us, hear us, or hurt us. We couldn't die again, although we were warned that our souls would shatter and just evaporate. *But from what? What could cause that to happen?* Obviously, the little red Corvette that Prince sang about sure couldn't make that happen.

What exactly were the rules now?

Reaching into my pack, I rubbed my lucky rabbit's foot. I knew we could use all the luck in this world—or any other. I rubbed it so hard that a little green fur came off in my hand.

4.

"We need to move fast," Daniel said, pulling me to my feet with his outstretched hand. "It's too dangerous here—and we don't even really know why. So we're going to do what we came to do and then go home. Maybe luck will be on our side." My mind fixated on one word. Funny, how this living realm felt like home and at the same time it didn't feel like home anymore at all. It was like going back to your old house that seemed so big and beautiful in your mind, only to find it much smaller and even a little bit shabby.

We had no other choice, but to walk toward the light—but not *that* light.

Downtown Lake Forest was in the near distance.

The city was located on the shore of Lake Michigan and had a long history, dating back to 1857, as a place where travelers stopped while making their way to Chicago. Hiking alongside the road actually felt good because it got the old blood pumping, although my teeth were still chattering. Taking my hand in his, and encasing it in his strong fingers, Daniel walked with me along a gravel path that lined the highway. In my mind, we looked like any other teenage couple on a preholiday date dealing with something as mundane as a flat tire.

As we got closer to the actual city, I could hear something that sounded so sweet and familiar that tears formed to my eyes. *"Just hear that those sleigh bells jingling, Ring-ting-tingling, too. Come on, it's lovely weather for a sleigh ride together with you. Outside the snow is falling and friends are calling yoo-hoo. Come on, it's lovely weather for a sleigh ride . . ."*

"Whoever wrote that about below-zero weather is a sadist," Daniel said.

372

"Or maybe a polar bear," I countered, shivering as we approached Main Street in the charming, upscale Illinois town where Daniel Reid grew up. Gazing up in awe, I could see a gargantuan Christmas tree proudly displayed in the center of town outside of what looked like an old-fashioned, charming, red-bricked courthouse. It was next to a big wooden sign that read: Welcome to Lake Forest, Illinois. Home of Friendly People Who Will Give You a Hand.

A tiny plaque explained that the town was settled as a scenic, historical, and architecturally significant suburb of Chicago. I learned that famed architects David Adler and Frank Lloyd Wright designed many of the estates and mansions that surrounded the quaint downtown. Market Square was built in 1916 as a commercial center and gathering place amid the virgin prairies and nature preserves dotting the town limits.

The public railway station, called the Metra, cut through the center of town and it linked Union Pacific trains to downtown Chicago. Tonight, the city of Chicago, where my mother was probably sleeping, was the least of anyone's concerns here in well-to-do Lake Forest. It hurt me to know she was so close, but still far away from me.

You'll visit her later, I thought. *For now, get Bobby.*

The charming downtown area was dotted with high-end dress shops and inviting small pubs, plus elegant, romantic bistros. There was even a little stationary store owned by a woman named Margaret and a pet shop where you could buy your poodle a fleecy winter coat and a new chew bone.

I stopped as we passed the twenty-foot Christmas tree, gasping when all of the lights on the bottom third sizzled like locusts and then popped, tiny sparks again flying everywhere. Glancing at Daniel, I said, "We seem to be having a strange effect on the electricity here."

"It's all you, Callaghan," he said, still holding my hand. "You're so pretty that lights are bursting all around to announce your arrival."

"Well," I blushed. "Okay, um, thanks. Let's go. We've got things to do."

He leaned over and kissed me on the nose and the middle third of lights blew out with several large pops. "Now that we've spread some Christmas cheer, let's get going. A.E. said he was only back here forty-five minutes and it's been way over that for us. Maybe the trick is to just keep moving."

We continued to walk down Main and then veered off onto a street named Fallon Lane, which was lined with houses so glamorous and large that my eyes popped just like the lights. Decorated in their holiday splendor, I could see into many of the windows, which made my heart ache. I watched families in brightly decorated, illuminated living rooms, wrapping presents, feasting, and laughing as they enjoyed the best time of the year.

"Oh, look," I cried when a blonde Labrador retriever with a big green bow around his neck came bounding down his long driveway. Maybe he was a Christmas present for some lucky little kid. In my mind, I named him Rudolph. "Come here, boy," I cried and young Rudy skidded to a stop a few feet in front of me before putting his tail between his legs, whimpering, and running back for his doggie door.

"So, we're not exactly popular with canines," Daniel said, his arms now wrapped around his chest for warmth, but he was still shivering. Meanwhile, I could see a scrappy little dog walking with her owner who was begging her to do her business.

"Muffin, you make pee pee now for Mommy," said the owner, but Muffin was obviously a rebel. She spied us, stopped in her tracks, and started to smell the air. In turn, I smelled my sweater, which still smelled pretty good. Muffin started whining.

"Muffin doesn't like us either," I said.

As the wind blasted its might, my boyfriend and first love was hopping from foot to foot to stay warm while I watched the living with great fascination as my body trembled. It was obvious that they couldn't see us at all, and I wasn't sure if I was grateful or sorrowful because of that fact.

We stopped by the personal mailbox of a well-dressed woman in high heels and a much-too-short red velvet party dress talking into her phone. "Bob, I don't even believe you when you tell me that you sent a card. It was the very least you could do," she cried, flinging open the little metal mailbox door and rifling through the contents inside. Putting his fingers to his lips to shush me, which was ridiculous because they couldn't hear us, Daniel walked right up to her until he was no farther than about an inch from her face. She didn't flinch.

He put his finger on the tip of her nose. She stopped and sniffed hard. When he tickled her nose, she scratched the bottom of it with a long, red fingernail. When he blew her bangs back, she stopped for a second, looked around, and seemed utterly baffled. I could see her peering into the bare winter trees covered with red Christmas lights. It was as if she wanted to gauge if a north winter wind was kicking up.

She ran a hand through her bangs to force them back into place. Then she returned to her iPhone and punched in another number without even saying good-bye to the first caller. "Jack, it's Melinda," she said in an accusatory voice. "What the heck did you give me to drink tonight? I think I'm totally looped," she said.

5.

Winding back around to the downtown shopping district, I glanced up at a government building sign to see it was now 9:45 p.m. and minus ten degrees. Obviously, a heat wave wasn't in our near future. I could see all the holiday shopping stragglers desperately picking up last-minute treasures.

"Bethany Marie, you get your *bee-hind* into the car or Santa won't come tomorrow night," a harried mother yelled as she dragged a despondent six-year-old behind her. The little blonde girl jutted her chin out in total defiance.

"It's too late to tell Santa I was naughty," she pouted. "He's probably too busy getting the sleigh ready and he can't focus on his e-mails."

"Then I'll text him," her mom threatened.

This time I decided to have a little fun. I tugged the little girl's ponytail ever so slightly so it didn't really hurt, but she did feel the pull.

"Hey!" Bethany yelled, whipping around and seeing absolutely nothing—or so I thought.

She did a full three-hundred-and-sixty-degree spin, which made me throw my head back and laugh. This was one of the fun parts of being in another realm. Invisibility was a powerful weapon. When Bethany turned in my direction, I took my finger and clucked her under the nose.

"Stop!" she yelled, even louder. I could see Daniel lower his head and laugh hard, which made him look momentarily carefree as his body shook with joy. He was still doing the cold dance, but was actually enjoying himself.

"Bethany, get in the car!" her mother demanded. "Right now or I'm cancelling Christmas."

"But Mommy, that girl is pulling my hair. Don't you see her? With the hunk," Bethany said, standing her ground. She lasered in on me. "I can see you!" she snapped. I just rolled my eyes and nodded "yes."

"Oh, please. Is this another one of your imaginary friends? It must be because no one is there," her mother insisted, grabbing her arm. "I don't want to hear you talk all this nonsense or I'll cancel New Year's, too."

Locked in the backseat of her mother's car, Bethany was determined to have the last word. When they passed us, she turned her head, looked into my eyes, and stuck out her little tongue.

"We've just been told off by a brat who can actually see us. I guess some people really are psychic," I marveled, looking down at my hands that were now shaking from the cold. Daniel wasn't psychic, but he still could see into our future. He pointed his index finger and motioned to me to follow him into the one place I never frequented when I was alive. "We're going into a pub to get a drink?" I marveled.

"No," Daniel said with a mischievous smile. "It's our turn to go shopping."

6.

Ronnie's Bar and Grill was a warm, inviting place that smelled like burgers that had been left on the grill for way too long. We snuck in when a couple of middle-aged patrons walked out of the heavy wooden door, and immediately I felt the wondrous rush of warmth from overheated air. Ronnie must have had the heater on ninety, and man, it felt good to thaw out. If only we could order one of those burgers. The smell of meat cooking was my undoing. I could see that the fries passing us in trays came in one variety: Well done and greasy.

Maybe we were in heaven right now.

Should we dare? Could we dare? Clearly, Daniel had no morals when it came to this stuff. He snuck up behind a young waitress in a low-cut top and grabbed four fries off the tray, handing me two sticks of heaven. We scarfed them down like castaways who hadn't had a decent meal in years. I couldn't believe we could actually eat them. They went down so easily that I wanted to shout out my own order for a plate of extra-crispy ones with a few onion rings on the side. Could someone get me a caramel milkshake, extra whip?

The waitress was a young redhead named Gwen, which we learned from her name tag. She served a burger and fries to an overweight, balding man in his fifties wearing a dorky reindeer sweater thanks to an office Christmas party. Maybe it was his lack of fashion that put him in a sour mood, but he decided to give her a hard time. "Is this what you call a drink? Did you run out of liquor in this place?" he fumed, slamming his empty glass on the table. "Why don't you tell the bartender to put a little whisky in it the next time. It's Christmas. It's about *giving.*"

He stared at the waitress, who gave us enough time to stand there and continue to eat his delicious, well-done fries. I laughed when Daniel lifted half of his double cheeseburger, which went unnoticed by the waitress and the man as they continued to lock eyes as they argued. I took a big bite when Daniel held the burger to my lips. Sweetly, he rubbed the running juice off my chin with his calloused index finger.

"Just bring me another drink—on the house," the man fumed, adding, "I'm starving. At least the meal smells good."

That's when he looked down. His horror was priceless. All that was left was a wad of lettuce, no fries, and a lonely sliver of onion.

"Do you think I'm on a diet? Do I look like a rabbit?" he accused the waitress. "What happened to my burger and where are my fries? What's wrong with this joint? I'm reporting you to the Better Business Bureau or the Restaurant Association of America. I'm telling my fantasy football pool."

"I'm so sorry," Gwen told him, looking down at the floor, which was clean. "Honestly, I don't know what happened. I'll be right back with fresh fries and an actual burger."

As she walked back to the kitchen in total confusion, Daniel was at another waitress's tray lifting all but three of the fries, which he left as a calling card. He returned with the loot and a small plate that he covered in ketchup. It was odd because once we held something in our hands it instantly became invisible to the living. Finally, I knew why—when I was alive—I could put my keys down one minute and then they suddenly disappeared the next. My late grandmother probably just moved them to have a little fun with me. And now we were the movers and the confusers. With our loot looking invisible to anyone but us, we sat down at a vacant table to eat what we lifted. The peril of "borrowing it" made it taste even better.

A few minutes later, we were forced to move when Gwen returned with a well-dressed young couple that was being seated "on" us. By then, Daniel had lifted a small pepperoni pizza from a woman who turned her back for a moment and several extra-spicy chicken wings from a guy who was a little drunk and obsessed with watching college football on the large-screen TV. He touched his plate to grab another wing, and looked baffled when all he felt was the actual plate.

By far, our best "get" of the night was when Daniel grabbed exactly what we desperately needed. He struck pay dirt by grabbing two North End parkas off that young couple who obviously had great taste. The coats were white, thick, and filled with extra goose down, which made them both stylish and extremely warm. Daniel lifted them from behind their chairs as "Joel and Linda" were having drinks while enjoying a heated conversation about if they would watch *White Christmas* or *A Christmas Carol* when they got home.

The parkas fit us perfectly. Digging my hands into the pocket, I found the most wonderful gifts including white leather gloves and a cashmere scarf that I knotted around my neck. I also felt Linda's car keys and carefully placed them by her side. It was one thing to take her coat. We couldn't mess with her ride.

As we began to slip back into the night outside, I could hear Linda, the proponent of *White Christmas* saying, "Bing Crosby is the best and it has that great Rosemary Clooney song and . . . Joel, wait a minute! My coat is gone. It was here two seconds ago. It couldn't have just got up and walked away!"

"It's Grandma Lee playing a trick on you," Joel said, without noticing his own missing parka.

"Right. My grandmother has been dead for fifteen years," Linda answered.

CHAPTER 28

1.

Soon we were outside again, wandering away from the charm of small-town life as we silently made our way to the outskirts.

It took us forty-five minutes to walk the two miles to the small, private Lake Forest Airport located on the north rim of town. There wasn't a light on in the any of the airport buildings in the distance nor was there a single living person around. Glancing at Daniel, I tried to see if he was having some sort of reaction to returning to the scene of his death, but his eyes were dark and dangerous. He was capping those emotions until later, or maybe until forever passed by him.

I knew from our research that Lake Forest Airport was a place that didn't look much larger than a couple of football fields lined up end to end. It was marked by one small terminal building where travelers could wait for small jets that raced down a medium-sized runway that ran the length of a prairie field that was almost all fenced in by tall evergreen trees.

For a moment, I could picture Daniel and the kids racing out of that building to their father's small, private jet on their way to a glamorous winter vacation in Florida. Maybe Andy had packed her favorite book. Pete probably brought his video games. I could imagine their father telling them to hurry up and yanking his youngest boy, Bobby, along in that way adults do when a child's feet barely touch the ground, so they can get to their destination as soon as possible.

Now that the Reid children were all dead, this place had taken on an entirely new meaning for them. It was their graveyard, although there were no markings. *Did Mr. Edward Reid ever drive by it thinking, "I can't look that way again"? Or did he find some secret relief in unburdening himself of his children?* In the distance, I could see several private planes. I wondered if one of them belonged to Daniel's father. *Was he still defiant about flying his own plane?*

We didn't talk much along this walk because we were both preoccupied by the reels playing in our minds. I thought about that little six-year-old boy who had been waiting for so long for anyone he loved to come and find him. *But where was Bobby Reid? As a spirit, he might have lingered at this site or . . . not. What if something else found him? What if he moved on to some place unknown?*

"Callaghan, stop."

Daniel's voice snapped me out of my mental "what if" game. But he wasn't calling me on my pessimistic thoughts. He meant stop in your tracks.

Something was about to happen. Something bad.

In the distance it was so dark, but when I blinked a couple times I could spot several private planes that were parked for the night, which meant that we had reached the actual airport. The planes didn't seem so odd because they were supposed to be here, and obviously grounded thanks to weather and the hour. Then I blinked again to focus, and that's when I knew why we were frozen in place.

It was the people.

The dead people.

2.

They were everywhere—like a convention of the deceased. They turned a desolate field into a virtual who's who of the dead. We took a few cautious steps forward and soon I could actually hear them.

"Come on, Jimmy. Time to pay up," said a cop in his 1920s wool coat and beanie hat. He was talking at some chain-smoking guy who looked like a Dapper-Dan gangster dressed in all black including a flowing wool coat. The Dapper Dan had what looked like a machine gun at his side. "Ay, boss, I got your money. Your blood money. Just stick out your hand," he said, putting something into the hand of the cop who was all but licking his chops.

"Jimmy, you wise guy," the cop said with a laugh. "Whadda you make me for? A schnook? You think I'm gonna take my hand off my gun to count the money? Keep dreamin'. I'll count it later, and my money better be all there. Or it's yer funeral."

We had no choice now, but to pass them as we continued on. We walked ever so slowly and surely, hoping that they couldn't see us.

There was no such luck.

It was the cop's turn to stop and glance in our direction.

"Whadda you two rummies lookin' at?" he said to Daniel

and then pivoted in my direction. "Look at Miss Fancy Pants over there," he shouted at me with glee.

Holding my hand tightly, Daniel pulled me along until we safely passed them, but neither moved to stop us. The cop was too keen on getting his blood money from his favorite wise guy. A few steps later, I could see what looked like an actual Native American Indian who was bare-chested and shoeless racing to the safety of the trees. Sensing us, he stopped. When I looked harder, I could see that he had a bow and arrow at the ready and pointed at us. Before we could duck down, he was running past us and disappeared into a cluster of evergreens. I pointed to the next clump of forest. Three of his tribe members were standing and waiting.

One stopped. Stared. Ran on.

Daniel put his hand in front of me like someone would do in a car where the driver was about to slam on the brakes. I stopped on a dime and looked the other way in horror. It was obvious that the others were looking right back at us—and there were many of them in different varieties. They saw us because we were one of them.

"Vote for Roosevelt," said a young demonstrator with a sign that read: FDR—Save Us from the Bread Lines. Happy Days Are Here Again. We walked past her as she reached out for us.

To the living this would simply look like an empty field at an airport that was shut down for the night. To the dead like us, we were just starting our evening amongst our peers.

"Young man." The words punctuated the loud din of the others.

"Yes, you, young man," said a solid man in raggedy denim overalls and a dusty white shirt. He approached us with a rope in his hand and in the darkness I could see he was leading a shadowy figure around. It was a brown, quite annoyed mule. Several layers of old grime and sweat covered the man's tanned brow, which was lined with the deep crevices of working outdoors in the elements.

"I don't know what parts you came from wearing that getup," the farmer said, looking at us in our modern parkas as if we were the ultimate curiosities. "But, if you're looking for work, I need a good field hand since it's spring planting time."

He eyed Daniel up and down in an appreciative way and said, "You look like a strong young man. I'll pay you fifteen cents a day. If you got any boy young'uns, they can work, too. I need all the field hands I can get."

When we didn't answer, he sweetened the deal. "You and your missus can have free room and board in the barn out yonder," he offered with hope in his voice.

I followed his thin, bony finger as he pointed somewhere in the distance to a barn that didn't exist. No one mentioned that in reality the field was covered with a few inches of gray snow and a light coating of ice. It was the middle of winter. Spring was a figment of his imagination. Or was it the truth to his reality?

"Is this your land, sir?" Daniel asked, dropping my hand for a moment. The older man took his craggy hand and wiped his forehead like it was a hundred degrees outside and he was sweating up a storm. "Born and raised on this land," he said, proudly. "My mama gave birth to me over there by the crick and I'll certainly die here. This farm has been in the Anderson family for three generations. Fought the droughts and the locusts here. We're still fighting those damn Injuns who think they belong here instead of the settlers. Well, we'll see about that."

"Do you have any family here?" I asked him.

He looked surprised for a moment and then it dawned on me. Womenfolk in his world didn't usually join in on these manly conversations. "I work the land with my son, and my eldest daughter, May. My younger girls are Beth, Laura, and Sally," he said. "My wife, Caroline, is around here somewhere. She's probably washing clothes down by the crick."

"Ma'am, my name is George Anderson," he said, bowing his head for a moment as a sign of respect. I offered my hand to shake his and he looked at me oddly. In turn, he took off his straw hat and nodded again as a courtesy.

"This is my partner, I mean, my wife, Walker," Daniel said.

"Walker!" George boomed. "Never met a girl named Walker."

"It's her daddy's name," Daniel said and then he introduced himself and explained that he was from Lake Forest.

"Lake what? We have lakes and we have forests, but I never heard of those parts put together to name a town," said George in a laughing voice. Obviously, he was proud of all members of his family, which is why he insisted on us meeting the rest of them. "Beulah is my prized mule. Aren't you girl?" he said to the animal that he tapped on the rump. She moved only a protesting inch.

"My boy is probably hiding. He needs to earn his keep, but the missus coddles him," the farmer told us. "Wait, here's my missus now."

Out of nowhere, a woman in her mid-to-late twenties seemed to materialize. She was a throwback to the 1800s and wore a long-to-the-ground dress that looked like it was made out of burlap and gingham. Her face was plain and devoid of any color and her dark hair was pulled back into a bun that was tucked neatly under a bonnet. It was obvious from her round stomach that she was pregnant. Her midsection was extended way out in front of her and she waddled when she walked.

Farmwife Caroline patted her stomach and smiled at me. "I know it must be a girl. I'm sure Pa told you that all we ever seem to have is girls," she said, smiling, as she continued to pat her tummy. Without another word, she seemed to drift away backward into the nothingness.

Before she disappeared, I saw her standing on what in reality was the edge of the runway. She turned and faced us again before she said, "Got some bread baking for dinner. A nice deer stew. Come! Eat! I know some weary travelers when I see them."

"You must have come from Poughkeepsie," she mused with a faint, tinny laugh. "I hear that in Poughkeepsie they have water that comes from the well and directly into the house. Can you even imagine?"

"Ma, she dreams of living in the big city," said George Anderson. "But I tell her that no matter what, I'll never leave my land. Even when I'm dead and gone it will still be my land."

We waved as we walked away. At last glance, George and his mule were about to plow what was actually a vacant asphalt airport parking lot.

3.

"Why didn't you ask him if he had seen a little boy?" I asked Daniel as we headed toward the one-story terminal building that looked like a giant L. It was nondescript, as most government buildings built back in the 1970s were, and the vanilla-colored bricks made it look dirty next to the fresh white snow.

"Let's leave the ghosts out of it. I'm sure they've seen a lot of little boys and little girls and everything else pass this way," he said.

It was clear that no one was landing here tonight. The building was dark with not an employee in sight. As we approached the side door of the building, we were passed by two Civil War soldiers returning home and a sixties hippie looking for a free concert he had heard about from some other "far out dude" at Woodstock. After they passed us we tried to open the door, but it didn't budge. We tried to jimmy the lock with no luck.

Motivated by sheer frustration, I kicked the door with all of my might.

When my right foot slid *through* the painted and peeling door as if I was moving through quicksand, I gasped and then I fell forward a few inches. It felt like I was swimming in molasses. *I didn't know we could do THIS!* It was clear that Daniel was as surprised as I was, and for a minute he looked so dumbfounded that my face burst into a joyful grin.

"Keep going," Daniel stammered, holding me by the waist just in case I got stuck as I jammed the rest of my leg directly *through* the solid door.

This time, I pushed my arm to the elbow through the hard substance and felt like it had become thick jelly. When I pushed harder, I felt nothing except warmer air from the other side. I was half inside the room.

"Shitballs," Daniel blurted out, borrowing his brother Pete's favorite word, as he held my waist harder and shoved both of us the rest of the way through the door.

We were walking through doors! This possibility never entered my mind, even after the Corvette ran right through me. Maybe at some point it wouldn't be this way, but for now going through solid objects was quite the adventure because we just weren't good at it yet. We were like kids on the first day trying a two-wheel bike—excited but cautious at the same time.

Now that we were inside, our eyes acclimated to the dim safety lights. It wasn't long before we were searching every nook and cranny of the actual terminal building, which was nothing more than a check-in desk, a large waiting room with hard chairs and a few tables, plus two bathrooms. A small coffee counter was wedged in by the chairs and offered everything from cold drinks and hot java to carrot sticks with hummus to the rich business travelers with private planes.

We saw other travelers in the terminal building, but they were harmless, including a woman in a perfect A-line skirt and a fancy, wide-brimmed, white linen hat that made it look like she was a sixties housewife on the way to an Easter parade. "Have you seen my lost luggage?" she cried out. "The bag is blue and says Pan Am. If I don't find it, my husband will just kill me!"

A handsome young man in a black leather jacket, looking like a greaser from an old movie, stood a few feet behind her holding a guitar. "Hey man," he said to Daniel. "Got any idea when one of these birds take off for Clear Lake, Iowa? I have a gig there. The other cats said if I'm late they're going to take off for the next gig without me."

"Go check in at the desk for the schedule," I told him. "Go on, now. Don't want to make those cats mad."

"Much obliged, ma'am," he said in a sweet, southern accent before disappearing into the men's room.

"Bobby!" Daniel called out in a curt whisper when we were alone again. But the only answer was a brisk north wind hitting the buckling terminal windows. Glancing outside, I knew if we had to explore the dense woods surrounding this place we would be sunk. It would take a full team of investigators to comb those woods. We were a team of two, armed with our backpacks, a few weapons, and no time. In fact, I was sure that the clock was ticking madly. Daniel must have been thinking the same thing.

"I hate to say this Callaghan, but maybe we should split up and search the airfield. It might go quicker."

"Yeah," I agreed. "I have a bad feeling that our little visit is getting stranger and more dangerous by the minute. And soon we'll run out of time."

"The story of our lives," said Daniel said with a quirky smile. Then we stuffed our heavy backpacks into one of the terminal lockers and moved our search outside.

As Daniel headed toward the empty tarmac, I explored the boarding area near the outside of the building. As I searched, I kept remembering that the only boy who had ever returned back to the living realm hadn't lasted here this long. A.E. was now serving eternity at ITT for doing exactly what we were doing now. He was only here for part of an hour before "the goons" came to get him. *What goons?* We had been here for way over two hours now and I had an uneasy feeling that we had already worn out our welcome. Yet, nothing had happened. *Maybe A.E. was lying.*

Maybe the goons were sent for him because he did something when he was alive that warranted goons. Maybe we were welcome visitors to this realm. Maybe I was becoming delusional the longer I searched for a pint-sized ghost.

Then I suddenly realized something else that sent a chill down my spine. Something we foolishly hadn't even considered. *How could we have been so stupid!* We landed by the side of the expressway: How would we ever figure out where the portal was back to the Academy? I didn't remember seeing a clown face when we landed in the muck of that ditch. Getting back to the Academy was the one thing that we never explored before we came here. *Getting* here was our obsession. *We found the portal back here, but where was the portal back there?*

While Daniel roamed the outer reaches of the airfield, I stayed close to the building where I quieted these questions for the moment.

"Bobby! Bobby Reid!" I cried, standing near the outside of the terminal's emergency exit. "Please come here. Your brother Danny is looking for you."

In the distance, I could hear Daniel scream for his little brother. "Bobby, come on! Come out. I'm here. I'm sorry," he cried.

Dropping my head, I leaned against the building because suddenly I was bone-weary tired, which was a feeling I hadn't experienced at all since I had been at the Academy. In the afterlife, I slept at night because it was a ritual and felt rather pleasant, but I was never really tired in that way where you can't keep your eyes open. Now, my bones ached and I felt like I could sleep for the next thousand years.

Maybe I could rest for a moment. Leaning against the outside of the terminal building, I planned on taking just a two-minute break.

I closed my eyes.

I opened them when I knew I wasn't alone.

Farmwife Caroline Anderson was standing inches in front of me. She was just *there*. That fact alone made me jump out of my skin. Patting her massive stomach, she ran one icy finger down my frozen cheek and her finger was so hard that I thought it might snap off her brittle hand. Then she said, "Miss Walker, I know about the boy you're hollerin' for. The little lost boy. I know all about him."

"Please," I begged her. "As a mother. Please tell me."

"Are you his mama?" she asked, her light-brown eyes wide and innocent under her bonnet. They were abnormally large eyes that jettisoned chills up my spine.

"Yes, he's my son," I lied. "He's my little boy. I'm his mama."

"Pa will be mad! Pa will tan me," she began to fret, toying with the string on her bonnet. And then she took a step back and I knew she planned on wandering into the distance once more where I would never see her again.

"Can I feel your stomach? Can I touch your baby?" I blurted out.

I knew it was the one request she would never deny me because she was so proud of her ability to create new little farmhands.

"You want to touch my baby?" she said in a soft voice, drifting closer again. "Oh, yes, that would be mighty fine. There are no women I know here to touch my stomach. I miss my sisters." She said those words while moving even closer, but again she didn't really walk. It was almost as if she was gliding on air.

Trying not to recoil, I placed a hand on her stomach and it felt cold and hard like that finger. Maybe there was a ghost baby in there, or maybe there was just a dream of something that wouldn't be possible anymore. At that moment, she surprised me and put her hand on my flat stomach that was rumbling a bit from those greasy chicken wings. "Oh, you have no baby in there," she said. "I know these things. I'm a midwife. I deliver all the babies in town. All the babies are so sweet. Even the dead ones."

When I looked closer, I could see that she only had a few teeth left in front.

"Caroline, please tell me where I can find my real baby, my son," I began. "He's all that I have. I've been looking and looking. Perhaps you've seen him wandering around here. His name is Bobby. He's only six years old and alone."

Then I stopped speaking.

Why would her husband be mad if she talked about some lost little boy? George Anderson told us that he had a son who helped him work his field. But his wife told us that they only had girls.

That left the boy.

"Mrs. Anderson, that boy is not yours," I stated, gazing hard into her washy eyes.

"But he belongs to us now," she replied, looking fearful. In the time it took me to blink again, I realized that Ma Anderson wasn't alone. At least not anymore.

Her husband was at her side holding a pitchfork in his hand. "That boy is mine," he said in a terse voice. "He works for his food. He's paying off a debt to me. Now, get off my land!" he ranted, slamming that pitchfork into what was the sidewalk of the terminal. "I won't have anyone taking my only son!"

Frantically looking over his shoulder, my eyes darted into the distance. Daniel was absolutely gone.

"He has a family that misses him," I begged Caroline Anderson while keeping an eye on that pitchfork her husband kept reflexively jackhammering into the winter-ravaged ground. "Little Bobby Reid," I told her. "He has two brothers and two sisters who are worried sick about him. You can't keep him. He belongs to his own family."

I could see tears forming in her eyes.

"Pa," she said to her husband. "The boy doesn't want to be here. You can't keep him like a slave. That's why he runs away every night. He's looking for his real family." And then she turned back to me. "We find him every morning in his hiding spot. He always goes there before they come. And in the daylight when they sleep, Pa drags him back to work the land."

"Before who comes?" I asked her in a frantic voice, my heart beating out of my chest.

"The demon ghosts. They mostly come after midnight," she said in an emotionless voice.

I did a quick calculation and knew that midnight was right around the corner.

"Ma, he's our boy now. No one claimed him for so long that the law says he belongs to us," George pronounced with a gleam in his eyes that said he meant to keep his smallest farmhand.

"He's not a dog. He's a boy," I said. His look reminded me that women in his world were for making babies and cooking. Not talking.

"Pa," his wife said, "forgive me." Then she turned to me and said, "He waits every night down yonder. Says he knows his big brother is looking for him."

"Ma!" George Anderson thundered.

"Where is yonder?" I yelled watching her take that long,

scrawny finger out of her skirt pocket and point toward nothing in the distance toward the trees. I tried to zero in as she continued to gesture in a vague direction northwest of the terminal building.

"Best be hurrying," she said. "A shadow just crossed the moon. Pa, we gotta go hide in the storm cellar. Call the girls inside. Can't worry about the boy now. We have to save ourselves."

George Anderson surprisingly allowed his wife to take the lead. He put his left palm over his wife's dead stomach and the two of them moved backward in slow motion. They continued to stare at me until they were so far back that they literally disappeared from my sight.

Even though she was far away now, I could hear Caroline Anderson call out to me, "You best hide, too."

"They will extinguish her," I heard George murmur. "Then the boy will be ours forever, Ma. As it was intended."

4.

As I rounded the corner to find the most northwest point of the building, I saw a small bench where on nice sunny days travelers probably sat and waited before their jets took off to Palm Beach and Long Island. Seeing no sign of anyone or any*thing*, I felt I had no choice but to sit down and wait. Daniel had to come back. And then we'd figure this out together.

So I sat in the cold on that old-fashioned wooden bench with three wide slats on the seat and three more on the back for support. I'm not sure how long it took me to fall asleep, but I could always fall into an almost instantaneous slumber when I was alive.

The worlds, both of them, faded to black.

I woke up with a start a few minutes later when my head fell forward hard. It was still freezing cold outside and Bobby Reid wasn't sitting on that bench.

I kicked my legs to wake them up. The back of my right heel knocked into something under the bench.

I glanced down without moving my head.

He was curled into a little ball and hiding under the bench, but he angled his head up and popped one eye out to look at my bum. I wanted to shout out to Daniel, but I didn't dare. One wrong move and I knew I'd never be able to catch him with my creaky legs that were still freezing cold. If he ran into the trees, we would never find him again. For a moment, I thought this could be any child.

But it wasn't any child. I could see from under his modern red hoodie, streaked with dirt stains, that he had the trademark inky-black Reid hair. That much I could register from his position, which looked like he was bracing for something bad. His tiny hands were over his head now, which was buried into his stomach and little, folded legs.

Quite purposely, I swung my legs again—this time, hard enough to tap him on the right kneecap.

"Ouch," he cried out.

"I'm not one of the demons," I said in a sweet, sure voice. "So you don't have to run off. In fact, I can prove it. I'm here with your brother Daniel. We've come to get you, Bobby Reid. By the way, nice to finally meet you. Peter, Andy, and Jenna can't wait to see you again."

He was stealth silent. And then as the wind stilled for a moment, I heard a small, whispery voice say words that I'll never forget.

"Go to hell," said little Bobby Reid.

"Wow!" I said in a mock-mortified voice. "If I said those words my mom would wash my mouth out with soap."

It wasn't really true because my mother had never used soap on me, but it was enough to make him laugh for a second before he added, "Piss off, lady."

"First of all, I'm not old enough for you to call me lady. Second, you're six," I said. "I know your brother is going to want to hug you and then ground you for saying this rude stuff."

In one fluid movement, a furiously angry Bobby Reid swung out from under the bench and stood a foot in front of me with his hands on his tiny hips. He couldn't have been more than three feet tall, but he was fierce and forceful.

"Shut up," he said. "You're just some stupid girl. And I don't have to listen to you. I was in a plane crash. Ka-boom! That means I don't have to listen to nobody anymore. I'm my own boss."

"Shut up?" I repeated. "That's not nice either. And for your information, I'm not stupid. Who do you think helped your brother figure out how to find you, you little toad face?"

"Hey!" he said, momentarily insulted. His small lower lip unfurled into a hurt frown. "I'm not a frog."

When I got a good look at him, I could see that he was one small bundle of emotion with a mop of jet-black hair, which was long past his shoulders now, and those searing Reid gray eyes. He was a compact little guy with a round face and a little pug nose. Bobby Reid was cute enough that you wanted to scoop him up and hug him, and defiant enough that you also wanted to ring his little neck.

"I don't know you, stranger danger," Bobby said, pointing his index finger at me as he read me the riot act. "I don't talk to strangers. Get away from me, you weirdo."

"Sorry, worm, I'm not a weirdo," I told him. "I'm a friend of your brother Daniel. He brought me here to find you. Don't you think I have better things to do two days before Christmas than look for smart-mouthed little brat who keeps telling me to shut up?"

"It's two days till Christmas?" Bobby said in a soft voice. "We all died at Christmastime. Every year I ask Santa to bring me my family. That's all I want for Christmas. My real family."

I decided to change the subject a bit. "I live with your brothers and sisters. They sort of adopted me," I told him. "My name is Walker, and I know you aren't going to believe me, but I can prove stuff to you. For instance, I know that your brother Daniel can't cook and loves dogs. He's a great soccer player. And he's pretty mad at your daddy. I guess those two don't get along."

Bobby seemed interested and said, "And what else do you know, walk the dog, Walker? What a dumb girl name. It's not even a *real* name."

"It's my family's name," I said, taking a deep breath.

"I know that Andy and Jenna like to hide in Peter's closet and jump out to scare him when he least expects it. They're really good at it because girls rule and boys drool." The kid was silent, so I continued. "I know that Pete is a really good catcher. Really good. He can catch anything without even really looking." Of course, I didn't add the part about his big brother Daniel being an excellent kisser. I could leave that out of it.

"Well, you tell Danny that I'm mad!" Bobby yelled as I kept one eye on him and another on the moon. The shadow was deeper and darker now over the light.

"Danny's in big trouble!" Bobby said, tears falling from his wide eyes and down his cheeks. "He better get his butt here because I've been waiting a really long time. A really, really long time and it's cold and I want a hamburger."

"You better tell me all that yourself," Daniel said as I glanced up and saw him towering over his little brother. What happened next wasn't what we expected. Bobby didn't run up to his brother and race into his arms. He looked shocked and gasped. And then he raced up to his big brother and punched him as hard as possible right in his upper thighs. He kept hitting him over and over again until the kid ran out of gas.

"Hey, tough guy, ow!" Daniel cried, crouching down and grabbing the little boy in a fierce bear hug.

"Do you know how much I've missed you?" Daniel said, and tears began to roll down my face as I saw the big man envelope the little boy.

"I've been sitting here for *forever*, Danny," Bobby cried. "Do you know how long forever really is?"

"Actually, I do, Bobby the Great. I really do," said Daniel, still hunkered down and rocking the boy who buried his face in his big brother's neck.

In a small voice Bobby said, "You told me to never go anywhere without you. I just waited and waited for you and I wanna go home. Now. Please. Pretty please with sugar on top. I wanna go home for Christmas."

"Bobby, there is no time to talk about this now. I love you, pal and I'm so sorry you had to stay here alone. You were right to wait for me—and here I am. And we're going home."

I wiped away my last tears that were threatening to freeze in place.

"We're all going to a new place—and it's great," Daniel said, hoisting his little brother up on his shoulder while quickly checking him for basic wear and tear. "You're going to love it there. You're going to live with me and Peter and Andy and Jenna. And Walker over there."

"She's a girl. We have enough girls," I could hear Bobby whisper into Daniel's ear.

"I've know she's a girl," Daniel said, giving me a little wink. "Sometimes that's good."

"Do you like her?" Bobby whispered to his brother, placing his pouting little mouth on Daniel's ear.

"Yeah, a lot," he whispered loud enough for me to hear.

"Gross. Do we have a pool?" Bobby asked, rubbing his eyes.

"No."

"Why didn't anyone tell me we were moving?" Bobby demanded, slugging Daniel again in the shoulder.

"Hey, Rocky Balboa Junior, knock it off," Daniel said. "And no one told me we were moving either. It just . . . happened."

"Can I have a dog?"

"Yes," Daniel said. "We have a dog. His name is Jake."

Bobby's immediate joy was suddenly replaced with a quick squirm and a curtain that seemed to come down over his eyes.

"We can't go anywhere now—even to our new house," Bobby said in a slightly panicked voice. "And you have to put me down. Right now. Put me down, Danny. Now!"

"I'm never putting you down again," Daniel said with a laugh, hugging him harder as he tried to toss him in the air.

"We have to go. We have to hide. We have to run," Bobby implored, squirming hard out of his brother's arms and shimmying down his body. Then he grabbed Daniel's hand. I was shocked when the little boy reached for my hand and started pulling us toward the terminal building as hard as he could.

"It's midnight. And they're coming," Bobby said in an oddly knowing voice.

"What is coming? Who is coming?" I implored as we arrived at the front door of the building, which was, of course, locked. Daniel pushed us back and grabbed my hand and his brother's. The experienced ghost that he was, Bobby yelled, "One, two, three," as he stepped back then yanked us along as he raced through the door like a little speeding bullet. Again, I felt a little wobbly-queasy from the jolt of parting solid matter.

"The demons. They want to eat us, you know," Bobby said in a frantic voice once we were inside. "Come on!"

Still holding our hands, Bobby raced us through the terminal and I could see that he was pulling us hard toward the lockers. When we reached the wall with the rows of tan little doors and bright-orange keys, he dropped our hands and scampered into one of the lower boxes. "Get in one of these and close the door behind you. Hide!" he cried, sliding into the small metal locker and winding his little fingers through the air vents to slam the door.

We were too big to fit into any locker—even the largest one.

"Bobby, listen to me," Daniel said through the slats. We could hear him breathing from the inside. "I'm here and no scary night shadows can bother you anymore. Monsters aren't real."

"Yes, they are," he said, his voice quivering like he was physically shivering. "They're realer than real. You have to hide or they will take you!"

"How do we know if the demons are here?" I asked him. I saw nothing but a vacant building.

His next words were a whimper combined with a whisper.

"They come at midnight to feed. Every night. They stay until morning," he whispered. "You have to be quiet now. They can see you, hear you, and smell you."

We had no recourse, but to stand in front of the locker housing the youngest Reid and wait for these night terrors to materialize in front of our eyes. Our backpacks were in one of the larger lockers and Daniel took them out as a precaution. He unzipped mine and handed me one of our man-made weapons—the morning star, which was the round club with sharp spikes sticking out of it. He armed himself with a large hammer and the caltrop, which was the club with sharp knives sticking out of it in a design that made the cutters look like an extra-large jack from a game of ball and jacks.

Not exactly satisfied, Daniel also passed me a Hunga Munga, the African weapon that had a c-curved Captain Hook blade that could create penetrating wounds. I could see him gripping the large metal hammer and testing its weight in his palm.

We braced.

Nothing happened.

We waited as the clock struck twelve. "Gear up," Daniel whispered, but his words faded away as the safety lights were suddenly cut and we were plunged into total darkness.

What I saw next—and I could clearly see it *and* hear it—made me drop flat to the ground.

CHAPTER 29

1.

Our first demon spirit was a little boy who looked exactly like young Bobby Reid, down to his little red hoodie. Two other Bobby Reids in the same getup, down to the dirty brown sneakers, flanked him. There was always something about twins in horror movies that completely terrified me. The idea of triplet spirits staring back at us was bone-chilling awful. Just looking at them made me feel as if I was plunging every ounce of my body into ice water.

"I'm your brother. Come here and hug me," cried one of the demon spirits.

"No, I'm your brother. Come over here and hold me. I missed you so," begged the second boy-devil.

"Don't move," Daniel whispered. From inside the small locker, I heard the real Bobby whisper, "Don't believe them, Danny. It's not me. They're here to eat us."

When my eyes adjusted to the only thin stream of moonlight coming in through the large picture window facing the runway, I was able to take a closer look at the third Bobby. He was trying to smile sweetly, but the light hit him at the wrong angle and I could see long, fanged teeth protruding from his mouth. His eyes were void of the whites; they were black orbs that looked as if they were created from molten tar. One glance at this "Bobby" and I could make out the hands of a shriveled old man attached to a shrunken body. The nails on his fingers were at least five inches long and sharpened into points that looked like daggers.

"What the hell?" I whispered as I moved into position, standing back-to-back with Daniel to defend what we had left.

A few moments after midnight, the others began to arrive. There were three girls and each was some form of . . . me. It was the freakiest thing I had ever seen in my time, and I knew this is what was meant by my Ka. Those ancient Egyptians were right about your soul fragmenting when you died. And what remained in the living realm were all your most heinous leftovers. Now, those fragments were red-hot angry and ready to annihilate any good that came into their path.

Finally. This was why Dr. King said we could never go back.

What was left behind was lurking. Waiting. Planning. If it couldn't ascend, it would extinguish.

Glancing at the other versions of me in horror, I could see that our faces were a curious mix. They were almost the same, but not exactly. The first girl was me, but in my most hideous form with a mouth that was an enormous, purple-black gaping hole and eyes that began at my hairline and dipped way down past my jaw. The second version of me had the sneer of a wild animal about to rip her prey apart, just for the sheer joy of the destruction. And the last me was the worst me because she was the most cunning of all.

She moved into position next to the little boys and their

flanking stances made it absolutely clear that there were at least two teams playing tonight. It would be three clueless optimists against . . . I wasn't even sure how many faces of evil.

Gripping his weapons in a crouched fighting position to defend his family, Daniel squinted at the third me because she was the vision that was the hardest to resist. It was a far more beautiful me than my real self. Her hair was long, shiny, and blonde like a princess. My new beautiful green eyes were the color of emeralds. She dented in exactly at all the right places and called out to him, making it sound like she was singing an alluring song. My gorgeous self knew the sheer power of her beauty, although it was a power I had never possessed in my awkward real life.

She called to him again in a voice that was as sweet as an angel speaking in verse.

"Danny," she said. "Help me. I need you to save me. I'm so afraid of giving in to the others. I can't give in if you save me."

Every jealous bone in my body raged as I allowed that monster to swallow my good sense and cloud my mind with blind, irrational fury.

"Danny, come with me. We can fight together," she called.

He didn't flinch or falter.

He knew only one thing.

I would *never* call him Danny again, which is why he took a step forward and drove his spike through her heart like a wild hunter spearing a vicious animal. I screamed when she exploded upon impact into tiny bits of particle dust. It didn't take a demonologist to conclude that one sure way to get rid of them was a direct heart shot.

Medieval? You bet your ass.

2.

We had to spread out or they would easily conquer. I ended up frozen in place at the far side of building away from the lockers. I was temporarily mesmerized by a vision of Daniel that stood with his arms open wide as if he wanted to hug me into extinguishment. Ducking to the left, I couldn't move fast enough to avoid his long, spiderlike arms that seemed to reach out for miles as they wrapped around me and clasped tightly behind my back. All I could think of in that moment was my mother going through eternity believing it was her fault that her only child was dead. Then I thought of Daniel and his warm, loving arms wrapped around me late at night. The beast hissed into my ear as it squeezed tighter and I could actually read its thoughts. It would extinguish me by squeezing me into oblivion.

Of all people, my friend Tosh popped into my mind as all the breath rushed out of my lungs. *Tosh would know what to do,* I thought. *She knew what to do during air hockey when she was cornered.* Unhooking its arms, the beast moved its tentacles higher and squeezed even tighter until my right arm went numb.

I dropped the morning star I clutched in my right hand.

Scrambling now, at least mentally, I focused on Tosh who remained in my mind. As it choked me harder in a full-body hug, I went absolutely lax, which was obviously a surprise to it because before it could readjust its pressure, I fell to the floor in a heap.

It reached down, fumbling to make contact and I rolled hard to the right until I was far enough away in the dark to stand up and then leap to the left in a Tosh-style ballet move that baffled the demon. I wasn't much of a dancer, but it was enough evasion to throw it off course. Before I could move again, I saw Daniel racing over at top speed, sliding across the waxed floors and then raising his muscular arm to fling a silver hammer at the beast, hitting the heart mark.

It evaporated in a burst of red light with those arms sizzling on the ground until they were nothing more than snuffed-out sparks.

Its friends were clearly not amused. Something that looked like a distorted Daniel who was at least eight feet tall with arms and legs as wide as tree trunks lunged furiously at the real Daniel, grasping him by the neck as it tried to choke whatever was left out of him. "The boy doesn't belong to you anymore," it moaned. "Give him to us. Otherwise, we will eat him whole right in front of you."

Winding my arm around Daniel's waist for support, I heaved the Hunga Munga with all my might, slicing the demon across its face and then jabbing him hard into his collarbone. "Lower," I could hear the real Daniel moan as he choked hard. Darting backward, I swung as hard as possible, pretending we were back in gym class taking batting lessons during softball season.

I closed my eyes and aimed for its chest, hoping that I didn't hit too low. Too low meant I got its stomach and too high meant it could easily grab my own weapon and use it against me.

I did it so hard that the stick flew out of my hands and into the air.

Contact! It was a perfect chest shot that splintered the thing into a billion tiny particles that just dispersed into the air.

As the thick cloud of demon dust settled around me an awful thought crossed my mind. My weapons weren't in my own hands anymore. I had tossed both of them and was now unarmed. I looked around frantically for Daniel, but couldn't find any sign of him or my weapons. Twisting hard on my right foot, I wondered if I could actually outrun the demons as I made my way to my backpack, which was now far away by the lockers housing the real Bobby.

Before I could burst off in that direction, the goon Bobbies scurried up from nowhere just like rats looking for the last bits of food. They were small, but lethal. Willing myself to look away, I couldn't help but be fascinated by their next move. Joining their wrinkled hands, they made a fast circle around me and did a high-speed dance jig that almost made me dizzy. *Get out! Get out of here!* my brain screamed, but it was too late because I felt myself being hypnotized by them. The Bobbies were opening the fanged holes in their faces and did a few test bites by snapping at the dead air.

They moved closer and closer until I felt their pointed feet kicking me hard in the shins, which was almost enough to make me buckle and fall for their feasting. Glancing to the side, I let out a cry when I saw Daniel fighting hard with a demented version of me that had picked up my Captain Hook slicer from the ground. Her face was three times as wide as normal, which gave her greater sight power to slice hard at Daniel's midsection. The little Bobbies weren't done playing with their prey. As they moved even closer, I could smell the death on them and shuddered when two of them reached out to grab handfuls of my hair, pulling hard. Sickly, delighted smiles played on their faces as they danced again while one of them struck out, kicking me so hard with his metallike legs that I crashed hard to the floor.

On my back now, with my hands covering my heart, I tried in vain to slide, but they had me flanked in all directions. Two of them jumped on my chest as if it were a bed, and they pounced hard while the third landed squarely in the center of my stomach. My eyes slammed shut. *So this is how it will end? They'll extinguish me and it will all be over? I'm so sorry, Mom. I'm sorry I couldn't tell you the truth, and I love you . . . I love you, Daniel.*

3.

In my last moments, I heard myself cry out, "You rotten little bastards!" When I opened my eyes again, I could see that one of the boys had what looked like a child's slingshot in his hand with a round, plum-sized metallic marble that was gleaming silver. I knew he was going to shoot and score a heart shot at me.

I closed my eyes hard.

And I heard it. I wasn't sure how particle dust like myself could hear anything anymore, but it was as clear as if the voice was whispering into my ear.

It was a deep, rich baritone that was commanding me to do his bidding and do it quickly.

"Walker Callaghan, stand up. There is nowhere for you to go, but Up," he said.

"Is this my maker?" I asked in a faint voice, my back still pressed to the floor and my eyes cemented closed.

"No, it's not your maker. It's your principal," stated Dr. Marvin King.

My eyes flew open. He wasn't just here with me in spirit. He was also here with me in reality, as real as Daniel and I were. I could see that Dr. King was neatly dressed in handsome black woolen slacks and a white turtleneck with a matching black overcoat that swept past his knees. Reaching deep into his pocket, he pulled out what looked like a palm-sized gold Frisbee fashioned into points on several ends. I knew exactly what it was from Daniel's list of ancient weapons. It was a throwing star with five deadly points that were as sharp as surgeon's scalpels.

By now, the spirit boys were fascinated and frozen in place.

The voice of authority mesmerized them and even the shooter had put his slingshot down in a random angle on my chest as he looked up at Dr. King in absolute awe.

"In this realm, we don't do detention," Dr. King said, savagely slicing the air as he flung the first throwing star into the heart of the shooter kid who burst on impact.

"We do permanent expulsions," said Dr. King as he grabbed two more stars out of his pocket and took care of his remaining little buddies by slicing their souls right in half. There wasn't much to extinguish as each burst into little puffs of dust.

"Doctor King," I stammered, closing my hand around the slingshot on my chest and leaping to my feet.

"Walker, we need to talk," he demanded, wiping the sweat from his brow. I saw that he wasn't walking right. In fact, he stumbled forward a few feet and then stopped to balance himself again with a gold walking cane. It was the type of instrument that you might find on a very old man, but Dr. King was never feeble or old at the Academy. He was ageless.

"Are you hurt, sir?" I asked, frantically looking to the left and right for any additional Ka visitors.

"I was born hurt," he said. "And this climate doesn't do much for my constitution. I hate the cold, but that's neither here nor there."

"Walker, what in the hell are you doing here? I want you to tell me why you would pull a stunt this insane," he demanded. "Did I not tell you the very first day that you must never even think about this—let alone end up here."

"I will tell you, sir. In just a second. It's actually a good story, sir. You're really going to enjoy it," I stammered, aiming and then pulling the cord taut on the slingshot and scoring a perfect bullet into the heart of Daniel's tormentor who exploded with a bang.

Wiping sweat from his own brow, I saw Dr. King gaze at me

quizzically, shaking his head. Slowly, he lurched forward to make his way with that hurt left leg over to his least-favorite student who was splayed on the floor breathing hard. Daniel didn't say a word. "I should have known from the start, Mister Reid, that you would be involved in something like this," said Dr. King who began to admonish Daniel.

The man I loved was half folded over in pain now, holding his knees and wheezing loudly.

At least he was in one piece.

And he wasn't alone.

"Stop being mean to my brother!" screamed a defiant Bobby Reid who popped out of a locker and did a quick scan of the room. When he saw a tall, stately figure who looked quite normal, he flinched because he wasn't sure if it was out to get him.

"Who the hell are you?" Bobby demanded.

"Who the hell are you?" Dr. King boomed.

"He's with us," I said to Bobby, giving him a quick thumbs up. It was enough of a distraction that I had time to kneel down near Daniel and throw my arms around him. I could feel from his ragged breathing that he had been banged up pretty good. When he caught his breath, he gave me the same once-over. Then he kissed me on the forehead and stood up.

"Who am I?" I could hear Bobby yelling in the corner at Dr. King. "I'm Bobby Edward Reid, which almost spells bear." Then in a meeker voice, he asked Dr. King, "Are you one of the bad guys?"

"Are you?" Dr. King asked, staring down at Bobby whose eyes were wide and defiant.

"Nah," the little boy said. "I'm just a kidnapped orphan who had to work my butt off for some stupid farmer guy."

"I don't have to do that anymore, do I?" he pleaded. "It was awful hard work and that mule was really mean and smelly." Then he leaned closer to Dr. King and whispered, "And the food was real mushy and terrible. So I runned away."

"No, you don't have to do that anymore, but no more running away," said Dr. King in a voice that sounded a bit amused. "Young man, you're going to come back with us and go to a proper school. I'm sure the Academy could use a tough, shrewd, short person like you who can take care of himself under the most dire of circumstances."

"Mister," Bobby interrupted. "What does shroo mean?"

"Shrewd means you are intelligent and can take care of things," Dr. King explained.

"Tell me stuff I don't know!" smiled Bobby.

"Bobby, you okay?" Daniel said, lifting him into his arms. "Shrewd means smart, which is exactly what we won't be if we stay here."

"Shrewd is exactly what Miss Callaghan and your brother were not when they came to this place, but now we're leaving. All of us. Immediately," said Dr. King.

Then Bobby looked around as if he was surveying the damage. Or was he just waiting for the next round? "It's safe. For now," he said in a most fearful voice. "But they'll be back. They're always back."

CHAPTER 30

1.

"No!" I screamed, stunned at the velocity of my own voice blasting through the terminal. "We're not leaving this place until I see my mother." The air in the room had turned cold now, and I felt myself begin to chatter.

"Walker, Mister Reid, Robert, we need to go now," Dr. King repeated, ignoring my outburst. "Those demons will be back with friends."

Nodding, Daniel scooped up the boy and put his arm around me.

"No!" I repeated as the others just stared at me. "That wasn't the deal."

I said the words while looking hard at Daniel. "The deal was that we find Bobby, go see my mother so I can talk to her, and then we go." The words came out hard, and I fought with all my might not to burst into tears as I said them. "Then we go home," I said in a much quieter voice. The truth of the matter was that the Academy was home now.

"Absolutely not!" Dr. King roared. "We won't be conducting any additional field trips in this realm, Miss Callaghan. I told you not to come here for a good reason. You could just as easily have ended up like those spirits that I—we—evaporated tonight."

"I'm not leaving until I see my mother," I said. "Ten minutes with her—or I won't go back to the Academy. You can go. But I'm staying."

"Is it worth eternity?" Daniel asked, putting Bobby down and taking me in his arms. Looking into his eyes, I knew he knew the answer.

"Doctor King, take Bobby back. I'll take Callaghan to go see her mother. I think I got the hang of this now," Daniel said.

Smiling at him, I allowed my head to fall forward onto his chest where a secret, silent tear slipped out. I wasn't going anywhere without telling her the truth about that night. I knew she would never rest again until she knew.

"No way, no fair, not happening," Bobby cried, now clinging to his big brother's leg. "You don't go anywhere without me. Never again."

Out of the corner of my eye, I saw Dr. King reach for his cane. "For God's sake," he boomed. "All three of you will be the permanent death of me. You're telling me that ten minutes with Walker's mother is worth it? Then let's just get this over with. All of us will go together."

"Move!" he commanded, but he moved the slowest as we wandered outside the terminal into the blustery winter freeze.

413

2.

The hard north wind was like a slap to the face. Bobby was clearly invigorated and like a young pup, he ran circles around us. Daniel held my hand and we moved quickly as Dr. King limped to keep up. I knew we couldn't walk anywhere with him. He could barely make it halfway across the small airport parking lot.

"How will we get to downtown Chicago?" I asked over the wind. "That's where my mom is living these days." Daniel glanced at me quizzically because I hadn't shared this recent bit of news with him.

I could see Dr. King's eyes scanning the lot, which was populated by BMWs, Cadillacs, a Rolls-Royce, and even an Aston Martin, the James Bond wheels. Dr. King pointed his cane at a brand-new black BMW that was in a handicapped spot. The windows on it were so dark that I couldn't see anything inside.

"Who drives?" Dr. King said and Bobby's hand jetted up.

"I drive. Big Wheels," he announced. "I drive really good."

I'm not sure how Dr. King did it, but suddenly the BMW's security system was disabled and a shrill blip told us that the doors were now unlocked. A second later, Dr. King opened the passenger's side door and then all the other doors followed suit.

"I'll drive," Daniel said. "My dad had a garage full of these cars. He was good at collecting things. Cars. Children." He slipped behind the wheel and with once glance from Dr. King, the car started. Bobby and I slid into our spots in the cushy backseat. I could barely see outside the backseat window because the tint on it was so dark. "Who owns this thing? Beyoncé?" I asked.

"Mister Reid," Dr. King began, "I'm sure I don't have to remind you to drive the legal speed limit, which is sixty-five and not one sixty-five. The last thing we need is for some cop to pull over this car and discover it's being driven by absolutely no one."

"Cool!" Bobby exclaimed. "It's like the headless horseman, but better. We have a DVD player back here."

"Yes, sir," said Daniel, who still insisted that we buckle up. What the hell? Who needed seat belts anymore? Before I could do anything, I felt Bobby slide over and then plop into my lap. Glancing backward, he wiggled even closer until I felt his little body relax. Running a quick hand through his silky hair, I felt my heart lurch down that slippery slope that led to love. "Tell me about my new dog, Walkie-Talkie," he teased me before stretching his mouth into a wide yawn.

"Well, his name is Jake and when he was a puppy he had the biggest ears," I said. "He looked like a Jackalope, but we call him a Jake-a-lope. By the way, he also weighs more than you and he likes to eat anything, including your socks. So put them away when we get home."

Throwing the car into reverse, the driverless car pulled away.

"And he slobbers a lake each day. More slobber than all the water in Lake Michigan," I whispered like I was telling him a great bedtime story. "He especially likes to slobber on little boys. He will drown you."

"Awesome," Bobby said, as his eyelids began drooping.

"Walkie."

"Yes?"

"You fought real good. For a girl," he said in the sleepiest voice.

"Thanks, toad face," I said, ruffling his hair again.

3.

The driverless car obeyed the sixty-five-mile-per-hour speed limit all the way down the Edens Expressway that led into the big city. This gave Dr. King ample time to express his true displeasure about our recent study-way-abroad plans. "Mr. Reid, I blame you for this because Miss Callaghan is too smart to do something this foolish—at least I thought she was too smart until I saw her on her backside being devoured by a demon child," he said.

That was just the beginning. As usual, the suburban route into the city was a long one, so there was plenty of time for Dr. King to explore all of his feelings on this distasteful subject matter. "What the hell were you thinking?" he boomed. Somehow Bobby snored through it. "I know there were extenuating circumstances," Dr. King ranted.

"But how did you even know where we . . ." Daniel began to speak, but Dr. King shot him a look and their eyes locked. For once, even Daniel backed down.

"Those trackers I gave you weren't for monitoring *where* you were going, only *when*. From day one, I knew what you were doing, Mr. Reid. I know what kind of research you were conducting because I knew of your little brother who was stuck," Dr. King said in a low, disgusted voice. "I just never thought that alone you'd be able to figure this out. And then enter Miss Callaghan with her natural curiosity and straight A average."

"You got straight As?" Daniel interrupted, staring at me from the rearview mirror. "Way to go, baby. I always liked smart girls."

"I told you from the start, Miss Callaghan, that doing this was breaking the most sacred rule," Dr. King began to rant again.

"Doctor King," I said, calmly. "How is it even possible—not to think about it?"

He didn't answer and the silence pushed my anxiety levels into the red.

"I do not govern your thoughts. I'm not a mind reader," he said, backing down a bit. "But I do rule over your actions, Miss Callaghan!"

"A few of you have tried this over the years. A.E., one of the strangest children I've ever known, bragged about it. There was no saving him from ITT," Dr. King said—and I had a feeling he was talking to himself now. "Now, what do I do? Turn you into the Higher Authority? Let this go? Hide any evidence of what you've done?"

We were silent as he wrestled with himself. And then it was decided. "If we somehow get back in one piece, I will consider keeping this strictly between the four of us. If not, both of you are incarcerated for eternity," he barked.

There was the one wild card.

"Can you keep a secret, Bobby?" Dr. King implored.

"Most of the time," the little boy said, holding up his hand. Bobby sealed the deal by shaking on it with Dr. King. "Tic tack, no take backs," he said.

"Tic tack, no take backs," Dr. King mumbled. "Whatever that means."

"Doctor King," I began.

"You're not even close to thanking me yet," he told me, turning around abruptly to shoot me a disgusted look. When he righted himself again, the car was plunged into absolute silence, so I allowed myself to just gaze out the window as I had so many times before when I was alive and my mom drove us into the city.

Once we passed the legendary Morton's salt plant, the bright lights of big skyscrapers came into view and dotted the skyline like millions of twinkling stars. Traffic was unusually heavy for the early morning hours of Christmas Eve and it soon it became apparent why we were inching to a crawl.

"Oh no."

The Chicago Police department had slowed down all the lanes and now we were being funneled into a sobriety checkpoint at the tollbooth before entering the actual city. I knew we were absolutely sunk. Yes, we were sober, but we were also *invisible*. I could see it now: "Hey Tony, go check out the black BMW. Those windows are so dark we can give them a ticket for that."

"If it comes to it, we'll all duck out and walk the rest of the way," Dr. King advised. But I knew he was the one who could hardly walk ten feet on a paved sidewalk, let alone hike miles down the side of a highway with goon spirits lurking everywhere to stop us.

"Sir, we can't," I began. "You can't."

Two burly officers approached the car. One took a billy club and began to tap on the driver's side window. I held my breath.

Before the cop had finished tapping, his partner yelled in a trademark Chicago accent, "Ay Gus, it's every other car we're checking. Let 'em go." We were spared, while the guy in the Bronco behind us with Wisconsin plates was hauled out to take a sobriety test. Thankfully, the Chicago cops always had it out for those cheese lovers.

4.

It took us another twenty minutes to drive to the heart of the city and into a neighborhood dubbed Greektown because immigrants from Greece lived there and many opened restaurants that offered some of the best food in Chicago, like lamb kabobs, hummus, and seasoned meat stuffed into grape leaves.

Before we had left the Academy for this mission, I went into the school office and talked to kindly Miss Travis about my mother and how much I missed her. "Oh dear, I know it's so extremely hard," she said, pouring me more tea and offering enough sympathy for ten despondent students.

"Walker, dear, you were very lucky and should count your blessings," she said. "You enjoyed what I call 'extra time' with your mother here. Most students don't get to bring parents to help them with the transition."

"What I'm really wondering is where my mother is living now," I posed.

Miss Travis gave me an all-knowing smile and said, "Why, she's back in Chicago." Knowing that I needed specifics for our trip, I pressed her for more information.

"Walker, you can come into the office anytime for this kind of information. It might just put your mind at ease," she said. "Someday, you won't need to link to our computers to figure it out. You'll be able to do that on your own. Until then, why don't you just think of me as your own personal GPS system. But, unfortunately, today our computer systems are down."

WT Frick. I couldn't believe it. I was in this limbo and even here they had computer issues. Who did they call here? Some afterlife Geek Squad?

I had to return for three days of all the tea I could drown in until Miss Travis finally provided an actual update. "Your mother was released from Michael Reese Hospital several weeks ago. She did live with your Aunt Ginny for a bit, but then she moved downtown to be closer to a rehabilitation center where she's learning how to walk again. Her back condition is much better."

"Do you have an address?" I asked. "You know. To make it

official. To put my mind at ease."

5.

My entire body was trembling as we all stood in front of 1501 Halsted Street in Greektown. It was a three-story, red-brick building next to the Greek Isles Restaurant where a tiny dancing Greek cook boogied on a neon sign. Outside of the building was a dirty white awning and a lonely, single strand of holiday lights adorning an almost-naked evergreen bush that looked like it would topple over if you breathed near it.

Christmas Eve was here. So was my mother.

Dr. King spoke first. "We have ten minutes, Walker. I'll let everyone into the apartment and we'll wait in another room until you're done. It's not safe for us to be outdoors for a long period of time."

Dr. King, of course, was a civilized, un-ghostly type of ghost. Walking through walls was clearly not his idea of a good time. Quickly, I discovered that our fearless leader had advanced powers—that had already come in very handy with the car—and I stared at him as he got to work. I'm not sure how he did it, but Dr. King was amazing at subverting locks by just running his index finger over them. His finger produced the solid click of the front door of the building, which opened easily. He also scrambled an inner door's security code, so it popped open without a struggle. When I raised my brow at him in awe, he simply lowered his head in a quick, but sure, nod. There was no time to discuss how he did it. He just did it.

Motioning us to follow, Dr. King quickly trudged down a

long, moldy-smelling first-floor hallway to apartment 1C with the three of us bringing up the rear. I could hear a loud TV from one of the apartments and smelled the putrid odor of some sort of fish cooking. The hallway was void of people, but messy with old newspapers and even a stray kid's bike leaning up against a wall.

1C.

Callaghan was on the door written on a white strip with black magic marker. Just seeing it made my heart pound.

Dr. King didn't waste any time. Quickly, he unlatched my mother's front door, sliding the dead bolt open with his thumb. It was as if the small piece of solid steel was nothing more than a piece of paper he was moving across a desk.

I couldn't wait to see her.

6.

Even Bobby was quiet when we walked into what looked like a shabby, but comfortable living room. The beige pile carpeting was worn and stained in spots, but our brown, lumpy antique of a couch hid some of the damage.

Just seeing that old, tattered piece of furniture made me smile because it was where I flopped every single day when I came home from school. I wrote my stories for the school paper on that couch and studied for history tests on it. I even flung myself onto it in despair when I thought my best friends had dumped me for no other reason than the sheer drama of it all. Next to the couch was our mostly scratched bookcase that we found at a garage sale and repainted a clean white. Those shelves held the pictures that told the story of our lives: There was me when I was a fat, bald baby;

pigtailed me at Lincoln Park zoo petting a goat; Dad throwing his laughing baby girl up in the air; Mom and me at Christmas last year with home-cut bangs and without a care in the world—or maybe we had cares that didn't really amount to anything at all. If only we knew then not to worry about any of it. So much time wasted. But it was too late to wish and wonder.

Now, I was gone. And my mom was here. We didn't belong together anymore.

At that moment, I felt afraid and I wasn't sure I wanted to see my mother at all. *Would she look different? Would she look broken inside and out?* Time was moving us along at different speeds now. *Would she feel me? Wake up and recognize me? Would she be glad? Would she be afraid of me? Was I still her daughter?*

Suddenly, I felt so bone-weary that I couldn't help but walk over to that stupid lumpy couch and sit down. Jostling around a bit, I tried to find my spot, which was a little groove where my body would just melt into the nubby fabric. Melting into that spot was only natural. I sat in that same spot for over ten years. It was mine. Or was it? There was no groove. No recognition. Not even from the fibers. Not anymore. The surface was flat. It might as well have been a new couch because my spot was gone. I didn't fit anymore.

And that was enough to make the giant ball of grief in my stomach launch into my throat. The sob that followed came from the depths of my soul.

Burying my head into my hands and weeping, I could see Daniel move quickly and helplessly toward me, but Dr. King abruptly stepped in front of him with great effort. The block seemed to work because Daniel allowed him to win. "Mister Reid, Robert, go into the kitchen," he insisted. "Do it right now. Please."

There was no discussion or resistance from either, which meant that Dr. King could take his time and painfully limp to where I was sitting. "Do you mind if I sit, too? I have never felt this tired," he said and I looked up. Nodding at him was my only recourse because I couldn't speak anymore.

Taking my hand in his creviced and worn one, he didn't speak for what seemed like a long time. And then he spoke in a low, sure tone. "This is the worst part," he said. "Why do you think we told you not to come back here? It's not just what happened at the airport. It's this exact feeling. It's the knowledge that it all goes on without you, which it does because it's supposed to go on. Until you learn how to gain control of your deepest emotions, this will break your heart every single time."

Pull it together, Walker, I thought. *Stop it. Don't cry anymore. Grow up.*

"What you're not realizing is that you go on, too. You ascend and someday they will join you in your new home. They've got a reservation, too. No cancellation policy. You just gotta wait until they show up. All things in their own good time."

"What about all the crap about us always being around them. Visiting them," I sobbed, wiping my tears on the sleeve of my mother's sweater, which was slumped on the back of the couch.

"All in good time for that, too," Dr. King repeated. "May I remind you, young lady, that you're still a freshman? You want me to teach you all the tricks when I'm still trying to intimidate you and get you in line? I gotta save some stuff for sophomore year."

I should have smiled, but instead I kept crying. "I don't know what to do," I finally whispered, pointing to a closed bedroom door, where I was sure my mother was sleeping.

"Why do we make everything so damn complicated when it's really so easy?" Dr. King posed.

And then he told me.

"All you need to do is go into your mother's bedroom. Lay down next to her. Close your eyes. And go into her dreams."

"What do you mean, 'go into her dreams'?" I asked.

"What do you think dreams were made for in the first place?" he posed. "Dreams are the great in-between. They're the real limbo."

CHAPTER 31

1.

There wasn't much room to walk. My mother's bedroom was the size of a postage stamp with just a tiny space for a full-sized bed, one wobbly nightstand, and a small TV on a wooden crate. With great trepidation, I stepped inside and shut the door behind me, which seemed to seal our fate. This was just between the two of us.

I heard her before I saw her. She was there breathing lightly just like I always remembered from all those times I wandered into her room late at night with some death-defying problem like a history test the next day or the fact that she forgot to sign a field-trip form. She was sleeping, looking so achingly beautiful to me that I just wanted to stand in that spot forever.

Mom wore an old pale-pink nightgown, the one with the small flowers on it that I had seen a million times. The worn cotton gown was big and baggy now and the short sleeves had fallen onto her arms. Her graying hair tumbled softly down her back and onto her broad shoulders that were milky-white from sickness. I could see her fragile veins that were like a road map to her soul.

I took a moment to savor this bubble in time. Even though her new bedroom was microscopic, the place smelled like my mother down to that lemon-verbena body wash that she loved, mixed with a faint mildewing scent of fermenting library books piled high on the small oak nightstand that had been ours for decades and counting. We polished it with lemon Pledge every Saturday morning because it was a so-called antique treasure found at a local garage sale. A small clock on that nightstand told me that it was 2:15 a.m.

I half expected my mother to look different, but that simply wasn't true. She looked like herself in the midst of a really bad dream. She slept fitfully now as if whatever was playing out in her head was horrifying to her. *Mom, wake up,* I thought. *I'm here. It's going to be okay. It's Walker. Just wake up for a minute and then you can go back to sleep and remember this forever like the very best dream.*

I could see that she slept on that same, ancient double mattress that she shared with my father, Sam, all those years ago when they were a young married couple with all the hopes in the world for a bright future. She already had to live through the loss my father when I was only five. He had been a strong building of a man. But even buildings tumble.

My eyes began to ache when I saw something else by the side of the bed that was illuminated by the silver moonlight. It was the unmistakable metal of a medical walker with tennis balls attached to the bottom of its legs. It hurt me that my mother was obviously still struggling with her physical recovery.

Oh, Mom.

My thoughts were interrupted by her words, although they

426

were garbled. "Walker, no. Baby, no," she cried in her sleep, tossing from her side to her back and then returning to her starting position again as she twisted in agony.

"Lie down next to her," I remembered Dr. King telling me. *"Breathe. It's like showing her a movie. Just hit the play button."*

And so I did.

Sliding into position beside her, I stopped for a moment to enjoy a feeling that was so familiar, yet also somehow different now.

"Mom," I said aloud. "Feel me. I'm right next to you."

It didn't register. All she did was breathe in a frantic way.

Taking her hand in mine, I concentrated on her thoughts, searching for her memory of our accident. I wanted to know what she remembered; what she couldn't forget. Then I saw it. It played like a movie in my mind because my mother was doing exactly what Dr. King said. She was doing what I was doing. *Breathe. Let the film roll.*

Tonight, I would join her. I was the unplanned visitor.

I stopped her film and began to rewind. When I was sure we reached the beginning, I began to tell her my story.

Death Story: Walker Callaghan
Age of Demise: 17

It was the first week of the school year and the hospital had finally given me my walking papers. A summer cold had turned into one of those scary bad coughs. When the wheezing had begun, Mom gave me extra cough medicine and she dragged my unwilling, lying self ("yes, I'm getting better") to the Walgreens walk-in clinic. We didn't have health insurance and I could see the mix of horror and dread on my mother's face when that nice young doctor from some foreign country said, "I'm sorry, Missus, but there is no other choice. You daughter has pneumonia. She needs to be hospitalized before you find her passed out, not breathing. I can't put it any other way. This is an emergency. It sounds like a freight train inside of her lungs."

Aunt Ginny opened her checkbook and soon I was in a semiprivate room at General Hospital. A few days of breathing tubes and IV meds finally did the trick and my poor, scarred lungs returned to a degree of normal where the wheeze was only faint. After a week, the wheeze finally ceased and I was sprung. They say that the day you get out of the hospital is like another birthday and it's true. Everything looked beautiful, even the gnarled, half-naked elm tree by Aunt Ginny's driveway. But I wasn't strictly out of the woods just yet. The doc told Mom, "I want to see her on a regular basis. Just to be sure."

One of those appointments was on a mid-September afternoon after school—when fate intervened. The doc had an emergency involving a kid, a skateboard, and a big pothole, and the nurse rescheduled three times. Mom had to settle for the late six p.m. appointment in the city. There was no other choice.

It was really cold outside—too cold for early fall—and Mom certainly didn't want to take my newly healed lungs out on a blustery, freezing-cold evening. She made me bundle up in a coat and a long, heavy cable-knit sweater over my T-shirt and jeans. "It's so cold today, it feels like winter already," Mom said.

After what could only be called a stellar medical report, including a clean chest X-ray, Mom and I could both breathe easily for the first time in two months.

It was colder than I could ever remember a September night as we made our way to the car. "How about we stop by the old-age home and then go out for dinner," Mom suggested. She volunteered at a place that took good care of her own late mother, and I knew Mom had to be there the following morning to drop off some stuff. Why not just get it out of the way tonight? Why make Mom drive twice. Of course, I nodded yes.

Mom had been collecting items to bring to the old folk's home, called Shady Gardens, including fabric and feathers for a project that weekend where visitors would sew colorful throw pillows for the elderly residents.

The minute we got inside the car, I crawled into the back so she couldn't see me nonstop texting my friends. Mom flipped on the news radio station to check on the weather. The DJ was squawking about how we were in the grips of a polar vortex that had made our late summer so unusually cool. And now, this polar thing was back with a vengeance. "I'm even expecting a dusting of snow tonight as the temps dip into the high twenties," he said.

As we drove down Milwaukee Avenue toward Shady Gardens, the DJ proved his point. A little dusting of the white stuff hit our car windshield, but then a mile later, thick white flakes began to burst from the clouds. In a matter of minutes, a fall evening had become a winter one as the snow began to cover the city in a white blanket of beautiful purity.

Mom decided to stay on two-lane Milwaukee Avenue all the way out to the 'burbs because it was less traveled than the highway.

I rolled down the window of the car to catch a few flakes. The snow was a natural beauty: porcelain, powered, and glistening. Glancing at my mom, I knew that driving wasn't exactly the same pristine experience. She was white-knuckling it now as it snowed harder. The dense flurry suffocated our tiny blue Honda as it wound down the twisting road that, once you got out of the city, was flanked on both sides by dense forest. The snow just wouldn't stop. The vortex meant that all plans were now cancelled. We were going home.

Mom was inching along in that little car, silent prayers probably racing through her mind. I could see the obvious end result of this evening: Mom breathing a sigh of relief as she parked, then the mad dash inside Aunt Ginny's apartment. I willed myself to think about a nice hot bath and a rerun or two of Raymond before heading off to *bed. Maybe tomorrow would even be a snow day and we could just hang out. I wondered if we still had coffee ice cream, my favorite.*

And then . . . there was no then.

I felt our skid before I saw it. It felt like the day I took a raft way out into the ocean during a trip to Florida. The waves made me sway hard to the side and there was no use in trying to control it. Nature is tricky that way. On the road, the asphalt seemed to disappear in the snow and we were airborne a few inches and slamming left—hard!

The next thing I heard was an explosion that rivaled the loudest firework ever set off on the Fourth of July. The heinous sound of metal grinding on metal filled my ears while I felt the sudden blast of winter-cold air hit my face because the windows in the car no longer existed. I felt myself jettison up high and fly out the window into the cold night until I was falling, falling, falling.

The Honda crash-landed upside down in a ditch that was packed with wet snow. Mom took flight next and landed in a bed of snow on the side of the road. The little car slipped down several inches, stopped, and then slipped the rest of the way until the exposed back end was packed with snow.

As for me . . . this is what I remembered next.

I fell with snow and feathers swirling all around me.

They were flying and so was I.

And then the world stopped.

2.

Mom, listen to me, I begged her in my mind. *That's not it. There's more.*

Now I know what really happened.

Again, I showed her the two of us driving home in that blinding snowstorm. Instead of her stopping cold on the road, as she remembered, and crashing into the truck, I let it play out the way it really happened, rewinding to Frank Wargo behind the wheel of an eighteen-wheeler. Again, my mind turned the story into a movie, and I hit the play button to show her. . . .

Deer emerging from the woods and gathering alongside the road in some sort of predestined formation, side by side, curious yet cautious—except for one.

Frank Wargo noticing the deer, the glint from their eyes illuminated by his headlights.

That one doe wandering onto the road where she stops and stands waiting, watching.

Frank Wargo locking eyes with the doe and grounding his foot to the brakes.

Frank's truck slipping out of control from the thick sheet of black ice concealed beneath the snow.

Headlights flashing wildly as mom rounds the bend.

The deer not moving a muscle, taking her last stand.

The truck jackknifes. Mom hits the brakes.

Skidding—sliding—metal hitting metal.

Flying.

Then nothing.

Stop! I commanded myself, refusing to allow my mother to see our broken bodies in a ditch on the side of the road. I focused on the big bag of feathers for the pillow project in the backseat with me. *Somewhere along the way the plastic burst open, and as I flew through the car window so did hundreds of tiny white feathers. Everyone and everything was airborne like we were flying away..*

And then I took it one step further and zoomed her right to our lovely Craftsman house near the Academy where I stood smiling.

I showed her all of it—and then some.

Her daughter with a championship hockey trophy.
Her daughter and her dog reunited.
Her daughter holding hands with her first love—her true love.
Her daughter and her new family.

"It's okay, Mom. It really is okay," I kept repeating. "It's actually beautiful."

In many ways, it was as if I grew up and moved out. I just moved further than anyone expected. I was there . . . and then I was gone.

I wasn't done showing her the scrapbook of my new life when I felt a firm hand on my shoulder. It was a wide palm that was warm to the touch and firm. He squeezed the bottom of my neck gently.

"Walker, you have to leave now," he said in a deep, masculine tone. Opening my eyes, I expected to see Daniel or Dr. King hovering over me.

It was neither.

Gazing into warm green eyes and a wide smile, I whispered in awe, "Dad?"

He was here. All of him. Whole. I remembered his broad, brawny frame; wide back; and large, muscular arms—courtesy of a fitness plan called "working all day in a Chicago steel mill."

My father was never a fancy business type. He was a worker. Before cancer invaded, he looked like he was made of steel himself at six foot two and brawny. At this moment, twelve years post death, my dad, Sam Callaghan, stood young, strong, proud, and sure. He still had one meaty hand on my trembling shoulder and in the other he was holding something metallic with dust all over it. It looked like an ax—one that had been used. Recently.

My eyes traveled over his face. The ravages of cancer were gone. He looked like his wedding picture again with sparkling eyes, a square jaw, and a mischievous Irish smile.

I hadn't seen him for over a decade, but it seemed like only a minute had passed. From the look of love in his eyes and the strangely smooth hand that now caressed my face, I knew he was here for a reason beyond a reunion. It was the look that only a father could give a daughter who was in grave danger.

"Babe, you have to hurry," he said. "You remember my friends from the steel mill? I got Joe McDoogle and Richie McGuffey out there."

"Out where?" I asked, thinking he would tell me about some jaw-dropping cosmic zone.

"Out there. In the living room. With your friends," he said with a concerned smile. "We've been keeping the goon squad away, but there are only a few of us—and lots of them.

"They'll be back here any minute," Dad said, holding my hand in his firm grip. I was still holding my mom's hand, which meant we were all united for the first time in over a decade. We were a family again.

"Babe, we got a lot of things on our side, but time isn't one of them."

"But Mom," I began.

"I'll watch over your mother. I'm always here with her," he said.

"Daddy, but," I started again.

"Not now, Walker Jane. Later," he said, actually pulling me forward now.

"There's plenty of time later for us. You go now. Please, honey—or there will be no later."

Softly, I dropped my mother's hand and saw that she was sleeping peacefully and breathing steadily. When I got off the bed and stood, my dad was the one who took a quick intake of breath. "Oh, Babe," he said, holding both of my hands now, but pushing me back just a bit as if he wanted to get one good look at me. "Just as pretty as a picture. Just like your mama."

I saw him take something out of the pocket of his worn jeans and lean forward to place it in my coat pocket. "Look at it later. Go now," he insisted.

I didn't obey my father. Instead, I turned away from him and stepped to the bedroom window, which was half frosted over thanks to more of Mother Nature's handy winter work. Pressing my finger to the glass, I finished what I came to do in the first place.

She had to be sure.

When I turned around, my father was gone. And my mother was . . . awake. Suddenly, she was sitting up, her legs slowly and painfully swinging over the side of the bed. I knew she couldn't see me. So I walked so close to her that when she reached out for the walker, I slipped into what seemed like an embrace. "It's okay, Mama," I whispered in her ear. "It's okay now."

The face I saw next was Daniel, leaning his head through the doorway. "Baby, it's now or never," he said.

"Yeah," I responded, leaning forward to kiss my mother on her forehead. Then I backed out of the room, so I didn't miss a second of seeing her. When I was almost outside the room, I heard it as plain as day.

"Walker?" Mom said in a quizzical voice.

By now, she was standing at that same window with her walker holding her up. I saw her touch what I had just traced.

In the frost, I had written a large "O" followed by a large "K."

"Walker," she repeated, but there was no question mark this time.

CHAPTER 32

1.

My dad was not in a better place. It turns out that he was actually in the living room, hanging out with his friends Rich and Joe from US Steel; otherwise known as two Chicago street palookas who graduated from the school of hard knocks located on the west side of the city. They flanked Dr. King like soldiers on a mission, but they weren't giving my brilliant principal many choices. Instead, they explained a simple escape route that we were about to embark on. They made it clear the mission could be dubbed "No Questions Asked."

For once, Dr. King took the backseat and allowed them to be in charge.

Dad returned to my side and placed one of his big, lumbering arms around me. The first person to break ranks and get personal with him was Dr. King. "Mister Callaghan, it truly is a pleasure to meet Walker's father. I just wish it was under better circumstances,"

435

he said. "Hopefully, we can meet again on parents visiting day at the Academy."

"I can't tell you what it means to me that you're with her," Dad said. "I studied up on you, Marvin. I mean, Doctor King. I'm glad you're the one taking her to the next pit stop, I mean, level."

Dr. King extended his hand to my father. "Marvin," he said warmly as my dad grasped it.

Bobby was next and my dad ran a hand through the kid's hair as a friendly way of saying hello. Daniel was hanging back, waiting to approach. When the field cleared, he walked up and put his hand out for my father to shake. My eyes darted from one to the other. What an awkward way to have your father meet your live-in, limbo boyfriend. It was a customary gesture—Daniel's long, tapered fingers at the ready—but Dad wasn't having any of it. Instead, he looked down at Daniel's outstretched hand and ignored it. Then my father gave Daniel the real death glare.

The look said it all. *Stay the eff away from my daughter.*

It was on, but it would have to wait.

I guess my dad wasn't thrilled that I was dating.

Diverting my gaze, I could see my father's work buddies dying to get the show on the road. These men were even bigger than Dad was. One of them was a former linebacker for the Chicago Bears way back in the day. The other one was the size of a small tank and he took it upon himself to help Dr. King to the front door of the apartment. Each of the big men was equipped with a long steel pipe that they grasped in one hand and a large metal steelworker's hammer in the other. These were men who looked like they could do some serious damage.

"Let's go," Dad said and Daniel wisely backed away, which gave him time to pick Bobby up in his arms.

"Kid," my dad said, but he wasn't talking to Bobby. He was talking to *Daniel*, although the way Dad looked he didn't appear to be much older than him. "Get your weapons out of your backpack. Whadda you think we're going to tonight, young man? A dance?"

Daniel's eyes went dark. This time he gave my father a matching death glare, but he didn't argue or say a word. He simply took out an ax, a bottle of something, and a large pick. He handed me our last Captain Hook claw and a small hammer that neatly fit into my battle-worn right hand, which Daniel squeezed gently on impact. Dad didn't miss much either and hissed, "Let's go."

Weapons in hand, Dad slowly peeked out the heavy, metal apartment door and surveyed the smelly, long, dark hallway that contained miles of worn, musty rose-colored carpeting. Turning around, he gazed lovingly at mom's bedroom door and then crooked his finger for us to follow him. "Walker, stay right behind me," Dad instructed, as all of us made our way into the murkily lit hall.

He firmly closed my mother's door behind us.

2.

For a beautiful moment in time, it was like leaving a late-night Christmas party with your family. You came, you had fun, you jawed with the relatives, and then it was back to your car and home. This wasn't exactly the same scenario. Rich, Joe, and my dad provided the first wall of defense and they blocked the rest of us as we cautiously took a few steps behind them.

Braced and alert, I was scanning the hall ahead of us. Then for some reason I decided to momentarily stop and focus on my feet. That's when I knew something was amiss. There was an extra dark and dismal cast over that rose carpeting that wasn't just normal wear and tear.

They were here. Lurking. But where?

Then it dawned on me. They weren't going to make it obvious and wait in the hallway. *They were inside the apartments!*

Of course, they didn't need to open doors. When they smelled us, they just floated through them. And now they were in attack mode, leaking from apartment doors like sinister shadows and fatal fog.

Two spirits that looked like demented versions of Daniel slithered from the door that read Perez; and three other smaller, long-toothed versions of me slipped out from an apartment labeled Murphy-Jones. As more entered the confines of that narrow hallway I felt like I couldn't breathe. We were neatly surrounded at every turn.

Quivering as I hovered behind my Dad, I was barely keeping hold of my weapons as my hands began to shake harder. Joe and Rich were not as easily frightened. They weren't rookies in the arena of a good old-fashioned street fight. In fact, they were masters at playing a game called chicken.

"You bastards been breaking and entering? Stealing little kiddie's Christmas presents," Rich said, swinging his ax expertly through the midsections of the two fake Daniels and then jamming upward toward their hearts. On contact, the demons dissolved together in an electric burst of light while my dad took on a young demon Bobby by smashing his hammer through him and then jabbing even harder to destroy his center. Jumping high into the air, another one of the bad little boys secured himself on my Dad's back like a monkey-beast from hell. Without hesitating, I swung my claw through the center of him with one easy swipe to his upper left.

Dad looked shocked, so I yelled, "I do sports now. Dad, watch out!"

The last little Bobby didn't stand a chance.

The real Bobby had possession of the high-powered slingshot

438

now, and obviously he had collected the bullets we left at the airport.

"Die suckers!" he screamed, scoring a perfect heart shot.

"You little maniac!" Daniel said in an admiring tone before pushing the real Bobby back into place. "Stay behind me, twerp."

"Another one bites the dust. And another one falls and another one falls," Bobby began to sing.

"I like this kid. Know any Tom Petty, son? " Joe said, opening the heavy steel front door of the apartment after slicing and dicing all the other versions of Daniel and me who were crashing our little Christmas Eve party. Joe began to sing in a merry voice, "You better watch out. You're gonna start to cry. I'm gonna take your ass out and I'm showin' you why . . . you rat bastard."

It was the Chicago version of that Christmas favorite.

3.

We got outside to Halsted Street, but the demons were already there and waiting for us. It didn't really matter, but there wasn't a living person in sight, which left more space for the monsters who were having some sort of predawn holiday mixer as they waited. There were enough of them to keep the party going strong into the wee hours.

A gauzy black spirit snuck up on me, stopped, and blew at me hard with some sort of fish-smell breath that made it seem like it drank half of Lake Michigan. I slashed hard, using the agility I had learned playing goalie, and turned it into sheer particle dust. Before it completely extinguished, it screamed a shrill sound that made my ears ring.

"We need to get to the train," Dr. King huffed behind us, as he tried to walk as fast as possible.

"Keep going north!" Dad yelled.

What we needed to do was make it a block and a half to a staircase that led up to the "L," or elevated train tracks that are a Chicago trademark. Unlike the subway in New York, the Windy City had tracks that ran above the streets. I knew that on the few days leading up to Christmas, the trains would be running all night long hauling last-minute shoppers to and from stores now open twenty-four holiday hours. I just didn't know where we were going once we actually made it there.

As Dad's buddies made dust out of a stray goon or two who popped out from between the narrow alleyways that separated the buildings, I watched Daniel ax a large shadowy female figure who towered over him. Meanwhile, Dad blocked a direct hit and swung that steelworker's hammer directly into the midsection of a wide goon, but he didn't shoot high enough. His friend Rich did the rest of the dirty work, by throwing what looked like a sharp metal pick into the creature's upper left chest quadrant. "That one looked a little like our old boss, Mister Fenton," he said to no one in particular. "I just fired him! Permanent-like!"

As they fought and seemed to enjoy it, I stared ahead of us and the asphalt city streets seemed clear. Behind us, it was a different story. An army of what looked like twenty goons united in a common cause were slithering their way down the desolate four-lane road. They were floating slowly, but surely, because they knew that seven were no match for their numbers.

"Babe, we're going to make a front line. The rest of you should run hard. We'll hold 'em as long as possible. Run like the wind!" Dad yelled to me, giving me a hard look that said he absolutely meant business.

"Run where?" I shouted, looking back at him wide-eyed.

"Where exactly are we going?"

I stopped near an abandoned lot covered in depressing gray snow. The glint of broken glass twinkled under the overhead city lights. "Daddy, come with us," I begged him. "Run with us. Come with us."

"Babe, you know I can't," he said, holding a pick and hammer in front of us as he scanned for imminent danger. I could see his friends were already fighting off the new demon hoard. "Run, Walker," he yelled, shoving me away with a force that surprised me. "It's the only way."

"But Dad, I don't want to lose you again," I cried, standing firmly in place. If it came to it, I wouldn't listen to him. I would make him run with me.

He stopped for a split second to put one arm around my waist while still crouched down low to fight. "Oh, I'll be around. You can count on that," Dad said, letting his guard down for a second to look into my eyes with pride.

"Babe, I'll catch you on the flip side," he said.

To Daniel, who was now next to me with Bobby in tow, he pointed the hammer and then lightly touched it to my boyfriend's chest.

"You watch yourself," Dad said. "And take care of my girl."

Hugging my father fiercely, I knew there were no options.

Slowly, I allowed his wide, thick hands to drop.

And then we ran.

4.

I ran with everything left in me while Daniel helped move Dr.

King along in a wheelchair we "borrowed" from the back of an SUV. Bobby led the race, careening at top speed until he practically made us dizzy again. Behind us, I could see Dad, Rich, and Joe fighting, but the line was holding. It was Joe's idea to also "borrow" a workman's bulldozer that was parked in an ally. I was sure he had the time of his afterlife plowing right through the demons that were fast approaching. It worked just fine because he could push them over as if they were nothing more than debris that needed to be cleared. And as they fell, Dad and Rich could finish them off.

Daniel hit the L stairs hard, and he carried Dr. King up the steep flight of thirty old-fashioned, worn wood planks. Bobby was already at the top screaming, "Hurry, hurry." I brought up the rear.

When we raced onto the platform we were three stories up in the air with empty railroad tracks on one side of us awaiting the next train, and billboards for Coke and *American Idol* at our other side. The road was way below us. On our train-station perch, there was a tiny bench under a roofed structure for commuters to take a load off and block themselves from the winter winds and rains while they waited.

We were on the L platform, which meant one thing: We were sitting ducks.

"Callaghan, stay sharp," Daniel whispered, handing Bobby a small hammer and a stake.

I could see that Dr. King had something in his hands, too.

The quiet was overwhelming. All I could hear was that fierce north wind that blew over the platform. It was the only sound as I stared at that staircase for unwanted visitors. *Nothing. Wait, was that shadow a . . . no, it wasn't. For now. Did I hear footsteps? No, I didn't.*

Bobby peered down the tracks, but he didn't see any distant headlights from a train. "Where is it?!" he demanded, hopping from foot to foot impatiently.

"It's coming, sweetie," I said, praying that I was right. We really didn't know the exact train schedule at three in the morning on Christmas Eve.

We waited as the minutes ticked by in painful slow motion. *How long could my Dad hold the line? Did they see us run up here? We were in the perfect spot for a goon ambush. Was that something or someone creeping up the stairs?*

Something or someone had arrived and she was walking toward us slowly and painfully as if she was wounded or very old. My reasonable mind figured that it wouldn't be uncommon to share this platform with the living travelers who actually had someplace to go in the wee hours.

To my relief, our visitor was an old woman whose lined, wrinkled face peered out from under the hood of an ugly green parka. For a moment, I felt almost sorry for her. Her coat seemed too thin and threadbare and her legs were short and naked underneath that coat. Her brown hair stuck out of the hood, going every which way just like mine did in this kind of weather. As she got quite close to me, I could see that her hands didn't look old at all. In fact, she had a small freckle on her perfectly smooth left pinky finger.

Just like the freckle I had on mine.

"Walker?" she said.

How in the hell could she know my name? How could . . . she . . . see . . . me?

Raising my hook, I took a giant step backward as she slowly advanced. Bobby must have felt my panic because he quietly snuck behind her. In one fell swoop he yanked off her hideous hood to reveal a face that was the color of rancid milk, with large black orbs where there should have been eyes.

It was the most grotesque me of all.

The old lady continued to advance, but a creaking sound from

443

the staircase made me look away for a split second where I saw the inevitable. Her friends were at the bottom. They were climbing in droves.

"Walker. Slowly, slowly, like molasses dripping out of a bottle, back up," Dr. King instructed. Grabbing Bobby by the shirt, I shoved him backward while my eyes scanned for Daniel.

Nothing.

He was gone.

5.

The evil me stared hard, her face shifting into several different forms of the original. She showed me all the versions of what had once lurked inside of me. Me frowning. Me jealous. Me angry. Me whining. Lifting her grotesquely long hands, which were the size of arms, she allowed me to watch as they morphed from young supple-fleshed appendages to old, wrinkled skin falling off what looked like bird-thin bones. This little circus show was only the start of her main stage of trickery.

Just like an intruder who was breaking and entering, I could feel her strolling through my mind.

"*Walker,*" she whispered from inside my head. "*We are one. Come to me. Let's be whole again.*"

Stay away from me, I thought. *You are not me! You are not part of me. Not now. Maybe once! But not ever again!*

"*I'm here to protect you,*" she whined, and I caught a whiff of her scent, which was old, dusty, and rancid like an overfilled ashtray.

Her voice trailed off into the night and that deafening silence filled my head again.

That's when I heard it.

I heard the air shift and the wind rush. The Others had arrived.

"Daniel!" I screamed, but there was no response. "Where are you?!" But Daniel wasn't here anymore and I tried to wrap my mind around it, although the mere thought of losing him was unthinkable.

"Walker, take three small steps backward and then wait for my command," Dr. King said, his voice breaking the silence. From the corner of my eye, I could see him bracing against the commuter's bench, a weapon in one hand, and a convulsively shaking Bobby under his arm. In that moment, I knew if a man with a battered body could try to make it then I had to fight on.

"But how?" I cried.

That's when I smelled it.

It was a smell so familiar that I stopped to take a second whiff to make sure that I wasn't dreaming. It was a putrid whiff of it, but it was also unmistakable. Someone had emptied lighter fluid onto those stairs as if they were about to barbecue them on a summer night. That someone was on the roof of the little makeshift train station, the roof that protected the commuters from the rain and the elements while they waited for their transportation.

That same someone had black hair blowing back off his face in the fierce winter wind. He stood in his heavy, ass-kicking boots, looking like he owned this world.

I smelled the sulfur from the match he struck—and the several other matches after that one. I watched the first little flame drift down until it reached the middle of the staircase. Like little missiles, he sent the other matches down, one after another. A bright-orange fireball exploded as the wood was set ablaze, flames licking each other as they built into a mini inferno.

Holding my breath, I prayed that it would work like that Greek flamethrower we read about on that badass ancient weapons list.

What was more badass than a makeshift flamethrower conceived in a place called Greektown?

I've never been much of a pyro queen, but it turns out that fire is different from a shot to the heart. But it is just as primitive. And just as effective.

The bursts of exploding soul-matter lit up the area like millions of sparklers with embers that drifted down to the street below until they were extinguished once and for all by wet pavement.

Bolstered by our little victory, I advanced on the woman in the cloak, but I moved slowly. In my most pleasant, singsong voice, I cried out to her, "I am coming to you. Help me. Save me. Let's be one again. . . . Consume me."

"I will help you, dear. I will be with you for all of eternity," she croaked.

It was a risk exposing so much of myself in an area that was prime destruction matter for her, but I opened my arms wide in a hugging motion. She easily moved into my embrace knowing that she could strike the moment she got close enough to my heart.

I banked on the fact that this victory would be so delicious to her that she would choose to savor it. Moving even closer into me, she laughed in a way that made my ears ring. It hurt my head and made the hair on my neck stand straight up.

At that moment, I remembered the words that came from one of our guest lecturers at the Academy, a smart philosopher from India. He told us that in any battle, "First, they ignore you. Then they laugh at you. Then they fight you. Then you win."

It was time for the fight.

I gave her a hook to the chest and dug in hard. She reared up, looming large, and it was clear that I missed her heart. Enraged, she descended on me, trying to trap me in that cloak of eternal hell with her. There was nothing to do but shove her as hard as possible backward. Her own clumsy feet did the rest of the work as she fell, but then righted herself. On her feet again, she took another staggering step forward.

Reaching out, I gave her one of my best hockey moves. I body checked her. In hockey, the other player usually just stumbled backward out of the goal. In this game, the demon fell backward onto the burning stairs.

"Watch your step. It's slippery in winter," I yelled as she became one with the inferno. She exploded on impact.

Jumping down from the roof, Daniel grabbed my hand before I fell into the fire from the force of her burst. He lurched us both backward as I heard another sound that made my heart sing.

It was a whistle.

Yes, that old, reliable L train was finally roaring toward this stop. "All aboard," the round-bellied conductor yelled, opening all the doors, though not seeing any passengers. I heard him say into his radio, probably to the engineer, "Jim, there's no one here. And there's a fire on the stairs that's moving toward the platform. Call 911 and get the train out of here, pronto." Quickly, we hopped aboard without notice and then I helped Dr. King into a seat close to the back of the train car. Daniel and I sat across from him while Bobby bounced into a seat behind us to watch the goons burn bright.

"Awesome," Bobby said, glancing out the window to see if anything or anyone was following us.

There were three.

Down on the street below us, I saw those determined, burly steel workers raising their hammers high in absolute, gold-medal victory. My dad was standing slightly in front of the pack, and I could swear I felt it when he blew me a big kiss.

6.

It didn't take long before the conductor approached the only living person in our steel train car. I didn't even see him when we got on board because he was slumped over, sleeping across the hard seats that were the color of orange soda.

"Okay, Marv, pony up your ticket or five bucks," the conductor said to the old drunk behind us in a foul-smelling sweat jacket with mustard stains on the front. He had a grizzled face, a long dirty beard, and a tattered Cubs ball cap hiding eyes that were bloodshot from booze.

"How's it *they* don't have to pay?" drunk Marv countered. "It ain't fair. I tell ya. It ain't fair that they ride for free."

"Who rides for free? There's no one else here," the conductor said.

"I might be a little bit relaxed, but I'm no fool," Marv slurred. "What about the black guy, two teenagers, and that annoying kid right over theres? They ain't got no tickets."

Sitting next to Daniel, I gasped, and even with his head leaning against the seat in front of him to rest for a few minutes, I could still see that he was smiling.

"Do something! The kid just shot me with a spitball," Marv said as Bobby turned around in his seat the right way and pasted an angelic look onto his face.

"Sleep it off, Marv," said the conductor, with the exasperated sigh of someone who works the night shift.

An exhausted Dr. King was sitting alone poring over some paperwork that he pulled from his pocket. Gingerly plopping down next to him as the train raced through night, I asked him one simple question: "Now what?"

I knew that if anyone had the answers it was Dr. King, who came to this realm with powers that we didn't yet possess including some sort of sixth-sense knowledge.

"Now, Miss Callaghan, we go home," he said.

CHAPTER 33

1.

I didn't want to grill our principal on the specifics of realm travel because I knew he might start playing the blame game. If it weren't for us coming here, we wouldn't require an escape route.

"The portal is up ahead," said Dr. King. His surefire response was comforting. For a moment. *At least he knew where the portal was and soon we'd be back at the Academy*, I hoped. "Trust me when I tell you that the last portal was a merry-go-round compared to what we're about to see next," he said.

A few moments passed on the train and we relaxed until Dr. King took it upon himself to heave his hurting body upward. On shaking legs, holding on to one of the silver support poles, he announced, "I believe this is our stop."

Again, we were defenseless and back out in the cold. The good news is it didn't look so frightening when we walked down a street called Belmont Avenue and stopped in front of a medium-sized city college with a large sign out front proclaiming we had arrived at DeVry University.

It was a strange time for an educational moment.

"Why are we stopping at a school at almost four in the morning?" Daniel inquired, his hand firmly holding Bobby's shoulder to keep him from wandering. "Is this another case of needing to use a library in order to figure out how to get back?" he asked.

"Mister Reid, this might astound you with your expert planning skills, but I know exactly how to get back, which is knowledge I'll assume you lack," said Dr. King, who walked stoically, in great pain, dragging his poor, useless leg, until he stopped cold near one of the modern blue-green glass buildings. Then he did something curious. He leaned down and picked up some black dirt that was peeking out from under a light coating of snow.

"Like the Academy, DeVry University has a rival school that's not far away called Illinois Technical Training," Dr. King said and then paused, which I knew was his way of allowing me to figure it out. Even with his own soul existence on the line, Dr. King couldn't pass up a teachable moment.

When I thought about it for a moment, the brilliance of it dawned on me. This rival school also went by the initials of ITT.

"We started at the ITT of our realm. We're now at this realm's ITT rival school, which is the equivalent of our school," I said with the kind of big smile that reminded me of my days as a reporter and getting the big scoop.

"Miss Callaghan," said Dr. King in a voice that was appreciative. "An excellent deduction, but you're dead wrong—and assuming could be the worst mistake you've ever made in death."

He bent down and grabbed another handful of that thick winter dirt that was coated with old snow. "It's not what this place is now," Dr. King said, putting the dirt to his nose to smell it. "It's what it used to be." He put a little of the dirt under my nose for me to take a whiff.

"It was a garbage dump?" I suggested.

"Miss Callaghan, imagination!" Dr. King implored. "This school opened at another location in nineteen thirty-one when it was called DeForest Training School named after Lee DeForest, a colleague and friend of founder Herman A. DeVry. In nineteen fifty-three, they changed the name; then in the early seventies, they moved locations when the city put this prime land on the selling block."

Nodding my head, I pretended to follow him, but I was tired, cold, and ready to end this adventure once and for all.

"Before this land became a school at all, this spot—where you are standing right now—was one of the world's most majestic spectacles. . . . Welcome to what was once upon a time ago Riverview Amusement Park," he said with great bravado.

Somewhere in the back of my mind, I remembered my Aunt Ginny talking about her mother, my grandmother, going on gigantic roller-coaster rides at a magical place in the heart of the city when she was a very little girl. She said that my great grandmother also went to this park when she was a girl. What they loved the most was a big water ride that promised a major drenching.

"With some things, you can close them down, demolish them, build over them," said Dr. King in a faraway voice.

"But they never really go away," he concluded.

2.

In a burst of mind over aching-flesh matter, Dr. King suddenly had the energy of men ten times younger than he was. He led us around the corner of the first building and through a courtyard that was like a winter wonderland of cold, snow, and ice. I almost tripped over my own feet as Dr. King continued to hobble along while telling us a story so incredible that even Bobby hit his own personal mute button.

On the exact grounds we were trudging along at that moment once stood a vast amusement park—one of the only ones ever built in the middle of a major industrial city.

Around the turn of the century, or 1904 to be exact, the park was created to give all the immigrants who populated Western and Belmont Avenues a place to enjoy after toiling for twelve hours a day in the stockyards or steel mills. This wasn't some corner carnival, but a seventy-four-acre massive amusement park that backed up to the Chicago River, a waterway that wound like a twisting ribbon throughout the city.

In 1907, Dr. King told us that investors named Nicholas Valerius and Paul Cooper helped the cause by raising five hundred and fifty thousand dollars—an amount unheard of in those days—to really put Riverview on the map. The park was known for massive rides that were impressive to this day including the Bob's Roller Coaster, the Comet, the Silver Flash, and the Fireball, which Dr. King said was pretty much self-explanatory. Men in dark wool suits and fedoras, and ladies in flowing dresses and wide-brimmed hats used to scream in joy, raising their hands in the air on roller coasters that sliced through the warm turn-of-the-century summer nights.

In a section of the park called Fairyland, Riverview offered one of its lasting signature rides called Shoot-the-Chutes. The ride was so popular that the line wound around the entire park and the waiting time was often several hours; riding twice in the same day was not permitted.

"You could only go once a day!" Bobby marveled, as we still trudged around the DeVry school grounds in the snow and dark.

"That's right, Robert. Once a day. No more," said Dr. King. "Being denied a second ride made people want it that much more, but isn't that always the case. Our nature is to want what is denied."

"Did you go to Riverview as a boy?" I asked.

"My family would drive here from Detroit every summer we could," said Dr. King, and then turned to Bobby. "My favorite ride as a boy your age was that Shoot-the-Chutes. It was built in nineteen-oh-seven. Imagine a five-story, high-in-the-sky waterslide. At the top you got in a tiny little boat and Riverview workers actually pushed you out over the edge. Your track was a rushing, slick, watery slide that provided the ride of your life."

"Then you crashed to the ground!" Bobby exclaimed. "Bang! Pow! Demolish!"

"No, young man," Dr. King said, laughing "You crashed your boat into the Chicago River and all that green river water splashed you in the face and nearly drowned you. But you would still scream, 'Again! I want to Shoot-the-Chutes one more time!'"

He told us that the other rides were just as spectacular including a five-row carousel, which, to this day, was one of the largest ones ever created. "I also remember the Tilt-A-Whirl and the Flying Cars where you actually drove on the walls and the ceilings. There was a crazy fun house where you could walk up stairs that collapsed right under your feet."

During the Roaring Twenties, Riverview added five more coasters, amazing since they were erected right in the middle of an urban city. The people of Chicago loved it and made it a habit to get done with their city business and then line up for the Big Dipper, the Skyrocket, and the Bobs. Of course, the Great Depression in 1929 forced new construction to come to a grinding halt because people didn't have money for food, let alone roller coaster rides.

"That wasn't the end of Riverview," Dr. King said, stopping to finish his story outside a red-bricked building that looked like a large dormitory. "The real end, or the death, of Riverview didn't happen for a few more decades," said Dr. King.

He told us that on a cold fall day, October of 1967, it was announced that Riverview would be closing that night. Forever. A shocked Chicago couldn't believe that there was no fanfare. There wasn't even a good-bye party or a last ride. As winter pushed its way into the city, the gates were padlocked and the giant coasters demolished along with the rest of the park. Soon after, the land was sold.

"It was greed," Dr. King said. "The land was worth far more than the park's revenue, so the investors decided to destroy people's memories and future memories of what was one of the most famous amusement parks ever to exist."

"No fair," Bobby cried. "Stupid heads wrecked it. I wanna go on the coasters."

"Yes, Bobby, they were foolish," Dr. King agreed. "It was the end of an era. The city was devastated."

All in all, it was a fascinating history lesson, but I still wasn't sure why we needed to know about it and why we were still standing out here in this winter freeze in front of a vacant college dormitory without so much as a hint of a plan.

"We're very close right now to the park's front entrance. I'm quite positive that the front gate was located at a longitude and latitude that matches up exactly to one of the rooms of this dormitory building. Do you know exactly under what circumstances one entered the park?" Dr. King posed in somewhat of a giddy voice. It was as if he was about to reveal some delicious secret to the three of us.

An agitated Daniel, who had given his parka to Bobby on the train, shrugged and shivered in place. I could read his mind. *Could we just get on with it since this place could explode with goons at any moment?* It was a reasonable worry when your principal seemed lost in reminiscing the good ol' days.

"There were the front gates that I just mentioned, and ticket takers in cheerful red-and-white-striped uniforms with newsboy caps," Dr. King said as we continued to huddle on the sidewalk outside this dorm. "At this moment, we're standing where the patrons lined up to initially buy tickets to enter the park."

"Okay, sir," I finally blurted out, "What do front gates of some ancient amusement park have to do with us getting back?"

"Miss Callaghan, I thought you would never ask," Dr. King said with a slight smirk. "Above those gates, guarding the park, there was a sight to behold. It was a face with no body. A gigantic, frightening, deranged-looking face that jutted several feet skyward—Gypsy Aladdin with his beady eyes, full eyebrows, and a royal-blue cap on his head greeted all visitors. He had a very large, bright-red mouth that looked like he fell into a vat of lipstick the color of a ripe apple. I'll never forget that as a boy that face frightened the stuffing out of me."

I began to tremble as I considered the similarities.

Dr. King chuckled to himself, then continued. "And his mouth would open . . . but never when the park was open. Only after hours—way after hours. Only when the time was right."

I knew in that moment that Aladdin was our new portal.

It was too perfect, except for just one thing.

Aladdin had been demolished five decades ago.

3.

When he was done with his tale of splendor as it pertained to exotic portals, Dr. King went back to business. "My calculations show me that Aladdin was directly above dorm room one-seventy-one, which is good because it's on the ground floor and my foot can't take another staircase."

"My feets hurt, too, and my tummy is drumming," Bobby complained. "Don't want to hear no more stories. Don't want to hear no more 'scuses. Just wanna go to my new home and meet my dog."

"Hang on, Robert," Dr. King insisted, moving to the front door of the dormitory building and disabling the lock with a quick wave of his left hand. When he wasn't looking, I tried to do the same thing to the next door. Nothing. When the heavy metal door opened, we scurried inside where I felt a welcome rush of overheated institutional air.

"Follow me," Dr. King said in a low voice, as we looked for dorm room 171.

"Lucky for us that it's Christmas Eve," Daniel said, holding my hand tightly and keeping a watchful eye on his brother. "We're not likely to find anyone in these dorm rooms. All the students are home for Christmas vacation."

In my mind, I could still see some little techie nerd hovering over a laptop, preferring to hang out with megabytes instead of his or her family. Who need Aunt Bea's cookies when you could curl up with code?

Inside Room 171, I wasn't disappointed.

The nerd was actually sleeping at his small wooden desk, which

457

his body was dwarfing, in a room that was pitch-black except for the greenish glow that emanated from his Apple MacBook. His hair was California beach blonde and wavy, and fell halfway down his neck. Obviously, they grew nerds in XL here and this one looked like a football player with a wide chest in a Hang Ten tee and nylon shorts. And then there were his glasses. Little round ones. And they had taken a ride halfway down his face. His computer screensaver was the starship *Enterprise* flying across the universe.

"May the force be with you," I whispered to Daniel.

"That's *Star Wars*, baby," he corrected me. "This guy is much more about 'Beam me up, Scotty.'"

My eyes scanned the room, which looked like a small tornado of dirty clothes just went through it. Apparently, this nerd liked to wear logo T-shirts and baggy shorts. My eyes settled on a little plastic name tag that was on his desk from some recent physics convention. His name was Caspian—just like the large and salty sea between Europe and Asia, and the princely C. S. Lewis character.

Ever the prankster, Bobby, raced up to him to pull his glasses all the way off his face.

Caspian was snort-snoring like a sleeping bear when Bobby made his move, but instead of those glasses slipping off entirely, the techie grabbed them midheist and slammed them back on his face, which was now upright. Flicking on his small desk lamp, he narrowed his eyes. "Hey kid, knock it off," he grumbled, his throat thick with enough growl that it was as if he had just been wakened from a thousand-year sleep.

Bobby did a little jig of a dance in front of him to test the situation.

"Kid, I see you and my mother dances better than you," said Caspian. To which Bobby put out his quivering bottom lip. "And I see the rest of you, too, especially that very pretty girl hovering in the corner."

"Um..yeah…thanks," I said. Technically, it was a compliment. Caspian just smiled.

"I'm not just the future Steve Jobs. I can also . . . see things," he said in a rushed way that indicated that he didn't really want us to focus on the last part. "In other words, I see dead people, as the saying goes. Have since I was a kid growing up in Encino. And I have one question for all four of you dead people visiting me on this night of all nights: Why the hell are you here? Is this my own personal version of *A Christmas Carol*? Is the black guy the ghost of Christmas past? I hope the girl is my own ghost of Christmas future."

"Keep dreamin'," Daniel said, stepping forward.

Placing my hand on Daniel's chest to stop him from doing anything extreme, I answered for all of us. "Caspian, it's a pleasure to meet you. We're not here to do your own personal version of *A Christmas Carol*. We're here to go home and we need to borrow your room to do something unusual."

"Cass," he said, standing up, shaking his head first and then shaking my hand. He was as tall as Daniel, and just as muscular. He was also . . . alive.

I wasn't exactly sure what we would be doing in his room tonight, but I knew enough to tell him that it wouldn't be like a normal night curling up with *The Big Bang Theory*.

"Want a beer?" he asked us. "No, I guess you guys don't drink beer."

"Later, on that one," Daniel said.

"We're here to bring back a place—a place that used to belong right here," said Dr. King, who added, "This is bound to get a little messy. Cass, I'd move your laptop to far higher ground. Just in case."

"I back up in the cloud. Hey, is the cloud where you guys live? No one really understands the cloud—or what goes on in there,"

Cass said, adding, "Okay, let's not even worry about that for a minute. I have a few questions starting with . . . so, you want to use my room like it's for rent? This is not some hotel for spirits."

"Everyone has a price," I countered, figuring all I had on me was my lucky rabbit's foot, which I just remembered I had moved to my coat pocket. So far, it had served me well here, so I produced it and Cass glanced down.

"I do have a price," Cass insisted, his eyes back on mine. "One kiss from a pretty girl. It's been a slow dating season." From the look of him, with all that hair and that square, handsome surfer-guy face, I found that hard to believe.

"Let's just take him out. We don't have time to waste on this crap," Daniel interjected moving forward, irritated and restless. "Any minute now this room could be filled with—" He stopped short. There was no need to put Cass on high alert.

In a room no bigger than the size of a walk-in closet, I kept my left hand on Daniel's chest and leaned right to kiss Cass on the cheek, but he turned at the last minute.

The kiss landed on Cass's lips and, although brief, it didn't go unnoticed. "Wait a minute," I said, and I physically blocked Daniel for the brawl I knew was coming next.

Cass just laughed, and when Daniel reached around me to try and grab him by the collar, he tried to grab right back. "Enough! You're both idiots!" Dr. King boomed.

It was Cass who stepped back and agreed. "Later, on that one," he said to Daniel who was now seething as Dr. King stood with a hand to his chest in warning. "Thanks beautiful, but our first date will have to wait," he added. "You don't have too long to hang out here. What a pity."

Quickly, I glanced at Daniel who knew there wasn't time to kick this guy's ass.

"Like I said, I see things," Cass continued. "And it's not frogs and locusts that are on the menu tonight, but some demon forces out for a nice holiday stroll with a score to settle."

He knew.

"I know your type and I have no fight with you. I respect you," Dr. King said to Cass before asking, "Anyone else here in the dorms? When you bring back seventy-four acres of the past, it's best not to have too many prying eyes around you. We don't need witnesses."

"This whole week, it's just me and the janitor. He's sleeping down the hall in his little closet," Cass said. "I think he lives in there and no one goes near him. Why are janitor's closets the creepiest places on Earth?" He stopped for a minute and looked at Daniel. "I guess you do know, tough guy," Cass spit out. "You've done your time in a janitor's closet recently. Nice of you to drag the girl with you."

"What kind of freak are you?" Daniel shot out.

"You can't fight genetics," Cass said in a wistful voice.

4.

Dr. King didn't waste any more time. First, he reminded us that when it came to portal travel, simple was always best. "People overthink realm travel," he said. "They make it more complicated than necessary. It's not complicated at all if you have the knowledge and the desire to get where you really want to go."

"Realm travel," repeated a seriously stunned Cass. "I heard about this stuff."

"Stand down, young man," Dr. King ordered. Then in a solemn voice, he lifted both hands, palms up to the sky, and began.

"Close your eyes," he told us.

Gripping Daniel and Bobby's hands hard, I didn't want to ask, but the words just seemed to slip out. "Why do you always have to close your eyes at times like this?"

"Haven't you learned that the best things in life, Walker Callaghan, are unseen?" answered Dr. King, his palms still raised as if he was waking up the dead in some sort of ritualistic ceremony where only he knew the results. "Think about it for a moment. That's why we close our eyes when we kiss, laugh, or dream."

"How do we know when to open them?" Bobby said, his own peepers cemented closed with little lines forming in the corners because he was squeezing so hard.

"I promise that you will know exactly when to open your eyes," Dr. King said in that merry, twinkling voice again as I gripped Daniel's hand even tighter. I hadn't closed my eyes yet and I could see that a dumbfounded Cass hadn't closed his either, but he did grab his nearest and only weapon, which was a giant bottle of Raid ant spray.

I closed my eyes.

But I couldn't stand it. I had to know.

Cracking them open only a tiny bit, I saw nothing. And then I glanced down at the floor. Dark shadows were billowing from under the door.

The goons were here.

We weren't going anywhere.

5.

Dr. Marvin King, former Detroit vice principal, was tired of being a victim. Or that was one way of looking at it. Reaching into the pocket of his black overcoat, he grabbed several throwing stars and whipped them under the door with all of his might. The brilliant light that drifted in after the explosions told me that they did their job.

It was as if Dr. King saw these things as an inconvenience that could potentially interrupt our travel plans. Ignoring them for a moment, Dr. King was chanting something that was indecipherable with his hands raised even higher to the sky. Struggling to hear only what an animal could pick up, I zeroed in on his voice, which now sounded as if he was recording a commercial for a place that didn't exist anymore except in a memory.

"Come to Riverview Park and laugh all your troubles away," he crooned. He sang it like the commercial jingle it once was all those decades ago.

In what sounded like a child's voice that didn't belong to Bobby, I heard Dr. King wail, "I want to Shoot-the-Chutes at Riverview Park! I want to Shoot-the-Chutes. Shoot-the—"

The floor under my feet began to crumble and my dry shoes were suddenly filling with the freezing cold, wet rush of river water. The entire room was flooding from the bottom up. Walls crumbled; doors blew off their hinges. When the plaster separating the dorm rooms flew away with a flourish, the red outer bricks of the dormitory burst away with several loud thuds.

Hold your breath! Hold your breath! I thought, as my body submerged completely in freezing green and murky Chicago River water that was now way over my head.

As I popped to the surface, I gasped so loudly that I nearly drank the entire river.

It was majestic! It was back!

I heard the carnival music and smelled fresh cotton candy. Blinking, I looked around at the acres and acres of gigantic

463

attractions that were bright, colorful, and reached high into the sky. I could smell the hamburgers and popcorn. And I heard the merry laughing of happy children combined with the occasional breathless scream of someone about to plunge down the metal tracks of a gigantic roller coaster.

It was Riverview Park. Reborn.

I looked high in the air and could see the Chutes, plain as day. It was right in front of us and so was the ride operator who looked like he stepped out of some turn-of-the-century novel. "Little Missy, watch your step," he told me, brushing off his red-and-white-striped uniform. He took off his newsboy cap and used to it wipe his brow as if the summer heat was really getting to him. "Little darlin'," he said to me. "You really got wet on that one, but that's what happens when you Shoot-the-Chutes." A woman in a sweeping green velvet coat that reached the ground stepped off the ride, vowing to go "again and again."

"Only one ride a day, little darlin'," she was told.

When I glanced to the left, I could see the Bobs ride, and when I looked the other way, I saw the fun house and the Flying Cars. Dr. King, Bobby, and Daniel were immediately at my side. Cass was standing near the fun house, his MacBook firmly in his hands, with his mouth open so wide that I thought maybe he was the portal now. That was the last I saw of him as he vanished behind bustling groups of turn-of-the-century Riverview patrons in wool suits and those neck-to-ankle dresses that brushed the streets. Friendly workers begged us to line up and try the Tilt-A-Whirl.

"Give it a whirl!" a man in a black cap insisted, crooking his finger at me. "If you dare!"

Rising up from nothing, it was all there: the Comet, the Silver Flash, the Fireball and the front entrance gates!

"Run for the gates! The face is the portal!" shouted Dr. King, grabbing his last few throwing stars, though he didn't need them now. I'm not sure why, but the goons didn't seem to follow. Perhaps they were denied admittance to this E-ticket mind meld.

"We don't have much time," Dr. King said, hobbling along, until Daniel put his arms around our principal and literally began to drag him along the asphalt.

"Bobby, Callaghan, run up ahead. Run!" Daniel yelled. "Go! Go through the portal!

"We'll be right behind you. I promise! Move!" Daniel boomed. "Faster! You can do this, Callaghan! For us!"

"Not without you," I screamed, running forward, and then stopping to turn around again, my heart pounding and my eyes filling.

Daniel stopped in his tracks, looked at me, and said, "I love you, Callaghan. Go. You promised."

"I love you, too. Say it! Say you'll be right behind us!" I demanded as the tears began to roll.

"Pinky swear," he said, his arm sloped around Dr. King's shoulders as they started to move again, limp-running together.

Bobby and I took off again, too—until our attention was diverted. We heard the most sickening sound in the world. The Chutes were still operating and a boat had just been sent down the massive slide. As plain as day, I heard the gigantic splash into the Chicago River of 1907. From the wail of the shrill, inhuman screams we heard, I knew it wouldn't be the locals with their hands in the air enjoying the ride as the boat descended.

The goons had arrived . . . again.

6.

I grabbed Bobby's hand and together we pounded that pavement as hard as we could until we reached the front gate. As we ran, day morphed into night and the other patrons seemed to fade from sight. Standing under the mammoth metal awning that was the front entrance, I gazed up at the menacing Aladdin face in awe. I couldn't be sure, but in the harsh glint of moonlight, it looked to me as if the ruby-red lips had opened enough to show just a hint of its teeth.

"Come on!" I yelled to Bobby as I dragged him around the back of the sign because it was the only way.

I prayed there would be some sort of fire-escape staircase for the workers who needed to clean that face, and I wasn't disappointed. There was a rickety, one-climber-at-a-time wooden staircase in back that was hidden behind one of the metal pillars. Wobbly stairs took courageous maintenance workers from the cobblestone on the ground to the top of Aladdin's crown. It was fifteen stories into the sky at the very least.

Already exhausted beyond the limits of endurance, with aching legs we climbed and climbed, only to be faced with more stairs. We ascended until we seemed airborne. Bobby was just inches in front of me, my hand on his back legs in case he buckled and fell backward, although there was little that I could do to catch him. One slip up and we were done.

When we were high enough, I had to look.

At the Chutes entrance, Dr. King was beating off the goons who had neatly surrounded him in devour mode. I could see him fighting on, tossing the rest of what was left in his deep trench-coat pockets. He must have run out of ammo because the last thing I saw was our beloved principal striking out with the only weapon available to him: His fists.

Larger creatures that must have stood ten feet tall were striking Daniel, who fought valiantly, disappeared for a moment, and continued to fight again. My heart was breaking. If I ran down to help, his little brother would never get home. None of us would get home. Daniel was axing away wildly when I heard his voice as plain as day in my ear. "Callaghan, I love you. Go, baby! Go home."

Tears running, I reached the upper platform with Bobby's help. Grabbing my hand, he helped hoist me onto a small, almost-invisible bridge that cleaners used to reach the front of this clown's face. When we positioned ourselves in front of the mouth and looked up into its eyes, nothing happened. A minute seemed to pass. Then two. "What if Doctor King was wrong!" I cried. "Open, dammit, open!"

It sensed our will. Those blood-red lips parted to flash jagged spikes that looked like teeth. "Close your eyes, sweetie," I said to Bobby, shutting my own, tightly this time.

And then we walked straight into the whatever.

CHAPTER 34

1.

We landed with a small thud inside John's clown emporium in the janitor's closet at ITT. Slamming my hand over Bobby's mouth, so he wouldn't say a word, I made the quiet sign and we tiptoed out of there without the slumbering bear being any the wiser.

"Bobby, this isn't Disneyland," I said, holding his hand as we emerged in the hallway near the chapel entrance inside D Block.

Maybe it was our crappy luck. Or perhaps it was just the way this worked. But none other than Eddie Wargo was in that hallway sweeping up. In our absence, Eddie was obviously being punished with clean-up duty. He took one look at me, blinked twice when he saw the kid, and let the drool building on his lower lip run down his triple chin. "Well, well, well, looky who we have here," he said. "It's that bitch Walker Callaghan who likes to have her boyfriend knock people out."

"Eddie, I'm having a real shitty day," I warned him.

"Every day is a bad day for me," bit out Eddie, who purposely jumped closer, blocking my path. After fighting demons from hell all night long, a Wargo seemed like just a minor inconvenience.

"Eddie, you're right," I said as he stood two inches in front of my face, towering above us. "I'm really sorry. Can you bend down a second, so I can tell you a secret? I'll tell you why we knocked you out."

"This better be good," he said.

"Oh, it is," I promised. As he leaned down, I took my fist and smashed it as hard as possible into his meaty forehead. He dropped like a rock. "You know what's the worst thing to be in life or death, Bobby?" I said to the impressed little boy. "Stupid."

"Walkie-Talkie, that was really good," he said, holding my hand a little tighter. "Should we wait right here for Danny and that doctor guy? They're coming right behind us? They promised. We have to wait for them to take me home."

Kneeling down for a second, I put my hands on his tiny shoulders, "We need to go, honey," I said. "We'll talk about the others later."

"Okey-dokey," he said. "I wanna meet my puppy. And Danny said he would take me to school. I'm not supposed to go anywhere without Danny, but I guess you'll do. For now. You seem like Danny's bestest friend . . . the girl kind."

2.

Slipping out of ITT was crazy easy because Dr. King had briefed us on the train—after he took his time admonishing me again for allowing my emotions to rule over my good sense, which he was hopeful I would develop when and if I returned to our realm. He knew about the second elevator located on D Block that took you all the way into one of the crevices of the mountain that led to a safe exit about half a mile away from the main entrance. Only those who were members of the Higher Authority Board knew about it—mostly in case there was ever a riot at ITT and the adults had to get out fast. We snuck down the D Block hallway, following Dr. King's explicit instructions to the letter, with Bobby hunkering under my long winter coat. Dr. King had been right in predicting the GF would assume we could never get back and wouldn't alert his guards to our breakout—he had to save face. No one even noticed when we walked to the very end of the hall and pushed a button hidden in the rock wall with the code Dr. King had given us: 1716.

Maybe our luck had finally changed. The elevator was already there. And there was no guard when the small car spit us out in a mountain crevice hidden by thick brush. The reset kicked in when I was scratched by the bushes crawling out. When I looked at Bobby, I didn't see a scratch on him either.

Bobby and I began the long walk back home. It was Christmas Eve here, too, and the farther we got from ITT, and the closer we were to the Academy, it became a festival of all festivals for everyone but me.

On Main Street, the Christmas tree was enormous and there were lights and decorations everywhere. A fake Santa was ho-ho-ho-ing in the distance while Angelina from Perks was serving free hot cocoa for anyone who cared to say, "Merry Christmas." When I walked passed her, she took one look at Bobby said, "Now who do we have here? It must be one of those Reid youngsters. You're as handsome as your big brother, Daniel. No offense, Walker. I know you two have a thing."

My heart was in my throat.

"I am so happy for the two of you, Walker. You make such a cute couple."

It took everything inside of my broken heart not to scream that maybe I wasn't a couple anymore. There was no way he could have fought off that many of them. And he would have tried to save Dr. King. That would certainly have been his undoing.

Daniel was gone.

I knew that there would be time for crying later. All the time under heaven and earth. Right now, I had a job to do. The man I loved would want me to fulfill this mission he set out to do. We got Bobby. And now I would bring him home to his family.

I didn't have to go far before there were others who were ready to welcome the newest member of the community with open arms. Jenna was the first one to spot her youngest brother and the way she yelled his name could have shaken the sky.

"Jenny-Bean!" Bobby screamed back to her and raced into his big sister's arms where he was smothered in hundreds of kisses. It was Peter Reid who scooped the little man up in a wild embrace that included several midair tosses that made Bobby scream with delight. Andy came running from a sledding race by the lake to see about the commotion. When she fell to her little knees in the snow to say a prayer of thanks, I almost unraveled.

"My Bobby!" she cried, tears falling everywhere as she formed a circle with her brothers and sisters. Jake came running with her. Bobby stopped, put out a hand, and Jake reared back to tackle him to the ground, showering him with doggie kisses. When he saw me, Jake made a beeline to repeat the process. "Down, boy," I said, trying not to cry as my body fell over into the snow.

It was all so normal.

And it would never be normal again.

"Where's big bro?" Peter asked as the girls continued to fuss over Bobby.

"Yeah," Jenna chimed in when she heard him. "He's gonna kill us. The house could be condemned if we had a Board of Health up here."

They saw the look on my face. The devastation was something I couldn't hide from them because they knew me so well. I was one of them now.

"No!" Peter screamed. "No! Goddamn it, no!"

"Why isn't he with you?" Andy said, tears forming. "Where is he?"

"Oh, it's gonna be okey-dokey, Andy," Bobby said. "Danny told me he was coming. He would never leave me alone again. He promised me. And he always keeps his promises."

In that innocent, happy philosophy that only a young child can possess, Bobby turned to walk his new dog down the street and Jake obliged. When he wasn't looking, I gazed at the others and shook my head.

Then I walked on.

Alone.

For some reason, I felt like putting my hands in my pockets. In one, I found a small gold locket in the shape of a heart. When I opened it, I saw a picture inside it of my mother and me. It was the gift from my father. Reaching for my lucky rabbit's foot in my other pocket, I searched, but it wasn't there. A strange panic set in and I took a deep breath. *It must have fallen out during the trip through the portal.* But then I felt something else, so I pulled it out for closer inspection. It was a small ripped strip of lined notebook paper with four words on it: Be seeing you, Cass.

3.

I made it all the way up the hill to the Academy and kept walking until I was in front of the school, which was covered in a wispy-thin blanket of snow. The mansion looked splendid in its holiday finery with green garland and tinsel everywhere, and a fifty-foot tree shooting up into the clouds.

"Hey Walker, there you are, stranger!" Tosh cried, racing up to hug me. "I've been looking everywhere for you. Did you hear the good news?"

"What good news?" I said in a hollow voice.

"Doctor King," she said. "I mean, we'll miss him and all, but isn't it wonderful that he ascended."

"What?" I held my breath.

"He's been gone for about two days now," she said. "He's never gone from this school. Ever. He always told the student body that if he missed even a day of school that meant he ascended. And that meant good-bye."

"The Academy will never be the same," she rattled on. "But Doctor King ascended! He ascended. He went Up and he earned it. We're having a huge farewell celebration for him in the courtyard. Come on! The cupcakes are *to-die*."

I couldn't believe that the entire student body was celebrating something that I knew was not the least bit true. Dr. King hadn't ascended. He didn't go Up, Down, or to some different In-Between. The simple fact of the matter was that monstrous demon forces extinguished his soul forever. He was millions of particles of nothing now. Evaporated. And Daniel Reid, the person who lied to me and said you couldn't die twice, was with him.

The truth was you could die twice. Three times. A thousand times.

In your heart.

In a trance, I continued to walk until I found the courtyard, which was decorated with balloons and streamers. In the center, a gigantic portrait of Dr. King was suspended from nothing with white and red flowers tossed around the bottom of it. Kurt was singing some rocking tune and many of the students were dancing recklessly in the snow having the time of their non-lives. Even Steve was doing some terrible half boogie that had to be seen to be believed.

In my exhaustion, I slipped away from the party and hid behind one of the large oak trees along the side of the great building. I couldn't think or feel anything. I was sure that I never would again. I closed my eyes for a split second and I willed myself not to think about anything but breathing.

His face filled that nothing. His whisper filled my ears.

And then I felt him. He brushed my cheek and ran his finger across my lips. All I could do was hold out my hand like I did on that first day in the music room. I wanted him to grasp it, so I knew this was real.

He took my hand, turned it over, and brought it to his lips. "Callaghan, do you have a middle name? It's funny what you think about when you're hovering between the life and death realms."

"Jane," I said, but I barely had time to get out that one syllable word. He crushed my lips with his. I opened my eyes.

It was real.

"Let's go, Walker," he finally said.

"Is this a dream?" I asked.

"Would we look like this in a dream?" Daniel said with a wry smile. "I do have to say nice shot when it came to Eddie Wargo. He was still confused and asking what happened when I knocked him out again and snuck out of ITT. I better keep our bathroom much cleaner in the future. Don't want to piss you off. Ever."

"How?" I asked, the tears rolling now.

Daniel lifted his finger to my tears and removed them as they fell. Then he pointed my entire body in the direction of the woods, stood behind me, and bandied his arms around my middle. I was sure that he didn't want me to see him cry, but I could hear the raw emotion in his voice and he began to tremble.

"Doctor King," he said in a thick tone. "He fought them off. Then he fought off the ones attacking me. We made it together to the staircase behind the Aladdin face. I don't even know how he found the strength. He insisted that I go up the stairs first and promised he would be right behind me. By the time I got halfway to the top, I turned to help him, but he was going in the opposite direction. He was climbing down again."

"Doctor King yelled to me," Daniel continued, "'We fought the good fight, son, but I'll never make it the rest of the way. You have to go now. Go for the both of us.' When I saw the goons at the bottom of the staircase, I started climbing back down to help him. He ordered me that I had to climb up and away. He said if I didn't, the first thing he would do is turn all of us into the GF at ITT. He told me not to worry. He would take care of business down below."

Daniel swallowed hard.

"He didn't make it," Daniel revealed in a grief-stricken voice. "He couldn't make it. There were thousands of them."

"But we don't know exactly what happened. He could still be there. He could still be whole," I said.

"No, baby," Daniel said. "He's gone."

And that's when I heard it. Daniel was quietly crying. But I wasn't thinking about him as Dr. King's face flashed in my mind. *He was alive.* I don't know how I knew, but I did. It was still possible. Anything was possible.

475

Staring ahead into the fields where spring had bloomed right before our eyes, I knew that I was lucky in a way that had nothing to do with a lucky rabbit's foot. Your real luck is the luck that you make in the moment that you have right now.

This was a bittersweet moment of love, loss, and everything that came in-between. Almost as if he was reading my mind, Daniel rested his chin on my head.

"Walker Callaghan, it's best now just to be," he said. "It's not how you start something. It's how you finish it."

"We have to start planning," I began.

"I knew you were going to say that," he said, turning me in his arms and briefly touching his lips to mine. "Tomorrow, we'll plan. For now, let's go home."

We were a little older now, although not in living years, but in experience, and we knew that this day was precious. We wouldn't think about the rest right now even though we were ghosts with ghosts. Our shadows lurked in the wounds we carried deeply within.

I've often asked myself what I didn't know in the living years that I can answer easily now: There are ghosts everywhere . . . in old houses, in that doll with the peculiar gaze, in the wispy clouds dancing across the night moon. Ghosts aren't frightening, but are our companions; and they wait patiently in those murky corners of our lives. If only the living knew that when a beam of light catches a shadow that shouldn't be there, they are not hallucinating. It *is* there. And it's not just a shadow.

As for me, I was here with Daniel, and for that I was grateful.

So I took my beloved's hand, and together, with all the pieces of our memory intact and our futures uncertain, we walked through the woods celebrating, in the most quiet way, the value of a open hand, a hopeful heart, and the stolen moments we were allowed to share.

476

To those no longer with us, because we were no longer with them, I bid them good night.

THE END

An Exclusive Excerpt from

ASCENDERS 2

**out in late 2015. Check
Ascenderssaga.com
for more information**

"Everyone's supposed to go to the auditorium second period. Victims of the Titanic are talking about the sinking of the ship. Attendance is mandatory," Tosh said to me as we exited our first class. That was one school-honored tradition I had yet to take part of at the Academy: an assembly.

When we reached the auditorium courtyard where the entire student body had assembled and were talking loudly, Tosh stopped to chat with some school buddies. I continued to walk into the courtyard, a circular meeting spot with wooden benches for lounging and enjoying nature, which today was alive with the smell of fresh spring jasmine. Stopping to pull one of the delicate white flowers off a branch, I gingerly placed it behind my ear, which was so girlie of me. Daniel brought out that side of me and I started to smile when I felt a large hand touch the middle of my back.

He would lean in to smell the flower, then give me a quick kiss. Now this was a great way to start the day. . . .

He pushed me from one side, slamming into me with all of his body weight. Then his friend wrapped a hand in my long hair and pulled down as hard as possible.

My head snapped back and I easily crumpled to the frozen

ground, landing hard on my knees. I could feel one of the men grab at my right ankle, fingers squeezing tightly like he was trying to break the bone. The sheer force of it threw me off balance as I wobbled recklessly to my side. He took his other meaty hand and slapped something cold and tight around the bottom of my leg. It was metal and he yanked on it with such extreme force that it cinched hard into my skin.

The pain made me see little white stars. The metal was now red-hot and burning me as it burrowed even deeper like some sort of flesh-eating disease, melting off the top layers of skin as it embedded itself into my leg. Some sort of heat-activated sensor worked its way down into my anklebone where it implanted with a loud clamping sound that made my stomach lurch and my breakfast rise to my throat.

I felt sick to my stomach.

I felt pain that made my nerve endings burn like fire.

That device changed everything. The reset was gone.

In the blur of what happened next, I saw the impossible: a small pool of my own blood on the pristine white sidewalk.

Reaching up to touch the fire in my right leg, I was toppled over again when the biggest of the men shoved me forward so hard that my face landing flat, kissing the ground. Biting hard into my inner lip, the impact was so seismic that my teeth actually rattled in my now-aching head. It was no match for my pounding heart.

Metallic-tasting blood leaked out of my mouth.

For a moment, everything went quiet. When I regained my senses, one of the foul men blew his stinking breath into my face as he squatted down to look at me, clearly enjoying himself.

"Get your skinny ass up," he ordered, tangling his hands in my hair again like he meant to yank me to my feet.

Then came five more words that I knew were coming.

"Walker Callaghan, you're under arrest."

ACKNOWLEDGMENTS

My deepest gratitude to the people I'm lucky enough to have in my life. Thank you to ….

David Pringle, my manager and friend. Thank you for being my champion, the voice on the other end of the phone line and for always guiding every step of the way. Your belief and expert guidance have made this possible…and so much fun.

Orian Williams, an amazing artist, visionary producer and friend. Thank you for taking this project to places beyond my wildest expectations. You were there from the start when I said, "Let me tell you this story." You've made this dream so fun and exciting, too.

Mary Altbaum, an extraordinary editor and friend. Thank you so much for your creativity, out of this world editing skills, and for reminding me to stick to my vision. You're a writer's dream editor and I'm so lucky that you chose to go on this journey with me.

Adrijus G from RockingBookCovers.com. What can be said about a writer and artist who have never met or even spoken on the phone? Well, a lot. Your creativity and vision knows no bounds. When you send me an email with your kick ass artwork, I can't wait to open it. You lived up to your promise to make a cover that would make a dent in the Universe. Thank you for a cover that truly is art.

Emily Tippetts. The inside worried me until I found you and your team. Thank you for making it so easy and giving me something beautiful and outside the box. A major thanks to the uber-talented Stacey Tippetts and Tianne Samson.

Autumn Hull. I spoke with a lot of book publicists and then was so lucky to find you, a kindred spirit, an amazing publicist and someone who loves words and truly wants to reach readers. Thank for your being this book's champion.

With great love, CL would also like to thank my great group of friends including Joyce Persico who heard some of these chapters read to her, Sally Kline, Vickie Chachere and Carrie Healy for all of your support and listening. And talking, talking, talking over so many great years. Thanks and love to my beautiful family including Gavin and Jill Pearlman, Reid, Cade and Wylie Pearlman and the best bro-in-law, Jack "Buzzy" Gaber.

Cody, Colt, Georgie…breaks are always better when accompanied by four legged loves.

Thank you to my parents, Paul and Renee, who always believed.

Sabrina, my bonus daughter, I could write a book on how great you are. Thank you for opening my heart and for just being the amazing, talented, smart, beautiful you! Love, Your bonus Mom.

Ron, my love, my heart, my husband, my everything and the first one who heard me say, "I had this really weird dream last night." The real dream is our life together. The other dream became this book.

Made in the USA
Middletown, DE
19 November 2015